A PLAGUE OF SECRETS

Also by John Lescroart

JOHN LESCROART

A PLAGUE OF SECRETS

A NOVEL

DUTTON

DUTTON
Published by Penguin Group (U.S.A) Inc.
375 Hudson Street, New York, New York 10014, U.S.A.
Penguin Group (Canada), 90 Eglinton Avenue East, Suite 700, Toronto, Ontario M4P 2Y3, Canada
(a division of Pearson Penguin Canada Inc.); Penguin Books Ltd, 80 Strand, London WC2R 0RL, England;
Penguin Ireland, 25 St Stephen's Green, Dublin 2, Ireland (a division of Penguin Books Ltd); Penguin Group
(Australia), 250 Camberwell Road, Camberwell, Victoria 3124, Australia (a division of Pearson Australia
Group Pty Ltd); Penguin Books India Pvt Ltd, 11 Community Centre, Panchsheel Park, New Delhi – 110 017,
India; Penguin Group (NZ), 67 Apollo Drive, Rosedale, North Shore 0632, New Zealand (a division of
Pearson New Zealand Ltd); Penguin Books (South Africa) (Pty) Ltd, 24 Sturdee Avenue, Rosebank,
Johannesburg 2196, South Africa

Penguin Books Ltd, Registered Offices: 80 Strand, London WC2R 0RL, England

Published by Dutton, a member of Penguin Group (U.S.A) Inc.

 REGISTERED TRADEMARK—MARCA REGISTRADA

ISBN 978-0-525-95092-9

Printed in the United States of America

Set in Simoncini Garamond
Designed by Alissa Amell

To my muse, mentor, partner, and true love
Lisa Marie Sawyer

A PLAGUE OF SECRETS

Men are not punished for their sins, but by them.

— Elbert Hubbard

Part One

Part One

1

Friday, the end of the workweek.

On the small deck outside his back door a lawyer named Dismas Hardy sat with his feet up on the deck's railing and savored a rare moment as the sun spent the last hour of its day lowering itself toward the horizon behind his home.

The house cast its ever-lengthening shadow out over the neighborhood to the east—San Francisco's Richmond District—and it threw into relief the bright west-facing facades of the buildings in the city before him as it stretched away to downtown. The random window reflected glints of sunlight back at him, fireflies in the gathering dusk, shimmering in the Indian-summer air.

He sipped his gin and ice, placed the glass down on the meshed metal of the picnic table they'd set up out here, and was suddenly and acutely aware that he could not be more content. His wife, Frannie, whom he still loved after twenty-three years, was inside the house behind him, humming as she did whatever she was doing. His two children were away and doing well at their respective schools— Rebecca at Boston University and Vincent at UC San Diego. The law firm of Freeman, Farrell, Hardy & Roake, of which he was the managing partner, was humming along as though it were on autopilot.

Hardy looked for a moment into the blue above him, blinking against a wave of emotion. Then, being who he was, his mouth cracked into a small grin at himself and he lifted his glass for another sip.

Inside, the telephone rang twice and stopped, which meant that it

was someone they knew and that Frannie had picked it up. Her
voice, with notes of sympathy and understanding, floated out to him,
but he didn't bother trying to make out any of the words. She had
begun to have a somewhat thriving career of her own as a marriage
and family therapist and often would wind up counseling her clients
from home.

Hardy drifted, not off to anywhere, but into a kind of surrender
of conscious thought. For a long moment he was simply there in the
same way that his drink or his chair existed; or the light, or the
breeze off the ocean a little over a mile west of where he sat. So that
when the door opened behind him, he came back with a bit of a
start.

Frannie put a hand on his shoulder and he brought his hand up to
cover hers, half turning, seeing the look on her face. "What's up?" he
asked, his feet coming down off the railing. "Are the kids all right?"
Always the first concern.

She nodded a yes to the second question, then answered the first.
"That was Treya." Treya was the wife of Hardy's best friend, Abe
Glitsky, the head of San Francisco's homicide department. Anguish
in her eyes, Frannie held and released a breath. "It's Zack," she said,
referring to Glitsky's three-year-old son. "He's had an accident."

Accompanied by her five-year-old daughter, Rachel, Treya Glitsky
opened the gate in the Hardys' white picket fence. Dismas Hardy, in
his living room watching out through the plantation shutters of his
front window, called back to his wife in the kitchen that they were
here, then walked over and opened his front door.

Treya turned away and, closing the gate, reached down for a small
duffel bag. By the effort it took to lift, it might have weighed a hundred pounds. When she straightened up, her shoulders rose and fell,
then she brought a hand to her forehead and stood completely still

for another second or two. With her tiny hand Rachel held on to the front pocket of her mother's jeans while she looked up at her face, her own lips pressed tight.

Hardy crossed his porch and descended three steps to the cement path that bisected his small lawn. The sun had gone down behind the buildings across the street, although true dusk was still twenty minutes away. As she turned and saw him now, Treya's legendary composure threatened to break. She was a tall woman—nearly Hardy's size—and strongly built. Her mouth, expressive and normally quick to smile, quivered, then set in a line.

Hardy came forward, took the duffel bag from her, and put an arm around her neck, drawing her in, holding her for a moment. Finally he stepped back and whispered, "How is he?"

She shrugged and shook her head. Then, her voice as quiet as his, "We don't know yet."

Frannie came up, touched his shoulder, and came around to hug Treya.

Hardy stepped to the side and went down on one knee to face Rachel at her level. "And how's my favorite little girl in the whole world?"

"Okay," she said. "But Zack got hit by a car."

"I know he did, hon."

"But he's not going to die."

Hardy looked up at the two women. Treya gave him a quick nod, and he came back to her daughter. "No, of course not. But I hear you're going to stay here for a couple of days while he gets better. Is that okay with you?"

"If Mom says."

"And she does. Is that duffel bag your stuff? Here, let me get it. If you put your arms around my neck, your old uncle Diz will carry you inside."

Then they were all moving up the path and into the house. "Abe went with the ambulance," Treya was saying. "We don't know how long we're going to have to be down there. I don't know how to thank you for watching Rachel."

"Don't be ridiculous," Frannie said. "We love Rachel." She reached out and touched the little girl's cheek where she rested it on Hardy's shoulder. "She's our favorite little girl."

Hardy and Frannie walked Treya out after they got Rachel settled in with cookies and milk in front of the television. They stopped again on the path just inside the fence. "Was he conscious?" Hardy asked.

"No." Treya paused, then lowered her voice. "He didn't have his helmet on."

"What happened exactly?" Frannie asked.

"We may never know," she said. "Abe had just brought down his Big Wheel bike and Zack was on it, but Abe told him to just sit still and wait a minute while he turned around and got his helmet, which he'd set down like two feet away on the stairs. But then as soon as his back was turned, Zack got aboard and either started pedaling or just rolling down the driveway, just as another car was coming up the street. One of our neighbors. He was only going like five miles an hour, but Zack just plowed into him and got knocked off the bike and into the street." She flashed a pained look from Hardy to Frannie. "He banged his head." She hesitated. "I've got to get down there now. You guys are great. Thank you."

"Go," Hardy said. "Call when you can."

At ten-thirty Hardy was shepherding the evening's last glass of wine, which he didn't need at all. He was sitting in his reading chair across from the fireplace in the living room. Rachel had gone down to sleep early and easily about an hour and a half ago. Frannie was in the family room now and for the past half hour had been talking to their son, Vincent, down in San Diego. She'd already called the Beck back in Boston, both calls not so much to share the bad news as to touch base with their own offspring, to make sure they were safe.

Neither Treya nor Abe had called yet with any report from the hospital. Hardy, hamstrung by his overwhelming sense of dread, had his hand around the stem of his glass but hadn't yet brought it to his lips. He simply stared at the fire.

Frannie must have hung up, because she was now standing in the portal that separated their dining and living rooms. "Diz?"

He turned his head toward her, perhaps surprised to see her there, appearing out of thin air the way she had. "Hey."

She crossed the remaining few steps to him and sat on the ottoman at his feet. "You've been just sitting there without moving a muscle since I've been in this doorway."

"Isometric exercise. Every muscle tensed for maximum effect." But there was no humor in it.

"Are you all right?"

He shrugged, his effort to smile halfhearted at best. "How's Vinnie?"

"Good. He got a B-plus on his first poly-sci exam."

"Slacker."

"He wanted to know if we needed him to come up. He said he would. I told him I didn't think so."

"Probably right. Nothing for him to do."

"You either," Frannie said. "Just be there for them if they need us."

Sighing, Hardy shook his head. "You think this stuff is buried so deep down, and next thing you know you're blindsided by it."

Frannie hesitated, but she knew what he was talking about. "Michael?"

Hardy's firstborn son had died in infancy thirty-five years before.

A precocious seven-month-old, he'd stood up in his crib well before he was supposed to be able to and had pitched over the guardrail that they'd kept at half-mast. He had landed on his head.

"I don't think I've consciously thought about him in five years, and now here he is, big as life. Bigger than he was in life."

Frannie rested a hand on his knee. "This may not turn out the same. Let's hope."

"I don't know if Abe could take it, how anybody does. I don't know how I did."

Frannie knew. Hardy's son's tragedy had marked the end of his first marriage and the abandonment of his law career. It had led to ten years behind the bar at the Little Shamrock, where he had averaged somewhere between one and two dozen beers a day, not to mention the rest of the alcoholic intake.

She squeezed his leg reassuringly. "Let's wait till we hear something. You want to come to bed?"

"I want to drink a bottle of gin."

"You could, but you wouldn't be happy about that tomorrow."

"No. I know. Plus, if Abe needs something . . ." He shook his head and looked away, then came back and met her eyes. "Shit, Frannie."

"I agree. But Rachel's going to be up early. We're going to want to be rested. I've got to go lie down. You're welcome to join me."

"I'd be lousy company." Then, softening it, he patted her hand with his own. "Couple more minutes," he said.

And the phone rang.

"The best bit of news," Treya was saying to both of them as they listened on the two extension phones, "is that he's out of his twos. Evidently the younger you are, the worse the prognosis. Three is way better than two. And this is a Level One hospital, so they had a neurosurgical resident in house, which is also lucky since he could go right to work." Her voice, while not by any stretch cheerful, was strong and confident-sounding. Conveying facts, honing to the bearable news, she was keeping herself together the way she always did, by sucking it up.

"They've cooled him down to make him hypothermic," she went on, "which is what they always do, and taken some scans, and they've got him on a continuous EEG and his vital signs are good, so that's all heartening."

"But he's still unconscious?" Hardy asked.

Frannie and Hardy heard Treya's quick intake of breath and flashed their reactions to one another. "Well, that's really not so much of an issue now, since they've induced a coma. He's going to be unconscious for a while. Maybe a week or more."

"He's in a coma?" Frannie, before she could stop herself.

"It's not as bad as it sounds," Treya said. "They induce it with some drug to let his brain heal. And they've got him on something for the internal swelling, but the doctor says they still may have to operate. In fact, probably."

Hardy, possibly leaving the actual ridges of his fingerprints in the telephone at his ear, asked, "When's that going to be, the surgery?"

"Probably pretty soon, maybe by the morning. They've got him stuck with a couple of catheters in his head to measure his cranial pressure. It gets above fifteen, whatever that means, they're going to have to go in. And it's at thirteen now, up from ten when he got here, so . . ."

"Do you need us to do anything?" Frannie asked.

"Watching Rachel is enough. I don't see either of us leaving here for a while."

"Take whatever time you need, Trey." Frannie's eyes were locked on Hardy's as they nodded together. "Don't even think about that. It's no issue. She's wonderful and we love having her. Both of us."

"Both of us," Hardy repeated. "So what's next?"

"I think probably the surgery."

"What are they going to do?"

"They take a couple of bones out of his skull to relieve the pressure."

"Not permanently?" Hardy asked.

"No," Treya said, "I don't think so. But I'll ask now for sure. Anyway, then they make some slits in the dura."

"What's that?" Frannie asked.

"Oh, you'll like this." Treya obviously wearing herself down trying to keep a positive spin on things. "It means tough mother."

"What does?"

"*Dura mater.* It's the outer layer of the brain. Tough and fibrous. They make some small slits in it to let the brain expand."

Silence collected in the line as this bit of horrifying, yet perhaps good, information began to sink in. Finally, Hardy cleared his throat. "So how's Abe?"

Treya hesitated. "Quiet. Even for him."

"It's not his fault," Frannie said.

"I know that. It might not be so clear to him." Again, a stab at an optimistic tone. "He'll get to it."

"I know he will," Frannie said.

Hardy, not so certain of that, especially if Zachary didn't make it, turned to face away from his wife. Stealing a glance at his watch, he did some quick math: If the accident had taken place at five-thirty, it had now been five and a half hours. After they'd gotten his own son Michael to the hospital, he had survived for six.

The women's words continued to tumble through the phone at his ear, but he didn't hear any of them over his own imaginings—or was it only his pulse, sounding like the tick of a clock counting down the seconds?

2

Bay Beans West enjoyed a privileged location, location, location at the intersection of Haight and Ashbury streets in San Francisco.

The large, wide-windowed coffee shop had opened in the summer of 1998 and from its first days became a fixture in the neighborhood. It opened every morning at six o'clock, except Sunday, when it opened at eight, and it stayed open until ten. Between the UCSF medical school a couple of blocks east, the University of San Francisco a few blocks north, the tourists visiting the epicenter of the birth of hippiedom, and the vibrant and wildly eclectic local neighborhood, the place rarely had a slow moment, much less an empty one.

The smell of its roasting beans infused the immediate vicinity with a beckoning aroma; the management provided copies of the city's newspapers—the *Chronicle*, the *Free Press*, and the *Bay Guardian*. The papers rarely disappeared before three o'clock. Even the homeless honored the custom, except for Crazy Melinda, who used to come in, scoop all the papers up, and try to leave with them—until the patrons started setting aside a copy of each paper at the counter for her to pick up whenever she wanted them.

Comfortable, colorful couches were available as well as the usual chairs and tables; the ethic of the place allowed an unlimited time at your seat once you'd claimed it, whether or not you continued to drink coffee; for the past five years or so customers could avail themselves of free wireless Internet service; and legal or not, pets were welcome. For many in the neighborhood BBW was a refuge, a meeting place, a home away from home.

At a few minutes before seven o'clock on this Saturday morning, the usual line of about twenty customers needing their morning infusions of caffeine was already growing along Haight Street at the establishment's front door. A long-haired man named Wes Farrell, in jogging pants and a T-shirt that read "DAM–Mothers Against Dyslexia," stood holding in one hand the hand of his live-in girlfriend, Sam Duncan, and in the other the leash of Gertrude, his boxer. They, like many others in the city that morning, were discussing the homeless problem.

For decades San Francisco has been a haven for the homeless, spending upwards of $150 million per year on shelters, subsidized rental units, medical and psychiatric care, soup kitchens, and so on. Now, suddenly, unexpectedly, and apparently due to a series of articles that had just appeared in the *Chronicle*, came a widespread outcry among the citizenry that the welcome mat should be removed. Wes finished reading today's article aloud to Sam and, folding up the paper, said, "And about time too."

Sam extracted her hand from his. "You don't mean that."

"I don't? I thought I did."

"So what do you want to do with them, I mean once you give them a ticket, which by the way they have no money to pay, so that won't work."

"What part of that statement, I hesitate to call it a sentence, do you want me to address?"

"Any part. Don't be wise."

"I'm not. But I'd hate to be the guy assigned to trying to diagram one of your sentences."

"You're just trying to get me off the point. Which is what would you do with these homeless people who suddenly are no longer welcome?"

"Actually, they're just as welcome. They're just not going to be welcome to use public streets and sidewalks as their campsites and bathrooms anymore."

"So where else would they go?"

"Are we talking bathrooms? They go to the bathroom in bathrooms, like the rest of us."

"The rest of us who have homes, Wes. I think that's more or less the point. They don't."

"You're right. But you notice we're loaded with shelters and public toilets."

"They don't like the shelters. They're dangerous and dirty."

"And the streets aren't? Besides, this may sound like a cruel cliché, my dear, but where do you think we get the expression 'Beggars can't be choosers'?"

"I can't believe you just said that. That is so"—Sam dredged up about the worst epithet she could imagine—"so *right wing.*"

Wes looked down, went to a knee, and snapped his fingers, bringing Gertrude close in for a quick pet. "It's all right, girl, your mom and I aren't fighting. We're just talking." Standing up, he said, "She's getting upset."

"So am I. If you try to pet me to calm me down, I'll deck you."

"There's a tolerant approach. And meanwhile, I hate to say this, but it's not a right wing, left wing issue here. It's a health and quality of life issue. Feces and urine on public streets and playgrounds and parks pose a health risk and are just a little bit of a nuisance, I think we can admit. Are we in accord here?"

Sam, arms folded, leaned back against the windows of the coffee shop, unyielding.

"Sam," Wes continued, "when I take Gertie out for a walk, I bring a bag to clean up after her. That's for a dog. You really think it's too much to ask the same for humans?"

"It's not the same thing."

"Why not?"

"Because a lot of these people, they have mental problems too. They don't even know they're doing it, or where."

"And so we should just tolerate it? You send your kids out to play and there's a pile of shit on your front stoop? Next thing you know, half a school's got hepatitis. You don't think that's a small problem?"

"That's not what's happening."

"Sam, that's exactly what's happening. They've got to check the sandbox near the merry-go-round in Golden Gate Park every morning for shit and needles. Some of these people think it's a litter box."

"Well, I haven't heard of any hepatitis epidemic. That's way an exaggeration."

"The point is the alfresco bathroom kind of thing that's been happening downtown for years. I think you'll remember we had a guy used our front stoop at the office every night for a month. We had to wash the steps down every morning."

"There," Sam said. "That was a solution."

"It was a ridiculous solution. It was insane. To say nothing about the fact that using the streets for bathrooms punishes innocent, good citizens and devalues property."

"Aha! I knew property would get in there."

"Property's not a bad thing, Sam."

"Which is what every Republican in the world believes."

"And some Democrats too. Dare I say most? And for the umpteenth time, Sam, it's not a Republican thing. You can be vaguely left of center and still not want to have people shitting in your flowerpots. Those aren't mutually exclusive."

"I think they might actually be."

"Well, no offense, but you're wrong. Public defecation and homeless encampments on the streets and in the parks are gross and unhealthy and sickening. I don't understand how you can't see that."

Sam again shook her head. "I see those poor people suffering. That's what I see. We've got a fire department with miles of hoses. We could deploy them to wash down the streets. The city could get up some work program and hire people to clean up."

"What a great idea! Should we pay them to clean up after themselves, or after each other? Except then again, where does the money to do that come from?"

"There it is again, money! It always comes down to money."

"Well, as a matter of fact, yes, sometimes it does."

"The point is, Wes, these people just don't have the same options as everybody else."

"And they never will, Sam. That's rough maybe, okay, but it's life. And life's just not fair sometimes. Which doesn't mean everybody else has to deal with their problems. They get rounded up and taken to the shelters whether or not they want to go, and I say it's about time."

Without either Sam or Wes noticing, several others in the line, both male and female, had closed in around them, listening in. Now a young hippie spoke up to Wes. "You're right, dude," he said. "It's out of control. It is about time."

A chorus of similar sentiments followed.

Sam took it all in, straightened up, and looked out into the faces surrounding her. "I just can't believe that I'm hearing this in San Francisco," she said. "I'm so ashamed of all of you."

And with that she pushed her way through the crowd and started walking up Ashbury, away from her boyfriend and their dog.

Sam was the director of San Francisco's Rape Crisis Counseling Center, which also happened to be on Haight Street. Her plan this morning

had been to take her early morning constitutional from their home
up on Buena Vista with Wes and Gertie, share a cup of coffee and a
croissant at BBW, then check in at the office to make sure there hadn't
been an overnight crisis that demanded her attention.

But now, seething, just wanting to get away from all the reaction-
aries, she had started out in the wrong direction to get to the center.
Fortunately, the line for the BBW stretched down Haight Street, and
not up Ashbury, and she'd gone about half a block uphill when she
stopped and turned around, realizing she could take the alley that
ran behind the Haight Street storefronts, bypassing the crowd and
emerging on the next block on the way to her office.

But first she stopped a minute, not just to get her breath, but to
try to calm herself. After an extraordinarily rocky beginning to their
relationship she and Wes hadn't had a fight in six or seven years.
She'd come to believe that he was her true soul mate and shared her
opinions about nearly everything, especially politics. But now, apparently not.

It shook her.

And, okay, she knew that she was among those whom most people would include among California's "fruits and nuts." She certainly
didn't too often doubt the rightness of her various stances. She was in
her early forties and had seen enough of the world to know that the
dollar was the basic problem. The military-industrial complex. Big
oil and corporate globalism. Republicans.

But here now Wes, who had registered Green and hated the right
wingers as much as she did, was arguing for something that she just
knew in her heart was wrong. You couldn't just abandon these homeless people who had, after all, flocked to San Francisco precisely because of the benign political environment. That would be the worst
bait-and-switch tactic she could imagine. She would have to talk to
him, but after they'd both calmed down.

She crossed back to where she wouldn't be visible to Wes or anyone else in the line as she came back down the hill. It was the kind of clear morning that people tended to expect when they visited San Francisco during the traditional summer months. Those people often left in bitter disappointment at the incessant fog, the general inclemency of the weather. But today the early sun sprayed the rooftops golden. The temperature was already in the low sixties. It was going to be a perfect day.

She got to the alley, squinting into the bright morning sun, when here was an example of exactly the thing she and Wes had been talking about—a pair of feet protruded from the backdoor area of BBW. Not wanting to awaken the poor sleeping homeless man, she gave him a wide berth and only a quick glance as she came abreast of where he slept.

But something about the attitude of the body stopped her. It didn't seem to be lying in a natural position, the head propped up against the screen door. She couldn't imagine such a posture would be conducive to sleep. Most of the weight seemed to be on his left shoulder, but under that the torso turned in an awkward way so that both feet pointed up, as if he were lying on his back.

Moving closer, she noticed a line of liquid tracing itself down over the concrete and pooling in the gap between the cement of the porch and the asphalt of the alley. In the bright morning sunlight, from a distance it could have been water. But another couple of steps brought her close enough to remove any doubt on that score—the glistening wet stuff was red.

Leaning over, Sam shaded her eyes against the glare and she saw the man's face; a face she recognized, had expected to see that morning behind the counter where he always was at BBW.

Her hand, already trembling, went to her mouth.

3

At a few minutes past seven-thirty a sergeant inspector of homicide named Darrel Bracco double-parked on Ashbury. He unhooked his squawk box handset and draped the cord up over the rearview mirror, so that a meter person coming by might surmise that this was a police vehicle and as such shouldn't get a parking ticket. Just to be double sure, though, he left his business card on the dashboard of his city-issue Pontiac. He knew from bitter personal experience that even these precautions might not be enough.

A crowd of perhaps sixty souls stood beyond the yellow crime-scene tape that the responding unit had strung across the mouth of the alley and again farther down. Bracco saw that the coroner's van hadn't yet arrived, but two black-and-white squad cars also helped to close off the entrance to the alley from the inquisitive populace.

His badge out, excusing himself as he went, he pushed his way through the mass of people and ducked under the tape. A no-nonsense guy, he met no real resistance—Bracco was forty-two years old, just under six feet tall, clean-cut, casually buffed. He nodded to the two uniformed officers who were keeping the crime scene from being violated.

Over by the body, obvious enough on the ground by the back door to one of the local establishments, another uniform with graying hair and the start of a gut, undoubtedly the lieutenant from Park Station, was standing talking with Bracco's new partner, Debra Schiff. Debra was thirty-eight, wore her sandy hair short, and possessed a very good if tough-looking face that looked tougher without makeup. For which reason she never wore any.

Bracco flashed his badge and stuck his hand out. "How you doin', Lieutenant? Darrel Bracco."

"Bill Banks."

"Nice to meet you. Thanks for holding down the fort. I miss anything fun yet?"

Schiff answered, shaking her head no. "Waiting on the techs. Story of our lives, huh? You'd think these people would have the good grace to get themselves shot during regular business hours. But here it is, first thing on a weekend. Time the techs get mounted and rolling, they might not get here till noon." She turned to Banks. "But Darrel and I can handle things here, Lieutenant, if you want to get back to your station or go home. Your call."

Banks clucked and shrugged. "Thanks, but if you don't mind, I'll just hang awhile. See where this goes a little."

"He was just telling me he knows the guy," Schiff said.

Banks nodded. "Everybody in the neighborhood knows him. Dylan Vogler. He managed this place."

"And what place is that?" Bracco asked.

"The coffee shop, Bay Beans West. Takes up the whole corner." Banks pointed. "This is the back entrance he's up against. Also, I was just showing Inspector Schiff, see on the side wall that hole in the stucco . . ."

"The bullet. But, hmm . . ." Bracco moved over to look more closely.

"What?" Schiff said.

Bracco, his face right up against the wall, said, "No blood?"

Schiff, now over next to him, pointed down and said, "Backpack."

"Backpack." Bracco repeated. "That'd do it." Then he went down into a squat.

"Darrel," Schiff began, a warning note in her voice.

But he put out a hand. "I'm not moving him, Debra. If my eyes don't deceive me, that holster on his belt's got a cell phone in it." He flipped the leather top open. "Aha!" Extracting the device from its holder, he stood back up and opened it.

"Ice?" Schiff asked.

Pushing buttons on the phone, Bracco nodded.

Banks's gaze went from Bracco over to Schiff. "Ice?"

" 'In case of emergency,' " Schiff said. "ICE. They're telling everybody to put that in their cell phones now. You don't have that in yours?"

Banks shook his head. "I'm lucky if I can keep the damn thing charged."

"Here you go." Darrel pushed the send button and held the phone to his ear. "Hello," he said after a brief moment, then identified himself. "I'm calling because you're the emergency number on a cell phone in the possession of a man named . . ." He raised his eyebrows at Banks, a question, and got the name again from the lieutenant.

"Dylan Vogler." Bracco paused, listened. "Yes. Yes," he said. "I'm afraid so. Well, at the moment I'm in the alley behind his place of business. Sure. Just tell the officers who you are and they'll let you through. No, you don't want to bring your child. Can we send someone up to your house to get you? Okay, then. Okay. There's no hurry, ma'am. We'll be here."

Closing the phone, he shrugged and let out a heavy breath. "The wife." Then, cocking his head and checking his watch, he turned to Schiff. "Not too bad for a weekend. There's a siren now."

By the time the first cops had arrived, there had been no question that Dylan Vogler was completely and absolutely dead—no hint of a pulse, the skin just warm to the touch, his eyes wide open and unresponsive to light or other stimulation. Nevertheless, the first responding squad car cops got some EMTs down to pronounce him. The photographer took a couple of dozen photos, memorializing the scene, before anyone else touched the body at all.

Behind Bracco and Schiff the three-person crime-scene investigation unit under Lennard Faro continued scouring the alley and its environs for evidence, although within the first minutes they'd already called Faro over to identify and bag as evidence a .40-caliber semiautomatic Glock pistol that had recently been fired and a brass bullet casing that probably went with it. After watching them poking around and letting the assistant coroner and the photographer finish, at long last Bracco got to the body.

The first thing he did was take off Vogler's light blue backpack so he could turn the body over and look at where the shot or shots had entered. He then turned the backpack over to verify the location of the bullet hole. And there it was, high up in the fabric adjacent to where the slug had exited Vogler's body, surrounded with the bloom of blood that Bracco had expected and failed to see around the hole in the stucco. After he flipped the backpack over and saw the corresponding exit hole on the other side, he sat back and turned to his partner, squatting next to him.

"I love opening presents." Bracco undid the clasp, pulled the top up, and held it open.

"Well, look at that," Schiff said.

"I am." The pack was filled to about the two-thirds mark with sandwich-size baggies of marijuana. Bracco removed one of them, opened it, smelled it again, and passed it over to his partner. "What I don't get," he said, "is why they didn't take this."

"Maybe they didn't know it was in there," Schiff said.

"They *definitely* didn't know it was in there," Bracco said. "They couldn't have known about this much weed and just left it. That'd skew my whole worldview."

Someone tapped him on his shoulder, and Bracco half turned. "Sorry, Inspector," Banks said, "but the wife's here."

Nodding, Bracco sighed, then straightened up. "Hide that backpack," he said to Schiff. "We don't know nothing about no stinking backpacks."

"Got it," his partner replied.

Debra Schiff dropped the backpack onto the asphalt out of sight behind Banks's squad car. Turning around, she saw that her partner had already gone over to greet the widow, who was standing just inside the crime-scene tape next to one of the uniformed officers.

From Schiff's distance the woman appeared young and very pretty. Her shoulder-length black hair, still wet—her morning shower?—framed a face of pale beauty, with wide dark eyes, strong cheekbones, red lips. She wore a long-sleeved 49er T-shirt tucked into her jeans, but the blousy shirt camouflaged neither her breasts nor her tiny waist.

Coming closer, though, Schiff saw something else around the eyes too—a swelling that might be from the crying but might have another source. And under the swelling did she discern a faint yellowish cast to the skin? An ancient, or not-so-ancient, bruise?

"I can see that it's him from here," she was saying to Bracco. Her left hand—no wedding band—was at her mouth now. "I don't know if I can . . . if I need to go any closer."

"That's all right, Mrs. Vogler." Schiff inserted herself into the conversation, identifying herself and laying a hand on Bracco's shoulder.

"I'm not Mrs. Vogler." The woman corrected her right away. "My name is Jansey Ticknor. We're not married. Weren't married. But just call me Jansey, okay?" Her shoulders sagged. "God."

Schiff wanted to get her away from her immediate reaction. "My partner mentioned a child when he talked to you."

Ms. Ticknor nodded. "My son, Ben. He's with our boarder. He's fine." Her eyes went back to the body. "My God, how did this happen?"

"We don't know yet, ma'am," Bracco said. "We did find a gun. Did your husband own a gun?"

Jansey Ticknor blinked into the sun for a moment. "He couldn't."

"He couldn't? Why was that?" Schiff asked.

Jansey's face went flat. She looked from one inspector to the other. "He served some time in jail when he was younger."

"What for?" Bracco asked.

She shrugged. "He was a driver in a robbery. It was the only time he ever did anything like that. Anyway . . . he went to prison. So, no, he couldn't have a gun."

Schiff threw a quick look at Bracco. There was a real difference, they both knew, between going to jail, which meant the city and county lockup downtown, and spending time in prison. Prison was hard time, and in San Francisco, the probation capital of the Western world, time in the joint argued strongly against Jansey's description that it had been the only wrongdoing of Dylan Vogler's life.

"Jansey," Schiff asked, "did you see Dylan before he went to work this morning?"

"No, he got up early with Ben, our boy. He lets me sleep in on weekends sometimes." The body over on the asphalt drew her gaze again.

Bracco spoke up. "Did Dylan have any enemies that you know of? Somebody who was mad at him?"

"Not really, no. I guess it's possible, but he didn't have any power. He just ran this coffee shop. There wasn't any drama in his life."

"Maybe he fired somebody recently?" Schiff suggested. "Something like that."

"No. The staff, it's like only ten people or so and they've all been here forever." She shook her head, dismissing the thought. "Whatever it was, it wasn't about his job, I'm sure." Her eyes went to the doorway. "Maybe somebody robbed him."

"His wallet was on him," Bracco said. "Cell phone. No sign of robbery."

"Maybe they were going to take his stuff and something scared them away."

"That's possible," Schiff said.

"What stuff?" Bracco asked.

She closed her mouth, pursed her lips, and shifted to her other foot. "I don't know. What you said, his wallet and cell phone. Like that."

Bracco kept it low-key. "He didn't have anything else particularly worth stealing that you know of that maybe wouldn't be obvious to us? A watch, maybe?"

"I don't think so, no." She turned her head back toward the body. "You can't just leave him lying there."

"We won't, Jansey," Schiff said. "The coroner's ready to take him to the morgue as soon as we release him." Lowering her voice, she moved in closer. "It might save you a difficult trip downtown if you wanted to give us a positive identification now. I'd be right next to you, if you think you can handle it."

Jansey was biting her lower lip and eventually nodded, putting her arm in Schiff's. "Don't let go of me," she said, "in case I fall down or faint or something. Please."

"I got you."

"Okay, let's go."

With BBW closed up, Schiff told her partner she'd meet him at a place she loved that had been serving breakfasts on Irving Street just west of Nineteenth Avenue for about eighty years. She and Bracco had been partnered up for only about six months and still had favorite haunts that the other didn't know.

As usual, the place was packed; but also as usual, they moved the customers along right smartly. So the wait for Schiff's table wasn't more than ten minutes. She'd just had her first sip of coffee when Bracco came in, caught her eye over the other patrons, and threaded his way over to her. When he sat down, she lowered her cup. "What took you?"

Bracco's normal sunny disposition sulked under a shadow. He was all but breathing fire but simply shook his head, his eyes dark. "You don't want to know."

She sipped coffee. "They gave you another ticket."

Bracco's head wagged from side to side. "They are twenty-four-karat idiots, Debra. I'm going to find out who wrote this one up and go after him."

"Or her," Schiff said. "Don't forget saying 'or her.'"

"I never would, of course, not in my real life. But I don't care if it's a him or a her. I'm going to take the sucker down, whoever it is. You didn't get tagged?"

She shrugged.

"But here's the thing. I parked in the street with my squawker hanging from my rearview mirror and my goddamned card on the dash. You know, Bracco, homicide, with the badge and all. You think it's possible they don't know that homicide is actually part of the PD? Maybe they think homicide is like the name of a pest control company."

"I wouldn't rule it out."

Bracco blew out heavily. "It's not right, Debra. It's just so incredibly demoralizing."

"It is, I agree."

"I'm not writing up another memo for another bullshit ticket like this."

The way it worked was that parking tickets incurred by city vehicles required the employee to fill out a form detailing the reason that the parking infraction had been unavoidable, and hence forgivable. The chief had issued a general order. Any officer who got a ticket had to fill out the form before leaving his shift for the day. Of course, a lot of times people couldn't be bothered, so about every six months they'd get a memo they had to sign and return, acknowledging in a sub rosa fashion that—officially—parking violations were, in fact, about as important as murders.

"I wouldn't write it up, either, Darrel. Call those bastards on it. Why don't you bring it up to Glitsky on Monday, let him handle it?"

"He'll go ballistic. He hates this stuff worse than me."

"Yeah, but that's why they pay him the big bucks."

"Good point. What else is he doing anyway, right?" The waiter appeared at his elbow and Bracco looked up. "Anything better here than everything else?"

Two minutes later, his eggs ordered, Bracco stirred his own coffee and looked across at his partner. "So, how about our victim?"

"I think he hit Jansey."

"How do you get that?"

"Her cheek didn't look right. Even under the tears. She didn't love him, I don't think. You see how she talked about him? 'He didn't have any power. He just ran this coffee shop. There wasn't any drama in his life.' That's not a woman who loves her man."

"So she knew about the weed?"

"Of course. How could she not?"

"You notice she didn't say anything about the backpack."

"She might not have known he had it with him. She didn't see him leave home, you remember. But as you said, the killing wasn't about the weed or whoever shot him would have taken it."

"If he'd known. If it was a 'him.' "

"Well, yes, that."

Their waiter arrived with their plates and both inspectors dug in for a moment before Bracco took it up again. "You believe her about the gun?"

"Not for a second. I ask if he owns a gun and she says he couldn't. Not he didn't."

"I heard that. So he was shot with his own gun?"

"We'll find out soon enough, but that's my bet."

"He know the shooter?"

"Maybe." She chewed for a minute. "No sign of struggle, anyway. He gave him his own gun and then the guy shot him with it? How does that play?"

"I don't know." Bracco put his fork down. "Actually, maybe Jansey."

"Pretty early for that, but maybe." She pushed food around on her plate before she looked up. "We have to search the house."

"I know." And Bracco added, "Like yesterday."

4

Joanne Ticknor sat next to her husband, holding her grandson Ben on her lap on the couch in her daughter's living room.

Jansey came back into the room behind a man and a woman, both of whom were dressed casually but who looked serious and professional. "Mom, Dad," she said, "these are inspectors Bracco and Schiff with the police department." At the introductions Wayne Ticknor stood and shook hands, and Ben wriggled out of his grandmother's arms and came forward to do the same.

Bracco went down on a knee to shake Ben's hand. "How you doing, big guy?"

"Okay. Are you going to find who shot my daddy?"

"We're going to try, Ben. We're really going to try." Then he looked up at Jansey's mother. "But we're going to have to have a little adult time to talk before we really get going."

Getting the message, she stood up. "Come on, Ben, let's you and Grandma go and find ourselves a snack in the kitchen. How's that sound?"

As soon as they'd gone, Wayne asked, "Do you have any leads yet?"

Bracco gave him a nod. "Well, as a matter of fact, we might, or at least a place to start." Including Jansey now, he continued, "Dylan was wearing a backpack that was full of marijuana. Did you know anything about that?"

She opened, then closed her mouth. Finally came out with it. "I

didn't know he had some with him this morning, but it doesn't surprise me, no. He was selling it sometimes. I wanted him to stop. I
asked him to stop. But he said it didn't hurt anybody and we needed
the money."

"That asshole," Wayne said.

"Dad."

"Putting Ben and you at risk like that? What a fool."

Schiff turned to the father. "You had other problems with him,
Mr. Ticknor?"

"You could say that."

"Dad!" Jansey repeated. "That's enough, okay? He's dead. Whatever he did, it's over now. Let's just leave it alone, can we?"

But Bracco wasn't of a mind to do that. "What else did he do, Mr.
Ticknor?"

Wayne looked to his daughter and shook his head. "Why can't
they know what he really was, Jansey? That he wasn't much of a father to Ben? Or that he beat you?"

"He didn't beat me!" She turned to Schiff, met her eyes. "He
didn't beat me," she repeated more softly. "He hit me a couple of
times, that's all."

"Recently?" Bracco asked.

"A couple of weeks ago, we talked about this marijuana thing and
he got mad at me. But it wasn't really a fight. He just got physical for
a minute. It wasn't really a big deal."

"No, no big deal at all," Wayne put in, with heavy sarcasm, "except for six months ago when she and Ben moved in with us for a
couple of weeks."

"He was under a lot of stress then," Jansey said. "He wasn't perfect, okay, but nobody is, you know?"

"True," Debra said, "we all have imperfections, but maybe one of
his made somebody want to kill him. You knew him better than anyone else. Maybe you could help us."

Bracco jumped in. "Was anybody mad at him? Jealous about his job? Anything like that?"

Nothing.

Schiff asked, "Jansey, do you know where he got the marijuana? If it's any help," she continued, "we brought a search warrant along with us."

This brought a bit of reaction. "What for?"

Bracco stepped up. "Dylan was on his way to work from here at home. Which means the weed was probably in this house last night. There might be more of it. He might also have left some records of where he got it or who he was going to sell it to."

Jansey looked to her father, indecision playing over her features. Finally, she came back to the inspectors. "It's in the attic," she said. "He grew it up there."

Debra Schiff climbed the stepladder and ducked through the small opening in the upper half of the closet wall and straightened up into a warm and humid room baking in a grow-light glow. She found a light switch next to the opening and flicked it, then spoke back over her shoulder to Darrel, on the steps of the ladder right behind her. "You're not going to believe this."

Bracco poked his head into the opening. "Lordy Lordy," he said.

The attic space the size of the house's footprint was filled with plants in various stages of growth, from just-germinated little shoots in cardboard egg cartons to full-blown, six-foot-high plants in raised planter boxes. The air was rich with the resinous scent of marijuana.

Bracco got through the opening and straightened up next to his partner, taking it all in. They shared a wondering glance and, at last, Bracco let out a breath. "Wow."

"You said it," Schiff replied. "How much is this worth?"

"Ten grand a pound, right? Or close." He turned around and peered across the space and into the recesses in the far corners. "And he's got a jungle of it up here."

Walking over to one of the closer tall plants, he reached out and picked one of the heavy and sticky buds, rubbing it between his thumb and forefinger, then smelling his hand. "Not that I ever inhaled any of this stuff, Debra, of course, and not to get too technical, but my limited experience tells me that this is some righteously good shit."

5

First thing Monday morning Bracco knocked on Lieutenant Glitsky's door on the fifth floor of San Francisco's Hall of Justice.

"It's open."

Bracco turned the knob, gave the door a push. "Actually, it wasn't."

Glitsky, a large-boned man with a prominent hatchet of a nose, an ancient scar between his lips, and a graying Afro, sat in semidarkness—room lights off, blinds closed up. Glitsky's elbows rested on his bare desk, his hands covering his mouth. Even with half of his intimidating facial arsenal covered up, Glitsky's eyes alone could do the trick—they gleamed like glowing coals, the window to his mind, announcing to anyone paying attention that it was scary in there.

Today those eyes stopped Bracco in his tracks. "You all right, Abe?"

Glitsky didn't move a muscle, still speaking from behind his hands. "I'm fine. How can I help you, Darrel?"

"Can I come in?"

"You already are in."

Bracco stood holding the doorknob. "If this isn't a good time . . ."

"I said it's fine. Get the lights if you want."

"Yes, sir." He reached over and the room lit up.

Glitsky didn't stir. Finally, his eyes moved and met Bracco's. "Anytime," he said. "Whenever you're ready."

The office featured a couple of folding chairs set up in front of Glitsky's desk, a few more leaning against the wall under the Active

Homicide board. Bracco took the nearest open one and sat on it, pulling a folded sheet of paper from his breast pocket. "Well, sir," he began, "I don't know how much you've heard about it yet, but we had a shooting out in the Haight Saturday morning."

"Vogler."

"Right. Me and Debra pulled it and here I am out there at seven-thirty or so and there's no place to park so I double up out on Ashbury—"

"And you got tagged."

"Yes, sir. Again." He came forward in his chair and placed the parking ticket on the desk. "The thing is, somebody's gotta talk to them and make them cut this shit out."

Glitsky lowered his hands, his mouth expressing distaste.

Bracco, who'd mentored under Glitsky in his first weeks of homicide duty, knew his lieutenant's disdain for profanity as well as anyone, and he shrugged. "You know what I mean."

Glitsky's shoulders rose and fell. "How many does this make?"

"For me? Like six or seven this year. Others guys might have more. I figured I had to talk to you about it."

Glitsky linked his fingers on the desk in front of him. "You think this is important?"

"Yes, sir. I do. Enough is enough."

Glitsky nodded. "And what would you have me do?"

"Well, number one, get these tickets erased. I'm out trying to do my job and I have to stop and fill in this totally bogus form. That's just wrong, Abe. So I thought maybe you could talk to somebody in traffic and just make it a rule that they can't tag us like this. Tell 'em that pretty soon it's going to cut into the time we need for our sensitivity training. That ought to do the job."

"Good idea, Darrel. They're always asking me how I can improve their operation, and now I'll have something to tell them." Glitsky scratched at his jawline. "Or, alternatively, of course, you can fill in the form. Or go to traffic yourself and make friends with whoever's running the place now, plead your case. That might work."

Not giving in, Bracco said, "I thought if it came from higher up . . ."

"Tell you what, Darrel, I'll mention the issue at the next chief's meeting, which is in about two hours. I'm sure they'll give it all the time it deserves. Meanwhile"—Glitsky pointed at the citation—"you hold on to that particular ticket. Call a reporter, maybe Jeff Elliot, have him come down and pitch him a 'CityTalk' column." Suddenly, the lieutenant pushed himself back from his desk and stood up. "I don't have you yet on the board."

Coming around, he went to the Active Homicide whiteboard and wrote the name VOGLER in the victims' column, then BRACCO/SCHIFF under inspectors. Finishing, he took a step back over to his desk and rested a haunch on the corner of it. "So where are you on that?"

"Couple of steps beyond nowhere, but only that." Bracco filled Glitsky in on some of the basics: the lack of signs of struggle, the backpack full of marijuana, the apparent murder weapon in the alley. "Because of the dope we got a warrant and searched his house on Saturday afternoon. And guess what? The guy had a full hydroponic pot garden in his attic." Bracco waited for a reaction, a nod, something to acknowledge this discovery. But Glitsky was just staring over his head, his bloodshot eyes vacant and glassy.

"Abe?"

"Yeah." Coming back. "What?"

"An attic full of pot plants."

"Good," Glitsky said.

"Yeah, we thought so. To say nothing of the computer records. The guy kept pretty good records on his clients and the wife, common-law, Jansey, didn't think to delete them before we got there."

"So she knew." Glitsky's gaze drifted back up to the ceiling.

Bracco nodded. "Well, yeah. Meanwhile, she, the girlfriend, Jansey, moved out with the kid, back in with her parents, about six months ago for a while."

"Why was that?"

"Just working things out with the relationship, if you believe her, which Debra doesn't." Again, since he wasn't getting anything resembling normal feedback from Glitsky, Bracco waited. After several seconds he went on reporting. "He beat her up. Sir?"

"Beat her up. Yeah. Go on."

"And because of the weed still there in the backpack, we're leaning toward some other motive besides that, maybe personal. Maybe like she got tired of getting hit. Jansey."

Glitsky nodded wearily. "Alibi?"

"That's another thing. They've got a boarder living in a room behind their garage. Young guy, med student at UCSF. Robert Tripp. Says he was with her. The kitchen drain was clogged up. He was helping her."

"Okay."

"Well, okay, except we're talking about six-thirty on a Saturday morning."

"Pretty early," Glitsky said.

"That's what we thought. Meanwhile, Vogler, the vic, worked all day six days a week."

"So Jansey and Tripp are hooked up?"

"Not impossible by a long shot."

"So what's next?"

"We talk to him, see if the alibi story holds up. If not, I go back and hit Jansey pretty hard. But on the chance that it's the weed in some way, Debra's got the list of clients she's working through."

"He kept a list?"

"He was an organized guy. Names, cell numbers, average buy disguised as coffee, dates. Of course, proving that this list was his marijuana customers won't be easy. Nobody's going to admit they were buying dope."

"How many of 'em are there?"

"Seventy or so. It might take a few days."

"So what'd he do, unload this stuff at the coffee shop?"

"That's the theory. He managed the place and had it all to himself, seems like."

"But he didn't own it?"

"No. The owner's a Maya Townshend. We're talking to her today, see what she knows, but the staff down there says they don't know her, she never came in the shop."

"If he's dealing to seventy people, maybe it's a turf thing."

"That might turn up. Oh, and last but not least, Vogler had a record. Robbery back in ninety-six. Jansey says he was just the driver and didn't even know what his friends were doing, but I pulled up the file and he was not an altar boy. They let him plead to one count, but the smart money says he was already in the life and just ran out of luck."

Glitsky took in that information in silence. After a minute, frowning at the effort to stay involved, he looked down at Bracco. "What about the gun on the street, with Vogler?"

"No idea, Abe, other than it was probably the murder weapon."

"Probably? They didn't run ballistics?"

"Sure. But it's our old pal the Glock hex-barrel. Bullet's consistent with the gun we found. The casing didn't have enough markings for positive ID. But we got one Glock .40 with a round fired, one bullet from a Glock .40, and one casing from a Glock .40. And we're running registration today. It's got a number."

"Will wonders never cease?"

"Well, we'll see." Bracco sat back in the folding chair. "So as I say, a lot's going to hang on Jansey's alibi, but if it holds up, we're about at square one."

Glitsky nodded and nodded.

"Sir," Bracco asked, "is everything all right?"

Glitsky looked through him, then focused on his inspector. "Fine," he said. "Everything's fine."

Twenty-six-year-old Robert Tripp's one-room studio was a narrow rectangle, about ten by fifteen, tacked onto the back of the garage. It featured a Formica counter with the butcher-block knife holder of a serious cook, every slot filled with high-end cutlery—carving, boning, and filet knives of various sizes, an impressive cleaver, and a sharpening steel. Also a sink and four-burner gas stove. A small shower-, sink-, and toilet-only bathroom in one corner.

He'd papered the walls with enlarged, full-color details of human body parts from his medical literature. The double bed was made up. A flat-screen television sat on a Goodwill desk below half a wall of Ikea bookshelf packed with CDs, magazines, paperbacks, and some folded clothes. A well-used bicycle hung from the ceiling.

It was a little after two P.M., and with the predictable volatility of San Francisco weather, the weekend's heat wave had been replaced by an Arctic afternoon, as an early fog had started to drift in just about when Schiff and Bracco had pulled up and parked on the street out front.

Now the two inspectors sat across from Tripp, in his medical scrubs, at his table in front of the solitary window that looked out onto a small grassless backyard bounded by a weathered brown fence, and with molded-plastic swings and a sliding board play-set erected in an island of tanbark.

"The disposal was backed up," Tripp said. "I already told you guys this."

"We believe you," Bracco replied. "We're trying to get the timing clear, that's all. You said this was at six-thirty?"

"Give or take. It was still dark out, so it couldn't have been much later."

Schiff, sitting back from the table with her legs crossed, canted forward a bit. "And Jansey felt okay coming over to knock at your door at that hour?"

The young man lifted his shoulders and let them fall. A couple of days' stubble darkened his cheeks and the bloodshot brown eyes said he hadn't been getting a lot of sleep; that combination lent a few years to an otherwise young face. "I was already up, studying. That's all I do, every waking hour, is study. Anyway, she probably saw the light was on."

"She couldn't fix the disposal herself?" Bracco asked.

He shrugged again. This seemed to be his default mannerism. "Ben. You know Ben? Her kid? He had a stomachache. He woke her up and told her about it right after his dad left for work. He'd been trying to do the dishes they'd left in the sink or something and then it overflowed and he left the water running. The place was a mess. The kid was a mess." He broke a smile. "It was a messy morning. Jansey was freaking out a little. That's all it was."

"And this was before she heard about Dylan?" Schiff asked.

"Of course."

"What was she wearing?" Bracco asked.

"When?"

"When she knocked on your door."

"I don't know. I don't remember. Jeans, I think, maybe a T-shirt. Why?"

Bracco came back with another question of his own. "So she was dressed? Shoes? Socks? A jacket?"

Tripp frowned. "Of course she was dressed. Why wouldn't she be dressed?"

Schiff supplied the answer. "If she'd just gotten woken up by her son and there was disaster going on below, she might have just thrown on a robe or something."

Tripp shook his head, impatient. "I just told you I didn't remember exactly what she was wearing. I thought it was jeans and a T-shirt. That's what she usually wears."

"You wouldn't have noticed," Bracco asked, "if she was in a robe? Maybe you were used to seeing her in a robe."

Tripp sat back and crossed his arms. "What's that supposed to mean?"

"It means maybe you were used to seeing her in a robe." Bracco came forward in his chair. "What is your relationship with her?"

"With Jansey? We're friends."

"Friends with benefits?"

"You mean am I sleeping with her? No, I'm not. Did I like her getting hit by Dylan? No to that one too. Did she come over here to talk about Ben or her life sometimes? Yep."

Schiff took over the questioning. "Did you know Dylan well?"

The topic shift slowed Tripp down. "To talk to. He was my landlord. He didn't treat Ben or Jansey right, but that really wasn't my business. I can't say I'm brokenhearted to see he got killed. He put on a good act, but he wasn't really that nice a guy. Jansey's going to be better off without him."

"So." Bracco, elbows on the table, asked, "So you were already up when Dylan went to work Saturday morning?"

"I don't know when Dylan went to work. But if it was after four, I was wide awake, in here studying until Jansey came to the door."

"And that was about six-thirty, you said?"

"I said I didn't know the time for sure. Only that it was still dark."

After the inspectors left, Tripp followed them outside to make sure they were leaving. When the car started up and headed down the street, he walked to the back door, opened it, and walked inside. "Jan!"

In a minute she was in the hallway coming toward him and then she was in his arms. They held each other for a long moment until finally Tripp pulled out of the embrace. "At the very least," he said, "they suspect. They asked me directly about us, but I said no, we were just friends. And how are they going to prove otherwise?" Looking back behind her, he went on. "So from the resounding silence I'm guessing they finished up there too."

She nodded. "They got it all, every leaf, every bud, every seed."

"Jesus."

"It's okay, actually," she said. "I can always start up again when this has all blown over. I've been thinking maybe it would be better if I didn't go back to it at all. The inspectors took all the records, all the buyers, so I'd have to start completely from scratch. And you know they'll be watching the house . . ."

"I doubt that. They've got better things to do, Jan. I mean, when they're done with this case. They're not coming back here to check your attic again."

She nodded. "You're probably right, but even so. It's no way to make a living. Maybe I'm just starting to realize that now, living in fear all the time that you're going to get caught."

"So how much are you getting from the insurance?"

"Three hundred. That's at least a few years. I could do something else."

"I'm sure you could," he said. "Anything you wanted, probably."

"And you wouldn't care?"

He laughed quietly. "Jan, I'm going to be a doctor. I'm going to make money hand over fist. You're going to be able to do anything you want." He drew her back into him. "So where's our little Benjamin now?"

"He's still at my mom and dad's."

"So we're actually alone? What are we waiting for?"

6

Maya Townshend's home was a big cut above average even in its very prestigious location. Behind a sculpted rose garden the residence rose four stories on the large northeast corner lot of Green and Divisadero. Behind it the escarpment dropped off precipitously down to the Marina, which meant that all of Maya Townshend's back and west-side windows—all forty-six of them—had killer views of the bay, the rust-red Golden Gate Bridge, the Marin headlands.

It was a multimillion-dollar property, and standing out in front of it, Bracco whistled. "There's more money in coffee than I thought."

Schiff stared at the immensity of the house, shaking her head. "This isn't coffee money, Darrel. Unless she also owns Starbucks. But in that case Bay Beans West would have been a Starbucks, right? No way she wouldn't have gone for the brand name."

It was closing in on one o'clock, the schizophrenic temperature back up near seventy. Above them, high clouds drifted in the blue. A fitful breeze, barely strong enough to ruffle Schiff's hair, hinted of another change in the weather, but for the moment it was nice.

The ornately carved door had an eight-toned ring.

"Lord, we thank thee. We bow our heads."

Schiff turned to him. "What?"

"Those bells. The song that goes with it. Lord, we thank thee. We bow our heads. You watch," he said. "She's Catholic."

"Maybe, but the Ferry Building, you might not have noticed, plays the same song."

"Maybe it's a Vatican plot."

Before Schiff could come back with a suitable wisecrack, the door opened to an attractive dark-haired woman in her early thirties who dressed as though she'd never heard of the Haight-Ashbury, or blue jeans, for that matter. In fact, she wore a grown-up, upscale version of the uniform for a Catholic girls' school—a plaid skirt over a white shirt under an argyle sweater. Her hair curled under at the shoulders. Green eyes, flawless skin.

Bracco and Schiff hadn't specifically told her when, or even if, they'd be coming by. Schiff had talked to her by telephone briefly over the weekend and said that the police might like to interview her sometime about Dylan Vogler and the business she owned, but she'd purposely refrained from making an appointment. There was the possibility that Maya wouldn't be in when they came to call, of course, but that downside was more than offset by the chance to catch her before she'd talked to a lawyer or given too much thought to what she might want to tell the inspectors.

"Hello," she said. "Can I help you?"

Bracco had his ID out. "Police inspectors, ma'am. Homicide. We wonder if we might have a word. On the Dylan Vogler matter."

"Sure. Of course." She stepped back, maybe unable to come up with an excuse on the spur of the moment why this wasn't a great time—and invited them inside, through a large square foyer with a thirty-foot ceiling.

Schiff stopped, agog at the panorama through the enormous windows. Apparently her reaction wasn't that unusual.

Maya stopped and presented the view as though it belonged to her. "I know," she said. "We're very fortunate."

"You must be selling a whole lot of coffee," Bracco said.

Maya's contralto laugh was unforced. "Oh, this doesn't come from BBW. This is all Joel, my husband. He's in real estate. The coffee shop is really more or less a hobby for me, to keep me busy."

Schiff came at her with a casual tone. "I understand you don't spend much time there."

Maya nodded. "Yes, that's true, very little. But I do most of the books, approve the ordering, sign the paychecks, that kind of thing." She shrugged apologetically. "It might not be really true, but I feel like I'm somewhat involved. It's good to have something keeping you busy besides the kids and outside of housework. Maybe you know."

Neither Schiff nor Bracco was married, so maybe they didn't. But Bracco kept the early patter alive. "But the place breaks even?"

"Oh, much better than that. Last year we grossed around forty thousand a month. It's actually quite a little gold mine, all things considered. People really like the place." Suddenly a pout appeared. "I'm sorry. What kind of hostess am I? Here we are all standing around. Would you like to sit down? Can I get you some coffee or something?"

"Sitting's good." Bracco lowered himself onto an ottoman. "Nothing for me, though."

Schiff took one end of the overstuffed floral-print couch. "I'm fine too."

For another second or two Maya stood expectantly, then she shrugged and took her place at the other end of the couch. "So all this business talk is interesting to me, of course, but that's not why you're here. How can I help you?"

Schiff threw a look over to Bracco, and he came forward slightly. "Well, let's get the hard stuff out of the way first. How long had Dylan Vogler managed BBW?"

Maya's lips turned up. "That's not a hard one. He pretty much started when I opened, which was ten years ago, and took over full-time about two years later."

"Were you aware," Bracco continued, "that he was selling marijuana out of BBW?"

All traces of animation left her face. "To be honest, I had heard a couple of rumors." She looked at Schiff.

The female inspector nodded. "They were evidently true. He was growing high-grade marijuana in his attic. He had a backpack full of it on him when he was shot. He's got records at his house for about seventy regular clients, a couple dozen of which we've already talked to. He sold it out of the store."

Maya's hand went to her mouth. "I didn't realize it was—"

"So"—Bracco kept up the press—"you didn't know that he had a criminal record?"

Her brow clouded as she whiplashed back to Bracco. "Well, yes. I knew about that. But that was a long time ago."

Schiff again. "Before he worked for you."

"Right."

Bracco, double-teaming. "You knew about his record when you hired him?"

"Of course."

"Of course?" Schiff asked.

Maya nodded. "We were friends. We'd been friends in college, USF. I knew he'd made a mistake, but he'd paid for it, and I had an opportunity to help him get back on his feet. It didn't seem like any kind of risk. He was a good guy and everybody liked him. He's been an ideal manager for all this time." She paused. "I can't believe he was selling dope over the counter at the store."

"That's pretty much established, ma'am," Bracco said. "Do you mind telling us how much he made working for you?"

For the first time Maya showed a reluctance to answer. Her back straightened for a second. "I don't see what that has to do with any-thing."

"Nevertheless," Schiff said, "it could save us some time."

Still rigid on her corner of the couch, now no longer smiling, Maya looked at her hands in her lap. "He made ninety thousand dol-lars a year. Seventy-five hundred a month."

"A lot of money," Schiff said.

"As I said," Maya responded, "the store made money. And largely because of Dylan's management. He did a good job, and I thought it was fair to pay him well."

"What's a manager of a Starbucks make?" Schiff asked.

Maya shook her head. "Less than that, I'm sure. But that doesn't matter. I'm not a big multinational corporation. I don't have stockholders. I can pay him whatever I want. He worked hard and I wanted to keep him happy, so I paid him well. As I said, we were friends in college. Once I got him set up, and especially once he started having a family, I felt a responsibility for him. Is there anything wrong with that?"

Schiff shook her head. "Nobody's saying there is, Mrs. Townshend."

But Bracco wasn't ready to stop mining this vein. He jumped in quickly. "So did you and your husband socialize with Dylan and his wife?"

"No," Maya said. "No. Not very much. He's my employee, after all. We have very different lives now." Suddenly seeming to realize that she'd exposed herself somehow, Maya relaxed back into the couch, trailed an arm along the armrest. "I'm afraid I don't understand what all these questions are about. Do you think I had something to do with Dylan's death? Or knew more about his marijuana business? I don't even know what's going to happen to BBW now. I may put it up for sale. Joel and I don't need it, and now that Dylan's gone, there's no real reason . . ." She shook her head and shrugged.

"Reason for what?" Schiff asked.

"I mean, to keep the place. I certainly don't have the time to go back in there and work it every day. I don't know what I'm going to do." By this time her eyes had taken on a brightness and shine—she seemed to be near tears.

"Mrs. Townshend"—Schiff laid a hand on the couch between

them—"we're trying to get some idea of who might have had a reason to kill Dylan. It's possible he said something to you, something he was worried about, a staff problem. Did he fire anybody recently, for example?"

"No. The staff's very loyal. He didn't mention anything like that. I really just don't have any idea. Maybe it was just a random shooting."

"Maybe," Bracco said, "but he wasn't robbed, so that leaves us scratching for a motive."

"If it's not something to do with the marijuana," Maya offered, "I just can't imagine what it would be."

"All right, ma'am." Bracco got to his feet. "One last quick thing. Just for the record, would you mind telling us where you were Saturday morning?"

Clearly, the question offended Maya, but she recovered. "I went to six-thirty Mass."

"On Saturday?" Bracco asked.

"I go to Mass most Saturdays. And Sundays too. It's not too fashionable anymore, I suppose," she said, "but it brings me a lot of peace."

"Well, here's to peace," Schiff said. "Can't have too much of that." She rose from her own seat, flashed a perfunctory smile. "We may need to speak with you again at some point."

"That'd be fine," Maya said, "if it will help you find whoever shot Dylan."

Bracco and Schiff were driving back downtown. They were stopped at a light at Van Ness Avenue, and Bracco was in the passenger seat. Schiff was talking. "So they're friends from college, and she feels responsible for him and his family, but they don't see each other socially and still she pays him nearly a hundred grand a year. This sings for you?"

"Why not?" Bracco said. "You notice her house? Her husband's doing okay."

"So why didn't she just sell the shop to him? Dylan?"

"I don't know. Maybe she hadn't thought of it. Maybe he didn't ask. It wasn't broke, so she didn't need to fix it."

They rode a few blocks in silence. Then Schiff said, "Another thing."

"You're really chewing on this, aren't you?"

"Tell me why there's no reason now to keep the shop. It's pulling in half a mil a year. She hires another manager, pays him half of what she paid Dylan, it's still making a half a mil a year. I'm not a business gal, but I don't see selling something that's making me half a million dollars a year."

"She doesn't need the money."

"Give me a break, Darrel. Half a million dollars to do basically nothing?"

In the passenger seat Bracco shrugged. "She'll sell it for five times that and it's out of her hair forever."

"I've got to think she owed him something. Dylan."

"What?"

"If she kept it open just to keep him getting paid."

"You're fishing."

"I am, but I got a license." They rode in silence for a half a block.

Then Bracco looked across at her partner. "I thought you were leaning toward Jansey."

"I was, maybe I still am. I like to keep an open mind. But something Robert Tripp said stuck with me."

After a couple of seconds Bracco said, "He didn't give us anything except the alibi."

"No. In fact, he did. He said Ben went and woke up his mother Saturday morning, remember?"

He nodded.

"Well," Schiff went on, "we can always double-check—and I intend to—by asking the kid about it, but that's the kind of detail I don't see Tripp or anybody else making up. That's the story as he knew it. And if it's true, it means Jansey hadn't left the house early to go down and lie in wait for Dylan at the store. She could have shot him way closer to home anyway."

"So how about Tripp?"

"As the shooter?"

Bracco nodded again. "He admits he was up. Maybe it's him who went to the store instead of Jansey. He could have thought he was protecting her, who maybe he's got a thing with, in spite of him saying no. Or wants to have one."

"Why?"

"Why what?"

"Why do it at the store?"

"I don't know. He says he's walking to school to study and they go down together. Then, maybe he knows Dylan's carrying a gun. And they're kind of friends, so he asks Dylan if he can just see it for a minute. And bang." He darted a quick glance at Schiff. "That accounts for the lack of any struggle. He caught him off guard, threw the gun away, ran back home in time to unplug the sink."

"Maybe," Schiff said. "Could have happened."

"But?"

"But nothing. As I say, I'm keeping an open mind."

7

The next day, Tuesday, Dismas Hardy sat at a small two-top against the back wall of Lou the Greek's, nursing a club soda and lime. As it was still well before noon, the lunch crowd hadn't yet materialized, and looking around him at the grungy, dark, semisubterranean watering hole and restaurant, Hardy marveled anew—as he did nearly every time he came here—that the place did any business at all, much less accommodated the booming daily influx of people who worked in and around the Hall of Justice just across the street.

After all, this was San Francisco, restaurant town extraordinaire. You could eat like a king at a couple of dozen places within a half-mile radius—elegant ambience, exotic ingredients, world-class chefs, superb professional service.

Where you wouldn't find any of the above was at Lou's. The eponymous Lou had a Chinese wife named Chiu who had all the creativity of any of the city's celebrated cooks, a fact she proved every day with the Special, which was the only menu item the place served. While showcasing Chiu's culinary wizardry, the Special also revealed a glaring blind spot in her originality—she believed that her creations should always and only include native dishes and ingredients from her own China and from Lou's Greece. Together.

It wasn't exactly what the rest of California was eating under the name Pacific Rim fusion, but within her rather limited universe, Chiu for years had been inventing meal after adventurous meal featuring often-bizarre combinations of wontons, bao dumplings, grape leaves, tsatsiki, cilantro, duck, squid, olives, yogurt—some of which were tasty, many not. It didn't seem to matter—the crowds kept coming, packing the place for lunch five days a week.

Today the Special, sweet and sour spanakopita with five-spice lemon chicken, had Hardy thinking about passing on that selection and walking uptown to Sam's Grill after his meeting, ordering some sand dabs and a nice glass of Gavi. If she'd only left out the sweet and sour, he was thinking . . .

"Hey, Diz."

Hardy, caught unawares in his daydreaming, pushed his chair back and stood to shake hands with Harlen Fisk, a member of San Francisco's Board of Supervisors and nephew of the mayor, Kathy West. Fisk, at a couple of inches over six feet, weighed in at around two hundred and fifty pounds and cut an impressive figure in his tailored Italian suit.

Hardy had first met him when Harlen had partnered with Darrel Bracco and worked for a time as a hit-and-run inspector in the homicide detail. The cop phase had been just another step in the man's political grooming—he was going to be West's handpicked successor and everybody knew it. At forty-one he was getting to be the right age now, but if he was impatient with the wait to become mayor, he didn't show it.

Now, sitting down, he glanced at the Special card and grimaced. "You know," he said, "spanakopita by itself is a fine dish. Why's it have to be sweet and sour?"

Hardy broke his grin. "I just was thinking the exact same thought. And here's another one—if it's five-spice lemon chicken, doesn't the lemon make it six spices? And what are the other five?"

"I think five-spice is more or less considered one spice. Like curry."

"I thought curry was one spice."

"No. It's a mixture. That's why you have different flavors and heats of curries. Different mixtures of stuff."

"Dang. Just when you think you've got it all figured out," Hardy
said. His eyes brightened. "Maybe they'd hold the sweet and sour if
we asked."

Fisk nodded. "We could always try, though history argues
against it."

Ten minutes later, they were served. It turned out that, as expected, the sweet and sour was integral to this particular version of
spinach in filo dough and couldn't be substituted out; less expect-
edly, when Fisk took his first bite, he discovered that it tasted pretty
good. He told a still-skeptical and reluctant Hardy, "My kids like
ketchup on spinach. This is kind of similar."

Hardy took his own small bite, chewed, shook his head in admi-
ration. "The woman's a genius." He forked a larger portion. "So," he
said when he'd swallowed, "what's up?"

"My sister," Harlen said. "My little sister, actually. Maya. Her last
name's Townshend now. She wants to talk to a lawyer and I thought
I'd recommend you, if you were interested."

"In all probability," Hardy said, "if it's not a divorce. I don't do
divorce."

"I don't blame you," Fisk said. "It's not that. What it is, is she
owns Bay Beans West, a coffee shop out on Haight. You know it?"

"I've driven past, sure." But then Hardy's brain caught up, and he
pointed a finger. "Somebody got shot there over the weekend. The
manager?"

"Right. Dylan Vogler."

"Is she a suspect?"

Fisk had a rich two-note laugh and he used it. "No, no, no way.
You've got to know Maya. Little Miss Junior League, mother of two,
sweetest thing you ever met. No, what happened is she just got a visit
from homicide yesterday—actually, in the small-world department, it
was Darrel and his new partner. A woman."

"Debra Schiff."

"Must be, if you say so. Anyway, they came and talked to her and after they left she called and said maybe she ought to have a lawyer if she was going to be talking to the police."

"I love people who think like she does. And she's not all wrong."

"That's what I told her. You can't be too careful on that front, although in her case, knowing her, I'd say it's a bit of a stretch."

"What'd they ask her about? She tell you?"

Fisk shrugged. "It all sounded general to me. Her guy gets shot outside her store, they're going to want to talk to her, right? It turns out, evidently, that Dylan was selling dope out of the shop, and she thinks because she owned it, that might get her in trouble."

"She might be right. What kind of dope?"

"Just weed, I think."

"How much weed?"

"I don't know. Does it matter?"

"It might if it was a major warehouse for distribution."

"I don't think it was that. It was mostly a happening coffee shop. But say it was."

"What?"

"A major warehouse or something."

Hardy fixed him with a wary look. "You know something you're not telling me?"

"No, no. Just to know so I can tell Maya if she asks. What if this guy Dylan was moving large quantities? What would be Maya's exposure as the owner?"

"I'm not sure," Hardy said. "I'd have to look it up. Offhand, I'd say she's probably okay if she can prove she didn't know anything about it. But landlords in crack neighborhoods—I mean, where they're selling out of every second apartment—they've been known to get their property forfeited."

The word jacked Harlen right up. "Forfeited! You mean the whole building?"

Hardy held up a palm to calm him. "Sometimes, but usually this is with bad guys, knee-deep in the business. If the feds get involved, they can take the whole property." Hardy knew that, actually, the city's own DA could try to take the property too; but they never would in this situation. He took a bite of his Special. "But that's usually, as I say, when they know they've got a live one they're trying to hassle. And that doesn't sound much like your sister's situation."

"Not even close, Diz. She didn't know much, if anything, about this, I'm sure. She's a Goody Two-shoes and would never have taken that risk. Her husband is Joel Townshend—Townshend Real Estate, struggling by on a couple of mil a year. Believe me, they don't need more money."

"I hate them already," Hardy said.

"Me too. But there you go. Anyway, the point is, the cops surprised her and got her nervous. You know how that is. So would you mind talking to her?"

Hardy told Harlen that that went without saying, then pulled a small grimace. "But it's just a shame she's already talked to them. That's all I was thinking. You know how long they were there, Darrel and Debra?"

"She didn't say. Half hour or so, I gathered."

"Well, probably not too much damage done. As long as she didn't lie to them."

Fisk nodded comfortably. "I don't think you have to worry on that score," he said. "She wouldn't have done that. That's just not who she is."

After telling Fisk to have his sister give him a call to make an appointment, Hardy crossed the street and walked into the massive gray stucco block that was San Francisco's Hall of Justice. He'd worked there as an assistant DA for a couple of years after law school,

and then for most of another year when he'd started practicing law
again after he'd woken up from his own grief-induced decade following Michael's death.

He thought it said something about the building's load of negative karma that after all the time he'd spent in it—it was also where
he'd tried the great majority of his cases as a defense attorney—he
still found the place oppressive. Back in the day the front doors at
least had lent an air of expansiveness to the front lobby area. But
since 9/11 the terrorism experts had closed all but one doorway, covering the rest of the front window glass with plywood.

Now everyone passed through the one door, waited in line, went
through the makeshift joke of a security checkpoint, metal detector
and all, and eventually emerged into the din and bustle of the ground
floor, which housed not only the line for traffic court, serpentining
its way out of the courtroom and past the elevators, but also the
Southern Station of the San Francisco Police Department.

So uniformed cops were thick on the ground, as were lawyers,
people visiting the jail upstairs, workers in the building. In its wisdom the city had also licensed a snack and coffee kiosk right out on
the lobby floor, and the line of cheerful folks queuing up for their
something to eat or drink often got tangled up with their counter-
parts happily awaiting their turn in traffic court. Hardy had heard
that the record for most fistfights in a day over spaces in one line or
another was six, although that was admittedly an anomaly. The average for actual blows struck was no more than one a week.

But because he'd met Harlen early to avoid the rush at Lou's, it
was high lunch hour when he got to the metal detector, and all the
various lines within and without the lobby seemed to have merged
into one cacophonous mob. Finally, getting to the front of his own
line, Hardy put his keys and his Swiss army knife onto the desk next
to the metal detector and walked through, picking them up without
any acknowledgment from the cop manning the station, who was

turned around the whole time, arguing with another cop about when he was going to get relieved so he could have some lunch.

Hardy felt he could have put a Stinger missile on the table, walked through the metal detector, picked up the rocket, and gone on his merry way, and no one would have been the wiser. He'd seen plain-clothes cops walk through with guns and had always told himself that this was because the station cops at the detector knew the plain-clothes, but really he wasn't so sure. Maybe it was just a stupid system that didn't work.

His sense of the surreal was heightened when he turned the cor-ner and watched the stream of people coming through the com-pletely unsecured back door between the Hall and the jail. The door was supposed to be locked, but anyone who worked in the building for more than a few months could get a copy of the key. And polite folks that they were, many would routinely hold open the door for anybody else trying to walk in at the same time.

Maybe, he thought, that's why the cops at the metal detector were so lackadaisical. They figured that anybody who had a gun would probably have the sense to walk around the building and come in the back.

Finally, entertained by his musings, Hardy made it to the elevator, pressed "5," and rode up pressed by the crush of bodies against the side wall, resolving he would never again come here for a social call, as he was doing now.

When he was being paid, okay, but this was lunacy.

By contrast the hallway on the fifth floor was a haven of serenity. Still with all the charm of an Eastern bloc housing project, still a ster-ile airless walkway with industrial green tile and fluorescent lighting, but peaceful nonetheless, somehow—strangely—comforting, even welcoming, after what he'd come through to get there.

He walked down about halfway and turned into the door mark-ing the homicide detail. Neither of the two clerks assigned there were at their positions, so Hardy lifted the hinged counter that separated the room and went through to the hall leading to Glitsky's office. With the metal detector still fresh in his mind and his Swiss army knife in his pocket, it occurred to him that he could quite easily take a few more steps into Glitsky's office and cut his friend's throat and walk out, and in all probability no one would ever know.

The thought brought half a smile. It was a funny world, Hardy thought, if you knew where to look.

Now here he was at Glitsky's door, but it was closed, locked up. He knocked once, waited half a second. If Abe was in, traditionally the door would be open or at least unlocked. He turned to leave and heard a drawer slam inside. "One minute."

Glitsky looked like hell—ashen and drawn—and for a moment Hardy thought that Zachary hadn't made it and that Abe had only just heard.

"Tell me he's okay," he said.

"The same."

"The induced coma?"

A nod, and Hardy took a breath of relief. Glitsky squinted out of the gloom of his office at his best friend. "What do you want?"

"Nothing. Just checking in."

When Treya came by his house to pick up Rachel and take her to school that morning, Hardy had been stunned to learn from her that Abe had gone in to work. Treya, as usual, had defended him—they'd done the brain-opening surgery on Zachary Sunday morning and there was nothing to be done with him now for at least the next several days, during which time they'd be keeping him in what was apparently called a pentobarbital coma. Abe could either sit in the waiting room at the hospital going crazy, or go to work and hope the day passed more quickly. He'd chosen the latter.

Now, after another few seconds staring at nothing, Glitsky turned back toward his desk and Hardy followed him in. Closing the door,

Hardy reached for the light switch, thought better of it, pulled around a chair, and sat. A diffuse light from the high windows kept the place from utter darkness, but reading here would be a stretch.

Glitsky sat with his arms crossed over his chest, his eyes focused somewhere a foot or two above Hardy's head. From time to time he'd draw a breath, but nothing so deep as a sigh. There was resignation in the wasted face, but no rage, usually Glitsky's default emotion.

The lack of anger worried Hardy.

"Yesterday morning Treya said they're keeping him unconscious for a few days," he said at last. "You got any more than that?"

"No."

"She said the operation was a success."

"In the sense that he lived through it."

"I thought it gave the brain room to swell."

"Right. That's what it does."

"Then what?"

"What do you mean?"

"I mean, what are you looking at? What's the prognosis?"

Glitsky brought his eyes to Hardy's. It seemed a long time before he spoke. "Either the swelling's going to go down and he gets better to some degree, although we can't know how much for a couple of months"—he hesitated—"either that, or one of the clots breaks up too much or any other random thing happens and he dies."

The silence gathered.

"You know," Glitsky said quietly at last, "I'm thinking it wouldn't have been the worst result if the heart thing had killed him when he was born." Zachary's birth had been accompanied by the discovery of a heart murmur, which, though later found to be benign, had raised the specter of his early death from congenital heart failure. "At least that wouldn't have been my fault."

"This wasn't your fault, Abe."

Glitsky shook his head. "You weren't there."

"Treya told me what happened."

"She wasn't there either."

"So tell me."

Glitsky's gaze went back to the ceiling. He unfolded his arms and put his palms flat on the desk. "He was right next to me. I mean, all I had to do was block him, one foot in front of that big fucking wheel." Glitsky's unaccustomed profanity hung in the room, a boundary crossed. "Instead I walked over to get his helmet, which should have been on him first." He leveled his gaze. "Five seconds, Diz. Five stupid seconds."

"You know why they call them accidents, Abe? They're nobody's fault."

Glitsky lived with that for a minute. Then, "I think I'm going to quit."

"Quit what?"

"This." Glitsky gestured around at the office. "Here."

"How would that help?"

"I don't know. Maybe it wouldn't." He brought a hand to his forehead, rubbed at the bridge of his nose. "What were we saying?"

"I've got an idea," Hardy said. "Why don't you go home and get some sleep? Take a few days off while this shakes out."

"And what? Just wait?"

"What else are you doing here?"

Glitsky looked through him for about five seconds. Finally, he nodded and started to push himself back from the desk, then stopped and reached for his telephone. He punched a few numbers, then after a moment spoke into the receiver. "Hey," he said. "No, nothing new. Diz is up here. He thinks I ought to go home and get some rest. Maybe you want to do the same thing." He waited, listened for another second or two, then said, "I'll swing by and pick you up on the way out."

8

When Hardy got back to his office on Sutter Street about twenty minutes after he'd left Glitsky, his receptionist/secretary, Phyllis, greeted him out in the lobby with a chilly smile and the comment that since she kept his calendar, it might be helpful if he shared his appointment schedule with her from time to time.

"But I do," he said. "Religiously." He put his hand over his heart. "Phyllis, I hope you know with an absolute certainty I would never, under any conditions, make an appointment without sharing every detail of it with you."

Phyllis cast her eyes heavenward in her perpetual exasperation over her boss's sarcasm. She threw a fast glance back over her shoulder, indicating a young woman sitting and perusing a magazine on the couch against the wall behind her circular workstation.

Hardy followed the glance. The woman turned a page in her magazine. "She's here for me?" he whispered with a bit of theatricality. "It must be a trick to make me look bad in front of you. I swear I've never seen her before."

Phyllis pursed her lips. "She says she has an appointment, referred by Harlen Fisk. A Mrs. Townshend."

"Aha! She was supposed to call and make an appointment, Phyllis. Maybe she misunderstood. But the real good news is that this was not my fault." At her skeptical expression he added, "Hey, it happens."

Leaving his receptionist with a conciliatory pat on the arm, he breezed around her and in a couple of steps stood in front of his waiting guest. "Mrs. Townshend? Dismas Hardy. Sorry to have kept you waiting."

She snapped the magazine closed and popped up to her feet, her mouth set in a prim line, her forehead creased with worry. Reaching out, she took Hardy's hand in a firm grip, as though now that he'd finally arrived, she didn't want to lose him.

"I asked Harlen to have you give me a call to make an appointment. I'm afraid I didn't expect you to come right on down."

She let go of his hand and brought her fingers up to her mouth. "Oh, I'm sorry. I just thought . . . I mean, he told me where you worked and that he'd talked to you and I was free and just gathered—"

Hardy held up his own hand, stopping her. "It's okay," he said. "Timing's everything and yours couldn't be better. I was looking at a long tedious afternoon of administration, and now instead I get to chat with Harlen's sister." He broke a welcoming grin and guided her toward his office with a hand under her elbow. "Does that also make you the mayor's niece?"

"Yes."

"Well"—Hardy led her into his office—"I'm a big fan of Kathy's as well. Since back in her own supervisor days." Closing the door behind them, he motioned to the more casual of the two seating areas, a couple of wing chairs by a magazine table. "Can I get you something to drink? Coffee? Wine? Something a little stronger?"

"Actually . . . well, it's a little early, but I'm . . . I think I must be a little nervous. Maybe a glass of wine wouldn't be too bad."

"You don't need to be nervous," Hardy said. "Nothing we say in this room leaves here if you don't want it to. Red or white?"

"White."

"White it is." Hardy crossed over to the mirror-backed, granite-topped wet bar that took up most of one of his walls. The bar was a bit of a showcase piece, with a golden inlaid sink and gold faucet, one open shelf for the oversized wineglasses and another for the china cups, a large commercial espresso-making machine, and a selection of teas, mixers, and spirits arranged along the rest of the free wall space. Opening the half-sized refrigerator, he stopped and turned back to her again. "Chardonnay or other?"

"Other, I think."

"I think so too. Maybe I'll join you." He pulled out a bottle of Groth Sauvignon Blanc. Serving her, he said, "If you think the bar service here is good, wait'll you see our legal work." He flashed what he knew was his professional disarming smile, sat down across from her, and took a sip of his wine, silently prompting her to do the same. "Now how can I help you?"

After her first small sip she held her wineglass on her lap with both hands. "I think I'm in trouble," she began. "I don't know what to do."

"Let's see if the first part's true first, then see where that leads us. Why do you think you're in trouble? Because the police came to see you about your manager's death?"

"Partly that. I don't know how much Harlen told you, but Dylan was selling dope—marijuana only, I hope—out of my store."

"Harlen told me you didn't know much about that."

"I didn't. Not really."

"Then you shouldn't be in trouble." He broke a smile. "That was easy. Next problem?"

"Really?"

"You mean really you shouldn't be in trouble?" He didn't feel he needed to go into the low-probability scenario of a forfeiture. "Yes, really."

"But . . . well, I mean, I own the place. I'm the legal owner. If somebody trips and falls there, I'm the one who gets sued."

Hardy sat back, put an ankle on a knee, and took another sip of his wine. "That's not the same situation. Nobody's suffering recoverable harm because they bought marijuana at your place. Who's going to sue you?"

But she shook her head again. "I'm not so worried, really, about getting sued. I'm worried about—about the police coming to talk to me again."

Against all of his training, and possibly because of the casual nature of Harlen's request that Hardy have a chat with his sister, Hardy was tempted for a moment to come right out and ask her if she had in fact killed her manager. Though he didn't for a minute think that this was likely, it was a question you normally didn't ask, an unspoken rule of the defense business. Because if you, the lawyer, didn't know, you would always be acting in technical good faith in your client's defense. And, of course, in theory it wasn't supposed to matter anyway. You argued the evidence that could be proved in court. Not necessarily the facts.

So, instead, he said, "I'm guessing you really don't have anything to worry about."

"I don't know if that's true." She saw her wine sitting there on her lap and brought the glass to her lips. "Why would that be true?"

"Because your inspector, Bracco, used to be Harlen's partner in homicide. Did you know that?"

"Okay, but what does that mean?"

"Well, the first thing it means in the real world is that Bracco's going to find out you're Harlen's sister. Knowing Harlen's inherent shyness," he said with irony, "he might even know by now. So unless Bracco's got something close to a smoking gun in your hand, he's going to be inclined to cut you some slack to begin with. You're the one who's lost your manager, so you've been victimized by this murder too. Plus, your connection to the mayor isn't going to make Darrel Bracco want to cause you any problems. Was he a little hard on you?"

"A little bit." She hesitated. "He seemed to think that there was something weird about how much I paid Dylan, or something about our relationship, I don't know what. But it just made me uncomfortable."

"It's supposed to. It's one of the things cops do when they interrogate people. They find a soft spot and go at it."

"But why did he think it was a soft spot?"

"I don't know. How much did you pay him? Dylan?"

When he heard the number, Hardy kept his face straight and took a quick breath to hide his surprise. "That's a real salary."

"I know. But he did a real job. He was good with the customers. I hardly ever had to be there. If ever. I felt he was worth it."

"Well, then, who's to argue? You own the place."

"Right. But Inspector Bracco, he wanted to know if we socialized together, Dylan and I."

"And?"

"And I told him no, which is true. But he seemed to think that was weird somehow. In spite of the fact that Dylan and Jansey had their own life and it's nothing like mine and Joel's."

"Lots of business owners don't socialize with their employees," Hardy said. "I don't see why Bracco would think it's strange that you don't."

"Maybe because I told him Dylan and I had been friends in college. This was before he did his time in prison, of course."

Hardy took a beat to let that settle. "I don't believe I've heard about that yet."

She shook her head. "It was a misunderstanding, a stupid juvenile mistake, call it what you will. He got involved somehow in a robbery and got caught. But long story short, when he got out, I was hoping to get the store up and going and . . . anyway, he started working for me."

"So you were close friends in college?"

Hesitating, she tightened her mouth, checked out the windows behind Hardy. "We weren't intimate, if that's what you're asking. We were friends."

Hardy brought his glass to his mouth, sipped, waited. She had more to tell him and he wanted to give her the space. She scanned the corners of the room, telegraphing to Hardy the jumble of her thoughts. He sat, unmoving, giving her time.

Finally, with an intake of breath, she met his eyes. "I suppose I wasn't exactly the same person then as I am now."

"I wouldn't think so," Hardy said. "That was what? About ten years ago?"

"Close enough."

"So you're saying that you and Dylan wouldn't have been friends if you met him now?"

She shook her head. "Not the same type of friends, certainly."

"And what type was that?"

"Well," she said, "we were a little wild, I guess. This crowd of us who just kind of found each other and got into doing stuff together, partying. Drinking, pranks, you know."

Hardy had an idea of what she was talking about. "Dope?"

"Mostly just weed," she said, "but, yeah. Some cocaine, too, once in a while, when we could get it." She picked up her wineglass and drank half of it down. "Hell, why am I sugarcoating this to you, Mr. Hardy?"

"Dismas, please."

"All right. Dismas. We would try anything we could get our hands on. Weed, coke, Ecstasy, alcohol, mushroom, pills—uppers or downers or whatever. It was funny," she went on, "it wasn't like we were all stoned all the time. I mean, we had classes and most of us generally did okay in them, I think, but then we'd get together on weekends and just kind of blow it all out. It was really stupid."

"And you're afraid, now that the police have this dope connection to Dylan, that somehow all this you did way back then is going to come back and bite you?"

Her expression of gratitude and relief at his understanding made Hardy realize how seriously she was taking all of this. "I really didn't want to know about him selling dope through the shop, but if they find out about the way we were in college, they're not going to believe me, no matter what I say. I don't know if *I'd* believe me."

"Belief isn't the point," Hardy said. "Is there anything on your books from the shop that might make it look like you were somehow profiting from his dope business?"

"No. There couldn't be. I wasn't."

Hardy sat back, consciously pausing. He had no intention of getting answers from his new client relating to the facts of her guilt or innocence, but that's where this discussion seemed to be leading them. He put on what he hoped would be a neutral expression. "Well, as I said earlier, given your connection to Harlen and the mayor, Bracco isn't going to be looking to open a can of worms investigating you." And then, in spite of himself, in an effort to give her a touch of comfort, he broke his own lawyer's rule and added, "Not unless he's got something tying you to Dylan's murder."

She took this as a question and, evading it, swallowed, tried a smile, met his eyes, and quickly looked down.

Hardy, who'd been about to stand up and walk her out with a figurative pat on the head, checked himself and settled back into his chair. "Is there anything else?"

"Not really. But I'm just afraid it might look . . . I'd so really rather not talk to the police again. It's Joel too."

"Your husband?"

She bobbed her head. "He didn't know me back then. I met him after that time was over. I haven't been able to make myself tell him about too much of it. He thinks . . . well, he'd never think that I could have been the way I was. I don't think he'd have an easy time accepting it. We're the Townshends, after all. He's got investors who count on that. So there's a certain expected"—she sighed—"behavior. He's always wanted me to sell the shop, you know."

"Why was that?"

"It just wasn't the kind of business he felt comfortable with. I think the bottom line was that he really just didn't like Dylan, didn't trust him, didn't understand why I kept him on and wouldn't let go of the place."

"Why wouldn't you? If you didn't need the money, and I presume you didn't."

"No. It wasn't the money." She hesitated, then finally came out with it. "But the shop was my own. It made me feel like I was contributing. I just couldn't ever convince myself that there was a good enough reason to give it up." She let out a breath of pent-up frustration. "Anyway, Harlen told me you could be there with me if the police want to talk to me again, just to make sure I don't say something wrong."

"I could do that," Hardy said, "and of course I will do that." He leaned forward in his chair and leveled his gaze at her. "But you and I both know you don't need a lawyer to keep the police from asking you about the hijinks of you and your friends in college. And practically speaking, no one's really going to think you were skimming from Dylan's dope business. If anything, people will feel sorry for you that he was abusing your confidence the way he was."

"So you're asking why I told Harlen I needed a lawyer."

"Never that," Hardy said with a small smile. "Everybody needs a lawyer all the time. That's my motto. But in this case, from what you've told me, maybe not so much."

"You don't think I'm telling you the truth," she said.

"It's not what you've said. Maybe it's what you haven't." He pointed down at her hands and added gently, "That's a fragile glass. If you squeeze it any harder, I've got to warn you, it's going to break."

For a long moment, her eyes glazed over and she sat utterly still. Finally, a small tremor passed through her body, she blinked, and a tear spilled onto her cheek. "Dylan called me the night before and said he had to see me first thing the next morning. That it was an emergency. So I went down there."

"You mean Saturday morning?"

"Yes." She closed both eyes, trying to regain her composure. "I went into the alley and saw him. He was already dead." Meeting Hardy's eyes, she went on in a rush. "I didn't know what I should do, other than I knew I didn't want to be there. I got back in the car and left. I mean, there was nothing I could do for Dylan. That was obvious. But then, when the police came to question me at my house, I told them I'd been at Mass, which is where I did go afterward, except I was very late, after communion, and somebody might remember that. And then I thought, what if somebody had seen me and they described me or my car to the police?"

Hardy let her sit with her words for a moment. Then, "What was the emergency?"

"He didn't say. Just that he had to see me."

"In person?"

"I know. I didn't know what to do with that—it didn't seem to make much sense—but it was the first time he'd ever called with a message like that, and I thought I ought to go."

Hardy placed his wineglass onto the small table in front of him. Suddenly things had turned serious. She had lied to the police about her alibi for the time of a murder. Her reason for wanting him to represent her in the event of another interrogation was now not only rational but powerful. Given a lack of other quality suspects, that fact alone might be enough to give her prominence in their investigation.

Whether or not she was politically connected.

"Plus," she went on.

He waited.

"If they check his phone records—and I guess they do that, don't they?—they're going to find out he called me, and they'll want to know about that, won't they?"

Hardy shrugged. "He managed your store. That wouldn't necessarily be incriminating." He sat back again. "How about this? When Bracco calls again, if he does, let me know right away and we'll see what he wants to talk about and then decide if we'd be well served by telling him you were there. If not, we won't. How's that sound?"

She attempted a shaky smile. "A little scary, really. I just want this to go away. Not have Joel and the kids have to find out the way I was."

"I don't know," Hardy said, finally getting up, taking one of his business cards out of his wallet, and handing it to her. "People surprise you. They might all understand and then you'd never have to worry about it again. And, you know," he added, "we were all in college and not all of us were saints. Maybe not even Joel."

Shaking her head, she said, "You don't know him." She'd followed him up and now crossed over to his desk, taking her own wallet from her purse. "I'm afraid Harlen didn't mention what this would cost. Do you bill me or do I pay as I go?"

"Whatever you'd prefer," Hardy said, willing in this case to break one of the major rules of defense law, which was get your money up front. But Maya was Harlen's sister and he thought a little professional courtesy wouldn't be out of order. Going to the file drawer behind his desk, he withdrew his standard contract and handed it over to her.

She scanned it quickly. "How does three thousand sound as a retainer?" she asked, opening her checkbook.

"That'll probably get you a refund when this is over," he said.

She handed him the check, and then they were standing facing each other by the office door. "So it's okay. I can call you?" she asked.

"Anytime, day or night." He pointed at the card. "All the numbers in the world where I can be reached."

The gratitude flooded back into her eyes. "Thank you," she said.

And he opened the door to let her out.

About twenty minutes later Hardy picked up the phone on his desk. "Yo."

"Yo yourself." The voice of his partner Wes Farrell. "What are you doing?"

"When?"

"Right now."

"Many things all at once," Hardy said. "Breathing, talking to you, figuring out our talented pool of associates' utilization numbers for the third quarter. Why?"

"Because I wondered if you might have a minute."

"Are you upstairs?" Wes worked alone on the third floor one level up, in an office that had once in a different world been Hardy's. "You could always just come on down like you usually do."

"I could, but then I'd have to pass the Phyllis test and I don't know if I'm up to it." Hardy heard something in the voice. Wes was nearly always upbeat, but he wasn't now. "If I'm really not interrupting you at something important, you want to come up for a minute?"

"Sure," Hardy said. "I'm on my way." As he passed the reception area, Phyllis raised her eyebrows and attempted a smile that nevertheless seemed somehow accusatory. Hardy pointed upward. "Just going to see Wes," he explained. "Firm business."

This was the password, he knew. Hardy was doing what she thought he ought to be doing, managing the firm. Phyllis graced him with an approving nod and swirled back to face her switchboard. Over the years Hardy had developed a faint and grudging affection for his receptionist/secretary, but as he mounted the stairway at the far end of the lobby, he wondered how sad he would actually be if she were, say, mercifully and swiftly executed by a large truck running a red light.

Farrell's door, festooned with left-wing bumper stickers, yawned open and Hardy knocked once before crossing the threshold. The office, such as it was, gave only the merest nod to the legal work Farrell supposedly did there. No desk, no files, just a couple of couches, a coffee table, some random easy chairs, a flat-screen TV on one side wall, a Nerf basketball hoop on another, a library table with more functional wooden chairs scattered roughly around it. One of the chairs was on its side at the moment.

Gert, his dog, slept in a corner.

In another corner by one of the windows Farrell did have a modern computer he never turned off, and he was sitting at that now, though facing away from it and toward him as Hardy came in. As usual when he wasn't going to court, Wes wasn't dressed much for success. Today he wore a pair of wrinkled tan Docker pants and wingtips that hadn't been shined since Watergate. And of course he sported his usual T-shirt, which today took Hardy more than the usual quick glance to read: "Haikus can be easy./But sometimes they don't make sense./Refrigerator."

Hardy had to break a smile, pointing to it and saying, "That might be one of the best."

Farrell looked down. "Yeah. I thought it'd get Sam laughing, but no."

"You guys okay?"

The shoulders rose and fell. "We'll probably get over it. I hope so."

"What?"

"This stupid argument. Or maybe not so stupid if it might really break us up. Which I'm starting to think it's got a chance."

"What about?"

Farrell rolled his eyes. Sitting in his ergonomic chair, he slumped.

His thick brownish-gray hair was unsecured and fell all around to the top of his shoulders. Hardy thought he looked about twenty years older than he was. "She thinks I don't care enough about the homeless."

"What about the homeless?"

"We shouldn't tell 'em it's cool to come here and then start making them go to shelters and stuff. We should respect them as individuals. Jesus. That's how it started, anyway. Now it's all she's not sure she knows who I really am or if she still wants to be with me."

Normally, Hardy would have asked why she wanted to be with him in the first place, but this wasn't the time. So he asked, "Because why, exactly?"

"I think in the last fight, I used the word *vagrant*, or maybe *bum*. Or maybe both. I probably did both, knowing me when I'm arguing. Anyway, somehow I betrayed my terminal insensitivity to the plight of . . ." He gestured in little circles with his hand. "Et cetera, et cetera." Farrell let out a long breath. "I don't know what I'm talking about, Diz. And that's not it, anyway. What I wanted to see you about."

Hardy pulled the fallen wooden chair upright and sat on it. "I'm listening, but I hope you're not going to tell me you're quitting, because Glitsky just told me he's quitting and if you both quit on the same day, I'll start to feel like all my friends are old, which would mean I'm old, and that would be depressing."

Farrell's head came up. "Glitsky's quitting?"

"Maybe not," Hardy said. "I might have talked him out of it. He probably didn't even mean it. He's having a bad time."

"Maybe we should start a club."

"You don't want to be in his club. His kid's in the hospital with a head injury."

"Shit. How bad?"

"Bad enough, but alive at least. For now." Hardy let out his own sigh, met his partner's gaze. "So. What do you want to talk about?"

Farrell came forward, elbows on his knees, his hands linked tightly in front. "There's this coffee place out near my house," he said. "Bay Beans West, maybe you read about it this weekend. The manager, this guy named Dylan Vogler, got himself shot on Saturday. Sam, in fact, discovered the body. Well, I just got a call on my cell from Debra Schiff, you know her?"

"Sure." Hardy nodded. "Homicide. Why'd she call you?"

Farrell hung his head for a minute. "Because Vogler sold weed out of the shop, and he evidently kept a list of his regular clients on his computer at home." He raised his tortured eyes. "It's gonna get out, Diz. Hell, it's probably already out. What I'm wondering is if you think it would be better for the good of the firm if I resigned."

9

Schiff couldn't let go of what she felt was Maya Townshend's crucial slip of the tongue: "There's no real reason to keep the place." Although admittedly slim pickins, she felt it was worth pursuing. Bracco and she agreed, however, that they could do their fishing elsewhere first, before coming back if necessary and taking on Maya head-to-head.

To this end, in the midafternoon, maybe ten other people in the shop, they were sitting up near the bakery products area of BBW with Eugenio Ruiz, who'd been one of the assistant managers under Vogler, and who'd opened the place this Tuesday morning and was currently functioning as the manager.

Eugenio was in his early twenties, small, wiry, and highly strung. He wore his thick black hair in a ponytail and had a couple of days of dark beard growth covering the acne scars. Today he was wearing black slacks, sandals, an incongruous button-down pink shirt, and a vest that looked like it came from South America. A diamond sparkled in his right earlobe. Though not handsome—not with the prominent and crooked nose and the gold-crowned front tooth—he had a confidence and a straightforward warmth that Schiff thought gave him some appeal.

She must unintentionally have been conveying that fact somehow, because even though she had at least ten years on him, he was definitely hitting on her. "She's okay," he was saying of his boss Maya Townshend, "nice enough, but not as pretty, say, as you."

Schiff did her best to ignore not just the comment but Bracco's quick smirk. "But you haven't really talked to her that often?" she asked.

"No. The longest conversation I had with her ever, really, was yesterday when she asked me if I would take over the place for a while until she could get a new manager. I told her I wanted to be the first to formally apply, and she said she appreciated that, she'd keep it in mind."

"So she's planning to keep the place open?" Bracco asked.

"I hope so. I haven't heard not. Why? Have you?"

But Schiff the cop was there to ask questions, not answer them. "How would you characterize Mrs. Townshend's relationship with Dylan?"

"What do you mean?"

"I mean, how did they act together? Like friends? Or more like boss and employee?"

Eugenio scratched at the corner of his mouth, a smile playing around his lips. "Boss and employee, but maybe not the way you think."

"We don't think any way," Bracco said. "That's why we're asking you."

Schiff shot her partner an unappreciative glance and came back at the witness, softening the rebuke. "What are you trying to say, Eugenio?"

"Well, just that if you didn't know and you saw them together, you wouldn't think she was the boss."

"You'd think he was?"

"Most people, I think, yeah." A quick shrug. "When I started here, the first time I see her come in, she's back in the office, doing some books or something and it's cooking out here—I mean, we got a line out the door and everybody's in high gear. So she comes to the office door and calls for Dylan and he's taking the orders and doing his schtick and he just waves her off, he doesn't have time. Makes a joke about accountants when we're the actual bean counters—get it, coffee beans . . ."

"I get it," Schiff replied deadpan.

"Yeah, so, anyway, the whole time she's back there and then finally she just finishes up and leaves without saying anything to anybody else. And when it finally slows down, I ask, 'So who was that, our accountant?' and Dylan about busts a gut laughing. 'That,' he says, 'is the owner. But I,' he says in that Godfather voice he could do, 'I'm the boss and don't you forget it.' But not really serious. That was the way he talked, that was all. He could be funny when he turned it on."

"So he was a good boss?"

"Definitely."

"Did you know he was selling marijuana out of here?"

Ruiz quickly looked from Schiff to Bracco and back. "Nope," he said. "No clue."

"Did you ever buy any from him?" Bracco asked.

"No way, man. I don't do drugs." A smile at Schiff. "Except caffeine, of course."

Since Ruiz's name did not appear in Vogler's computer, Schiff was willing to let this answer pass. It might even be true. "Let's get back to Dylan and Mrs. Townshend, if we can, all right? Did he always treat her as though he was the boss, and not vice versa?"

"Pretty much."

"And she took it . . . how?"

"I think mostly . . . I mean, I don't know for sure . . . but if you ask me, it's why she didn't come in too often. She was nervous, like. I don't think they really liked each other."

Schiff told him that Maya had told them she and Dylan had gotten along.

His eyes went to both inspectors in turn. "Well, I don't want to get her in trouble. She seems like a nice enough lady. Maybe they saw each other out of work."

"No," Bracco said. "But she did tell us that with Dylan dead, now there was no reason for her to keep the shop open. You have any idea what she meant by that?"

The young man shook his head. "She didn't tell me she was going to close it up. I don't know why she'd do that. The business is great. That just doesn't make any sense."

In the passenger seat of their car just after the interview with Eugenio Ruiz, Bracco hung up his cell phone. "Well, that's interesting."

"What?"

"Guess who's the registered owner of our purported murder weapon? I'll give you a hint. By all accounts she's not quite as pretty as some men find you."

"You caught that, huh?"

"I'm a trained detective. Nothing escapes."

"You want to go by again and say hello?"

"I was thinking maybe we should."

Slammed by the admission of Wes Farrell that he was one of Dylan Vogler's marijuana customers, and still worried sick about the Glitskys and the fate of Zachary, Hardy couldn't make himself concentrate on his junior associates' utilization figures. So he decided to leave work early and on the way home to seek an hour or so of solace in the company of his brother-in-law Moses McGuire, who would be behind the rail at the Little Shamrock, the bar they co-owned out on Lincoln near Ninth Avenue.

He'd just found a miraculous parking place around the corner on

Tenth and pulled into it when his cell phone rang, his most recent client calling in a panic to tell him that the police had just shown up at
her door again and she didn't know what she should do. It was getting
late and the kids were underfoot and Joel would be home soon too.

"Where are they now?" Hardy asked. "The cops?"

"Still out on the porch. I told them I had to talk to my attorney
before I could let them come in and talk to me again, and Inspector
Bracco said that that was fine but I should know that they'd identified what they think is the murder weapon and found out it was
mine. I mean, registered to me."

"Is that true?"

"I don't know. It could be, I suppose. I had left a gun I bought a
long time ago down at the shop, but I hadn't seen it in years. I didn't
know it was there anymore, but I guess it was. Anyway, they said
maybe I should talk to them here and now if I didn't want to have to
come downtown."

"That's a bluff," Hardy said. "They can't take you anywhere you
don't want to go without a warrant. And they can't make you talk to
them under any circumstances. Do they have a warrant?"

"I don't think so. They didn't say so."

"Are they still out there?"

"Yes. I mean, it's only been . . ." He heard her talking away from
the phone. "That's okay, honey, Mommy's just . . ." He missed the rest
of it, and then she was back with him. "I'm sorry, where were we?"

"Are Bracco and Schiff still there?"

"I think so." A pause. "Yes, they're just standing outside, talking."

"Could you let me speak with Inspector Bracco, please?"

"Sure, if you think . . . just a second."

"Darrel Bracco here. Who's this?"

"Darrel, it's Dismas Hardy. How are you doing?"

"Fine, maybe a little cold standing outside in the fog, but okay.
Call me a mind reader, but Mrs. Townshend's your client?"

"She is. I could be there in fifteen minutes. How does that sound?"

"Frankly, sir, it sounds like she's got herself lawyered up."

"Every citizen's right, Darrel."

"No question, sir, no question. Though as you know, it sometimes gives a cop pause."

Hardy well knew. "Sometimes it should," he said. "But I don't think this is one of those times. Although I'll tell you frankly I don't know how much I'm going to let my client say to you until I've had a chance to talk to her a little more. Maybe not much."

"Why am I not shocked?"

"Experience, Darrel. It's a beautiful thing. Can I talk to Mrs. Townshend again?"

"Sounds like it's your show. Here she is."

"Maya," Hardy said, "why don't you ask the inspectors in and I'll be there very shortly. But don't answer questions until I get there. Is it really your gun?"

"It might have been. If they say so, I'm sure they're right."

Hardy wondered why she hadn't seen fit to remember that detail in their earlier interview, but this wasn't the time to bring that up.

"But what about Joel?" she asked.

"What about him?"

"He's going to be coming home. I mean, maybe we could meet someplace else later. You and me and these people."

"We could do that," Hardy said evenly. "What time does your husband get home?"

"Sixish. Six-thirty. Usually. But sometimes not. It's hard to predict."

Hardy took a beat, checked his watch. "It's just past four now. I'm sure we can get this all cleared up by five if I come right over."

"But if Joel gets home early . . ."

"You're going to have a hard time keeping this from him in any event. Maybe you want to get that part over with now. But meanwhile, I'll be there in a heartbeat."

"Or sooner if you could," she said.

The two unknown guests in the living room—a man and a woman—stopped Joel Townshend in his tracks as he was coming in. He looked a question at his wife, who was sitting with them making small talk.

She had turned and now she stood up, wiping her hands nervously on her skirt. "Oh, Joel. You're early." Walking back to him, her face a map of her worries, she kissed him on the cheek, then turned to present the couple on the couch as they were getting to their feet together. "These are inspectors Bracco and Schiff. They have some questions about Dylan and BBW."

Joel put on a welcoming smile, took a few steps forward, and shook hands all around. Thirty-five years old, tall and thin with short-cropped brown hair, he projected an easygoing, casual style only slightly belied by the perfectly tailored tan business suit, light yellow shirt, and brown and gold tie.

In fact, though, he gave no sign that these unexpected visitors bothered him in any way. They were guests in his house, and he was their host. End of story. "Please," he said, "sit back down. I didn't mean to interrupt you."

"That's all right," Debra Schiff replied. "You didn't interrupt anything. We're waiting for your lawyer anyway."

Joel's face clouded in confusion. "My lawyer?"

"Actually, mine." Maya reached out and took her husband's hand, facing him now, cutting off any further response. She added, "A friend of Harlen's. He thought we ought to have a lawyer if we're going to be talking to the police about a murder."

Joel made a dismissive gesture and shook his head with a bemused humor. "That's ridiculous. You know I love your brother, My,
but sometimes he's a bit too much of a drama junkie, don't you
think? I hardly believe we need a lawyer to tell these people the simple truth, do we? You didn't have anything to do with Dylan's death."

"No, but—"

"Well, then? And now we're making them wait here in their busy
day. And for what?"

"Well, Harlen thought . . ." She tried a conciliatory smile. "Mr.
Hardy will be here in just a minute anyway. He thought it was worthwhile me calling him and asking him to come by."

In a bit of theatricality Joel cast his eyes to the ceiling. "Well, of
course he did. You ask a mechanic if he thinks you need a brake job.
Ninety-nine times out of a hundred, guess what? You do. New pads
all around, more brake fluid and lots of it, maybe balance the tires
while he's at it. Oh, and PS, that'll be five hundred dollars." He
looked at the inspectors. "Am I right?"

Bracco wasn't completely successful hiding his appreciation at
this response. But he kept it low-key. "We're not encouraged to argue
when citizens say they want their attorney, sir," he said. "But I think
it's fair to say they're probably overused, especially in situations like
this one, where your wife is not a suspect."

"Well," Joel said, "her brother's a big, important city supervisor
now and when he gets dumb ideas, nobody ever calls him on them."

"I know Harlen pretty well, sir," Bracco said. "I used to be his
partner when he was a cop." Now he broke a broad grin. "The ambition thing makes him a little cautious."

"There you go," Joel said. "Excessive caution. Sometimes it's just
unnecessary." Still holding Maya's hand, he gave it a little confident
squeeze. "I'm sure my wife will be happy to talk to you. What do you
want to know?"

"Joel." Maya now squeezed his hand hard, warning him off.

"Really, My. Come on. This is silly."

And the doorbell rang.

"There he is now." Maya jumped as she let go of her husband's hand and ran to the door.

Townshend watched her for a second, then turned back to the inspectors and shrugged with some exaggeration. "Fantastic," he said.

Hardy, walking in to a cool reception at best from both the inspectors and the husband, didn't make matters any better when, first thing after the introductions, he asked Maya if he could speak to her alone, or with her husband if she wanted.

"I don't think we need to do that," Joel said. "Maya doesn't have anything to hide. She can say anything she needs to in front of me and these inspectors."

"Absolutely," Hardy said. "If she wants to, of course she can. Maya? Your call."

They stood in a frozen tableau for a long moment, until she finally turned to face Hardy and said, "Maybe Joel ought to come with us."

After his initial stunned expression Joel took in the cops again with an apologetic shrug, then came back to Hardy and Maya with a terse, "All right. Let's go, then."

Maya led the little party of three off to a front working den—flat-screen TV, bookshelves, fireplace. Closing the door, they remained standing because Joel gave no one any time to sit down before he more or less exploded, although he kept his voice in check. "Maya, you want to tell me what this is about?"

She threw a glance at Hardy—and again, clearly, this didn't get her any points with her husband—nodded, took in a breath. "Mr. Hardy knows that I went by BBW on Saturday morning and saw the body, and then got scared and drove away without calling the police."

Joel's mouth went tight. "You went to BBW Saturday morning? Why?"

"Because Dylan called me Friday night and said he needed to see me first thing, that it was an emergency."

"What kind of emergency?"

"He didn't say that."

"But you went?"

"Yes. I went. But the real problem, ask Mr. Hardy here, is that the first time I talked to those people, I didn't say anything about that. I told them I went to Mass."

"The first time you talked to who? Those inspectors out there? This isn't the first time?"

Hardy finally felt that he could join the conversation. "They talked to your wife yesterday morning."

Joel couldn't take his eyes off his wife. "Why didn't you tell me you'd talked to them? And not told them the truth?"

"I don't know, Joel. I don't know. I panicked. I was afraid, or embarrassed, or something. I thought you'd be mad at me being in this on any level, for getting you involved." She had her arms crossed over her chest, displaying more defiance than her words indicated. "The point is I'm telling you now, all right? I don't know what I should do *right now*. And by the way, you should know, Joel, that the gun they think is probably the murder weapon is the one I left down there back when I first opened the place, like ten years ago, and it's registered to me." She looked from one man to the other. "And in case either of you are thinking it, if I were going to have shot Dylan, which I never would have done under any conditions, period, I never would have been so stupid as to throw it away where the police could find it."

For a minute no one spoke. Eyes flashed between husband and wife. Hardy kept his own counsel in silence until he felt again that he would be heard. "The thing to do right now, in my opinion, Maya, is to go out there and tell the inspectors the truth. As your husband has said. If you don't do that, and somebody did witness you in the alley on Saturday morning, it will look much worse and be a lot harder to explain. As for the gun, you owned it. So what? If you kept it at the shop, Dylan undoubtedly knew about it and probably had it with him illegally for protection while he was carrying the weed."

"What weed?" Joel asked.

Maya shook her head in anger and frustration. She spoke under her breath. "Oh, Jesus!"

"Dylan was selling marijuana out of your wife's store," Hardy said in his most neutral voice. "I don't know why it hasn't been in the papers. The cops have known this all along."

"How special for them," Joel said. Clearly seething now, he spoke in a near whisper. "How long were you going to keep all this from me, Maya? What is that about? I thought we talked to each other."

"We do."

"Not so much, though, as it turns out." Finally, Joel brought his attention to Hardy. "So you're suggesting we go outside and tell these people that my wife lied to them, is that it?"

"Omitted," Hardy said. "Not lied. At least then we start over with a clean slate."

"But Maya's at the murder scene within, apparently, minutes of the crime."

"That's true. And in point of fact, she was."

Now Joel came back to her. "And you don't know what the emergency was?"

"No."

"No idea?"

"No, Joel, really."

This wasn't enough for her increasingly furious husband. He kept at her. "So the situation here, correct me if I'm wrong, is that Dylan called you on Friday night saying he needed to see you first thing next morning, and you dropped everything and got up at five-thirty, lied to me and the kids about going to Mass—"

"But I did go to Mass, after—"

Joel waved that off. "After you went to see Dylan first, for some reason that he wouldn't even tell you. Is that what you expect me to believe?"

Tears glistened in Maya's eyes. "That's what happened, Joel. That's exactly what happened."

"That twerp calls you, doesn't even give you a reason, and you come running, and now we've got the cops sitting in our living room and your lawyer here says we need to tell them the truth, except that the truth leaves you going down to visit the murdered man just about the time he was killed, and with essentially no reason." He turned to Hardy. "How can we tell them she went down there if we can't tell them why? Can you answer that for me?"

"Keep it simple. He asked her to, that's all. Some problem with the business, some decision she had to make in person." Hardy slowed himself down. "I'm sure Maya thought it was going to be a quick little meeting and then she'd have time to make it back to Mass. Isn't that right, Maya?"

Hardy had given her the answer and was glad to see her embrace it. "That's exactly it, Joel. I didn't think it was anything really important. I wasn't hiding anything from you. It was just a small business hassle that I thought I'd take care of like I have a million others."

Another silence, finally broken when Joel asked Hardy, "You really think this will fly?"

"It's the truth," Hardy said. "All things considered, honesty's still the best policy."

Husband and wife stared at each other for a long beat. Maya reached out and took Joel's hand in hers. "That ought to be the end of it," she said.

"Not exactly," Joel said, extricating his hand from his wife's. "You and I are going to have to have a discussion."

"We can do that." She looked up at Hardy. "Meanwhile, let's go tell 'em," she said.

He nodded, no-nonsense. "All right," he said. "But let me do the talking."

At ten-thirty that night Hardy threw the next-to-last dart of his round at the Little Shamrock bar and it landed in his "out" spot of double eleven. He plocked the next shot directly in the center of the bull's-eye, ending the game. He was playing "301" and he'd gone out ahead of his opponent, Wyatt Hunt, by hitting his last eight throws in a row, a fairly nice run.

And all too underappreciated by Hunt, his firm's private investigator, who now owed him not only the tab for the three beers they'd each consumed in the three-game minitournament, but the extra hundred bucks they'd put up as the pot. No sooner had Hardy's winning shot landed than Hunt handed him the Franklin and offered to go double or nothing.

"That's a sucker bet, Wyatt, as you well know." Hardy took the bill and put it into his wallet. "But I'll buy you a consolation drink to help assuage the agony of defeat."

"*Assuage* is a good lawyer word," Hunt said. "You don't hear people say *assuage* every day."

"No indeed, you don't," Hardy replied. "And yet, sometimes it is the perfect choice, *le mot juste*, as Hemingway would have said."

"Or me if I spoke French."

The private eye went about six three, two ten, an athletic hunk comprised of about equal parts gristle and testosterone. If you could be handsome in an ugly way, that's what Hardy would have said he was. He'd grown up in foster homes, done a stint in Iraq I, then worked a dozen or so years in Child Protective Services, taking kids from abusive environments away from their parent or parents, pretty much the apogee of thankless jobs. Now, and for the past seven or eight years, he ran a private investigations business called The Hunt Club, and Hardy's firm used it almost exclusively.

Wyatt was leading the way as the two men moved from the dart area and into the narrow recesses of the bar proper, which was having a relatively slow night. Two stools stood open in front of the taps, and they got themselves seated. "That was an obscene run of darts, you know."

"Admittedly. I'm sure I couldn't do it again. Although you've got to figure that a guy who's got a board on the wall of his office and his own customized darts probably spends a few minutes playing the game. He's going to get a lucky run from time to time."

Hunt was grinning. "I'll try to keep it in mind."

Moses McGuire appeared in front of them and they ordered—a club soda for each of them. McGuire, on a club soda regimen himself for the past couple of years, still couldn't help himself. "Whoa," he said. "Katie, bar the door. Want those babies full-strength up or on the rocks?"

"The great thing about drinking here"—Hardy ignored his brother-in-law and spoke directly to Hunt—"is the commentary."

"I knew there was something," Hunt replied.

"Rocks," Hardy said, coming back to Moses, "and hold the pithy observations, thank you."

McGuire pulled the drinks, and Hardy held up his glass to clink Hunt's. "I feel a little guilty inviting you down here and then taking your money, but thanks for coming."

Hunt sipped his soda. "Long day?"

"Actually, fairly brutal." Hardy filled him in on the dramas surrounding both Glitsky and Wes Farrell, which had continued into the night as Hardy, after dinner at home, went to the hospital to check on Abe and Zachary—Abe still a zombie, Zachary unchanged.

Hardy had stayed on with Abe for a long half hour, then patted his friend's knee and told him to hang in there, call if he needed anything, and left. Unable to make himself go back home to Frannie, Treya, and Rachel, he'd stopped by the Shamrock and called Farrell, who'd apparently turned off his telephones. Getting an idea, then he had called Hunt. "Anyway, between Abe and Wes, it's like I'm knocked off my horse. I can't seem to get my arms wrapped around this Dylan Vogler situation. Not just what it's done to Wes, or potentially could do."

"You're really worried about that?"

"A little bit, yeah."

"Well, let me lighten your load, Diz. You can get over that. Nobody outside of Singapore cares about who smokes weed. Certainly nobody in law enforcement in this town. 'Course, the bad news in Singapore is they hang you for it. But the good news is we're not there. Not even Wes. But I'd warn him if he's thinking about making the trip."

"I'll do that," Hardy said with a strained tolerance. "But in actual fact Wes is an officer of the court. He's a rainmaker for the firm, he's—"

Hunt held up a hand. "It's only going to increase his street cred among his potential clients, Diz, all of whom probably light up a doob with some regularity. The guy's one of them."

"Judges won't think that's a plus if it gets out. I promise."

"How are they going to prove it? So his name's on a list. So what?" Hunt drank. "He's not really thinking of quitting, is he?"

"He offered." A shrug. "I told him to think about it some more."

"Well, before he does anything dumb, at least he ought to talk to Craig." This was Craig Chiurco, one of Hunt's operatives, working on his own private investigator's license. At Hardy's look Hunt went on. "This guy Vogler had a good book, I'll give him that."

Hardy's eyebrows went up in surprise. "Craig was on this list too?"

Hunt bobbed his head. "Yeah, and he's actually a pretty big number. He came and told me about it yesterday. I mean that the cops had called him about it. He was worried it might affect his license chances."

"Same story. If they could prove it, it might, but without a confession, forget it."

"Right," Wyatt said. "And I don't really see anybody going to go out of their way to bust these guys, even if they could prove anything. At the most it's casual use, and then only if they in fact catch 'em in flagrante. Hundred bucks if anybody actually cares enough to write you up, which they won't. Not in this town."

"So what'd you tell Craig?"

"I told him to dump his stash and give it up. But really, Diz, it's a nonissue. Vogler, maybe not. But Wes and Craig and whoever else, nothing."

Hardy glanced over at his companion and lifted his glass. "Okay, since you've got all the answers tonight, let me ask you another one. There's a piece missing somewhere and I can't put my finger on it." He ran down what he'd learned about Maya up to this point—the mysterious call from Vogler on Friday night, the early morning trip to BBW, Maya driving away from the body, her concern about her supposedly profligate fling in college, and then bringing the story around to Dylan's exorbitant salary, the gun, and so on.

When he finished, Wyatt nodded. "Can you say 'blackmail'?"

"Okay. For what?"

"I don't know. Something she's ashamed of or worried about. Probably when she was having her wild time back in college."

"That's pretty much what I'd come to. But I didn't want to let myself believe it."

"Why not?"

"Because blackmail comes with implications."

"She's done something bad?"

"In the past, yeah. But nearer the present is the real concern."

"You're thinking she did it?"

Hardy hesitated for a few seconds. "If he was blackmailing her and she went down there on Saturday morning? The blackmail was the missing piece. If it's in there, the picture gets a lot more clear and maybe real ugly in a hurry."

"You think Bracco and Schiff have put it together?"

"If they haven't already, they will soon."

"So what do you want to do?"

"I thought I'd ask you to see what you could find out."

"About her college years?"

At Hardy's nod Hunt went on. "Not that I couldn't use the work, but why don't you just ask her? Tell her you figured out she was being blackmailed, see what she does."

"Well, I could. But a couple of things. First, her husband kind of made it clear that he didn't want her seeing me without him being there too. So if he's the one she doesn't want to know whatever it is—and that's a decent bet—she doesn't tell me no matter what. Next, I might be wrong and the accusation might piss her off. Maybe even enough to where she wants to fire me, which would be letting a potential big one get away. Finally, if whatever she did was bad enough that she killed Vogler to stop it coming out, no way she's just giving it up, even privileged, to a lawyer she barely knows. I'd be wasting my breath even asking. Better if I find out what it is on my own, then hold on to it and use it as things develop."

"Knowledge being power and all."

"Truer words," Hardy said.

"And why do you want to know all this, exactly?"

The question seemed to stump Hardy for a minute. "If I'm going to defend her, it would help to know who she is."

"But you're going to bill her to find out something she doesn't want you to know?"

"If it's going to help her in the long run. If it turns out I need her history, which now I'm thinking I might. Otherwise, I step in it without ever seeing it coming. And she winds up screwed." He tipped up his glass, brought it down slowly. "So what do you say?"

Hunt nodded. "I could give it a couple of days. See what pops."

"That's all I'm asking. She gave me three thousand as a retainer. You can spend a good chunk of it. How's that sound?"

"Doable," Hunt said. "I'll give it a run."

10

Hardy wasn't wrong when he said that Schiff and Bracco wouldn't be far behind him in coming to the conclusion that Dylan Vogler was blackmailing Maya Townshend.

They'd gotten to it almost by osmosis the next morning. At a few minutes after nine A.M. they knocked at the front door of Jansey's house, figuring that she would most probably have known what dirt her man had had on his boss that he had used not only to keep himself gainfully employed, but that also allowed him to treat her as an underling when she came into her own store.

Last night, in spite of their great frustration at having Dismas Hardy show up at the Townshends' to limit the free flow of information, the inspectors had learned a great deal. Most importantly, Maya had lied to them about her alibi on Saturday morning. Beyond that, she'd admitted that she'd actually been called down to the murder scene by the victim and had discovered his body and then opted not to call the police and report it. In the eyes of the inspectors these two revelations elevated Maya in a hurry to a person of interest in the homicide.

She had had both the means and the opportunity to have killed Dylan Vogler. If Bracco and Schiff could establish a compelling motive, they would be well on their way to establishing her as their prime suspect. And the fact that Maya had apparently been at Vogler's beck and call—coming down to the store before dawn on a Saturday morning?—argued strongly, in spite of Hardy's disclaimers, that theirs was not a simple business relationship.

Vogler must have had something on Maya that she didn't want revealed. And maybe he'd been threatening her with just that—upping the ante on what she was paying him, making new demands. Maybe she'd just had enough and decided to put an end to it.

It wasn't much of a leap for either of them to imagine her killing him. And the why of it led them to Jansey's door again this morning.

She was barefoot in cutoff jeans and wearing her usual T-shirt. "You guys put in some serious hours, you know that? You got another warrant?"

"Not this time," Schiff said. "We were hoping you'd talk to us about Maya."

Her forehead crinkled. "Why? I don't even know her."

"You know who she is," Bracco said.

"Well, yeah, of course I know who she is. She owns the shop. Do you guys hang out with the chief of police?"

"I take your point." Schiff didn't want to antagonize Jansey, who was at this point about their best hope. "Do you think we could come in and talk for a minute?"

"About Maya? Look, I really don't know anything about Maya." But the cops simply nodded until Jansey hesitated, looked behind her, then shrugged, indicating they should follow her. "Robert's over having some coffee with me," she explained in advance.

As Maya turned to lead the way back into the house, Bracco flashed his partner a knowing look, and Schiff acknowledged it with a nod as they fell in behind their witness.

In the kitchen Robert Tripp sat at the table, again in his green medical scrubs. He'd heard the doorbell and then the discussion at the door and appeared, if not actively enthusiastic about the police presence, then at least engaged. "Hey." He stood up, coming around the table and shaking both of their hands. "Jansey and I are just having a cup," he said. "It's hot and fresh. Bay Beans's finest."

"Sounds good to me. Black." Schiff would take anything that would give her and Bracco more time to chat with Jansey and Robert. "Where's Ben this morning?" she asked.

"Preschool. Eight to twelve." Jansey looked at Bracco. "Inspector? Coffee?"

"Sure," he said. "Why not? Two sugars, please."

Jansey was grabbing mugs and putting them on the counter when Tripp declared, "White sugar'll kill you."

Bracco let out a halfhearted chuckle. "That," he said, "or something else. I promise you, sugar's the least of my worries." He pulled a chair around and straddled it backward. "So, Robert, let me ask you this. When do you go to school?"

The question, perhaps intended to get a rise, drew only a muted reply. "I got off at midnight. I'm back in at noon. Twelve on, twelve off, this week. Oh, and I'm on call during the off hours every third day, lest we start to catch up on sleep. That would be wrong."

"They don't want you to sleep?" Schiff asked. "Isn't that dangerous for patients?"

"If it turns out it is," Tripp said, "you're out of the program. If sleep's more important to you than medicine, you don't want to be a doctor bad enough anyway. If lack of sleep affects your performance, you don't have what it takes. I don't think there's an American-trained doctor in the world who hasn't gone through five years of serious sleep deprivation. It's part of the culture. If you can't hack it, get another gig."

Jansey set the mugs in front of the inspectors. She put a quick hand on Tripp's shoulder. "Robert's record is four days without a minute of sleep."

"That's a long four days," Bracco said.

Tripp broke a tired smile. "That was a long month, Inspector, let me tell you. I finally fell asleep outside an OR, standing up in the hall, which I didn't think was possible until then. Luckily, one of the nurses noticed and got me onto a gurney, pushed me into an empty room."

Schiff blew over her coffee. Bracco took his first slurping sip and pulled his tiny portable tape recorder out and put it on the table.

Jansey got herself settled into the chair next to Tripp, reached over and touched his hand on the table, then brought her hands back, clenched in front of her. "So, back to what you came for, I don't really know what I can tell you about Maya. I've only met her a couple of times."

Bracco and Schiff exchanged a glance and Bracco took the lead. "We're looking at the possibility that Dylan might have been blackmailing her."

The news didn't seem to startle Jansey. Still, she asked, "Why do you say that?"

"Couple of reasons," Bracco went on. "First, his salary. She paid him ninety grand a year. For comparison the same job at Starbucks pays around forty."

"Yeah, but he'd been there nine years."

"Okay, so say he got raises every year. That brings him up to fifty, or even sixty. Ninety's still a good ways out of the box. Second, some employees at the shop have told us that when Maya came in, which wasn't very often, Dylan treated her like she was the help, like he had something on her. And if he did, it's hard to believe he wouldn't have mentioned at least something about it to you at some time."

The young woman stared down at the table.

"Jansey," Schiff put in, "if he was blackmailing her, it may have been part of the reason he was killed."

This brought her head up. "You mean she might have killed him?"

"We don't know," Bracco said. "If we've got a blackmail situation, that'd be something we'd be forced to consider."

Schiff expanded on the theme. "It might have just been an ongoing thing covered in his salary. So it wasn't like she was paying him every month out of her own cash."

"Even the ninety wasn't enough," Jansey said. "It was only sixty after taxes, you know. Why do you think he needed to sell weed? If he was blackmailing her, he could have just asked for a raise, and she would have had to give it to him, right?"

"Maybe," Bracco said. "But also maybe she told him she was at the limit, she couldn't or wouldn't go any higher. Her husband wouldn't let her, I don't know, something. Did he tell you he wanted to ask her for more money recently? Something that would have made him a danger to her again?"

"He always wanted more money." She looked across from one of them to the other. "You're right, though, about him not being afraid of her, or of losing the job."

"But he never talked about why?" Schiff asked.

"The most he ever said was that she owed him."

"There you go." Bracco leaned forward. "Did he say what she owed him for?"

For a second she appeared to think about it. "It wasn't like we really ever talked about it," she said. "Once or twice he might have said something like, 'She won't fire me. She owes me her life.' But that was just Dylan being dramatic. She owed him her life. I'm sure."

"If that's a grieving woman," Bracco said as soon as they were rolling in their car again, "I'm the shah of Iran."

"I don't think there's been a shah in Iran for a few years, Darrel."

"Lucky for me," Bracco replied. "And I don't really want a leadership role in Iran anyway. Just think about it, no booze, no women. Talk about dull parties. I can't even imagine what the inaugural ball must be like. But I wasn't so much talking about Iran as the grieving part. If those two don't have something going on, they will soon, don't you think?"

"If body language talks, it's already happening. And the little kid's gone every morning for four hours when Tripp's home. I'm tempted to give them fifteen minutes and go back and catch them in the act. Then we'll at least have caught the future Dr. Tripp in a lie, and it might lead to something else, like their meshing alibis."

"You think it might have been them together?"

"I think that if they're an item, and let's pretend they are, they both wouldn't mind seeing Dylan dead."

"Why wouldn't she just have left him?"

Schiff, driving, thought for a while. "This isn't a complete list, but offhand here are the first reasons that occur to me. Because of the beatings he had power over her. Two, Ben was Jansey and Dylan's kid together. Or maybe Tripp wasn't that serious, just some recreational sex while the old man was at work. Then, finally, Dylan brought in the money and lots of it, where Tripp's a destitute student. That enough?"

"It'll get us started, Debra. In fact, assuming Tripp and her are serious, killing Dylan's a solution to three of their problems, maybe even all four if Tripp's good for taking over the father role. But I'll tell you something else."

"What's that?"

"I'm getting sick of all this theorizing. You ever get tired of people lying to you?"

"No. It's my favorite. But who this time?"

"Jansey."

"You think she knows what the blackmail's about?"

"You don't? She's lived with the guy for like five or six years and doesn't know something that basic to Dylan's work? To their whole situation? If Dylan was blackmailing Maya, she might have known about it, might have even been part of it."

"Might might might."

"I know. I agree. And if she—Jansey—and Dylan were in cahoots on that, where does that take us?"

"It gives her less of a motive to shoot him, if that's their business together. And that puts Maya back square in the middle of the picture."

"Except if Jansey's really in love with Tripp and wants out with Dylan."

"So we've got Maya alone? Or Jansey alone? Or Jansey and Tripp together? Or a random shooter out for a stroll?"

"I'm not leaning toward random shooter."

"No, me neither."

The two inspectors rode along in silence for a couple of blocks, until at last Schiff said, "We've got to figure out a way to turn up the heat."

11

Hardy showed up by surprise with deli sandwiches and Diet Cokes in Farrell's office, but they'd barely unpacked the lunch when Hardy took the call from Frannie. The partners were both sitting on the dilapidated couch, their food and napkins and bags of chips and cans of soda untouched on the low table in front of them.

Frannie told him that she'd just gotten off the phone with Treya and they had brought Zachary out of the induced coma and done something called a "pinch test" and that he'd reacted, which apparently was very good news. The swelling had gone down considerably and they were now talking about reinserting the dura mater and closing up the brain again within the next couple of days.

The doctors were starting to think, and had told Treya and Abe, that their son appeared to be out of immediate danger, on the mend, and that he might recover completely. Although with these types of injuries there would be a long watch-and-wait period to determine if there were going to be any ongoing problems with development, cognition, or motor skills. This still sounded quite serious to Hardy, and Frannie agreed with him that it was, but compared with what they'd been looking at for the past four days, it was the best possible news.

Hanging up, Hardy, with a great sense of relief, reached for his drink and sat back on the couch. "See?" He recounted the gist of the conversation, concluding with, "Things sometimes do turn around for the better."

Farrell still wasn't much in the mood to agree with him. In fact, his confidence and spirits had retreated so far that he'd worn a regular business suit to work today, and without a funny T-shirt under it. He'd gone out earlier in the morning and trimmed his thick gray-brown hair to a length that qualified as relatively normal. Now Wes hunched on the couch, holding his sandwich over the table in front of him, shredded lettuce spilling, condiments dripping. "Sometimes they do, and I'm glad as hell for Abe's kid, and for him. But I haven't even told you yet about Jeff Elliot's call this morning."

"What did our paper's most esteemed columnist have to say?"

"He just wanted to give me a heads-up 'cause we're friends. The *Chronicle*'s talking about running the weed story and including the whole list of us alleged dope-smoking fiends."

Hardy was shaking his head. "Can't happen. Won't happen. Never in a million years."

"Why not?"

"Because your name on a list on somebody's computer doesn't mean anything. You didn't admit anything to Schiff when she called and asked you about it, did you?"

"I'm sure." Farrell rolled his eyes. "What, I'm retarded?"

"That's my point. You're not. So you didn't cop to it. So she's got nothing she can prove. Besides, no way does this make 'CityTalk.' That doesn't sound like Jeff."

Farrell chewed and swallowed, chasing with Coke. "No. He was talking regular news. And you might be right about the libel problem, but the *Chron*'s got to be tempted. It's a great story."

"It's a nonstory. They can't run it."

"Okay, good. But evidently there's more than a few semipublic figures on the list, not including yours truly and Wyatt's guy. And the public would like to know."

"Like who?" Hardy asked.

"Jeff, God bless him, didn't want to name names to me. But at least one judge, more than a couple of city department heads, several prominent educators, two supervisors, a few actors and like that, public personalities, and, oh yeah, some DAs . . ."

"You want to talk screwed," Hardy said. "Just on the innuendo, those DAs are screwed. At least the ones that didn't have the sense to get medical marijuana cards."

"Yeah, heads are gonna roll for sure. If I still worked here, I'd swoop and scoop 'em up cheap and get 'em on our payroll."

"You're still working here, Wes. Don't worry about that."

"I'm not worried about getting fired, Diz." He looked sideways down the couch. "Tell you the truth, I'm just embarrassed as all shit to have exposed the firm like this. You and Gina don't deserve it, and it doesn't exactly put on the best face for the associates, either, does it?"

Hardy waved that off. "Wes, it's marijuana in San Francisco in the twenty-first century. It's going to blow over in a week, maybe two. I appreciate your feelings but truly, nobody really cares."

"They will if this murder turns out to be about a little benign weed."

"It won't come down like that. Whoever shot Dylan, he didn't steal any of it."

"How do you know that?"

"He was still wearing his backpack, which was full of it. How about that?"

"How about if he also happened to be pushing a shopping cart loaded with the stuff and the shooter ran off with that?"

That proposal stopped Hardy short for a second, but then he shook his head, banishing the unwelcome thought. "That didn't happen, Wes. Look, worst case, if the *Chronicle* does the story, it'll sell a few papers, but it's a nonissue to everybody else."

In fact, it wasn't a nonissue to at least one San Francisco official—the newly minted special assistant United States attorney, Jerry Glass.

The previous U.S. attorney in San Francisco, construed by the attorney general's office to be too liberal, had been one of the notorious Alberto Gonzalez fires. Upon taking office his replacement wanted to waste no time establishing his credentials as a hard-line prosecutor, aligned four-square against the permissive culture of the city that Herb Caen, the legendary columnist for the *Chronicle*, had christened Baghdad by the Bay. For some years after his graduation from law school, Jerry Glass had been an assistant district attorney in Orange County, following his boss the district attorney to Sacramento as a speechwriter during the first appointments of the Schwarzenegger era, eventually catching on as an assistant director of one of California's dozens of bureaucracies, the Department of Alcoholic Beverage Control.

Glass, thirty-five by now, was a well-built though slightly overweight, plain-looking specimen with an office worker's pasty complexion. He shaved close and wore his light brown hair short, parted low on the right. He trimmed his sideburns up around the top of his ears. He was also aggressive and ambitious and had seen his ABC assignment—accurately—as a dead end. He'd had résumés out and was in a holding pattern when his ex-boss, now an assistant attorney general in Washington, D.C., tapped him for the San Francisco job, and he jumped at it. With this plum in his lap Jerry had no intention of following in the footsteps of his predecessor and, among other priorities, set to work immediately making efforts to shut down the city's medical marijuana parlors, of which there were dozens. This was always a somewhat delicate endeavor, since the state of California, as well as the city and county of San Francisco, either sanctioned or at the very least turned a blind eye to these so-called compassionate use facilities.

But Jerry was there to enforce U.S., not local, law, and the use of marijuana was a federal crime. He got his name in the paper several times during his first year in office for busting some of the

medical marijuana folks, but except for burnishing his conservative credentials—not exactly a plus in the San Francisco cultural
environment—these actions did little, if anything, to raise his profile.

And suddenly, here in his office this cool Wednesday afternoon,
all by herself, was Debra Schiff. He'd run into the very attractive
homicide inspector a couple of times at the bar at Lou the Greek's
and he'd planned to meet her there some more if he could, but here
she was now, telling him about this murder of a coffee-shop manager
out in the godforsaken Haight-Ashbury.

To date, Glass had only been aware of rumors and what he'd read
about this particular murder in the papers. Astoundingly, he thought,
Schiff was telling him with a straight face that she and her partner,
Bracco, hadn't brought up the dope connection to the news media
before because it simply *didn't occur to them* that it might be of some
special importance—since apparently no marijuana had been stolen,
it couldn't have been part of a motive in the case.

She waved off his objection. "No, listen, Jerry, there's *always* dope
somewhere in a homicide picture. A roach in the drive-by car, some
paraphernalia around a DD"—domestic disturbance—"gangbangers
loaded up with coke or heroin. So it's always there someplace. You
don't comment on it any more than you'd talk about the weather. 'In
other news tonight,' she said in her best anchor voice, 'Shawahn
Johnson was shot seventeen times in an apparent drive-by shooting
in Hunters Point when the fog was in.' Generally, we don't mention
the fog."

"But this fellow, Vogler, he had an entire marijuana garden in his
attic, didn't he? Thousands of dollars' worth, right?"

"Right. But again we didn't have any reason to believe that was
part of our case at the outset. We handed the dope part over to the
narcs and that might have been the end of it."

"But for what?" Glass adjusted his spectacles.

For the next few minutes Schiff ran the highlights of their investigation. "The bottom line, though," she concluded, "is that we think . . . in fact, we're morally certain that Maya, Jansey, and Robert Tripp have lied to us, in some cases more than once. We have motives for each of them, both alone or possibly together in the case of Jansey and Tripp, but almost no evidence and certainly nothing we can use to bring any leverage to bear on getting anybody to talk. We're pretty sure, for example, that Vogler was blackmailing Maya, and that Jansey may have known about that, but if they both say, 'No he wasn't,' we're stuck."

"You can't just lean on them harder?"

"We could, but as I say, it's kind of pointless without some new leverage, some change in the status quo. There's no physical evidence that's very compelling." She shook her head. "Besides, we've already gone back and talked to all of them at least twice, but Jansey and Tripp are at the very least well-rehearsed, and Maya's got herself a lawyer. Plus, you know, we've got to walk a little easy around her anyway."

"Why's that?"

"The whole political thing, which I hate, and Darrel hates, but there you go. The plain fact is, Darrel and Harlen Fisk used to be partners, and she's Harlen's sister."

Jerry's eyes lit up. "Are you talking Supervisor Fisk?"

"Right."

"Which also makes her the niece of Mayor West?"

"I guess so, yeah."

Jerry Glass pulled himself up straight in his chair, his attention now riveted. "Is Mr. Fisk interfering with your investigation? Is he talking to your partner?"

"Not that I know of, no. That would be a little awkward, even if . . ." She stopped.

"What?"

"Well," she said, "Harlen, among many other names you might recognize, was one of Vogler's regular customers."

This stopped Glass dead. He squinted through his glasses, across at her. "Marijuana customers? You're sure of that?"

"Absolutely. He's on the list."

"The list?"

"I'm sorry. Haven't I told you yet about the list?" She gave him that news, the incriminating computer records. "Anyway, in short it looks like there's a ton of connections between all these people, and we'd like an excuse to shake their trees and find out if we can what those connections are. The blackmail, for example. What was that about? Was it serious enough that Maya might have killed to keep it quiet? Or, on the other hand—"

"No"—Glass raised his palm to her—"hold up a minute. Let's go back to what might really make a difference. You've told me that Maya says she didn't know this weed was sold out of her shop, right? How credible is that to you? Especially if her brother was one of the customers." He waited, a smile beginning to play at the corners of his mouth. "That's what I thought. And beyond that, if the mayor—I'm kind of new in town, but Harlen's her protégé if I'm not mistaken—I mean, she'd know as well, or might know. How much was Maya paying Vogler again?"

"Ninety thousand," Schiff said.

"Well, that's enough, or almost enough, to live on, right? Do you think it's actually possible that he *didn't* kick back some percentage of this drug money to Maya, who had, after all, set him up in business?"

Schiff kept nodding. "You're saying Vogler—"

"I'm saying it sounds to me like he was her partner on the dope side as well. Which would explain his cavalier attitude toward her as much as blackmail, wouldn't it? He can treat her any way he wants and she can't fire him, can she? Since he's her supplier. They're in it together hip deep."

Glass was making sense, although neither she nor Bracco had yet considered the possibility that this whole thing might, in fact, be about the weed. Schiff's hope, and the reason she'd come to visit Jerry Glass today, was that he could start some kind of a U.S. prosecution on the marijuana issues that would make the principal witnesses nervous enough about the possible dope charges against them that in exchange for lenient treatment on that score, they would perhaps be inclined to trade information they might have about the murder.

But now Jerry's take took it to a different level, contemplating that Maya herself might have been the prime mover, and armed with political connections and possibly even police protection, she would have been all but invulnerable to suspicion, much less prosecution.

And then—instead of this imagined blackmail about what she'd maybe or maybe not done in her past—the murder had simply been the usual dope deal gone bad. Maya had killed her employee because of any number of common reasons—he wanted a bigger cut, he was selling to his own customers and leaving her out, he was either getting sloppy or hard to control.

Now Jerry Glass settled back into his chair, his hands clasped on the desk in front of him, a faraway glint in his eyes over a tight-lipped smile. "I know how we can get these people to talk," he said.

Back in his office once again, Glitsky sat slumped, his elbows on the armrests of his chair, his hands joined in front of his mouth. He was back in at work because what else was he going to do? Zachary was coming out of the coma, although they were going to operate on him again to close up his skull tomorrow. Rationally, he knew that there was reason for hope, and yet all he could feel was a deep self-loathing. Regardless of what Treya or Hardy or anyone else said, he knew that all of this was his fault.

Through his lack of attention he'd allowed his son to be hit by a car—there was still a reasonable chance that his boy could die. Even if he didn't die, he might never be completely right in the head again. And they might not know the extent of those injuries, if any, for years.

He'd left the lights off at the door, so again the high windows provided the only illumination, and not much of it at that.

He clearly wasn't welcoming guests.

Nevertheless, somebody knocked and he straightened up and intoned, "Come in."

Bracco poked his head in. "Sir? Lights?"

"Sure."

Glitsky covered his face with one hand against the sudden brightness, then lowered the hand and faced both of his inspectors with a flat eye. "Come on in. Have a seat."

Bracco was on his way over to a chair, but Schiff saw him and noticed something and stopped in the doorway. "Are you okay, Lieutenant?"

He turned to look at her and surprised himself when he said, "My son's in the hospital. He got hit by a car. He came out of a coma this morning, but he's got another operation tomorrow. I'm sorry I've been out. What can I do for you two?"

Both of the inspectors broke into condolences and questions, and he responded and answered dutifully without really hearing many of the individual words. They were just noise against the constant thrum of the guilt in his head.

And then finally he became vaguely aware that they were talking about something else, something to do with their case, and after a couple of minutes of that—mostly more white noise—he held up a hand. "Whoa up," he said to Schiff, who appeared to be acting as spokesperson. "Can you repeat that last part? Are you talking about Jerry Glass? Federal Jerry Glass?"

"Yes, sir, but that's what makes this so good, at least potentially. He says the dope is enough, especially in the quantity we found at Vogler's place, to trigger a forfeiture."

"Forfeiture?"

Schiff nodded with enthusiasm. "Confiscating their property."

Glitsky said, "I know what forfeiture is, Debra. But whose property?"

"Maybe Vogler's, if for example we can prove that he used any part of the profits from the drug sales to pay off his house. But also Maya Townshend's, and even better, maybe her husband Joel's."

"Townshend Real Estate?" Glitsky asked.

Bracco finally spoke. "It could be huge, Abe. Millions and millions."

"They were in the drug business? I thought she didn't know anything about that."

"Well, that's her story," Schiff said. "But Darrel and I don't really believe it. And Jerry Glass doesn't believe it. And he thinks he can get a federal grand jury motivated to prove it."

"Well, all that's well and good, but how's it relate to the homicide you're trying to bring to trial? We're still doing homicide here, right? That hasn't changed during my short absence?"

"Jerry thinks there's much more going on, and that Vogler's murder's in the middle of it. He gets these people into a forfeiture situation on the civil side, then he gets to ask them anything on the criminal side in secret with the grand jury, they look into their assets, get connections we wouldn't have a chance at."

"Plus," Bracco added, "the threat alone. It's pretty powerful leverage. They tell us the truth or—"

Glitsky cut him off. "I get the concept," he said, "but I can't say I really like it."

"What's not to like?" Schiff asked.

"Well, for starters, if you don't have any evidence, how do you decide that these people are your suspects? Or that one of them is. You leaning toward any one of them?"

"Maya doesn't look bad for it, Lieutenant," Schiff said. "She was down there, it was her gun. We know her relationship with Vogler was squirrelly at best."

"So bring her downtown and sweat her."

"Not so easy," Schiff said. "She's already lawyered up. Your friend Diz Hardy."

"Wonderful." Glitsky studied the ceiling for a moment. Then, "What about this list of Vogler's customers? You don't think it's reasonable he was killed by one of them?"

"Why?" Bracco asked.

A shrug. "The usual stupid reasons, Darrel. He cut the dope with parsley and somebody didn't like it. Or one of 'em graduated to crack and just went psycho. Or he stiffed a guy for five bucks. Or any one of a hundred other reasons. Have you talked to any of these people?"

"Some," Schiff said. "There's seventy-two of them, Abe."

He nodded soberly. "I'm sorry about that, I really am. But it seems to me that at least you've got to talk to them, if only to eliminate. Find out who was where on that Saturday morning. I know it's tedious, but that's the job. Sometimes we've just got to grind it out."

"What about Jerry Glass?" Schiff asked.

"I don't know," Glitsky said. "If I'd have been here, I might have suggested you two hold off on going that route for a while, at least until somebody pops up as a bona fide suspect that the forfeiture or the grand jury might squeeze. Now I think we just gotta hope he doesn't get too much in the way."

12

As was often the case early on a workday, Craig Chiurco was loung-
ing in the small reception area of The Hunt Club, Wyatt's office in
the heart of Chinatown, chewing the fat with his girlfriend, Tamara
Dade, who answered the phones and occasionally did fieldwork—
taking pictures, tailing female witnesses. Tamara, twenty-six, tended
to dress for the office in brightly colored miniskirts with form-hugging
tops, and there was ample form to hug over the tight, and often exposed, stomach with its tasteful little gold naval ring. Today only the
ring's shape showed under the orange leotard an inch or two before
it disappeared into her black skirt—Halloween was coming up.

Craig, maybe five years her senior, had been going out with her
now for about three years, although they still maintained separate
apartments. After four years working with Hunt, doing anything he
was asked to do, but mostly subpoena service and stakeout work,
Craig had acquired enough hours in the profession to start the application process for his own private investigator's license. But, of
course, being on Vogler's list, his career plans were in jeopardy. And
he was saying so to Tamara.

Who dismissed the idea with a wave. "Wyatt already told you not
to worry about that."

"Oh. Okay, I won't then."

"Craig. Really. He's the one paying you, so if it doesn't bother
him, how is it going to hurt you?"

"It goes on my record and I have to put that on my application . . ."

Tamara shook her head. "It's a misdemeanor at most, Craig."

"That would do it, though, Tam, which is kind of the point."

"But you don't even have that. The only way that happens is if they catch you with the actual weed. Being on this list isn't proof of anything. And you've gotten rid of all your stuff, so even if they come and search your place—as if—then so what?" She gave him a tolerant look. "You're just upset because you got caught. And because now Wyatt knows."

"Maybe some of that."

"Except he doesn't care. You don't think he's smoked a little weed in his time?"

"I'd bet not much."

"Well, you might be right there. But don't you think he supposes you and me maybe were together a time or two that your alleged dope-smoking took place?"

Craig, reclining sideways with his knees up over the edge of the small love seat that was the only place for a guest or a client to sit, broke a small smile. "I didn't rat you out, Tam. Promise."

She favored him with her own smile. "I didn't say you did, Galahad, and I know you wouldn't. But that doesn't mean that Wyatt wouldn't have put two and two together—or in our case, one and one." She picked up an emery board from her desk blotter and started working on one of her fingernails. "I think the smart thing for you and me to do, which we've already done, is just take it as a wake-up call to be a little smarter, give the stuff up altogether."

Chiurco, arms crossed, pursed his lips at that request.

"What?" Tamara asked. "Would that really be so hard?"

"Not really hard. More like just unnecessary. I like the stuff. *You* like the stuff. Everybody agrees it shouldn't be illegal. So why should I be coerced to give it up entirely?"

Tamara held up one finger. "Me, me, Monty, call on me. How about because it *is* illegal? Whether it should be or not. And you want to work around law enforcement. You get caught with it—you said it—it's on your record. It can affect things—your application, for example. So there's a reason to give it up right there." She pushed back her chair and turned to face him. "The thing is, though, in real life nothing's going to happen around this. Your name is on a list that may or may not have been this guy Vogler's clients. It might have just been people who owed him money."

A short laugh. "That too."

"Well, that's fine. You may know that. But the police just can't know anything, or prove anything, about anybody on that list. Even if everybody else owned up and said they were his customers, that still wouldn't prove that you were. And, by the way, if you're worried that the paper might print it, forget it. They'd get sued from here to Italy. It won't happen."

"Okay," he said. "I'm convinced."

"Good. I mean, bottom line is we just don't do it anymore. Easy enough, right?"

"It should be," Chiurco said.

"Well, there you go. Done deal."

Wyatt Hunt looked briefly out onto Grant Street through the one window across from Tamara in the reception area, then turned back to his employees. "I will entertain even the smallest crumb of an idea."

"Do we have a hint," Chiurco asked, "of what we're looking for? Or some kind of timeline?"

"Hardy thinks when she was in college, so ten to fourteen years ago. In the city here. Something she was embarrassed by, or worse. Obviously, he thinks, something she could still get in trouble for if word gets out."

"Well," said Tamara, who had taken her share of criminology

classes as well, "the statute of limitations would have run out on almost anything she did back then, except if she killed somebody.
What did Vogler do that got him in prison? Could she have been involved in that?"

Hunt pointed a finger at his secretary. "There you go. There's
someplace to start. If she was any part of that, and Vogler took the
fall for it . . . how well did you know him, Craig? Did he ever talk
about that?"

"Not to me. I barely knew him at all, except through the coffee
shop. Maybe we could get our hands on that list and ask some of
those people what they know?"

"I wouldn't bank much on that. Besides, I'm thinking what Tam
suggests is probably going to be more productive. See if he had an
accomplice or two and go talk to them."

"Hardy should just ask her," Chiurco said. "Whatever she tells
him, it's privileged, right? Nobody else would have to know. I don't
see the problem."

"Well, one problem, Craig, not to sound mercenary, is if he asks
her and she tells him, there goes our fee. But the other thing is that
she's evidently cut a deal with her husband—his name's Joel—that
she's not going to be seeing Diz except with him there with them too.
So what's that leave?"

Tamara raised her hand like a good student and spoke right out.
"She doesn't want Joel to find out."

"Ten points." Hunt nodded. "That's my guess too. Which of
course means it might not be a criminal thing at all. Just some behavior she'd rather he never knew about."

"She had an abortion," Tamara said.

Again, Hunt nodded. "Not impossible. Especially being a good
Catholic and all like she is, like they are."

"Wait a minute." Chiurco swung his body around and sat up.
"She pays Vogler ninety thousand dollars a year just so he won't tell

her husband that she had an abortion? And Vogler's the only one who knows? I don't think that flies."

"I don't know, Craig. Stranger things have happened. Maybe Vogler was the father." Hunt pushed himself off the window ledge. "But why don't we see what we can find out about this prison time he did, who he might have been hanging with, see if it leads us back to Maya in any way?"

"I'll take that," Chiurco said.

"Fine. Meanwhile, I'll dig around and see if I can talk to somebody who remembers her from school. I talked to Diz about this yesterday and he's a little worried, beyond everything else we've talked about, that if Vogler was blackmailing her, she might know something dangerous that she doesn't know she knows. So there's a bit of urgency."

Chiurco was on his feet. "I'm all over it," he said.

At a little before noon, with a full blustery fall day building up around them, Bracco and Schiff were back out in the Haight-Ashbury, this time talking to an elderly woman named Lori Bradford. They were all sitting around a small wooden table with a lace tablecloth in a nook off her kitchen. She lived on the second floor of an apartment building looking out over Ashbury, several structures up and across the street from the alley where Dylan Vogler had died.

She'd of course seen the police and the crowd last Saturday and since then had read about the murder, following the story rather closely in the newspaper. Over the last couple of days she had been trying to decide if it would be worthwhile to call somebody about a possible discrepancy that she'd noticed, and finally thought that, yes, it would be, and here they all were.

"Are you sure about this?" Schiff asked her.

"Yes. Absolutely. There were two shots, not just one." Mrs. Bradford, in her late sixties, had dressed for her appointment with these inspectors in a pair of purple slacks over sensible black shoes, and a black turtleneck. "I thought at the time I heard them that I should have called nine one one, but then there wasn't any more noise, and no screaming or anything like that, so I just assumed it must have been a backfire or cherry bombs or something. If it was a real emergency, someone else would have called nine one one anyway, I thought. It wasn't that I didn't want to get involved. People always say that, I know, that they don't want to get involved, but I don't have a problem with that. But I think I just convinced myself that it was probably nothing. I looked out the window there—you see how you've got a clear view of the first twenty or thirty feet of the alley anyway—and didn't see anything moving. Or on the street either. And then I didn't want to send a false alarm, which would have been worse than not calling at all. Wouldn't it? Anyway . . . ," she said. And trailed off.

"Well, it's good you called at whatever time, ma'am," Bracco said. "But we haven't heard anybody else talking about more than one shot." Bracco's face reflected his frustration with San Francisco's laissez faire reality. This wasn't Hunters Point, exactly, in terms of gunshots per minute, but Bracco thought it wasn't such a high crime area that a couple of gunshots would be a completely normal event. And yet, apparently, no one among the citizenry had seen fit to rally to report them. If it wasn't napalm, he figured, nobody paid attention.

Mrs. Bradford looked from one inspector to the other, as though soliciting their forgiveness. "Nobody else called nine one one, then?"

"No, ma'am."

"Oh, then I really should have, shouldn't I?"

"I wouldn't worry about that, Mrs. Bradford," Schiff said. "The point is that you called now and we're here. Inspector Bracco and I will check with dispatch and see if anybody called to report these shots or make a noise complaint on Saturday morning. Maybe they didn't think it was an emergency, and then it wouldn't have come to us through dispatch."

Bracco leaned forward, elbows on the table. "Could you tell us a little more about these shots, ma'am? How far apart were they spaced, for example?"

Mrs. Bradford sat back and stared off into nothing for a second or two. "I'd say about a minute. A fairly long time, anyway. They weren't right away, one after the other. I was awake, I remember, but still in bed, when I heard the first one, and I kind of lay there wondering what that was for a while, and if I'd really heard it. You know? The way you are when you're half awake. And then I decided I'd really heard something and got up to see if I could see what it had been and I was just in the hallway there when the second one went off."

"And what did you do then?" Schiff asked.

"Well." Mrs. Bradford's face grew animated at the recollection. "Well, then, I of course got to the window as fast as I could and looked down at the street here, and I could see the alley, too, but I didn't know that's where the shots must have come from. I couldn't tell anything, really. Anyway, but then when I didn't see anybody moving and hear anything else down below there, that's when I decided it was probably nothing and not to call nine one one."

"Mrs. Bradford," Schiff asked, "did you happen to notice the exact time of these shots?"

"Yes," she said. "It was ten minutes after six. The second one, I mean. The first one, just before that. Six oh eight or nine." She pointed. "There's the digital on the stove."

"And how sure are you," Bracco asked, "that it was the same kind of sound?"

"Oh, the same, definitely. If the second one was a shot, the first one was a shot, and vice versa. Loud, and sharp. Louder than TV." Back to her recurring theme, she said, "I really should have called nine one one. Someone might have gotten here in time to catch the killer."

"Really, Mrs. Bradford"—Schiff patted her hand on the table—"I wouldn't lose one minute of sleep over that. You've done the right thing to call us now, and this is a very important bit of information that we didn't have before." She cast an eye on Bracco. "This may change our entire theory of the case, and it's all because you're a good citizen. We thank you very much."

On the second flight down the stairs, out of earshot, Schiff started talking about it. "You believe her?"

"I think she heard something."

"There was only one bullet missing from the murder weapon."

"*Maybe* the murder weapon. Consistent with the murder weapon. And I kind of vaguely remember, Debra."

"Vogler didn't shoot somebody in that alley."

"Nope."

"And there was only one casing."

"Yep."

"Which means what?"

"It means the woman's going on a hundred. She's bored living alone. She heard some noises maybe the same morning Vogler was shot."

They came out into the overcast and windy day and turned down-hill toward Haight, where, even though they'd parked legally in an open metered space, Darrel had gone through his radio-over-the-rearview-mirror and business-card-on-the-dashboard routine. They were walking on the opposite side of the street from Bay Beans West, and as they came abreast of the place, Schiff hit Bracco on the arm. "Darrel," she said, "wait up. Look at that."

They both stopped.

"What?" Bracco asked.

"On the door."

Bracco squinted to look, then stepped off the curb and started across the street. "What is that?"

When they came closer, the answer presented itself. Taped to the front door was an official yellow-colored single sheet of a government document with the heading "Posting of Real Property," declaring that the establishment was subject to forfeiture to the federal government, as the proceeds of trafficking in controlled substances.

"Jerry Glass," Schiff said. "I fucking love that guy."

13

Dismas Hardy hadn't thought to bring his trench coat to work with him this morning, and on general principles he'd be damned if he was going to take a cab from his office the dozen or fewer blocks to the Federal Building on Golden Gate Avenue. But now he was paying for his stubbornness, leaning into the teeth of a minigale as he walked, suitcoat buttoned up, hands in his pants pockets.

After the ten-thirty A.M. emergency cries for help, first from Maya and then minutes later from Joel Townshend, Hardy had immediately placed his own high-priority call to Jerry Glass, who did not seem inclined to discuss much about the forfeiture situation on the telephone—"It pretty much speaks for itself" was all the explanation he was ready to volunteer. But Hardy had an ace or two up his sleeve, as well, in the person of his former DA friend and mentor Art Drysdale, now one of the Grand Old Men of the U.S. Attorney's Office, and ten minutes after Hardy got off the phone with Art, Glass called him and told him he'd give him some face time if they could do it in Glass's office in the next half hour.

Hence the hike.

But the exercise did serve a couple of small purposes. It gave Hardy time to think. And walking into the gusts and grit really pissed him off.

Now, as he walked down the perennially sterile hallway on the eleventh floor, Hardy found himself forcefully reminded of the last time he'd been down to this neighborhood on business. It had been directly across the street in the State Building. At that time, probably the best part of six years before, he'd essentially been accused of setting fire to his own home for the insurance. An arson inspector and a couple of detectives had three-teamed and threatened him with arrest until he'd called their bluff and simply walked out on them in the middle of the interview.

He wondered, not for the first time, if there was some kind of bland but powerful psychic karma in these two governmental edifices—one federal and one state—that attracted heartless, deceptive, self-righteous bureaucrats. For all of his dislike of the physical layout and general tone of the Hall of Justice at Seventh and Bryant—which is where he normally did his business—no one could argue that the place didn't thrum with almost the very heartbeat of humanity in all of its flaws and grandeur. By contrast these fat faceless rectangles of glass and granite—the halls were silent—seemed the embodiment of the anonymous power of the state to harm and to meddle wherever it saw fit under the rubric of enforcing the rules.

An aphorism of someone he'd once known sprang to his mind: The essence of fascism is to make laws forbidding everything and then enforce them selectively against your enemies.

It wasn't that bad, of course. Hardy had several friends, including Art Drysdale, who worked in one or the other of these buildings. But he himself avoided them whenever he could, all but unconsciously. And getting to Glass's outer office, he could neither ignore the bile that had risen in his gut nor the frisson of what felt like fear tickling at the base of his brain.

Glass evenly carried twenty extra pounds on a frame about the same size as Hardy's. Today he wore a gray suit, white shirt buttoned tight at the neck, a light blue tie. With some effort he shook Hardy's hand over his desk, then sat back down and indicated either of the two beige faux-leather chairs facing him.

Hardy generally thought it best to start out civilly. "I appreciate your taking the time to see me."

Glass turned a hand up. "Art Drysdale's a legend, Mr. Hardy. He recommends that I talk to you, that's what I do. Although I'm not sure how I'm going to be able to help you."

"Well, then we're a bit in the same boat."

"How's that?"

"I think this forfeiture action you're contemplating is going to turn out to be an embarrassment and a mistake. I don't know how I'm going to help you avoid making it."

Glass's mouth tightened, the lips conveying a mild distaste. "I'm not just contemplating going forward with the forfeiture process, Mr. Hardy. I've got plenty of grounds and it's a pretty cut-and-dried precedent. You deal in drugs, your profits and whatever you buy with your profits are subject to forfeiture."

"Fair enough," Hardy said. "But my client hasn't been dealing in drugs. One of Maya Townshend's employees evidently sold marijuana out of her coffee shop, but she didn't know anything about it."

"No?"

"No."

"And you're sure of that?"

"It's not a question of whether I'm sure of it, which I am. It's a question of whether you can prove it, which I don't see how you can."

"Well, that's another matter and what I've already convened the grand jury about. As I'm sure you know, I can't talk about what goes on in those proceedings at all. But as to whether your client knew this was going on—and let's leave for a minute the question of whether she was profiting from the sale of this marijuana herself—it would be hard to imagine that she didn't."

"And why is that?"

"Because Bay Beans West has been the subject of no fewer than

twenty-three nuisance calls from neighbors in the past five years.
Almost all of them concerned flagrant marijuana use, much of it in
front of children and adolescents. The nuisance complaints were, of
course, conveyed not just to the manager of the business but to the
owner of the establishment, who happens as well to own the building. Beyond that, and leaving out the stabbing that took place in the
alley behind the place two years ago, to say nothing of the murder
last week, would you care to guess how many citations for marijuana
smoking have been issued in the past twenty-four months on the
street directly in front of the coffee shop?"

"*In front of* isn't *in.*"

Glass waved that objection away. "Forty-three. Forty-three tickets. The place is a well-known dope den, Mr. Hardy."

"Be that as it may, sir, and I'm not denying it, the fact remains that
my client didn't know much about it. She rarely went there. She was
a silent partner in running the place, that's all."

"She knew it well enough to have her civil lawyers come to the
Zoning Commission when some neighbors tried to lift her business
license three years ago. It went all the way to the Board of Supervisors, Mr. Hardy, and some say that if it weren't for her brother, they
would have shut her down then."

This was completely unexpected and bad news to Hardy. Neither
Maya nor Joel had mentioned anything about it to him. "Okay,"
Hardy said, conceding the point, "but this is marijuana on Haight
Street. You can get it in any doorway. You can't seriously claim that
BBW was the source or even a major contributor to all these tickets."

Glass sniffed his displeasure. "Your client is the sister of one of
our supervisors and the niece of the mayor. And mustn't that be
nice?" His lips turned up, but no one would have called it a smile.
"Your client certainly knew the kind of place they were running,
believe me. It's a plain and simple narcotics operation, complete with
the gun that's the purported murder weapon for the latest problem

there, huge amounts of cash—far more than you'd expect in a coffee shop—and substantial quantities of marijuana on the premises."

Hardy took in this information in silence, masking his concern with a nonchalant posture—sitting back now, arms on the chair rests, his foot resting over its opposite knee. "Mr. Glass," he said, "I'm not here to dispute whether or not the place was a source for marijuana. Obviously, it was. But it's a long stretch—even if my client knew about it, or had a hunch about it, or anything like that—it's a hell of a long stretch to prove that she profited from the dope at all. Do you know who Joel Townshend is? He doesn't need dope money, believe me."

"You mean on the theory, Mr. Hardy, that people who have a lot of money don't want to have more?"

"He doesn't need to take that kind of risk to get it. He wouldn't take that risk. Neither would she."

"Which came first, I wonder, the real estate or the drugs? Mr. Townshend may have a fortune, Mr. Hardy, but we intend to claim every dollar of it that came from the narcotics business. Then we'll see how much he's got left."

"Why would they take the risk?" Hardy repeated.

Glass had a hand stretched out casually in front of him as he scratched at his desk blotter. "One could make the argument, I think you'll agree, given the, shall we say, personal relationship between your client and the mayor's office, that there was no risk here in this city in running any kind of illegal operation." Now he came forward, his eyes narrowing, a hint of real anger ruddying up the pale flesh of his face. His voice, though, remained controlled. "She was paying the man ninety thousand dollars a year, for Christ's sake."

"That's right."

"To manage a coffee shop."

"Correct. Last time I checked, that wasn't a crime."

"No, but money laundering is. He gives her his dope money, she puts it in her or her husband's account, and they pay him back out of that."

"That wasn't happening," Hardy said flatly.

"I intend to show that it was. You get people worried about their assets, you'd be surprised what turns up."

Hardy uncrossed his legs and came forward in his chair. "Mr. Glass, have you met these people? They didn't do any of this."

"No? Well, we'll see. But what's your point? That I'd like them if I met them socially? That it would matter to me? I'm sure they're charming. People who deal in cons tend to be."

"You've got this completely wrong," Hardy said. "You don't have any facts that implicate my client in any of this. And meanwhile, you've got her threatened with this forfeiture. It's just a blunt instrument at this point."

"Well." Glass folded his heavy hands on the desk. "It'll get us on the road to finding out what we need to know. And sometimes you just have to use the tools you got."

"You can still do that?" Hardy asked from the office doorway.

"It's like riding a bicycle," Art Drysdale replied, "once you've got it . . ." He caught the last of the three baseballs he'd been juggling at his desk, tucked them into one enormous paw and, with a lot more enthusiasm than Jerry Glass had evinced, sprang up from his chair to shake Hardy's hand. "But, hey, you're looking great. How you doin'?"

"Any better and they'd have to change my medication," Hardy said. He cast a quick eye around the premises, which sported a lot more personality than Jerry Glass's digs. Of course, that might have been because Drysdale himself had a lot more personality than his gung-ho new colleague. Drysdale—no relationship to the ex-Dodger Don—had been a professional baseball player in his youth, making it up to the Giants for a cup of coffee in the mid-sixties, before deciding to go into the law. The bookshelf that covered his left-hand wall was packed with sports memorabilia, trophies from the PAL coaching days, photos with the great—McCovey, Cepeda, Mays!—and with his family, four boys, himself, and even his wife usually attired in some kind of sports uniform.

"If I hadn't just come from Jerry Glass," Hardy added, "I might even be positively glowing."

Drysdale boosted himself back up onto his desk, motioned that Hardy might want to get the door behind him. When that was done, Drysdale clicked his tongue. "Mr. Glass didn't give you much satisfaction, did he?"

"Oh, no. To the contrary, he was nothing if not informative. The problem was that the information sucked. You guys can really just take property?"

Drysdale grimaced. "We're the federal government, Diz. We can do anything we want. Why? Because who's going to stop us?" Then, in a different tone, "I admit, it's a bit of problem for some of us. On both sides. That little, tiny potential for abuse of the system, since if you play it close enough, you don't really get seriously called on anything."

"And that's what Glass is doing? Playing it close?"

A nod. "From what I hear, he's pretty much on his game, let's say that."

"So what do I do?"

"What do you mean?"

"I mean, I've got a client involved here, Art. In theory I'm supposed to keep her and maybe even her family out of this trouble."

Drysdale let out a dry chuckle. "Well, there's your problem. The system's kind of set up to keep you out of it. Especially if he's using the grand jury, which I happen to know he is."

"Yeah. He told me that too."

"Okay. So you'll never find out what happens there. Don't even try, Diz. No lawyers allowed. No witnesses. No talking about anything said there, ever ever. But you know this."

"Okay, but how's he do the forfeiture?"

"Well, actually, that's pretty slick. He's only asking for a civil forfeiture."

"As opposed to criminal, I presume. But what does that mean?"

"It means, basically, that he posts the property . . . you know anything about this at all?"

"Not really. It doesn't come up every day."

"No. I'd guess not. Which is why Glass can have so much fun with it. Just for starters, you want to guess what the forfeiture rules are administered under?"

"The Little League?"

Drysdale cracked a smile. "Closer than you'd think, actually. The Rules of Admiralty."

"That was my second guess."

"I'll give you partial credit, then. And you know why it was Admiralty rules? Because since Elizabethan times, the British Empire allowed an action against a ship as a way of getting at the owner. They would literally 'arrest' the thing, the ship, before it took off, and make the owners in some faraway country post a bond before they would release the ship back to the high seas. Then they could collect whatever was owed from the bond. In rem jurisdiction. Latin for 'against the thing.' Just like here. Grab the store. Make the owners come to court to free it in a civil case. So basically, your clients are going to have to sue to get their shop out of this limbo, and, surprise, the burden of proof is now on them. The good news is that they get to stay in business—their legitimate business—until the final ruling."

Hardy walked over and settled himself into a rocking chair in the corner by the bookshelf. "So what's the point? What's it get Glass to just post the place?"

"Not much, if that's all he's doing. He might win, he might not. But either way, he gets their attention."

"So what?"

"Aha!" Drysdale held up a finger. "'So what' is that he's allowed to talk about a civil case. To the newspapers, TV, to your clients, to the cops, to anybody. He's doing the public a service by talking about it. Meanwhile, he's stirring the pot to see what rises."

"But as opposed to what?"

"I'd tell you, but I know you already know."

Hardy paused, and of course the obvious truth emerged. "The grand jury."

"Ta da!" Drysdale spread his hands in a victory gesture. "Two prongs. One public, one secret." His face went dark. "It is a serious, no-bullshit press, Diz. And my sources tell me that old Jerry is playing it so far like a maestro. You know, he got his homicide inspector—Schiff, is it?—designated as a special agent of the grand jury?"

"He can do that?"

Drysdale tsked. "I believe we've mentioned that he can do anything, haven't we? He can get the grand jury to designate anybody as its agent. And what does that agent have access to? Grand jury documents, including financial and bank records, which, by the way, in real life the feds—us—can subpoena anytime and the state can never ever get its hands on." Drysdale turned a hand over. "Now, of course, that agent can't reveal what's in those documents—that's secret—but she can act on her knowledge of them. Including—you'll love this—based on this private knowledge, she can argue for a judge to order release of these otherwise secret docs. And also, PS, if that doesn't work, once the documents leave the grand jury room, sometimes they get leaked somehow. Though that, of course again, would be wrong."

Hardy could listen to Drysdale's commentary all day, but he wasn't even slightly amused. "This isn't right, Art."

Drysdale laughed with some enthusiasm. "We've barely started, Diz, and if you can't laugh at it, you're in deep shit."

Hardy sat back. "What else?"

"You really want to know?" At Hardy's nod Drysdale settled himself on the desk. "Jerry's got so many ways he can play this, it's just gorgeous. You said Kathy West may be involved here, right? And Harlen? Okay, first, he has them talk to one of our agents a few times. They're not targets, he tells them. He wants them to roll over on your client, but they're not themselves part of the investigation. So what's that get him? Well, first, if either of them tells even a little fib to the federal agent, they are in felony land. And guess what? Federal agents don't have to tape-record interviews."

"Now you're kidding me!"

"Would that I were, my son, but that was J. Edgar's original policy and it's in force today, so it's always your word against that of a federal agent, and guess who the grand jury is more likely to believe? They've even got a cute little name for this cute little strategy—the Perjury Trap. Isn't that special?"

"Beautiful. And I'm guessing we're still not done yet."

"You catch on fast, Batman. You really want to know?"

"I want to know where they teach this stuff. I've been a lawyer for thirty years and I've never run across it."

"That's not a coincidence, Diz, I promise. This is some *très* arcane shit. But anyway, since you asked, let's say your people—Kathy and Harlen and even your client—avoid lying to their friendly federal agent. Now they go in front of the grand jury as individuals, where, you remember, they are specifically not targets. Glass gives them immunity for anything they say, and what's interesting about that? Now they can't take the Fifth! Now they've got to answer every single thing Glass asks them; if they refuse, they go to jail for contempt. Is that great, or what?"

"Why is that somehow familiar?" Hardy asked.

"Because you, as a lawyer, will remember that this is almost exactly what happened to Susan McDougal in Ken Starr's Whitewater investigation. The grand jury called her up and even gave her immunity, but she refused to answer questions because she was concerned her statements would be viewed as false—"

"There's a nice distinction," Hardy commented. "Viewed as."

"Isn't it? Well, anyway, if they were viewed as false, then she'd be indicted for perjury, so she didn't answer, and so for her troubles she got slammed with civil contempt, where you stay in custody as long as you refuse to answer or until the grand jury term expires, which in McDougal's case was eighteeen months."

"Holy shit." Hardy rocked gently, his hands gripping the armrests, taking it all in. "So it's way more than just this forfeiture stuff? What's Glass going for? Money laundering?"

"At least. Plus distribution, conspiracy, you name it—where you're looking at major hard time."

"Jesus."

Drysdale wasn't smiling anymore either. "And I'm afraid it just gets worse, Diz."

"I can't really imagine how."

"No. You probably can't. So let me tell you the real ugly truth. You should know for your client's sake, and Kathy and Harlen's, too, for that matter, that you want to do everything you can to keep them from getting charged at all. That's what Jerry wants—he wants to force them to cop a plea to maintaining a place."

"Even if Kathy or even Maya had nothing to do with the dope?"

Drysdale shook his head. "Doesn't matter. They can still both be criminally liable."

"How's that?"

"Because if any of them has reason to believe there was the criminal activity, but didn't ask, the jury is allowed to impute knowledge."

"Under what possible guise, Art?"

"Simple and glorious. They should have asked, so it's deliberate
ignorance."

"Deliberate ignorance. I love that."

"And why would you not? It's a lovely thing."

Hardy sat still for a long moment, his feet planted to the floor. "So
let me get this straight. They're going to get them at least for maintaining a place, pretty much automatically, it sounds like. Is that
about right?"

"Close enough."

"Then why wouldn't they want to duke it out in court on the
money-laundering and distribution and conspiracy charges?"

"Good," Drysdale said. "I love a guy who pays attention. That
was just hanging out there, wasn't it?" He absently threw up one of
the baseballs and caught it. "I was saving the best for last. I bet you
think that if you get acquitted in federal court, you can't be sentenced."

"Well, yeah. That's kind of what *acquitted* means, doesn't it?"

"Ah, the naïveté of youth! In federal court, as it happens, if you're
convicted on even one count of anything—perjury, maintaining a
place—the judge can base a sentence up to the statutory max on your
acquitted conduct. So one small white lie to a federal agent—which,
by the way, may not have ever been actually told—could get your client *five years* federal time. And keep in mind that the max for maintaining a place is twenty years. And, oh yeah, there's no parole with
the feds. So of course they try to plead it out, even if it costs them the
property. Maybe that's all Glass wants anyway, but probably not. Is
that a lovely squeeze or what?"

"It's unbelievable, Art. There's got to be a way around it."

"Well, if and when you stumble upon it, my friend, get the word out and you'll make yourself a quick million bucks the first week. I guarantee it."

Glitsky said, "Yeah. I told Debra maybe she moved a little too soon on that. Glass."

"You know him?" Hardy asked.

"Never had the pleasure."

"It wasn't."

"If it's any help, I kind of tried to call her and Darrel off."

"That would have been good if the horse wasn't already out of the barn."

"I told her this being an agent of the grand jury wasn't really rec-ommended SOP. For what that was worth. Which, from her reac-tion, I gather wasn't much." At the table at Kokkari, Glitsky turned a hand over. "Another failure, I'm afraid. I'm going for a record."

Hardy killed a minute lifting a perfect backbone out of the whole sea bass he'd ordered for lunch. Hardy had cabbed back from Glass's office and picked up Glitsky in front of the Hall of Justice, thinking maybe some great Greek food would cheer them both up. But so far, halfway through the meal, it wasn't working too well.

They'd covered Zachary's situation on the drive over. The doctors were recommending a few more days in the hospital before proceed-ing to the next operation to replace the dura mater early the next week. The boy had apparently recognized everybody in the family on the visit last night, going so far as to reach out and poke his sister, who'd come along to the hospital for the first time, in the arm, after which he'd broken into a short-lived smile. He still hadn't spoken yet, which everyone agreed might be a little worrisome—Glitsky loved the word, *worrisome!*—but his other motor skills had clearly improved.

The diagnosis had moved from critical to guarded, and the general tone of the medical team was one of optimism.

Although very little of that optimism had rubbed off on Abe.

The usually glib Hardy kept his peace as he squeezed lemon on his fish. Self-loathing was about the last reaction he'd ever expected to run into from his hard-assed longtime best friend. Glitsky hadn't before harbored too many doubts about who he was or what he was all about.

Or if he did, he didn't show it.

Now Zachary's accident seemed to have unleashed a pride of demons set upon undermining his confidence and self-respect.

Hardy chewed, then put his fork down. "You know," he began, "I was the one who changed Michael's diaper before I put him in bed that last night. I had all the time in the world to lift the side of the crib. I mean, there I was, leaning over the damn thing, tucking him in. It was halfway up and all I had to do was stand and pull it up the rest of the way. Easiest thing in the world. Piece of cake. Unfortunately, the thought never crossed my mind."

Glitsky put his iced tea down halfway to his mouth. "*Unfortunately.* Think that's strong enough?"

Hardy's heart thumped in his chest with an unexpected jolt of rage that it took several seconds to control. Finally, he let out a breath. "It's how I've come to see it, Abe. It's what I've had to get to so I could live with it. You think I've been lying to myself all these years?"

"You said it yourself—the thought never crossed your mind."

Hardy took a sip of his club soda, picking his way with care. "So you're standing there being a good dad, taking Zack out on his new bike. You get him settled on the seat and think, 'Oh, yeah, the helmet . . .'"

Glitsky cut him off, his volume up a notch. "I know what I did."

"I don't know if you do."

"Don't push me, Diz. I mean it."

Hardy drew a breath. "I'm not pushing you. I'm saying you didn't do anything that caused it. *The thought never crossed your mind.*"

"It should have."

"Why? Anything remotely like that ever happen before? You've got to think of every single contingency that can happen? If that were true, you'd never let your kids out of your sight. Ever. Hell, you might not let 'em get out of bed because something might happen."

"Something did happen."

"You didn't make it happen."

"I could have prevented it. If I'd have thought—"

Hardy put a flat palm on the table between them. "If you'd have thought," he said. "But there was no reason you should have. Nothing like that had ever happened before. Next time, okay, you'll think to put the helmet on first. But not thinking of it then wasn't negligence, Abe. It was a freak accident. You could do everything exactly the same a thousand times and nothing bad would ever happen again. It wasn't your fault."

Glitsky sat hunched forward over his plate. Their table was by a window and he glared out at the blustering day. Finally, he came back to Hardy, seemed to force the words out one at a time. "How can it not be my fault when he was my responsibility? If it happens on my watch, I'm at fault."

"This isn't police bureaucracy, Abe. This is your life."

"Being a cop is my life."

"Don't give me that shit. Being a cop is what you do. The rest of you is your life. The problem you've got here is this really happened to you, to your boy. So you're both victims of it. And since the one thing you won't do, ever, is be a victim, that leaves you holding the bag and taking responsibility for it. 'Cause that's who you are. That's what you do. It's automatic."

Glitsky spit it out. "It's not wrong either."

"I'm not saying it is. Not all the time, not usually. But this once, this one time, it's beating you down when you're going to need to be strong, when Treya and Rachel and even poor fucking attorneys like me need you to get over it so your troops don't go riding roughshod over their cases. You didn't do this. You didn't cause it. It happened, that's all. You're a victim of that, okay, fine. Legitimately. But that doesn't make you any kind of unworthy human, not if you don't let it."

Glitsky's scar burned white through his lips. His heavy brows hung like a precipice over hooded eyes, which remained fixed on the plate before him and refused to meet Hardy's, who thought it wasn't impossible that his friend would suddenly either physically explode at him across the table or throw something and storm out. Instead, though, the eyes came up. "You done?"

"Pretty much."

Glitsky nodded. "I'll give it some thought."

It was a bit of an extra drive—several other churches, and even St. Mary's Cathedral, were closer to her house—but Maya Townshend felt a special energy connecting her with St. Ignatius, the church at the edge of the USF campus, and it was where she had driven now. She needed all the divine intervention she could get, and here is where she most often came to pray for forgiveness. Those prayers she had prayed here had, for the most part, been answered.

Answered in the form of Joel and her life with him. Their healthy family. Their wonderful home and financial security. If God had not forgiven her, surely he would not have showered such beneficence upon her.

Or so she had come to believe.

But now she was suddenly not so sure. She knew that killing was a mortal sin and wondered if God's apparent acceptance of her penance and prayers was really just the first stage in a punishment that would strip from her all that she loved and cherished. If, because of all this, if she lost Joel now, or the children, or even their home and fortune, it would be far more devastating than if she'd never known such love and contentment. God demanded justice as well as he dispensed mercy. The Church taught that there was no sin that God would not forgive, and that the failure to believe that was the worst sin of all—despair. God's mercy was infinite. But the key to any claim to that mercy was confession. And she could not confess.

She could never confess.

And that truth, she believed, stood to damn her for eternity.

A regular here, she went to her usual back pew and knelt, making the sign of the cross, then bringing her hands together and bowing her head.

But no prayers would come. Her mind kept returning to the lies she had told Joel just last night; the lies she'd been living now for so long; the truths that were even worse.

The padded wooden rail on which she knelt had a gap in the middle of the pew, and after only a minute of attempting to pray she moved down and again went to her knees, but directly onto that gap now, putting all of her weight onto it, offering up the pain even as it shot up her leg and became nearly unbearable.

"Please, God. Please, please forgive me. I am so, so sorry."

She raised her head and through tearful eyes tried to focus on the crucifix above the altar far away up front, on the suffering of Christ.

But Christ had never done what she'd done. Christ knew that God's mercy would save him.

After the events of the past few days she no longer harbored that hope for herself.

14

Not two hundred yards away from where Maya suffered and tried to pray, Wyatt Hunt turned another page in the yearbook, thinking that private investigators in the future would have an easy time of it. All they'd have to do with kids who were going to school now would be call up their MySpace or Facebook accounts, and they'd have a blow-by-blow account of everything their subjects had done from about sixth grade on.

Maya Townshend, though, at thirty-two, was just a bit too old for that approach. So Hunt was reduced to searching for clues in the hard copy of her college years. Of course, first he'd Googled her and her husband, and though there had been three thousand or so hits, the majority of them by far concerned Joel's business and their philanthropy. For such a politically connected couple there was very little about either local or national politics, nor were they particularly active in San Francisco's high society. Hits for Bay Beans West appeared a whopping four times—all of the stories variants on the Little Local Coffee Shop That Could standing up to the Starbucks giant and making it work.

Not a whiff of marijuana or, indeed, troubles of any kind.

On a whim Hunt had done a search for Dylan Vogler, and the coffee shop manager had come up completely empty except for references to his death recently—one of the country's very few invisible men, Hunt thought.

Maybe Craig Chiurco, he thought, checking the criminal databanks, would have more luck.

His next stop was the library at USF, where he started on the 1994 yearbook and found the standard posed picture of Maya Fisk looking about fifteen—fresh-faced, perfect hair, big smile. She was one of her class's representatives in student government her freshman year, on the debate and IM soccer teams, active in music and theater, appearing in two student productions. She was also a cheerleader. Sophomore year was basically freshman year redux.

The change must have occurred late in her sophomore year or in the succeeding summer, because her picture as a junior was so different from the others as to be nearly unrecognizable. Though the hair color had turned light and the style more untamed, the main change from Hunt's perspective was the facial expression. In place of the adolescent with the sunny smile of the previous two years, now a young woman stared defiantly at the camera with a bored smirk. Seeking another view of this chameleon, Hunt turned to the club and team pages, but here again something drastic had changed—Maya had stopped taking part in extracurricular activities.

In her senior year her photo placed her more closely with the girl from her first two years—she wore a passive toothless smile and she'd combed her still-light hair—but it was a more formal portrait than the others had been. And again, she'd joined nothing.

Pretty much striking out with the yearbooks, Hunt turned to the microfiches of the student newspaper, the *Foghorn*, for the first couple of years, when Maya was still active, and might have appeared in some captioned photographs with other students. In this he was luckier right away. Here was Maya, in her freshman year, mugging for the camera with three other cheerleader friends at a pep rally. Hunt took down all the names. And three others that he found captioned throughout the rest of her freshman year. Obviously, at the beginning, Maya had been a popular and involved student.

She'd costarred in *Othello* her sophomore year, and there was a

picture of her with her leading man, a handsome African-American
kid named Levon Preslee. In an accompanying story entitled "It's in
the Genes," Hunt read about Maya's introduction to acting and to
the theater through her aunt, the truly famous actress Tess Granat,
who'd by that time been the star of sixteen movies and had appeared
in four leads on Broadway.

Hunt sat back, intrigued by the connection about which he'd previously been unaware. He'd seen some of Granat's films before, he
was sure, but he couldn't remember any titles. Or whatever happened
to her. Probably the same thing that had happened to so many former talented beauties who lost enough of their looks to become un-
desirable and uncastable in Hollywood.

Or had she died? Some tragedy?

The name tickled a vague memory of that, but he just couldn't
remember for sure. In any event there was no mention in the article
that Granat had played any kind of a day-to-day role in Maya's life
back then, but she was another someone who may have known what
the young woman was like or what she had done in those days, and he
wrote her name in his notepad.

Sure, he thought, if she was even alive, he'd just call up the
once-famous movie star in Hollywood or wherever she was and chat
about old times. That was going to happen. Not.

But the afternoon, after all, had not been a total loss. When he was
finished, he had nine names of people Maya's age who had known her
in college.

It was someplace to start.

Back in his office downtown Hunt realized that having nine names
to work with was all well and good, but seven of them were women,
and this made it likely that some of them, like Maya, had changed

their last names since college. Meanwhile, he had Levon Preslee and
one other male, Jimi d'Amico, and Levon was listed in the San Francisco phone book.

Hunt called the number, got the young man's answering machine,
left a message, and decided that it was time he got Tamara working
with him on this tedious business. There were several d'Amicos in
San Francisco, and Hunt and Tamara called all of them, hoping to
find a Jimi, but since it was the middle of the afternoon on a week-
day, between them they managed to talk to only one human being,
who didn't know a Jimi.

They left more messages.

As he thought it would be, finding even one of the women turned
out to be a chore. He and Tamara were hoping that one of the last
names would reveal at least a set of parents who might be inclined to
pass Hunt's name along to one of their daughters, but this was going
to involve quite a few phone calls and, again, messages, messages,
messages.

By four-fifteen they'd been at the whole business for better than
three hours when Hunt punched up the twenty-third telephone number under Peterson and a woman's voice answered.

"Hello," he said, "I'm trying to reach a Nikki Peterson."

"This is Nikki."

Hunt punched a fist into the air, threw a paper clip at Tamara to
get her attention and let her know he'd finally gotten a hit, then went
into his spiel, identifying himself and stating his business. When
he'd finished, she said, "Sure. I knew Maya. We were cheerleaders
together. I don't know where she is now, though. I haven't seen her
since college. Is she in trouble?"

"Why do you ask that?"

"Well, you're a private investigator asking about her. I wasn't great
at math, but I can put two and two together. So she is?"

"What?"

"In trouble."

"Not yet," Hunt said, "but she might be getting there pretty quick."

He told her he was free if she was, and within an hour she was sitting across from his desk. No longer a cheerleader, but from looks alone she would still have a good shot to make the team.

"So," Hunt asked her, "I'm talking to people who knew her back then. Did you know a guy named Vogler? Dylan Vogler?"

She hesitated. "I don't think so. Was he a jock? Mostly I hung out with the jocks."

"Did Maya? Hang out with the jocks, I mean?"

"Not really. She started out with us, then dropped off the team."

"Why?"

"No idea, really. Maybe it was too much practice. I don't know. Maybe she just lost interest. That happens."

"You don't remember any rumors or gossip about her sometime around the time she quit? Pregnancy, abortion, anything like that? Drugs? Arrests?"

"Not really, no. But we weren't really that close, you know. I mean, I knew her when she was on the team. But after she left, like I said, I haven't heard from her since."

"Were there any other cheerleaders who might have known her better? I've got a picture of her with you and two other girls in the *Foghorn*, Amy Binder and Cheryl Zolotny."

"Amy, no, I'm sure. Cheryl? Maybe a little. But she's not Zolotny anymore now. Just a second, let me think."

"Take all the time you need."

In the reception room, at Tamara's desk, the telephone rang. Tamara put her own call on hold and answered, then said, "Just a minute, please. Can you hold a sec?"

And then Nikki answered Hunt's earlier question. "Cheryl Biehl.

That's it. Biehl. B-I-E-H-L. I think she's still in the city. She was at the reunion last year. You can try her."

"Okay. Well, thanks, Nikki. You've been a help."

She'd no sooner left the office when Hunt gave Tamara the high sign and immediately was on the telephone again. "Hello."

"Mr. Hunt?"

"That's me."

"My name is Jimi d'Amico. You left a message for me?"

And it started all over again.

"Nothing?" Gina Roake asked.

"Nothing."

It was six forty-five and Gina, Dismas Hardy and Wes Farrell's law partner and Hunt's somewhat clandestine girlfriend, had her shapely legs curled under her on the couch in her well-appointed one-bedroom condominium on Pleasant Street just down from the peak of Nob Hill. Hunt sat across from her, in one of her matched brace of reading chairs. They'd pulled closed the drapes in the picture window behind him and she'd turned on some of the room's lights and the gas fire-logs as the now-fierce wind rattled the panes. Gina, barefoot but otherwise still dressed for work in a tan skirt and a beige turtleneck, sipped her Oban scotch and sighed. "That sounds like a long day, Wyatt."

Hunt sat back, shaking his head. "I don't mind long if I get something for it. But we finally got to only five of them before I gave it up. Tamara's still at it and I must say it's great to have workaholic employees. But it's a little weird. It's like Maya almost didn't exist after her sophomore year. And there's no way, or at least it's unlikely, she was involved in some kind of scandal. Whatever it was, if she was being blackmailed by Vogler, he was one of the very few who knew about whatever it was."

"Maybe the only one. Maybe that's why it worked. And nobody knew him either?"

"Not so far. The mystery man."

"And you're sure he went there? USF?"

"Diz says so."

"Did you check the yearbook and the student paper for him too?"

"No." Hunt made a face. "The reason I like you is that you're so much smarter than me. But say he didn't go to USF, so what?"

"I don't know. You might be able to find out where he actually went, which might tell you something you don't know about him."

"I don't know anything about him, except he did hard time for a robbery—which Craig's checking out—then came back to town and ran this coffee shop and evidently moved a hell of a lot of dope."

Pensive, Gina absently turned her scotch glass around and around on the arm of the couch. Finally, she looked up at Hunt. "You're saying he went to prison from San Francisco?"

"Yep."

"If he was sentenced to prison, he had a presentence report, and the background section of that is going to tell you everything they could find out about him at the time. Surely you have a close personal friend in probation."

Hunt considered for a moment. "Have I already told you you're way smarter than me?"

15

At Hardy's house, less than twenty blocks from the ocean out in the Avenues, the approaching storm decided to get serious. A heavy, wind-driven rain raked the rooftop, turning the skylight over their kitchen into a booming kettle drum that reverberated through the rooms. Hardy, on the wall telephone, trying to hear his client over the din, stood frowning with his finger in one ear and the receiver at the other.

"The best advice," he said, "is don't panic. I got the impression that Mr. Glass sees a political opportunity here. He wants to get his name in the paper, and he thinks tweaking you to get at your brother and the mayor is as good a way as any."

This, Hardy knew, was easy for him to say, but not so easy for the Townshends to live with. The truth, verified that afternoon by Art Drysdale, was that Jerry Glass was moving with an almost unheard of dispatch to bring pressure to bear on Joel and Maya. Seen in the kindest possible light, maybe Glass was motivated by a desire to help Schiff and Bracco solve their homicide.

But Hardy didn't really buy that, and by the time they both hung up, he didn't feel like he'd done much of a job consoling or reassuring his client. Still angry about Glass and the way he was operating, Hardy thought a beer wouldn't hurt him and he opened an Anchor Steam and then placed a call to Harlen Fisk.

The supervisor picked up on the second ring. "Yo, Diz. What's up?"

"Have you talked to your sister recently?"

Hardy heard a sigh.

"I talked to Joel earlier today."

"Well, if it was before noon, it's gotten worse since then. Now they're looking for a court order to freeze Joel's accounts."

"Jesus. Why?"

"Because they can. They're saying they've got a money-laundering case. But I'm thinking the real reason is so that Jerry Glass can finally get some national profile for being a good conservative prosecutor with the guts to be tough on dope. He busts the compassionate use spots, the only people who care at all think he's wrong, and none of them are in the media. But he ties you and your aunt into a bona fide dope operation, I don't care how obliquely, and you watch, he's a household name in a week or so."

"Joel and Maya aren't running a dope operation, Diz. Guaranteed."

"Right, but the problem is that he doesn't have to prove it to make noise about it."

"Can he do that? I mean just freeze assets?"

"He's the U.S. government. He can sure try. I don't think he'll actually find a judge who'll approve it, but he's got your sister half around the bend with worry."

"But what about the forfeiture?"

"Forfeiture is a civil case, so in essence he's just filing a lawsuit. I haven't turned on the TV yet, but the smart money says this gets covered tonight and tomorrow it's in the paper."

"Shit."

"I agree. Which is why I called you. Maybe there's something we can do to keep this from exploding any bigger than it has to."

"Like what?"

"Like, the first thing is call him on it, get him back on defense a little. You and Kathy get together and make a strong public statement that this is just a political ploy, another partisan attack on liberals. Then you get the medical marijuana or compassionate use people to go nuts. It's about politics, pure and simple. The second thing is something I've already got my investigator working on, but maybe you can help me with it better than anybody else."

"If I can, I'm in. What?"

Hardy tipped up his bottle. "Well, it looks like both me and homicide have come up with the same theory, and that's that Vogler was connected to Maya in something that happened a long time ago. The bad news would be if that connection gives her a motive to have killed him."

"Jesus Christ, Diz. Maya didn't kill anybody. That's crazy."

"I hope you're right, but—"

"You *hope*? You're her lawyer, Diz. You've got to do more than hope. She's not some kind of a murderer. She's my little sister, for Christ's sake."

Hardy kept his voice modulated. "This hasn't come out yet, but you've got to know that she was down there that morning, Harlen. Vogler might have been squeezing or threatening her. The homicide inspectors went to Glass to try to get Maya to start talking."

"Darrel did that?"

"Glitsky said it was Schiff, but Darrel's on board with her."

"That's bullshit. I'm going to call him."

"Don't do that. Please don't do that. They haven't arrested her yet. They don't have enough. But if you try to pressure them not to, I guarantee it won't help. They'll think she ran to you for protection because she's guilty and you could pull strings."

"This is insane."

"It's the way it is, Harlen."

"So what did you want me to do? About this connection?"

"See if you can get her to tell me what it was."

"What, exactly?"

"What was her history with this loser, who treated her so badly? Why was she paying him ninety grand when the going rate is about half that?"

"I've already heard her answer to that. It was a point of contention between her and Joel. At first, she felt sorry for him and wanted to help him get back on his feet after he got out of prison, and then he did such a good job."

"I've heard that one too."

"You don't think it's true?"

"Maybe I would if he hadn't treated her like the help. But he did."

At this, Fisk went silent for a long beat. "So if and when we find out, assuming she'll tell me, then what?"

"I don't want her to tell you, Harlen. She can't tell you. You're not her lawyer. There's no privilege. You'd have to repeat anything she told you in court if you got a subpeona. You have to get her to tell me or one of my investigators. Then at least we've got answers. We're dealing with the reality of what was going on down there. Glass is going on the theory that the ninety grand was money laundering through the drug business. We need to explain away the high salary without any reference to the dope."

"But, as you say, it also gives her a motive to have killed him."

This, of course, remained a true source of concern, but Hardy spun it the best he could. "I'm hoping if we can somehow defuse Glass, Darrel and Schiff won't get enough."

"You're saying you think she might actually have done it."

"I'm her lawyer, Harlen. I'm trying to keep her out of jail. Jerry Glass is trying to make her a drug dealer. If she's a drug dealer, she's a much more likely killer to Darrel and Schiff. At this point it's mostly a matter of perception, and admittedly it isn't much, but it's about all we got."

The Hardys rented a double garage only a couple of blocks from their home, and most of the time this was an advantage over having to drive around the neighborhood for long minutes in search of a parking place. Tonight, however, the short walk through the ongoing monsoon had delivered Frannie, soaked and freezing, to her home about five minutes after her husband's talk with Harlen Fisk.

He poured her a glass of wine to go with his second beer and suggested she go upstairs and run a hot bath while he made them one of his extemporaneous "black-frying-pan meals." Since these were usually great-tasting and an absolute snap to clean, Frannie agreed, gave him a shivering kiss and a quick hug, and disappeared up the stairs.

The heavy, well-seasoned cast-iron pan was the one possession that Hardy retained from his childhood, and he treated it with great care. Normally it hung on a marlin hook behind the stove and now he took it down, and after admiring the look of it for a moment, he ran a finger over the cooking surface. As always, it was silken to the touch, shiny with a micron brush of oil from its last use, unmarred by any scratch or even the hint of residue.

Rummaging, Hardy started in the refrigerator—perennially bare now that the kids had gone—and after pulling out a half head of iceberg lettuce, he fixed his eyes upon a carton of eggs and a decent-sized half wedge of triple-crème d'Affinois cheese, which he knew would turn the blood in his arteries to the consistency of tar, but he cared about as much as he had a few days before when he and Frannie had split the first half of it, which is to say not at all. Something was going to get him someday, and if it happened to be the d'Affinois, he could think of lots of worse ways to go.

They had other only-in–San Francisco staples on hand—butter, truffle oil, sourdough bread in the freezer, some packaged dried mushrooms in the pantry. Hardy dumped the mushrooms in a bowl of warm water to reconstitute, carried his beer with him over to the family room, where he fed his tropical fish, and sat down on the couch to wait for Frannie to descend.

He was still wrestling with the idea of why he wasn't asking Maya himself.

The reasons he'd given Wyatt Hunt had, at the time, seemed reasonable, but now he wondered. True, he didn't want to get Maya defensive with him. And one of the main tenets of defense work is that no lawyer wants to put his client in a position where she has to lie to him. But he was dimly, naggingly aware of another motivation that made him feel morally uneasy—and that was that he didn't want to lose her as a client because she represented perhaps a quarter of a million dollars in fees if she got arrested, which he was starting to consider at least as a possibility.

Hardy billed a hell of a lot of very expensive hours every year, as did his partners and their associates, but even so, a quarter million dollars or more wasn't something to risk if you didn't absolutely have to. To say nothing of the publicity surrounding a case with such a high-profile client. And if he got her off, it was probably worth another half million or more to the firm, plus the gratitude of the city's mayor and one of its supervisors.

He was hyperaware of the money. That was it.

He didn't like to think that he'd become strictly mercenary, not when for so long the law had been a passion for him—first as a beat cop and then a lawyer on the prosecution side, then for the next two and more decades as a defense attorney. Of course, it was also a business and had turned into a fairly lucrative one, but the business side alone had never been the point. And he didn't want it to be now.

He wondered if for all the wrong reasons he had sent Wyatt Hunt and now Harlen Fisk off to do a job that should by all rights have fallen to Hardy himself. Or maybe should not be done at all. He knew that he could argue blackmail to Glass without revealing or even knowing the actual fact of it, and thus refute the money-laundering theory upon which the U.S. attorney was building his forfeiture case. But some instinct told him that there had in fact been blackmail, and that the nature of it might be at the crux of this case.

He sat sipping his beer and staring at his tropical fish, which didn't provide him with any kind of answers by the time the telephone on his belt went off—Wyatt Hunt atypically calling him off-hours. He must have come up with something.

"Tell me you've got it already," Hardy said.

"We got something, all right," Hunt replied, "but it won't make you too happy."

"I'm listening."

"The guy who did the robbery with Dylan Vogler? He was a friend of our client when she was in college, name of Levon Preslee."

"Okay."

"Well, not so okay, as it turns out. Levon's dead."

16

A gust of wind pulled the door of Darrel Bracco's car out of his hand and slammed it for him just as a fresh volley of rain peppered the blacktop all around him. Lowering his head, he pulled up the hood of his yellow parka and jogged at a good clip toward the obvious destination—the coroner's van parked in front with a squad car, lights on at the porch and in the front windows. It was ten forty-three when Bracco flashed his badge at the two patrolmen standing by the door.

Debra Schiff was already there inside, clogging up the hall by the kitchen with some coroner and crime-scene people, including Lennard Faro, and the original team of inspectors who'd pulled the call—Benny Yung and Al Tallant. They were all trying to keep out of the way as the photographer finished her work.

Schiff, at a glance, was wet and, by the looks of her, none too happy either. Darrel looked around as he came in out of the rain—the murder had occurred in a ground-floor front unit on the right-hand side of a Victorian building on Potrero Hill. There weren't any obvious signs of struggle in the living room to Bracco's right. A distraught-looking young man was sitting on the couch with his hands clasped between his knees, while another patrolman sat across from him, unspeaking.

There was similarly not much sign of struggle as Bracco came and looked over Schiff's shoulder, except for the one overturned kitchen chair and the body sprawled out on the floor, the puddle of blood underneath Levon's head.

"Not that I'm not thrilled to be here," Bracco announced to all and sundry, "but does somebody want to remind me again why we need Deb and me?"

Tallant was a mid-thirties distance runner with big teeth, a long, jowly face, and a perennial shadow that he couldn't ever seem to shave off completely. "Not our call," he said. "We ran it by Glitsky and he said to bring you in."

Debra turned back to her partner. "Listen to this, Darrel," she said. "Why don't you hit it, Ben?"

Yung, heavyset and normally cheerful, at the moment seemed stretched thin and exhausted. He reached over and pushed a button on the telephone unit on the kitchen counter. "Levon," a voice said, "I am a private investigator named Wyatt Hunt and I'm working for a lawyer here in town who's representing a woman named Maya Townshend, maybe known to you as Maya Fisk, who I believe went to school with you at USF. If I could have a couple minutes of your time to ask you a few questions, I'd appreciate a callback. My cell number, anytime, is—"

Yung hit the stop button and turned back to his colleagues. "We called Hunt and asked him what he was working on and eventually got around to Dylan Vogler. I recognized the name and we talked about it and decided to call Abe."

"It was a good call, Benny," Schiff said. "Don't mind Darrel. He gets crabby when his beauty sleep gets interrupted."

"Hey," Bracco said, "I'm not crabby. I said I was thrilled to be here. And if this is part of Vogler, even more so." He pointed back toward the living room. "Who's the kid out front?"

"Boyfriend," Yung said. "Brandon Lawrence, says he's an actor. He called it in and waited for us to arrive. Had a dinner date and a key, but this was over before he got here and I think I believe him."

"Well, let's keep him on a while anyway."

"That's why he's still here," Tallant commented with some asperity. "He's not going anywhere till we let him."

"Hey, no offense, Al. I see a fresh body, I get a little pumped up." Bracco looked across and down to the body, spoke to the crime-scene boss. "So, Len, what do we got?"

Faro, the squad's token metrosexual with his well-trimmed goatee, spiky hair, and multiple gold chains around his neck, was in his early forties but looked and dressed a decade younger. He'd been leaning against the kitchen wall and now came off it. "He got hit hard and hit at least once again, best guess is by the back of the cleaver we found rinsed off in the sink. Maybe dead before the second blow, although that'll have to wait for the autopsy, not that it matters much. He's dead enough now."

Faro moved away to the far side of the kitchen table. "Whoever did this, our victim almost undoubtedly knew him. Or her. No sign of forced entry." He pointed down at the table. "Note the condensation ring, still here, across from where Levon was sitting. Maybe they were sitting here together having a glass of something. We bagged up some clean and dried glasses that were in the tray by the sink. Maybe find a print on one of 'em, but unlikely. So whatever else you might say, your killer's a pretty cool customer, washing up after. Michelle," he asked the photographer, "you get all this?"

She nodded, then pointed and shot at the ring on the table one last time and stepped back to survey the room and make sure she'd captured it.

"So what's his connection to Vogler?" Bracco asked. "Besides Maya?"

Al Tallant knew that one. "None that we know of. Not yet."

"Is that why we got invited to this party?" Bracco asked.

Tallant nodded. "Pretty good guess."

"Anything else?" Schiff asked.

"Nope," Yung said. "Levon was clean, with a job and everything."

"Where?" Bracco asked.

Yung nodded. "ACT." This was the American Conservatory The-ater. "He had business cards in his wallet. Associate director of de-velopment. He was moving up."

Schiff looked down on the body. "Not anymore."

"How about dope?" Bracco asked. "You see any sign of mari-juana?"

"Funny you should ask," Faro said. "He had a half-full Baggie in the drawer next to his bed. Anybody else, hardly worth talking about. But if he's connected to Vogler . . ."

Bracco nodded. "I hear you."

"Well," Tallant said, "if you guys won't be needing us anymore, it's been a slice."

Bracco and Schiff stayed on the scene until the coroner's team re-moved the body well on toward two o'clock in the morning. Faro and his crime-scene unit stayed on as well, poring over the house from stem to stern but adding little to their store of information.

Out in the living room the inspectors tag-teamed Brandon Law-rence, who in fact had his own key to the apartment and had called nine one one when he'd discovered the body. He told them both, verifying the obvious, that Levon lived alone and that they were in a "wonderful, committed relationship." He told them that he hadn't touched anything after coming upon the body and, not being able to stand the proximity to his lover, had waited outside the whole time for the arrival of the first squad car. He would do anything he could—anything!—to help them find who'd done this. But he'd seen nothing suspicious, either in the neighborhood or once he'd let him-self in. Until he'd seen the body. Bracco and Schiff made sure they had his ID, DNA, and fingerprints. They told him these were for elimination purposes and let him go home.

Bracco walked Lawrence to the door and then returned to sit at the end of the couch, catercorner to where his partner sat back in an armchair in the well-lit living room. Schiff's face wore a pained expression, and she sighed. Finally, she looked over at Bracco. "I'd hate to think that getting Jerry Glass involved and shaking things up at the Townshends' had anything to do with this."

"Maybe it didn't, Debra. Maybe Maya doesn't have anything to do with this."

"Do you believe that?"

"No. You?"

"Based on the rule of never a coincidence, me neither."

"I'd love to call her right now, find out if she's got an alibi."

"Not yet. Not in the middle of the night, without more than this."

"I know. But still . . ."

"We could pull an all-nighter and hit her at seven sharp. If she's got no alibi, we sit her down for a serious chat."

"She'd just call Hardy and he wouldn't let her talk."

"Fine. Wake him up early too. And by the way, I've been meaning to ask, how do you get to be friendly with a defense attorney?"

"I wouldn't go so far as friendly. He and Abe are pals. I worked with him a time or two. He used to be a cop, you know."

"Who did? Hardy?"

"Yeah. Then a DA."

"Get out of here!"

"True."

"What made him go over to the dark side?"

Bracco gave her a sideways glance. "You're more mad at yourself than at me or Hardy or anybody else, aren't you?"

She shook her head. "I shouldn't have gone to Glass. Levon might still be alive."

"I'm not going to say you might have wanted to discuss it with your partner first."

"Good. Don't."

Bracco took a beat. "What do you think of the cleaver?"

"As a murder weapon? It seems to have worked."

"You think it's a woman's weapon?"

"Spur of the moment? It'd do."

"But it couldn't have been spur of the moment. Whoever it was knew him and if they came over here to kill him, they would have brought something to do it."

Schiff nodded. "Either that or she knew he had the cleaver. All she had to do was get him into the kitchen and get behind him. In fact," warming to her theory a little, she went on, "I think I like that she used the wrong side, the dull side. A guy maybe doesn't do that."

Bracco sat back on the couch. "Maybe not. I don't know. But we could talk about this all night and never go anywhere. As opposed to what we do know."

"Which is what?"

"Well, keeping it simple, let's assume that Levon hung out with Maya in college. We've been thinking that Vogler was blackmailing Maya, so let's call that a fact too. What does that say to you?"

"She's the connection, back when they were all in school."

"That's what I see."

"She didn't own the coffee shop then."

"Yeah, okay. So the blackmail didn't start then. It wasn't until she had money."

"Maybe she was paying Levon, too, somehow."

"And then he finds out Vogler's been killed and suddenly he's a little uncomfortable."

"No, he's a lot uncomfortable." Bracco sat with his thoughts for a moment, then suddenly came forward, stood, and went over to a lamp table across the room where he'd left some small Ziploc evidence bags and other stuff from Levon's pockets, including his cell phone. As a matter of course he and Schiff were going to go through the recent history of calls received and made, which were automatically logged, but they'd both thought they'd wait until the next morning when people would be awake. Now, though, he picked up the phone, turned it on, and brought it back over to where he'd been sitting. "I love these things," he said. "Remember what a hassle it used to be to get phone records on people? Days, weeks, subpoenas. Now, push a button, bingo. Ah, here we go."

The very first number in Levon's recently made calls menu was a 415 area code that struck Bracco as familiar. He took out his own cell phone and ran down his own recently called menu until he came to the same number.

"It looks like Levon got uncomfortable enough to call somebody we know," he said.

17

Debra Schiff wasn't the only person feeling some responsibility for setting events in motion that had apparently and very suddenly gotten out of control. At three A.M., Dismas Hardy still hadn't gotten to sleep.

He'd come down for the first time after an hour's tossing in bed, made himself a warm Ovaltine, gone into his front room, and rearranged the caravan of glass elephants that trekked across the mantel over his fireplace.

Sitting in his reading chair with the lights off, though, he'd convinced himself that really he had had no choice. All he'd done was send his own investigator team out to try to pry loose one of his client's secrets. He would need to do that, to have that information, if he was going to help her in her defense.

Should it come to that.

Which—pretty obviously—was looking more probable every minute.

Just before Hunt had received the call from the police at Levon's place and called Hardy with the news, he'd learned from his own employee Craig Chiurco that the same Levon Preslee that Hunt had already identified as a friend of Maya's during their time at USF was the guy who'd been arrested with Vogler in the robbery they'd committed at about that same time.

Chiurco had gone out to Levon's apartment in Potrero in the late afternoon, but no one had answered his knock—he might have already been dead. Chiurco was in the process of reporting back to Hunt, planning to track the potential witness down either later that same night or in the next day or so to question him, when the call had come in from Inspector Tallant with the news of Levon's death.

As soon as Hardy heard this, it had immediately become clear that if Maya did not have an alibi—and of course no one knew even the approximate time of Levon's murder—she was going to be even more squarely in the sights of Bracco and Schiff as a suspect not just in this latest crime, but with Vogler as well.

Part of Hardy wished that Wyatt hadn't been so forthcoming with the police when they'd called him. But then again, what else was he supposed to do? They already had the message he'd left on Levon's phone—that he was working for the lawyer who was representing Maya Townshend. He couldn't very well deny that, and once the police recognized her name, along with any connection whatsoever to the dead man, she was going to assume a higher profile, and there was nothing at all he could do about that.

The Ovaltine finished, Hardy had gone back up to his bedroom and tossed for another hour and change, his mind ping-ponging willy-nilly between Maya and her husband and Jerry Glass, then Bracco and Schiff, and Glitsky and Zachary, and Wes Farrell and then back through the litany in a different order. Everybody either in trouble or making it, or both.

Until finally he got up again, grabbed a robe, and padded downstairs. The rain still fell heavily onto the skylight, drumming away. He went back up to the front of the house and settled himself down in his reading chair in the dark.

He couldn't afford a sleepless night. He had a feeling he was going to get a call from his client in the very early A.M., was somewhat surprised that he hadn't gotten one already. But maybe she didn't know yet about Levon.

Or maybe she knew all too well.

And at this thought—the actual admission of it to himself as a possibility—all of Hardy's random imaginings about the troubles of his friends or those making trouble for them coalesced into a tiny pinpoint of something that suddenly felt like a certainty.

Whether or not she was in fact a killer, he was sure that Maya was involved as some kind of active participant in all of this. In both the deaths of Dylan Vogler and of Levon Preslee.

And it was starting to seem that regardless of what Hardy chose to do, and however cooperative Maya was with the police, she could be arrested for both murders.

Still sleeping in his reading chair up at the front of his house, the rain and wind pounding at the bay window three feet from his right hand, Hardy never heard the telephone ring. And now suddenly here was his wife first touching his shoulder, then shaking him gently. "Dismas." Opening his eyes, everything out of focus, he saw her standing there in a bathrobe, the receiver in her hand, concern writ large on her features. "Maya Townshend," she whispered.

Straightening up, his neck cricked with a stabbing pain, it took him a few more seconds to get his bearings. All right, he was still downstairs, must've fallen asleep trying to figure . . .

"Hello?"

"I'm sorry. Did I wake you?"

Hardy cleared his throat. "No, of course not." What the hell time was it anyway? He glanced outside, where the heavy storm clouds kept it looking like half-night. "This is just my precoffee voice. Don't mind it. How can I help you?"

"They're here again."

"Schiff and Bracco?"

"They're unbelievable, these two."

"I don't know. I find myself believing in them lately. What do they want?"

"Apparently they've got a search warrant. They want to look through the house. Joel's furious, of course. We haven't even finished breakfast, and the kids are all upset. I don't know who's going to take them to school now."

In fact, Hardy heard children crying in the background. "What time is it, actually?"

"Ten after seven. They got here at seven sharp."

Hardy knew that this was a bad sign. Generally speaking, police were not permitted to serve warrants in the middle of the night. In fact, search warrants were not valid for service between ten P.M. and seven A.M. unless a judge specifically found evidence that justified the extreme intrusion into someone's home. Absent an emergency, judges were reluctant to issue such a warrant. They would do that, of course, if there was cause to believe that a suspect would destroy evidence or flee under cover of darkness. So the fact that they'd waited until seven—the first allowable minute without that extraordinary finding— was ominous.

"So where are they now?"

"Right here. Joel's trying to reason with them. They said we had to let them in. They have us all sitting on a couch in the front room. They won't let us move. If we try to move, they said they'll put us in handcuffs. They wouldn't even give me my cell phone until I said I needed to call Harlen to get the kids and then you. Can they do all this?"

"If they have a warrant, they can. Did they say what they're looking for specifically?"

"Shoes and/or clothing that might contain blood . . ."

Which meant, Hardy knew, that she was now a suspect.

". . . phone and financial records, computer files—a lot of the same kind of stuff they wanted for the other—" The woman's voice suddenly broke. "Oh, God. I don't know why all this is happening to us all of a sudden. I don't know what's going on. It's like we're living in a police state. Can they just come in here and look through everything?"

"Not without a reason, so they must think they have one, and they must have convinced some judge too. Have they talked to you at all?"

"To get in, yes. Before they told me they had this warrant, they asked me about what I did yesterday."

"When yesterday? What time?"

"Afternoon."

"And you didn't tell them anything, right?"

"I said I'd gone to church, that's all."

That was enough, Hardy thought, wondering anew about his client's predilection to lock herself into a position that might incriminate her. But he kept his voice mild. "You went to church again?"

"I know. Most people don't, I suppose. But I do all the time. St. Ignatius."

"And how long were you there?"

"I don't know. A little while. Before I had to pick up the kids. But I told them, the inspectors, that I wouldn't answer any more questions until you got here."

Open barn door, let horse out, close barn door after it. Check. But there was nothing to do about it now, so Hardy merely said, "Good for you, Maya. Try to stick with that. I can be there in a half hour. How's that sound?"

"Like a long time."

"I know. I can't help that. I'll get there as fast as I can. Promise."

"Okay." Hardy heard her breathe.

"Maybe between Harlen and Joel they can stop them before that."

"Harlen? Your brother Harlen?"

"Yes. I told you I called him first, didn't I?"

"Yeah, but you said it was something about the kids."

"Well, that too. But he and Sergeant Bracco are friends, you know."

"Right. I'm aware of that. They were friends, but now he's—" Hardy stopped before he said anything else, such as that given the presence of Jerry Glass around this case, Harlen Fisk was possibly the worst imaginable choice of a person to confront the police, and especially Schiff, about the legality or reasonableness of a search warrant in Maya's house.

"He'll be good with them, Mr. Hardy. Harlen's good with everybody."

"Okay, then, but even after he gets there, if it's before me, can I ask you please not to say anything to the police until I get there? Can you promise me that?"

After she did, Hardy pushed the button to ring off the phone and went to straighten himself, but the crick in his neck asserted itself again and he sat back down with some care, twisting his head to find an angle that didn't hurt.

"Are you all right?" Frannie coming through the dining room with two steaming cups in her hands.

"Except for the icepick in my neck." Taking one of the cups. "You're the best, you know that?"

"I've heard rumors. So why again were you sleeping down here?"

"I wasn't sleeping upstairs and didn't want to wake you up."

"You can always wake me up."

"That's what they all say, but they don't mean it."

"I mean it, Dismas. You know that."

"I know. I'm sorry, just kidding." He sipped his coffee, and sighed. "But all kidding aside, this isn't starting to look too good."

"Maya Townshend?"

He went to nod but stopped himself before he got too far. "I need to get over there right now. They've got to have something new or they wouldn't have moved like this."

"You think it's this guy Glass?"

"I don't know. Maybe. Maybe I should call Abe."

"And what?"

"Finesse him to get some inside dope. Failing that, see if he can slow things down." Realizing the absurdity of that possibility, he added, "Which he's just plain not going to do, is he?"

"Not if they have something on her, which they must, right?"

"Right. I wish I knew what it was." Grimacing, he reached over and put his cup down on the windowsill. "I've got to get moving." He started up again, and again his hand went to his neck, but this time he fought through the pain, got to his feet. "One step at a time," he said half to himself. "One step at a time."

18

Arriving at the premises, Hardy convinced Bracco to let him sit with his clients in their kitchen in return for a vague promise that they might have something to say to the inspectors.

Maya set her mug of coffee down on the countertop. "Even if he did call me, that doesn't mean I went and saw him afterwards, does it? I don't even know where he lives. Lived."

"So you couldn't have gone there," Hardy said. "You're absolutely sure you didn't go there, right?"

"Well, yes. Of course. I don't see why there has to be a connection between him calling me and me going to see him. He just wanted to talk about Dylan and if anybody suspected him."

"Because you all used to be friends," Hardy said in a low voice.

The police had let them give the children to a neighbor—Harlen hadn't made it there yet—to take to school. They were probably just as happy not to have the kids underfoot anyway. The three of them—Joel, Maya, and Hardy—sat around the island stove in the Townshends' ultramodern, supergourmet kitchen. Every appliance, from the refrigerator and stove to the toaster and coffeemaker, was of brushed steel; every flat surface a green-tinged granite. Outside the wraparound back windows the storm swirled and eddied around them. The lights had already blinked twice as gusts of wind hammered at the glass.

Along with two other search-specialist cops Bracco and Schiff were somewhere back or up in the house behind them. Occasionally the disembodied voices from one or more of these people would carry in to

the trio in the kitchen—thrumming undertones of a somehow unde-
fined menace and conflict. The uniformed officer left at the door of the
kitchen to watch them didn't appear to be either interested or listening.

Nevertheless, they kept their voices low. "It made perfect sense to
me, Dismas. Even if it doesn't to you." She motioned back toward the
rest of the house. "Or to them."

Hardy nodded. "Although you must admit," he added, "that the
timing doesn't look too good. He calls you the day he's killed."

"I can't help when he called me," Maya said, "or what he wanted
to talk about. And it wasn't like I spent a lot of time talking to him.
He was mostly afraid somebody, like those inspectors, might think
he had something to do with Dylan, you know? And had I heard
anything? He was worried."

"I know. That's what you said. And it looks like he had reason to
be. Look," Hardy said. "As long as you didn't go there, and they can't
prove you did . . ."

"Come on. I told you. I was at church."

"For two hours?" Joel asked.

"I didn't time it, Joel. As long as it took. I don't know."

"It's all right." Hardy held up a hand. "If you were at church,
that's where you were. All I'm saying is if that's the case, there's nothing Schiff and Bracco can do. If you weren't at Levon's, you weren't
there. End of story."

Maya stared hard at her husband. "That's what I'm saying, Joel.
And there's no dispute about whether I was there, so the phone call
doesn't matter anyway."

No doubt, Joel wanted to help his wife, but he obviously didn't
believe yet, as Hardy had come to, that Maya could possibly be going
to jail, maybe in the very near term—possibly today.

When Hardy had arrived, he'd asked what had changed in their
investigations that Bracco and Schiff needed to serve a search warrant
on his client first thing in the morning. They had told him about the

call from Levon's cell phone to Maya's home number. After a flus-
tered minute she'd admitted not only to her past friendship with
Levon and the connection between Dylan, Preslee, and herself, but
that he had in fact called her yesterday, out of the blue. Before that
she hadn't heard from him in a couple of years.

The good news from Hardy's perspective was that now he felt
sure he understood in a general way what the blackmail had been
about. The specifics might not ever be forthcoming, but given Levon
and Dylan's criminal conspiracies, and the fact of Maya's close
friendship—and perhaps more—with at least one of them, it was
pretty clear that she'd gotten herself involved in some kind of illegal
activity, that she'd made deals with each of them to keep herself off
the radar.

The bad news, of course, was that her involvement on any level
with two men murdered within the same week made her an extremely attractive candidate as a suspect in the killings.

Except that, according to her, she'd never been to Levon's home.
"Maya," Hardy now said, "it might be helpful if you could write
down as much as you can remember about the phone call. Just to
give it added credibility."

The police packed up and left, taking with them a lot of clothing, their
computers, phone books, and financial records. Joel was on the phone
in his office calling his place of business to see if perhaps the police
had been there, and trying to decide how to reconstruct the financial
records the cops had carted off. Hardy and Maya had just sat down in
the kitchen when the doorbell rang, and Maya got up to answer it.

She came back in trailing her brother, who parked his bulk on a
counter chair and sighed. "I don't like this, Diz."

"I can't say I'm wild about it either, Harlen. But if she's never been
to Levon's . . ."

"Yeah, but you can't prove a negative."

"True, but luckily, the burden of proof isn't on us. It's on Darrel and Debra."

The doorbell rang again, and again Maya went out to answer it.

"You think she's telling the truth?" Fisk asked, his body language saying he didn't.

"She's my client," Hardy said. "I have to believe her. If there's no evidence placing her at Levon's, no blood on her shoes or clothes . . ."

"That's not what I asked."

"No, but—"

Maya's returning footsteps closed out the discussion as Hardy turned to see her coming back into the kitchen. "It's your investigators," she said. "They're wet and said they're good waiting out in the lobby. You asked them to come out here?"

Hardy shrugged, standing up. "I didn't know what was going down exactly when I called them. I knew your children needed rides to school. But sometimes cops serving search warrants get carried away. It never hurts to have backup. Witnesses tend to keep things copasetic. Although it doesn't look like that's needed today. I'll go and talk to them."

Out by the front door Wyatt Hunt stood dripping in hiking boots, jeans, and a Giants slicker, and Craig Chiurco looked a bit more well-defended against nature with a natty tan trench coat. But the weather wasn't foremost on their minds. They didn't even notice Hardy as he approached them, so intent were they on their conversation, whispering back and forth.

Until he stopped two feet away from them, and hearing Chiurco's last words, ". . . don't have to say anything about it?" Hardy said, "About what?"

Hunt shook him off. "Nothing."

"Ah, the famous nothing."

"You don't want to know, Diz," Hunt said. "Really."

"I like knowing stuff," Hardy countered. "It's one of my hobbies."

"You really might not want to know this, Diz. I promise. The only way you want to know this now is if it comes out some other way later and you didn't hear it here first."

"You're saying I'd be pissed?" Hardy leaned in toward them and lowered his own voice. "Maybe I should get to decide. I hate surprises later. So I decide yes now."

Hunt motioned off with his eyes behind Hardy, over toward the kitchen. He stopped, turned to Chiurco, and shrugged, then shook his head. To all appearances, he had a bad taste in his mouth.

"You're the boss," Chiurco said. "Your call."

Hunt hesitated another moment, then finally let out a long breath. "Craig saw her."

"Who?" Hardy asked, his empty stomach suddenly bunching up on him. For of course he immediately knew who, and when, and where.

Two minutes later they were all back in the kitchen. Joel had appeared from his duties elsewhere in the house and now stood over by the sink, holding Maya's hand. They'd all been in a spirited conversation talking about something but stopped when a firm-jawed Hardy trooped in with Hunt and an especially disconsolate Chiurco in his wake.

Without any preamble Hardy looked around to Joel and Harlen and said, "If you don't mind, I'd like to speak to Maya alone for just a minute if I could."

Joel, on edge in any case and perhaps emboldened by his interactions over the past hour or so with the police, moved a half-step over in front of his wife, protectively. "That's not happening. We've already told you our decision on that. We're fighting this together, Maya and me, all of it."

"All right, then," Hardy said. "But if that's the case, I have to tell you that you'll be doing it without me."

"Fine," Joel said. "We didn't—"

Maya held up her own hand. "Wait!"

"Maya." Joel, warning her, scolded her back into her place.

"No!" She turned her gaze to Hardy. "Dismas, can't you just say whatever it is in front of Joel? We are in this together." She turned to her husband, met his eyes. "We really are, Joel. But"—coming back to Hardy—"but I'll go talk with you if you need me to. If that's the only way."

"There's no only way, Maya. There's no one way. There's just the way it's worked for me. The way I do it."

Joel, adopting a reasonable tone, said, "Mr. Hardy, all right. Maya wants to keep you on, we'll play it your way if you need to. But I'm telling you that you can say whatever you need to in front of me. And Harlen, for that matter. He's family too."

Hardy, exhausted from the lack of sleep and the postadrenaline slump after what he'd just heard from Chiurco, felt his shoulders sag, and this tweaked the crick in his neck anew. This was not the way the practice of law was supposed to work. To be effective you had to maintain control over the client, the family, the flow of information. And now he was feeling it all inexorably swirling away from him. "I very much appreciate all of your cooperation with one another," he said, "and your mutual trust. But as I've told you, this is just not how I do it. I've got to talk to Maya first and alone. She's my client and I've got no choice." He turned to her. "Maya?"

She looked around at the room full of men, brushed her husband's arm, and moved around him. "We'll be right back," she said.

"He's sure?" she said.

"He said he's one hundred percent sure. You've got a memorable face, Maya. You passed right by him as he was going in."

"I don't remember him."

"No," Hardy said, "maybe you don't." Thinking that it was probably because she had just killed someone. "But you were in fact there,
weren't you?"

She didn't say anything.

"Maya?"

She looked up at him. "I didn't think anybody would believe me
if said I went there but he wasn't home. But that was what happened."

"Why did you go there?"

"He asked me to. He told me he needed to see me. That he'd tell
about me and Dylan and him if I didn't."

"Just like Dylan?"

"What do you mean?"

"That's what Dylan threatened you with if you didn't come down
too."

"No. That was different. That was the shop. I already told you
that."

Hardy took a beat. "You also told me you didn't go to Levon's."

Again, silence. Finally, "So what are you going to do?"

"What do you mean?"

"I mean, are you going to tell the police?"

"No. Of course not. I'm on your side here, Maya. We can't let the
police find out about this at all. We're just lucky it was my investigator who saw you. He'll never tell a soul. I'll never tell a soul. And
there is no way we can ever be made to testify against you. But I
think it's time we stop answering any more questions at all. Someone
wants to talk to you, you refer them to me."

But no sooner had they walked back into the kitchen than Maya
walked and then ran the last few steps up to her husband, hugged
him, and started crying.

"Hey. Hey," he said, holding her. Then, at Hardy, "What did you
say to her?"

Hardy stood his ground. "There were things she had to understand. She'll be all right."

"She'll be all right! She'll be all right! Look at her. She's crying now, for God's sake. She's not all right at all."

"I'm sorry," Hardy said. "I didn't mean to make her cry."

"Well, whether or not you meant it . . ." He brushed his hand down over her hair. "It's okay, babe. It's okay."

She pulled away and looked up at her husband, her voice breaking, hysteria coming on. "It's not okay. It's not going to be okay. Maybe not ever again."

"Sure, it will. We'll get through this and—"

"No, Joel. You don't understand. I was there. I was *there*." She turned and pointed to Chiurco. "He saw me. Oh, God! Oh, God! I'm so, so sorry."

Three days later, after the lab confirmed that both Maya's fingerprints and DNA were on the doorknob of Levon's apartment, Schiff and Bracco took Maya into custody.

Part Two

19

There were Superior Court judges Hardy liked a lot, and a very few that he'd prefer to avoid if at all possible, but only one he actively despised, and that was Marian Braun.

The history between the two of them was so extreme that it included a contempt violation and actual jail time for Hardy's *wife*. He honestly believed that he might prevail on appeal, should it come to that, if he argued that Braun should have recused herself when she discovered that Hardy was going to be defending a murder suspect in her courtroom. Of course, the flip side of that was that if Hardy was worried about the impossibility of getting a fair trial from Braun, he could have exercised his 170.6.

That section of the California Code said that any lawyer assigned to trial could excuse one, but only one, judge, without giving any specific reason. The lawyer was sworn and simply declared under oath that he believed the judge to whom he'd been assigned was prejudiced against himself or the interests of his client to the point he thought he couldn't get a fair trial.

That was it—no hearing, no evidence. The declaration itself caused the judge to be removed forever from the case. And challenges were reported to the judicial council. Obviously, a judge with too many challenges acquired the unfavorable attention of that supervisory body.

But the move had its price.

First, the courts hated challenges. They not only dinged one of their colleagues, however deservedly, but screwed up the scheduling for everyone else, because another judge had to take the case, and someone had to take their cases, and so on. And even if the judges personally despised the object of the challenge, they despised more the hubris of a mere lawyer who dared to suggest that one of their own tribe might not be fair.

So if Hardy exercised a challenge, he would likely immediately find himself in the courtroom of the most antidefense judge that the presiding judge could find available, and that judge would have an additional motive to make Hardy's life as miserable as he or she possibly could. Hardy knew he challenged at his peril.

So Hardy elected to roll the dice with Braun. Call him superstitious or crazy—he'd also pulled Braun for his last murder trial, nearly four years before. She hadn't liked him any better then, nor he her. And that trial had never been given over to the jury because a key prosecution witness had changed his testimony at the eleventh hour. Nevertheless, Hardy's client had walked out a free woman, Braun or no Braun. He'd already proven that he could win in her courtroom, and if he could do it once, he could pull it off again.

Now, as he sat in Department 25 on the third floor of the Hall of Justice, waiting for his client's appearance in the courtroom, Hardy found himself marveling anew at the thought that they were about to begin a full-blown murder trial. He felt vaguely responsible and not-so-vaguely incompetent that things had come to this point. Surely a better lawyer could have closed the case after the PX—the preliminary hearing—which they'd had a little over four months ago, within two weeks of Maya's arrest.

At the end of that fiasco, Maya had been held to answer. In Superior Court he'd filed the pro forma 995, which called for the dismissal of the two first-degree murder charges against Maya on the grounds that the prosecution had failed to present even probable cause to suggest she'd committed these crimes.

Hardy had even permitted himself a flicker of optimism. There might have been technically enough evidence to justify a trial, but surely the court had to see the same weaknesses in the evidence that he himself saw. That was why Hardy had demanded, as Maya had a right to do, that the prelim take place within ten court days of her arrest. He had felt that on the evidence, he might win, and in any event, the case wasn't going to get any better for the defense. But now, here he was in Braun's court.

He'd been wrong.

The other, political, reason that he'd pressed for the speedy PX was that Maya's arrest had set off a news frenzy in the city that Hardy thought could only get worse over time, and in this he was right. The secret grand jury investigation that Jerry Glass was conducting on the U.S.-attorney front, along with the public threats of forfeiture of the properties of one of the town's major development and political families, had by now neatly dovetailed into a narrative that had captured the public's imagination, as Hardy had suspected it would.

Knowing that the body politic of San Francisco in general, and probable members of jury pools specifically, tended to have little sympathy and lots of hostility and envy for the two aligned, and—in the public eye, generally malignant—classes of developers and politicians, Hardy had wanted to hurry up with a jury trial before every single person in San Francisco had been so exposed to innuendo, insinuation, and the venom of the press that they had all long since made up their minds. Juries didn't always return verdicts based on the facts; sometimes they voted their prejudices. So, given the dearth of evidence for the actual murders, he'd believed back in October that a quick defense was his best chance to free his client and cut short the debate about the kinds of people the Townshends and other developers and power brokers must be.

And now, in late February, here they were, with Braun presiding, about to begin exactly what he'd strategized and labored to avoid and yet called down upon himself. He had demanded a speedy trial, and now he was going to get it.

Even moving as quickly as he could, he couldn't avoid the collateral damage that continued to wreak its havoc on the extended Fisk/ Townshend/West families—Harlen's, Maya's, and the mayor, Kathy West's. It appeared that the U.S. attorney's power to subpoena— particularly financial records—in capable hands like those of Jerry Glass could be a blunt weapon indeed.

By the time the preliminary hearing had begun, Glass had barely had time to look into the Bay Beans West bookkeeping, much less Joel Townshend's wider business affairs, and how, if at all, they might relate to one another. But since the marijuana connection with Dylan Vogler was intimately connected with BBW, and this was needed by the State to establish a purported motive for Maya to have killed him, Glass and his conduit Debra Schiff had obviously been supplying the prosecution with whatever they could in terms of questionable financial dealings between the coffee shop and the Townshend household.

This hadn't hurt anyone too badly during the preliminary hearing— although the money laundering possibility had apparently been part of the court's decision that a jury should weigh the evidence and reach its own conclusions in Maya's case—but over the past months, and especially in the past couple of weeks, Glass's investigators and accountants had finally unearthed what appeared to be a treasure trove of sophisticated financial relationships and arrangements that now appeared to implicate Townshend, Harlen, Kathy West, and some other large players in at the very least questionable, if not to say unethical or illegal, conduct.

Potential kickbacks, preferential treatment, undocumented meetings about matters of public interest in violation of the city's Sunshine Ordinance.

Very little, if any, of this had been proven yet, except that Glass had succeeded in crippling BBW, and the government was preliminarily close to attaching the entire building as the probable proceeds from a drug operation, although the place itself was still open day to day. Because Maya had a Fifth Amendment right not to answer any questions in the forfeiture proceeding while her criminal case was pending, any final decision was on hold for now, but the questions alone raised a spectre of criminality over Maya and everything she touched.

The BBW accounts were incredibly sloppy. As just one example, Maya had cut Vogler a check from her own personal checking account for $6,000 for emergency repairs from water damage in July and another personal check for a half month's pay, $3,750, last March. There was no record he had ever given her back the money. There was at least $30,000 worth of checks from Vogler to Maya over the past two years with no explanation at all in their records. The only question seemed to be what precise illegality was being funded by the operation.

Maya told Hardy she'd been busy with the kids' school and on vacation and hadn't been able to make it into the store to sign the business checks, but she'd also neglected to reimburse herself from the company account during the many visits when she'd had a chance to do so. She had no idea what the checks from Vogler to her represented. She had left it to Vogler to keep the books. In the current climate this explanation was widely discredited.

The victory for Glass and the accompanying widely perceived truth that the Townshends were in fact in the drug business had then in turn played a huge role in people's perception of the Townshends, and public opinion shifted away from presumption of innocence. Suddenly, if you did business with Joel Townshend, or Harlen Fisk, or Kathy West—in fact, if you did business with the city—you were going to get cheated. That's just the way "these people" did things.

Just this morning Hardy had read the *Chronicle*'s editorial and letters page, and it was fully one-third choked with vitriol—Supervisor Fisk and the mayor should quit or, failing that, they should be impeached. The drumbeat was picking up; even in Hardy's office it was water-fountain talk.

And though none of this had anything to do with Maya's guilt for the crimes of murder of which she was accused, Hardy knew that it was going to have a lot to do with Paul, aka Paulie, aka "The Big Ugly," Stier—the assistant DA who'd pulled the case—and how he played the evidence. From an untutored perspective the entire court-room drama could unfold as a large multi-tentacled conspiracy fueled by drugs and moral turpitude in high places.

Hardy glanced over at his opponent.

Despite his flamboyant nicknames Stier was in his mid-thirties, earnest, and, from Hardy's dealings with him so far, possessed of little personality or sense of humor. The nicknames remained worri-some, though.

It was a truism in the courtroom that what you didn't know *would* hurt you, and Hardy hadn't been able to pick up much in the way of gossip or dirt on The Big Ugly, which probably meant he kept his personality—and his possible clever moves and dirty tricks—well hidden until he needed them, when they could inflict the most dam-age. Of course, it was also possible that the nicknames were sarcastic—that Stier was what he appeared to be, a hard-charging, fair-minded, good-looking working attorney. Certainly, he didn't look dangerous now, leaning back over the bar rail chatting amicably with Jerry Glass. They were simply two clean-cut, hardworking, self-righteous, ambitious guys doing the people's hard work—one for the country's government, and one for the state's.

Hardy felt a twist in his stomach.

There, also, in the front row, was Debra Schiff, who, Hardy knew, had started to see Glass socially, if not intimately. Leaning around further, Hardy briefly caught the eye of Darrel Bracco, who gave him a quick ambiguous look and then looked away—clearly all along Bracco had not been as gung-ho as Schiff about Maya's guilt and the wisdom of her arrest, but in the maelstrom that had developed, his doubts, if any, had surely been laid to rest. Still, though, to Dismas the look somehow felt heartening.

Or maybe it was pity.

At a signal from the bailiff Hardy got up and walked through the door at the back of the courtroom leading to the corridor and the judge's chambers. There, out of the sight of the jury, the bailiff took off Maya's handcuffs, and Hardy entered with his client, followed by the bailiff, and they took their places at counsel's table.

In what Hardy thought was a show of judicial nastiness if not downright personal affront to him, Braun had considered denying Maya the privilege of "dressing out," or wearing normal street clothes when she appeared in the courtroom. For the duration of the trial, she opined, his client would sit next to Hardy at his table in her yellow jumpsuit.

Hardy, insane with rage, had had to file a fifteen-page brief before he could convince Braun that a variety of federal and state cases held squarely that his client had an absolute right to appear in front of the jury in civilian clothes. Dressed as a convict, she would present to the jury an image that was at odds with that of a citizen who was presumed innocent. She must be already guilty of something, went the not-so-subtle psychology of it. She wouldn't be in jail, wearing that outfit, brought into the courtroom in handcuffs, if she hadn't done anything at all, if she weren't a danger to the community. Braun's position was ridiculous and had been repudiated by courts for a good fifty years. Even so, she had conceded this absolutely undebatable point grudgingly and with bad grace.

The gallery noise behind them abated slightly. Maya gave Hardy a lost look and then scanned around behind her, nodding at her husband in the first row on "her" side of the gallery, or maybe it was that she was relieved not to see her children, who had been living with Fisk's family all the while she'd been incarcerated.

The whole thing was awful, Hardy thought. Simply awful.

And what made it worse, all but intolerable from his perspective, was that in spite of the lack of evidence he'd finally come to lose almost all of his belief that she was not actually guilty of both murders.

Certainly, he knew, she had done something she was unwilling, under pain of life in prison, to reveal.

Also, while her family and her outside world appeared to be imploding around her, as the weeks had passed, she seemed to have grown more and more acquiescent, and less concerned with her defense, as though she deserved whatever happened to her. She still professed a desire to be found innocent, but mostly because she thought the children needed her. She didn't want them to have to live with the fact that their mother was in jail, convicted of murder. For herself, though, it didn't seem that critical an issue.

Hardy stood and pulled out her chair as all the parties rose while another bailiff brought in the jury from their room farther back along the same corridor Hardy and Maya had just used to enter the courtroom. When all the jurors were seated, she sat and Hardy pushed her forward until she was comfortably up at the table. As he'd coached her, she cast a look over to the newly empaneled jury and nodded a few times, making as much eye contact as seemed natural.

It was, from his perspective, a decent jury. Nine men and three women. Five whites, four African-Americans, three Asians. All between forty and seventy, and Hardy guessed from various nuances that seven or eight of them had at least tried marijuana. Nine of them held full-time jobs. Two of the men and one woman were retired and had been moderately successful in business. Hardy was surprised that Stier hadn't peremptorily dismissed any of these, but maybe he hadn't factored the antidevelopment prejudice adequately into his jury-selection strategy.

Although sometimes, Hardy knew, you just got lucky.

The way things had been going, though, Hardy didn't think that was it in this case.

But before Hardy had a chance to sit again, behind them the gallery energy shifted, and both Hardy and Maya turned around to see what had caused it.

"Well, look at this," Hardy said, a small grin toying with the sides of his mouth as Kathy West, the mayor of San Francisco herself, came walking down the center aisle toward them, accompanied by her nephew Harlen Fisk and a small procession of both of their staff members. Beyond them flowed a steady stream of reporters, courtroom groupies, and the simply curious, such that by the time Kathy and Harlen got up to the front row and began moving in beside Joel, the gallery was standing room only and the buzz in the room was constant and formidable.

The bailiff, obviously at a loss as to what he should do, especially after Kathy West shook his hand, allowed the mayor to further ignore the rules and reach across the bar rail to shake hands with both Hardy and her niece, while Harlen pulled Hardy a little closer and whispered, "This is Kathy's spur of the moment inspiration. Maybe put our friend Stier over there a bit off his feed for his opening statement."

"Couldn't hurt," Hardy said. The grandstanding, coming as it did after weeks of inactivity and silence from Maya's extended family, was in fact far from unwelcome. A smile creased Hardy's features and he glanced over in time to catch Stier, Glass, and Schiff in what were to him sweet expressions of disbelief and shock.

But the energy had no time to gather momentum as the door by the judge's bench opened and the bailiff up there at the far end of the room intoned, "All rise. Department Twenty-five of the Superior Court of California is now in session, Judge Marian Braun presiding."

And Braun swept in and up to her chair behind the bench, glanced out at the crowd, then glared as she became aware of her visitors. After a second's hesitation she lifted and slammed her gavel and said, "Attorneys, my chambers, immediately!"

The judge, in her black robe, was standing waiting for both of them as they came in. She didn't even ask the court recorder, Ann Baxter— sitting on the couch with her magic machine—if she was ready to take down every word that was said, as was required in a murder trial, before she started in. "Mr. Hardy. Because of our long history together, I thought I'd made clear that there wouldn't be any show-boating in or around my courtroom. And now I come in here on the first actual day of trial and who do I see out in the first row but the mayor and one of our city supervisors, and if you think—"

"Your Honor," Hardy said.

But she raised a hand. "I'm not finished talking yet, and I don't want you interrupting me. Ever. Here or in the courtroom. Clear?"

It was unprofessional and might even be counterproductive in the short run for his client, but if Braun was going to insult him and act like a tyrant whose malice toward him might provide grounds for an eventual appeal, Hardy was going to be happy to help her along. So, knowing that decorum demanded that he respond aloud to her— otherwise the court recorder couldn't put his answer in the record— he nodded with an exaggerated solemnity.

And waited.

It didn't take Braun long. Her eyes went nearly shut as she squinted across at him. "I asked you a question, Mr. Hardy. I asked if it was clear that you were not to interrupt me."

"Yes, Your Honor. Of course. I'm sorry. I wasn't sure you'd fin-ished and I didn't want to interrupt." Straight-faced.

She pointed a finger at him, schoolmarmish, her voice a hoarse and controlled rasp. "I'd like to know what you mean to accomplish by having the mayor and Supervisor Fisk sitting out there. This is exactly the kind of circus environment that I've cautioned you that I want to avoid, and here it is before we've even begun."

Hardy stood at attention.

"Well? Are you going to answer me? Or not?"

Hardy canted his head slightly, leaning forward. "I'm sorry, Your Honor. I didn't hear a question and didn't know you required a response."

"What are they doing out there?"

"I don't know, Your Honor. Intending to take in the trial, or at least part of it?"

"Why?"

"I don't know. I wouldn't care to hazard a supposition."

"I don't believe you. I sense your hand in their presence here."

"Your Honor, you flatter me to assign me such influence, but I assure you that I have no control over the movements of the mayor. Or Mr. Fisk. Their appearance here is as much a surprise to me as it is to you."

"They are sitting on your client's side. You don't think this is going to influence the jury, seeing them sitting rooting for her?"

"I don't know about that and I can't help how the jury will react. Ms. West and Mr. Fisk are both related to the defendant." He turned. "As Mr. Stier and, I believe, you, well know."

Again the finger. "Don't you presume to tell me what I know or don't know."

"Of course not, Your Honor. But regardless of your knowledge or lack of it, it's only natural that as Ms. Townshend's relatives, they should sit on the defense side of the gallery."

Braun turned her angry eyes to the prosecutor. "Mr. Stier? Do you have anything to add to this conversation?"

The clean-cut and quite possibly cutthroat attorney, who had come in the door behind Hardy and remained slightly behind him until now, stepped up beside him, cleared his throat, but remained silent.

"Your Honor, with respect," Hardy began, "first and primarily, this is a public courtroom. Anyone has a right to be here. We fought a revolution about this sort of thing. Further, there is an argument to be made that their presence might be calculated to combat the pretrial prejudice that the prosecution has been abetting throughout the lead-up to this trial."

"What are you talking about?" Stier snapped.

Hardy kept himself at attention, eyes forward.

After a satisfying five seconds Braun finally came at him. "Did you hear Mr. Stier's question, Mr. Hardy?"

"Of course, Your Honor."

"Well?"

"I'm sorry. Well what, Your Honor?"

"I asked you if you'd heard Mr. Stier's question."

"Yes, of course, but you've instructed me many times to address my remarks only to the court. I'm trying to hone to the court's protocol, Your Honor. As to Mr. Stier's question, I'm certain he knows full well what I was talking about."

"Would you care to enlighten the court what that is?"

"Certainly, Your Honor. It's no secret that for the past several months Mr. Glass, the U.S. attorney here in San Francisco, has been prosecuting a campaign in the civil courts, in the media, and with a federal grand jury, trying to link my client and her husband to her brother and to the mayor and trying to implicate all the families in a money-laundering, dope-dealing, and racketeering conspiracy. That's why I submitted all the questions for your voir dire about which of our prospective jurors follow the news closely. I had assumed you were aware of this, Your Honor."

For an answer Braun turned to the prosecutor. "Mr. Stier?"

"Nonsense, Your Honor. It's true that Jerry Glass has been following his own trail of malfeasance that appears to lead through some of these same individuals, including Mr. Hardy's client, but to imply that we've colluded to prejudice—"

"Excuse me, Your Honor. I didn't mean to imply any such thing. I meant to state it as established fact."

Stier wheeled on Hardy. "That's absurd."

"To the contrary," Hardy replied evenly, facing Braun. "It's demonstrable, Your Honor. Debra Schiff, the homicide inspector who arrested my client, has been designated a special agent for Mr. Glass's federal grand jury. Some would call that collusion."

Braun glowered.

"But more to the point, Your Honor, Ms. West's and Mr. Fisk's right to be here, and my client's right to have them here, is absolute. Of course, if you or Mr. Stier would like me to pass along a message to the mayor and a member of the Board of Supervisors that you want them to leave, I'd be happy to oblige. I'd actually be kind of interested to hear what they had to say to that."

A longish pause. Then, "All right"—Braun bit off her words— "that's quite enough. I won't condone this type of bickering, either here or in my courtroom." Hanging her head for a second, she shook it in disgust, then came back to the attorneys standing before her. "This situation infuriates me, but I don't see any help for it. You gentlemen are excused. I'll be out there again in just a minute."

Word had evidently spread quickly, and by the time Hardy was back next to Maya at his table in the bullpen, there wasn't a seat to be had in the gallery. A line stretched out through the door that led from the hallway into the courtroom, and Hardy was more than a little surprised to see Abe Glitsky standing in it, just inside the door, having come down to check out the show. He gave Hardy an infinitesimal nod.

Because they were scheduled to appear as witnesses and could not remain in the courtroom, Schiff and Bracco had both abandoned their earlier front-row seats in favor of a couple of reporters, who were among the number of people questioning both Harlen Fisk and Kathy West in what appeared to be a virtual impromptu press conference. Indeed, the gallery was fairly humming on all sides, so much so that the bailiff's ringing call to order as Braun reentered the room and ascended to the bench went largely unheeded.

Hardy, up front, heard it and turned, but the noise behind him continued and, if anything, increased. Until Braun, standing, used her gavel, at first once, gently. And getting no response, then with a more imperious and forceful *Bam! Bam! Bam!*

"Order!" she called out. "Order in this court!"

Until gradually, finally, the place grew silent.

Braun waited until the last whisper had died, then put her gavel down and, still standing, leaned forward onto her hands, scowling down at the crowd. "This is a court of law," she began, her voice strained with emotion. "There is no place in it for bedlam. I would ask those of you who have seats now to please take them, and for those of you standing along the sides, find a seat or I will be obliged to ask you to leave."

After giving the gallery time to comply Braun finally took her seat. "Thank you. The court," she went on, "recognizes Her Honor, the mayor of San Francisco, Kathy West, as well as City Supervisor Harlen Fisk, and welcomes them both to these proceedings." In a convincing display of graciousness the judge nodded through a tight smile, then turned immediately to the prosecution table.

"Mr. Stier, are the People ready to begin their case?"

"Yes, Your Honor."

"Mr. Hardy, the defense?"

"Ready, Your Honor."

"All right, then. Mr. Stier, you may begin."

20

For all of his low-affect demeanor and appearance, Stier's public persona projected the first hint of the enigmatic Paulie—a real authority that seemed based on equal parts confidence in who he was and the certainty of his position. He spoke in a normal, conversational tone with few oratorical flourishes, but his down-home sincerity created a simple eloquence that rang with conviction.

"Ladies and gentlemen of the jury." He was standing just in front of and sideways to Hardy and Maya, facing the jury box. As he began, he held his hands in a relaxed manner down and slightly out in front of him, reminiscent of a shortstop in the ready position, from time to time bringing them up, clasping them for emphasis, or sometimes pointing a finger from one of them for clarity or effect.

"The evidence and facts in this case are fairly simple, straightforward, and unambiguous. They concern a significant drug-dealing operation and long-standing relationships among three individuals that for some unknown reason suddenly went bad, with tragic, in fact fatal, results for two of them. And they point to an inescapable conclusion—that the defendant in this case, Maya Townshend"—and here he turned and pointed a finger directly at her—"willfully murdered her accomplice in her marijuana business, Dylan Vogler, and then several days later she willfully murdered another former accomplice in the marijuana business, Levon Preslee.

"Here's how we know this.

"At nine forty-seven on the night of October twenty-sixth of last year, a young man who is one of the two victims in this case, Dylan Vogler, the manager of a coffee shop called Bay Beans West on Haight Street here in the city, placed a phone call to his employer, the defendant Maya Townshend. We don't know precisely what he told her during that phone call, but whatever the message, it was important enough that Defendant first lied to the police about ever having received the call, and only when caught in the lie did she admit that it was enough to convince her to get up before dawn the next morning and drive to Bay Beans West."

Hardy squirmed. Maya had not been caught in a lie but had admitted her deception to the police on her own, on his advice. He made a note to make the point later through Bracco or Schiff. But for the moment the accusation rang unchallenged in front of the jury.

Stier went on. "Less than one hour later, by the time it was just starting to get light, Mr. Vogler was dead, shot once in the chest at point blank range in the alley that runs behind Bay Beans West. There was no sign of a struggle. Police investigators discovered a gun in the alley from which one shot had recently been fired. One bullet was recovered. One shell casing was recovered. Both matched the gun. This gun belonged to Defendant. It was registered to her and her fingerprints were on it, as they were on cartridges inside the gun.

"So why did Defendant do it?

"They had been business partners for nearly ten years. Why did Defendant wake up on this particular Saturday morning and decide that she was going to have to kill Mr. Vogler? We may never know the precise reason. But we do know with certainty about the life of crime they were leading together, a life where violent death, even at the hands of partners and associates, is as common as this city's morning fog in June."

Stier smiled politely at his homespun witticism but didn't pause. "At the time of his death," he continued, "Mr. Vogler was wearing a backpack into which he'd packed fifty Ziploc snack bags, each containing a few grams to up to half an ounce of high-grade marijuana that he grew himself in his attic. It seems that Mr. Vogler used Bay Beans West, the coffee shop owned by Defendant and managed by himself, as a cover for a thriving marijuana business, a business whose books and accounting ledgers will show operated with the complete cooperation and collusion of Defendant."

Maya was beginning to fidget and Hardy reached over and put a hand on her arm, squeezing gently. Everything Stier was saying was old news to both of them by now, but that didn't mean it wasn't disconcerting hearing it laid out in a smoothly flowing narrative. And he didn't want a member of the jury to pick up on Maya's discomfort, which any one of them might construe as guilt.

For his own part Hardy wore a practiced expression of barely disguised disgust at this reading of the purported "facts." Without lapsing into anything like true theatricality he let his head, as though of its own accord, shake back and forth ever so slightly whenever he sensed a juror checking him for his reaction.

Stier went on. "But Defendant wasn't done yet. Her drug business went back a long way, and it would take more than one murder to keep it secure. Unfortunately, the murder of Dylan Vogler aroused the suspicion of another of her confederates named Levon Preslee. Until his death Mr. Preslee worked as a fund-raising executive at the American Conservatory Theater. Like Defendant and Mr. Vogler, he had attended the University of San Francisco in the nineteen nineties. While they were students there, several witnesses will testify that the three of them—Defendant and the two victims, Mr. Vogler and Mr. Preslee—first got involved together in a marijuana distribution business. Eventually, the law caught up to Mr. Vogler and Mr. Preslee and they were both convicted of robbery in connection with a dope deal gone bad and sentenced to prison."

Hardy had fought vigorously to keep Vogler and Preslee's prior marijuana dealings and the robbery away from the jury. There was no evidence, he'd argued, that connected Maya to that in any way. As with almost every other motion he had tried to make, Braun had brushed him aside: "Goes to the relationship among the parties," she'd said, as though that either made sense or had something to do with the legal ruling.

Stier picked up the narrative again. "But not Defendant. The evidence will show that she remained a silent partner, and that silence had a price. In the early afternoon on Thursday, November first, Mr. Preslee got a phone call and abruptly left work at ACT in an agitated state. At two-oh-five that afternoon he placed a call to Defendant on his cell phone. Although Defendant—again—initially denied to police that she had ever been to Mr. Preslee's apartment, DNA and her fingerprints will in fact place Defendant at Mr. Preslee's home right around the time of his death."

At their table Hardy's hand closed around Maya's wrist, and she cast him a downward look and let out a sigh.

This last bit of evidence, of course, had caused Maya's arrest and was in many ways the low point of the past several months. The prosecution had developed its theory about the supposed relationships and possible blackmail between Vogler, Preslee, and Maya, but without any physical evidence tying Maya to Preslee's home, even with his telephone call to her from his cell phone, there was no practical chance that she could ever be charged with Preslee's murder. And possibly not even with Vogler's.

"Ladies and gentlemen," Stier went on, "we have here nearly the exact same pattern of behavior from Defendant in two related homicides. When she was in college, Defendant became involved with both victims in the sale of marijuana. You will hear evidence that Defendant both used and sold this and other drugs, and hear eyewitness testimony that her criminal partners, Vogler and Preslee, participated in robberies of other drug dealers.

"Since those days Defendant has masqueraded as an upper-class mother, a good wife, a regular churchgoer, and a law-abiding citizen. This new life was all-important to her for many reasons, but most particularly because she is a member of one of San Francisco's most prominent political families."

Here at last was Hardy's first chance to stem the onslaught. "Objection, Your Honor," he said. "Irrelevant and argumentative."

Judge Braun frowned down at him and let him know how the wind was going to blow. "I think neither," she said. "Overruled."

Stier nodded at the bench, continuing smoothly. "Defendant paid dearly to keep her past secret. You will hear another eyewitness— the victim Mr. Vogler's common-law wife—testify that her husband, with whom Defendant had been intimate, was blackmailing Defendant over an eight-year period. The blackmail mostly took the form of an exorbitant salary that he took as manager of Bay Beans West, but lately, Defendant's financial records will reveal a pattern of money laundering through the coffee shop that corroborates the bare fact of the blackmail and provides a compelling motive for Mr. Vogler's murder. And, in fact, for Mr. Preslee's.

"The evidence overwhelmingly supports the People's contention that Defendant killed both Mr. Vogler and Mr. Preslee because one had been blackmailing her and the other was about to do the same. She used her own gun to kill Mr. Vogler and—with that gun in police custody—used the nearest thing that came to hand, a kitchen cleaver, to kill Mr. Preslee. But both of these were premeditated acts that the state of California defines as first-degree murder, and that is the verdict I will ask you to deliver at the end of this trial. Thank you."

Glitsky sat, feet up, behind his desk, which was getting pretty much littered with peanut shells. He'd opened the high blinds up sometime over the past six weeks since Hardy had last been up here, once it had become reasonable to assume that Zachary would recover, so the room was at last adequately lighted again.

Hardy and Frannie had been at the Glitskys' home two weeks before, and while Zack still wore a football-type helmet during his every waking moment, to both Hardys he seemed absolutely normal, back to what he had been before the accident.

It was Abe, Hardy felt, who had irrevocably changed. Not a man whom anybody would mistake for Mr. Sunshine in any event, Glitsky couldn't seem to absorb the reality that Zachary was better, and that this was good news for him and for his life. Instead, his focus tended to be on his own responsibility for the accident in the first place; his general incompetence as a human being; his unlucky star. Whatever it was, much of what had always been at best a dark and cynical spark now had ceased to throw any light at all, and Hardy found it disturbing and wearying. Not that he was giving up on his best friend, but he was constantly trying to come up with ideas that might help restore Abe to something like what he used to be.

Stopping up here unexpectedly at lunchtime today on the first day of trial with a fresh supply of peanuts, for example. The peanuts that Glitsky had always kept in his desk drawer—top left until Hardy had surreptitiously moved them one day to top right—had run out just before Christmas, never to be replaced. So even though he had his own opening argument to deliver when court resumed after lunch, he stopped by to drop off the gift and chat for a few minutes.

And it had started, of course, with a discussion of Stier's opening, which Glitsky thought was pretty compelling. "Admittedly, though," he said, popping a nut, "I'm the choir he was preaching to. You probably didn't really want to ask me."

"Oh, right, I forgot for a minute. What was the part, though, that convinced you?"

"Of what?"

"That Maya's guilty."

Glitsky's hands rested together on his stomach. He leaned back in his chair. "I've got one for you. What part of it didn't you believe?"

"I believed all of it," Hardy said.

"There you go. Don't worry about it. You're due for a loss anyway. Nat"—Glitsky's eighty-something father—"says the occasional loss strengthens the spirit."

"The old 'What doesn't kill us makes us strong'?"

"Right." A shadow fell over Glitsky's face. "I have to admit, though, sometimes not."

"When did you get a loss recently?"

Glitsky's face went a shade darker. "Hello? You been around the last few months?"

"You're taking Zack as a loss? Last I saw, he was bouncing off the furniture."

"Last I saw, he was walking around in a football helmet. Maybe you didn't notice?"

"Maybe you didn't hear what you just said: He was walking around. The football helmet was against future injury, if I'm not mistaken. Is there something you aren't telling me?"

"About what?"

"Zack. All I've heard is that all signs point to complete recovery."

Glitsky shook his head. "They don't know for sure."

"But they say what I said, don't they? All signs point, et cetera."

"They say they're 'cautiously optimistic.' That's 'cause if they say he's all better and something happens, they're afraid I'll sue 'em."

"How about if it's because they don't think anything else bad is going to happen?"

"They can think it all they want. Nobody's saying they know it. Nobody can know it. Why again are we talking about this?"

"You were calling it a loss, that's why."

"Yeah. Well, it's what it is, whatever you call it." Glitsky pulled his feet off the desk. "What were we talking about before that came up?"

"Stier's opening."

Staring off into the middle distance between them, Glitsky absently cracked another peanut shell. "That's the main thing. I used to have a pretty good brain. Now, my attention span . . . I get one thought. It goes away. Another one stops by. I can't string any of them together. It's just like I'm endlessly distracted. I can't seem to get myself out of it."

Hardy asked, "You talking to somebody?"

"Sure. Treya, Nat, you from time to time."

"I mean a professional."

Glitsky almost smiled. "That's not happening. It's not something I can figure out and decide to change."

"How do you know that?"

"I just do, all right." He ate a nut. "And I'm kind of done with this topic, okay?"

Hardy could take a hint. "Sure. What do you think about the mayor being down there?"

"Pretty bold statement."

"I can't figure out if it helps or hurts. Me, I mean."

"It's a jury," Glitsky said. "Only takes one. How'd Braun take it?"

"Like you'd suspect. She blamed me, of course."

"Naturally. I would have too."

"Well, there you go. But however it plays with Kathy and Harlen, bottom line is it's just another distraction. And my client's only chance is if this thing starts being about the evidence at some point."

"I thought that was the PX."

"Never got there. Not even close." Hardy shook his head and threw a baleful look across the desk. "This might be a good time to remind you that you never signed off on the arrest, if you recall."

"Let's not go there, Diz. You know I didn't have to. Bracco and Schiff had more than enough. The PX confirmed it. And, PS, didn't you just tell me about five minutes ago you believed every word Stier said?"

"Yeah. I think he's right. It all works as a theory. But I don't think he proves any of it—the evidence doesn't prove it, that's for sure. And that's kind of what he's supposed to do."

"Well." Glitsky suddenly realized they'd eaten all the peanuts he'd left out, so he stood up, stretched his back, started gathering the used shells for the wastebasket. "There's the beauty of the system. If there's no evidence, you'll get her off."

"I'd say, 'Isn't it pretty to think so?' Abe, except the line's already taken."

After Hardy left, Glitsky's short attention span still worked well enough to jog him into writing himself a note to go over the Maya Townshend file just to make sure that Bracco and Schiff had presented their case as clearly and with enough evidence as they could to Paul Stier. Hardy was right—Glitsky had been out at the time with Zachary's medical care issues, and his troops hadn't run their evidence by him even once. If they'd left anything out, Glitsky wanted to be sure he got it back in, not that it would break his heart for Hardy to lose one.

The guy, God knew, was due.

21

If Hardy thought it had been madness in and around the courtroom for the morning session, in fact it had been as a mild and peaceful meadow compared to the riotous frenzy that greeted him as he got off the elevator on the third floor after his talk with Glitsky.

Evidently, Kathy West was going to be staying around at least for the afternoon session and clearly this was making some big waves out in the real world. The mayor didn't come down and sit around in open court very often, and her presence had become just what Hardy didn't need right now—the biggest news story of the day, perhaps the biggest nationwide.

The entire hallway was stuffed with humanity—lots of the press variety—and Hardy was trying to elbow his way through. Should he be even one minute tardy, he would face Judge Braun's wrath and possibly a contempt fine. Hardy didn't know whether it was police paranoia, Braun's need for control, or one of the mayor's staff trying to protect the boss, but someone had ordered a makeshift metal detector station outside the courtroom door, and what had at first appeared to be an amorphous mob was in fact a restricted and organized line waiting to get in.

Very, very slowly.

At near the head of the line he made out the figures of his two partners—Gina Roake and Wes Farrell—unexpectedly coming down for the show. As if he needed it, here was a true litmus test for how quickly the news of the mayor's attendance had spread throughout the city. But he didn't think he could push his way through enough to get to them in any event. The crowd didn't strike him as one that would be tolerant of cuts.

Hardy might not have been a fan of the architecture of the Hall of Justice, but he knew his way around the building. Hewing to the back wall of the wide and echoing hallway, he inched his way along against the current and eventually found that the door to Department 24 was open. Court wasn't yet in session there, and he walked up through the deserted courtroom and into the back corridor that connected all the departments on this floor. Unchallenged by bailiffs, all of whom were doing crowd control in Department 25, he approached the door through which they would later bring his client.

As he came abreast of the judge's chambers, he stopped. The door to Braun's chamber was open about halfway and Paul Stier and Jerry Glass were coming out of it, still in amiable conversation with Braun. When they saw Hardy, both their progress and the discussion came to an abrupt and awkward halt.

"Gentlemen. Your Honor," Hardy said, and held his ground, actually more shocked than angry, waiting for the explanation that would have to be forthcoming. One of the most sacrosanct rules in jurisprudence was that attorneys with active cases before a judge were not to have any ex parte interaction with that judge.

Any.

And it went both ways. A judge should not allow or entertain the possibility of such interaction.

What Hardy had just witnessed was an apparently flagrant violation of that rule—enough that he might on those grounds alone immediately move for a mistrial and, later, the judge's recusal of herself from the case.

Glass came around Stier and stepped right into the breach with what Hardy considered a pathetically cavalier approach, an offhand wave, a light tone. "Counselor. This is not what you think it is."

This was unworthy of a response, since obviously it was what it was. Hardy, in no way tempted to be forgiving or friendly, looked around the two men and into the room. "Your Honor?" he asked with a hint of demand in his voice.

Braun came forward, embarrassed but clearly determined to brass her way through. "Mr. Glass is right. Nothing untoward occurred here, Mr. Hardy. These gentlemen happened to pass my doorway and I heard them talking about the mayor's appearance in the gallery and we exchanged a few casual words about it, that's all. Much as you and I are doing right now."

"With respect, Your Honor. You and I are talking right now in the presence of my opponent, and overtly or not, we are discussing the case before your court. As a matter of fact, before we go on, and if we are to go on, I'd like to request that the court recorder be present."

"That's ridiculous," Glass blurted out.

Hardy ignored him, focused on Braun. "Your Honor?" he said again.

After an excruciating five seconds, the judge's eyes having squinted down in concentration, she nodded and with a touch of ostentation checked her watch. "Court's back in session in six minutes," she said. "I'll see you gentlemen out there."

And with that she closed her door.

In the courtroom Maya had yet to be brought in. Hardy greeted Kathy and Harlen cordially through the press around them and thanked them for their show of support. He said hello to Joel. Then, excusing himself, he caught Gina Roake's eye back a few rows and motioned both her and Farrell up to the bar rail.

When they got there, he said, "I'm going to believe you both came down here to take notes on how a master does an opening statement."

"What else could it have been?" Roake asked with a straight face, then gave a little wave over at the mayor and Harlen. The bonds among all of them had of course become a bit strained over the years and all of these individuals evolved into new relationships, new jobs, even—it sometimes seemed—new selves. But seven or eight years before, when the city was in turmoil over the resignation of District Attorney Sharron Pratt and the grand jury indictment for murder of her chief assistant, the then-mayor had appointed a new district attorney. Clarence Jackman had come on board from the private sector to restore some semblance of order—getting the department back on budget, prosecuting crimes, litigating the city's business problems. Jackman had gathered around him a kitchen cabinet that met most Tuesdays at Lou the Greek's. That group had included, among a few others, Hardy, Roake, their now-deceased partner David Freeman, Kathy West, who was a city supervisor back then, Glitsky, the *Chronicle* columnist Jeff Elliot, and Jackman's secretary, Glitsky's future wife Treya.

"Although," Gina continued, "it is always nice to see Kathy. She's looking particularly perky today, don't you think?"

"I do, but enough about Kathy," Hardy said. "I need a little advice. I've got a question for you guys."

Farrell was ready for him. "Berlin," he said.

"Good answer," Hardy replied. "Wrong question, though. The real question is what do you do if you see your judge schmoozing with your opposite number?"

"Yeah, Berlin would be wrong for that one," Farrell conceded. "You're talking ex parte? When did it happen?"

"Just now. Five minutes ago. Braun and Stier and Jerry Glass, back in her chambers."

"What were they talking about?" Roake asked. "Not that it should matter too much."

"That's my point," Hardy said. "I think at the least I've got to have her memorialize what went on."

Farrell asked, "Doesn't she already hate you?"

"I believe that's accurate. So in that case, how could it hurt?"

"It could always hurt," Roake said. "Your judge hates you, she can fuck you in myriad subtle and unreviewable ways, as I know you're aware. You really don't want her hating you more than she does."

"Yeah, but this happened. If she doesn't memorialize it, it goes away."

"All I'm saying," Roake went on, "is compare it to what happens if she does. Could be a lot worse, and you wouldn't even know it. And more to the point, Diz, what do you get for pissing her off? They're going to make up some kind of bullshit explanation no matter what they were doing, and no court of appeal will ever give you a reversal. You get nothing for your trouble, so anything you could lose is not worth it."

"Maybe," Farrell put in, "you could ask her if she wants to recuse herself."

"That would just piss her off too."

Farrell made a face. "Okay, then, how about going to Thomasino?" Oscar Thomasino was the presiding judge of the Superior Court and, more importantly for these purposes, a reasonably warm acquaintance of Hardy and both his partners.

"I thought of that," Hardy said. "But I didn't hear anything they said, and Braun will just say it was a casual conversation that had nothing to do with the case. And guess what? That, too, will piss her off. Knowing that I get out of bed every morning probably pisses her off, now that I think about it."

"Maybe you should have challenged," Farrell said.

"Thank you," Hardy replied with heavy irony. "If only. Maybe I'll whip into my time machine and go back and do it when I could."

"Do you really want her out, Diz?" Roake asked.

Hardy turned to her, his voice barely a whisper. "Nothing would make me happier. But one ex parte communication seems a little thin, as grounds go, to get rid of her. Especially if they weren't, in fact, talking about the case."

"It might be smarter," Gina said, "to let her keep on knowing that you've got something on her."

"I like that," Farrell said. "Better to have her think she owes you."

"And I'm guessing," Roake added, "that you want to decide right away."

"Actually, I think I've decided. But the last thing is I don't want her thinking I'm a wimp and she's frightened me off."

Farrell grinned at that. "I think she already knows you better than that."

"So I just keep this in my pocket? That flies for both of you? No memorializing? No recusing?"

His partners silently conferred with each other, glances back and forth, consensus.

As soon as she ascended to the bench and got the courtroom under control, Braun called the attorneys up to her bench for a sidebar. "Mr. Hardy," she began, "we're on the record now. Is there anything you'd like to bring up before the court?"

Calling him right away on what he'd seen. If he was going to make trouble for her, it would start now. And she'd have it in her mind while he was delivering his opening statement.

Hardy, his blood rushing with what had somewhat surprisingly turned into rage-tinged frustration, tried to slow his breathing. He finally came out with it. "Nothing, Your Honor."

Hardy saw Braun's eyes narrow. If he looked, he was sure he could have seen the wheels spinning in Stier's head as he tried to figure out what trick the legendary Dismas Hardy was pulling now.

Braun could see no reason not to accept the Trojan horse, and actually looked as though she felt a moment of relief, if not gratitude, that Hardy had decided to let her off the hook. "Mr. Stier?" she asked.

Just at that moment a camera clicked loudly in the gallery, followed immediately by a cell phone going off, and Braun looked up and exploded, rapping her gavel several times in quick succession. "That's all I'm going to tolerate of cameras and other disturbances! I granted permission for a number of news cameras to be in this courtroom. At the slightest further disruption that permission will be revoked. I want no more pictures taken. I want all cell phones turned off." Here she looked over the front of her podium. "As a matter of fact, now that I think about it, for the remainder of this trial, after today—bailiffs, please note—I will not be allowing cameras into the courtroom."

At the mild rumble of protest that arose in the gallery at this edict, she banged her gavel again. "I am this close," she said, "to expelling people with cameras right now. But in the interests of keeping things moving I'll hold off on that order, unless someone abuses it." She glared through her glasses for another ten seconds or so, scanning the gallery right to left, left to right, for signs of disobedience.

Finding none, she returned to the prosecuting attorney, standing next to Hardy in front of her. "Mr. Stier?"

"Yes, Your Honor."

"I believe before that interruption that the court was asking if the People are ready to begin?"

The Big Ugly for an instant took on an expression that somewhat explained the nickname. Nervous, and with a light sheen of perspiration on his high forehead, Stier cleared his throat and threw a quick glance at Hardy, then came back up to the judge.

He finally decided that while he couldn't figure out what Hardy was doing, if Hardy wanted something, any smart prosecutor wanted the opposite. "Your Honor," he began, "I call your attention to a meeting that took place just minutes ago at the door to your chambers, where you and I exchanged a few pleasantries relating to the mayor's appearance in the courtroom today, but outside of the presence of Mr. Hardy."

Hardy couldn't believe his ears. But he wasn't inclined to interrupt.

Braun looked for all the world as though she was going to have a stroke right there on the bench. "Go on," she said. "What do you think is so important that it needs to be memorialized at this point in the proceeding?"

Oblivious, Stier kept digging his grave. "I believe that in the interests of precluding a defense appeal on grounds of this technically ex parte communication between you and myself, it is in the interest of justice that that discussion be memorialized and entered into the record. Then, if Mr. Hardy's got any objections, he can raise them now."

Hardy stood with the muscles in his jaw locked against breaking into a victory grin. This was the kind of moment that his old mentor, David Freeman, had lived for. You plan and you plan and then you strategize and plan some more and then something completely unexpected happens and you're back in the ball game in a way you had never imagined possible. Sometimes you just had to love the majestic insanity of the law.

Stier had just overstrategized himself into a truly dumb move and Judge Braun, never subtle, was letting him know it by her body language and withering expression. "Very well, Counselor," she clipped out through lips tight enough that it didn't appear she was moving her mouth at all. "By all means, let's memorialize that conversation. Court reporter and attorneys in chambers. Ten-minute recess."

Finally Hardy stood to deliver his opening statement. He had the option of either delivering it now or waiting until the prosecution closed its case in chief. But like most experienced defense attorneys, he didn't want to give the jury too much time to live with the version of the crime they'd just heard described in the prosecution's opening statement.

Even with many murder trials under his belt Hardy expected that he would be struck by opening-day jitters—the familiar hollowness in his stomach, the deadness in his legs—when he first stood to address the jury. Especially with the large and captivated crowd in the courtroom, the sudden sense that something of major import was transpiring here. When he rose to come around his table and face the panel, though, he found himself possessed of an almost unnatural calm, even a confidence.

The easy camaraderie between Braun and Stier had just suffered a serious blow and while the prosecutor was probably still reeling from it, Hardy could use this small but real advantage to push the envelope a bit—maybe throw in a little argument, which was forbidden in opening statements—and, while Stier's attention was focused elsewhere, perhaps escape without too much interruption in the form of objections from the prosecution table.

He began in an amiable fashion, wearing an easy smile and making eye contact with every juror he could before he started. "Good afternoon. This morning Mr. Stier related to you an extravagant scenario of motivation and coincidence that he hopes will convince you that Maya Townshend is guilty of two counts of first-degree murder." Much in the same way that Stier always referred to Maya as "Defendant" to dehumanize her to the jury, Hardy would strive at every opportunity to refer to her by her given name, underscoring her humanity and personhood. "Unfortunately for the People's case, but fortunately for Maya and for justice, what he left out of his story were the gaps and holes and inconsistencies in the so-called chain of evidence upon which the prosecution relies. The prosecution cannot and will not prove that Maya killed Dylan Vogler or that she killed Levon Preslee, because she didn't.

"Did Maya know Dylan and Levon when she was in college? Absolutely she did. Did she do some things she's ashamed of now, as Mr. Stier alleges? Yes. Will there be evidence, such as direct eyewitness testimony, to prove these things? Again, the answer is yes."

Hardy, always conscious that he had a tendency to go too fast and gloss over elements of syllogisms that might be crucial to jury members, had trained himself to slow down, timing his restrained pacing from one end of the jury box to the other, getting back to his table ostensibly to consult notes or take a drink of water, sometimes just to touch it to keep him in his rhythm, center him for another lap.

Now he touched the wood of his table, gave a quick confident nod to his client, and turned back to the jury. "So the prosecution can prove that Maya Townshend"—he walked over to her, putting his hands on her shoulders—"small-business owner, wife, and mother of two young children, made mistakes when she was in college.

"We know that she was a student at the University of San Francisco because there are records supporting her attendance there. She appears four times in four years in the school's yearbook, and several times in the university's newspaper, the *Foghorn*. Similarly, we will learn from her classmates at the time that she associated regularly with both Dylan Vogler and with Levon Preslee, and we will hear from other eyewitnesses that these young students were not exactly members of the choir. These are facts supported by both documentary and eyewitness testimony."

Hardy didn't dare glance back at Stier. He was well into argument here and so far he was getting away with it. The prosecutor, still licking his wounds, hadn't engaged yet. He was no doubt listening, but he wasn't hearing.

"But that's not what she's accused of. She's accused of murder.

And for that accusation the prosecution has no evidence. The district attorney tells you that it has evidence to support the charges it has brought against her, evidence that directly ties her—and this is important—that ties her, and no one else, to these crimes. That is simply not so.

"The actual truth is that unlike the story about Maya's earlier life, which the prosecution can back up with witnesses and documents, there is nothing to tie her to evidence of these murders except innuendo and speculation. And why is that?"

Hardy paused, taking a moment up by the witness chair, again meeting the gaze of juror after juror. "The answer, ladies and gentlemen, is quite simple. The prosecution won't provide you with this evidence because none of it exists. There are no eyewitnesses who will claim they saw her in the presence of either of the two victims on the day of their respective deaths. There is no documentary evidence—say a time stamp or video recording—analogous to the USF yearbook or the issues of the *Foghorn* that places Maya in the company of either of these two victims at the time of their deaths. Nearby? Yes, by her own admission. But nearby, ladies and gentlemen, is not good enough to meet the legal standard that will take you beyond reasonable doubt."

This time Hardy stopped at his table for a quick sip of water. He glanced out at the gallery, at Kathy West and Harlen and Joel in the front row right in front of him. Nodding to them soberly, he came back to the jury.

"Now, I can see some of you asking yourselves: Wait a minute. This is a young woman without a criminal record. If she didn't do it, if there were no proof that she did it, why would she be on trial? Why would the state of California expend all this enormous time, energy, and expense if there is no physical evidence tying her to these crimes? These are excellent questions, and unfortunately they go begging for answers. Because the real truth of this prosecution is that there is no physical evidence proving that Maya ever fired the weapon that killed Mr. Vogler, or held the knife that killed Mr. Preslee. No eyewitnesses. No fingerprints. No physical evidence. No incriminating bloodstains on Maya or on her shoes or on her clothing. No nothing.

"She was in the vicinity of both deaths on the times they occurred, yes. But both times she was summoned to those places—as her phone records will attest—by the victims themselves, or by someone calling her on their telephones. That someone is, I submit, the person who should be sitting where Maya is now, charged with these murders. He or she is every bit as real—in fact, more real—than the so-called evidence you will hear connecting Maya to these murders. The police simply haven't found or identified this person as a suspect."

This—the theory of the case that Hardy would be arguing whether he believed it or not—brought a significant buzz to the packed courtroom, as he'd known it would. The pundits, the reporters, the Court TV and other television crews—and with Kathy West's presence he knew there'd be vanloads of them now in the next few days—would dissect this strategy from every imaginable angle. Was Hardy wise to show his hand so early? Was this pure cynicism? Did he have any proof of his own to support what he was saying? Wasn't the SODDIT—"some other dude did it"—defense one of the most hackneyed and noncredible strategies in criminal law?

Hardy didn't care. Whether he could prove it or not—and he couldn't—he still felt that he could make it sing to at least one of the jurors, and that was the name of the game.

And incredibly, he thought, Stier still hadn't said a word.

Well, Hardy was going to give him another chance.

He took another sip of water, set the glass down carefully, turned slowly to face the jury panel again. "All this brings us back, of course, to the question of why Maya has been arrested and charged with these murders.

"Unfortunately, the answer is cynical at best, and despicable at worst: Maya Townshend owned the coffee shop Bay Beans West, out of which Mr. Vogler sold marijuana. Although there is, again, no evidence tying Maya to Mr. Vogler's marijuana business—the documents to which Mr. Stier referred in his opening, purportedly proving some marijuana business connection between Mr. Vogler and Maya, are inconclusive and ambiguous at best—Maya proved an inviting target as a suspect for a number of reasons, none of them having to do with evidence. All of them having to do with political ambition and expediency."

If Stier had been asleep to this point, he was all the way awake now, and seemingly in full fettle. "Objection, Your Honor! Argumentative. This is an outrageous accusation, offered without proof. It has no place in an opening statement or, indeed, anywhere in this trial."

And again, Braun, revealing the depths of enmity one encountered if one got on her wrong side as Stier had obviously done, surprised Hardy. "I was wondering when you'd notice, Mr. Stier," she said. "But you're a few beats late. Mr. Hardy is simply presenting his theory of the case, as you did in your own opening. Objection overruled. You may proceed, Mr. Hardy."

"Thank you, Your Honor." Hardy wasted not a second before getting back to his tale. "From the outset of their investigation the two homicide detectives handling this case were hampered with—guess what?—lack of evidence. In an effort to shake up one or more of their potential suspects—and the testimony of those inspectors will reveal that there were more than a couple of them—one of the detectives, Debra Schiff, happened upon the strategy of contacting a gentleman named Jerry Glass, the United States federal attorney based in San Francisco.

"She persuaded Mr. Glass to use the very tenuous marijuana connection between Bay Beans West and Maya Townshend not only to impugn Maya's character and reputation, but also to provide her with an apparent motive for these murders—one that has no basis in reality or in evidence. But almost worse, it also attempts to explain away this lack of evidence by the implication that Maya's close relatives—who include a supervisor and the mayor of this city—somehow colluded with her to cover up her transgressions."

"Your Honor, I must object again." Stier rose at his table. "All of this high-flown rhetoric is just a smoke screen meant to confuse the jury."

Braun, humorless, looked down over her eyeglasses. "Objections, as you know, Mr. Stier, must be on legal grounds."

"Argumentative, then, Your Honor."

She appeared to consider for a moment, then shook her head. "Overruled."

Hardy nodded quickly to the bench, acknowledging the ruling. Stier might not have realized it, but he'd just insulted the jury and questioned its intelligence by implying that Hardy's "smoke screen" would fool them into giving the wrong verdict. Now Hardy thought he'd play the other side of that coin, praising their sagacity and collective wisdom. "Finally, ladies and gentlemen," he continued, "I need hardly point out to you that this trial has taken on a very high public profile. A glance at the size of the gallery here, the number of reporters, and even some of the spectators"—he paused for a ripple of appreciation to flow through the gallery—"all of these things make it clear that this trial has the potential to be a career-making moment—"

"Objection!"

Hardy heard the word behind him, but he was too energized to stop himself now, and not inclined to in any event. He was speaking what he believed to be the absolute truth and he wanted the jury to hear. In fact, he raised his voice and continued. "A career-making moment for people whose ambitions—"

"Your Honor!" Louder still. "Objection! Irrelevant and argumentative!"

"Mr. Hardy!"

"—whose ambitions exceed their sense of fairness and whose thirst for fame and recognition blinds them to the simple demands of justice."

Bam! Bam! "Mr. Hardy, that's enough. Mr. Stier, objection sustained. Mr. Hardy—"

But he was a step ahead of her. "I apologize, Your Honor. I got a little carried away."

"Apparently," she said. "Please don't let it happen again. Jurors will disregard that last outburst of Mr. Hardy's." Then, back at Hardy. "All right. You may proceed."

Hardy took a small breath, having made it at last to what had become almost his boilerplate closing. "This trial is about determining who caused the deaths of two people—Dylan Vogler and Levon Preslee. One died by gunshot wound and the other by the stroke of a cleaver. The evidence is quite clear on these points. But where the evidence is not clear, and in fact where it altogether fails, is where it purports to connect Maya Townshend to either of these murders. It is neither clear nor clean. Where it needs to be unambiguous, it is open to interpretation. Where it needs to dispel reasonable doubt, it only adds to it. No real evidence inexorably connects Maya Townshend to these murders."

Now, his own adrenaline storm having passed, Hardy thought he could maintain his less dramatic tone and lull Stier into failing to object on argumentative grounds one last time. "As you were seated on this jury, you all swore an oath that you would presume the innocence of Maya Townshend. She must remain innocent in your eyes until the prosecution presents you with enough hard, physical evidence to prove to you beyond a reasonable doubt that she in fact committed these crimes. That means you must be sure of the intimate details of these crimes. When Mr. Stier tells you that he can't say exactly how Maya killed Mr. Vogler or Mr. Preslee, he is admitting that he doesn't have that proof. And without that proof there is doubt. Where there is doubt, there is innocence. My client, Maya Townshend, is innocent—and she will rely on your sworn oath to presume that innocence and, after you have weighed all the facts in this case, to return a verdict of not guilty."

22

Braun called a recess as soon as Hardy sat down. While Maya was in
the restroom, Hardy pushed his chair back to the bar rail and turned
around, resting his elbow on it. "Well," he said to what he hoped was
his private little fan club of Kathy, Harlen, and Joel Townshend, "I
think I got a few licks in, anyway. How'd it play out here?"

"Excellent," Joel said.

Joel had become a rather more enthusiastic partner in Maya's
defense since the arrest. Of course, this had come at the expense of a
seismic shift in his worldview. Before the weekend of Dylan Vogler's
death he'd never had occasion to think that the world wasn't at base a
fair and equitable place. He'd always had enough money and social
standing to remain above the little mundane headaches that most
people faced constantly—household bills, fights about money or time
or chores. If he wanted to go out to dinner, they hired a babysitter and
didn't care what the meal cost. If he and Maya were tired or bored,
they'd go spend a night or two in Napa or Carmel to rejuvenate themselves. Their friends were people more or less like them. And other
people he met tended to be polite, at least to him personally. Perhaps
even more fundamentally, he never really had to prove himself to get a
loan or make a connection; he got the benefit of the doubt.

And now, not just suddenly but seemingly instantaneously, all of
that had ended. The properties against which he'd taken out more
loans to finance other properties and ventures were no longer rock-
solid as collateral. His social life, with his wife incarcerated in the

county jail, essentially vanished. He found himself amazed by how completely life changed when you got accused of wrongdoing. At first he'd held to the belief that this whole affair was just a mistake and if he could just find the right person to talk to and explain everything, it would all go away. He and Maya would go back to their real life.

But by now he had come to realize that this wasn't going to happen. He and his wife were somehow "in the criminal justice system," and this more than anything meant that the benefit of the doubt had evaporated. No one in the system was inclined to believe anything he said. The motivations for anything he did got skewed and twisted by people who started out by considering him, if not a criminal, then at least a shady character. And once they had that mind-set, nothing was going to change.

Now he was going on to Hardy: "I like the way you laid this conspiracy these people have cooked up right out there."

"Me too," Hardy said. "I couldn't believe Braun let it in, but if she was going to let me, I sure as hell was going to run with it."

"My concern," Harlen Fisk said, "is it's going to turn up the heat on Glass."

"Let it," Kathy West declared. "Harlen and I showing up here ought to be enough to do that. I welcome it. And, Diz, you just declared open war, which also suits me fine. Jerry Glass has got nothing on us. This will all get litigated away in civil court, but in the meanwhile this is where we fight it, where it can do Maya the most good."

"It's great you both came down for this," Hardy said to Kathy and Harlen. "It was really a good idea, Kathy. Let them know we're not cowering and hiding and plotting some backroom deal. I think it's really shocked them."

The mayor nodded. "That was my intention."

"Are you planning on coming in every day?" Hardy asked.

This brought a smile. "When I can, maybe I will, if it will have some strategic value for you. But day-to-day, I've still got this city to run."

"I should be here most days," Fisk said. "Wave the flag for my sis."

"So what's the next step?" Joel asked.

"Witnesses," Hardy replied. "We get down to it."

If Paul Stier felt he'd taken a few hits from Hardy's opening statement, or harbored any residual resentment at Judge Braun, he showed no sign of either as he stood in the center of the courtroom. "The People call Sergeant Lennard Faro."

The head of Crime Scene Investigations stood up in the second row of the gallery and came through the door in the bar rail and up to the witness stand. Well-dressed as always in snug tan pants, a pink dress shirt, and a subtly shimmering light brown sports coat, he cut a dashing figure very much at odds with that of most other cops. With his spiky dark hair, gold stud earring, and well-trimmed goatee, he might have been a young graduate student or fashion designer; but even so, his experience and ease on the witness stand soon verified the credentials he outlined to Stier as they began—fourteen years on the force, the last eight with the CSI unit, the last six in charge of it.

"Now, Sergeant, what is your role at these crime scenes?"

"My team of three officers and I search the general area for physical evidence that might be related to the crime. We collect as evidence anything of interest. We also photograph the victim and the scene to try and create a record of everything at the scene as it was when we found it."

Though a bit unusual, since murder trials often began with forensic and medical evidence, Hardy thought Stier's decision to call Faro first was a good bit of strategy. This would put evidence at the crime scenes into the trial at the outset, potentially rebutting Hardy's contention in his opening statement that there was little or no physical evidence tying Maya to the murders. It was also a prime opportunity to get pictures of the victims in front of the jury—real human beings who'd been murdered.

"Sergeant, were you present at the scene of Dylan Vogler's murder?"

"Yes, sir."

"And would you tell the jury how you proceeded?"

"Sure." Faro, the consummate witness, nodded and came forward in the witness chair, turning slightly to be facing the jury. "I arrived at a few minutes before eight with three other crime-scene technicians."

"Would you describe the scene as you found it?"

"It was a Saturday morning, nice day, and patrolmen from the local precinct had already cordoned off the site with police tape. Their lieutenant, Bill Banks, was also at the scene."

"Did it appear that officers had appropriately preserved the scene so that you could begin your investigation?"

"Yes, it did."

"Describe, please, the body of the victim."

"Mr. Vogler's body was lying on the ground in a paved alley by the back door of his business. He showed signs of a gunshot wound in the chest."

"Showing you People's One through Six, do these appear to be photographs accurately depicting Mr. Vogler's body in the alley as you first saw it?"

"Yes, they do."

"After the scene was photographed, did you conduct a search of the alley to determine what, if any, evidence might be present at the scene?"

"Yes, I did."

Hardy knew that, in fact, all four crime techs had searched the alley. But if any of the other three located something, they would call Faro over without touching it, and he would photograph and collect the evidence. That way, Faro could testify to finding each piece of evidence without needing to have the other three come to court. "Among other debris, I found one .40-caliber brass bullet casing and a .40-caliber Glock semiautomatic handgun."

Stier went through the same process of authenticating and introducing the photos of the items as they were found at the scene. Then he went to his counsel table and retrieved two evidence containers that held the items. He had them marked as People's Exhibits and showed them to Faro. "Now, Sergeant, do you recognize these?"

"Yes, I do."

"Please tell the jury what they are."

This allowed Faro to repeat for the third time—in case one of the jury members was actually so dense that they'd missed it the first two times—his account of finding the gun and the casing in the alley. Whatever else Stier might be, he was professional and methodical. He went through the same process having Faro describe where and how he found the bullet in the stucco wall. Photos of the bullet hole and the projectile itself went into evidence.

For the next twenty minutes they went over all of the things Faro had not found in the alley, although he had looked for them. No other casings, no other weapons, no other bullet strikes on any of the walls or surfaces. No signs of blood, no footprints. Absolutely nothing out of the ordinary in that alley. He even described, though they did not physically produce, the bag of garbage they packaged up for later examination at the lab—the Coke cans, cigarette butts, and, not surprisingly, about a dozen coffee cups.

Having finished the crime scene, Stier moved on to work Faro had done at the lab. As well as working at crime scenes Faro wore a second hat as a firearms examiner in the lab. Stier went through his extensive training and experience and qualified him as an expert, and then led him through the process of comparing the bullet from the wall to the gun—test-firing the weapon and comparing the known bullet microscopically to the bullet in evidence.

As Hardy knew he would, he said that although the bullets appeared similar in class characteristics and likely came from the same sort of gun, there were insufficient details on the recovered slug to say with absolute certainty that it had come from the gun in the alley.

Stier knew that this was not his strongest point, and he moved to buttress it. "Tell the jury, please, what tests, if any, you ran on the spent casing, and what results you got."

"The brass casing is part of a round of ammunition used in the .40-caliber Glock. The marks on the base of the casing—caused by the weapon's firing mechanism—were consistent with other markings we could create on other bullet casings fired from the same weapon."

"Does that mean the casing necessarily came from the weapon found in the alley?"

"No. Like the bullet, it came from a Glock .40, but I can't say with certainty it was that same Glock .40."

"But of course, Sergeant, you found no other bullets or casings in that alley, correct?"

"Right."

Hardy knew that this was a repetitive and therefore objectionable question, but that objecting would only draw more attention to something he hoped the jury would not focus on. So he let it go.

Stier saved the best for last. "Sergeant, is there a database that firearms examiners can access to determine ownership of a handgun?"

Hardy knew that this was gilding the lily—any cop could access this database. Even a clerk could access the database. Stier's question suggested that this was some sort of secret database and that you had to be a member of a club to look at it. But there was nothing Hardy could do about it. Once again, he had to tip his hat to Stier for know-ing his business.

"Yes, there is a database. The gun had a registration number, and I ran that."

With a brightness implying that this was all new to him, Stier glanced over the jury, sharing with them his enthusiasm for the hunt. "A registration number? You mean the gun was licensed to an indi-vidual?"

"Yes."

"And who is that person, Sergeant?"

"The defendant, Maya Townshend."

A wave of energy swept through the gallery. Stier paused just a moment for dramatic effect, until the room was dead silent again.

Hardy knew that this was a low point, and that it was just going to get worse when the fingerprint examiner told the jury that Maya's fingerprints were on the magazine that held the ammunition on the weapon from the alley. The best Hardy could hope for from the fin-gerprint expert was going to be a discussion of an unidentified par-tial fingerprint on the spent casing.

But since Hardy knew that ultimately that print could have been left by anyone who ever handled the ammunition, who worked where it was manufactured, or clerked in the store where it was sold, that was precious little.

Stier took the opportunity by a sideways glance to include the jury in his acknowledgment of the witness. "Thank you, Sergeant." Then, somewhat to Hardy's surprise, Stier half turned to look at him. "Your witness, Mr. Hardy."

Hardy's surprise came from the fact that he'd expected Faro to re-main on the stand to testify about the Preslee crime scene, but appar-ently Stier had an alternate strategy in mind for that portion of the

People's case. For now, Hardy had a job to do, and he squeezed his client's arm and rose with a show of confidence from their table.

"Sergeant Faro," he began, "in your testimony today, talking about the alleged murder weapon, the Glock .40 and the brass casing and bullet that you found at the scene of Mr. Vogler's murder, you used the words *consistent with* several times, did you not?"

"Yes, I think so."

"Tell the jury, please, what you mean by that phrase."

After a moment's hesitation Faro shrugged. "I'm not sure I know a better word. We fired a few rounds from the gun in the lab and compared the indent left by the firing pin on those casings to the gun from the alley and they were virtually indistinguishable from one another."

"Virtually indistinguishable? Do you mean to say that they were exactly the same?"

"Yes."

"But you can't say that the casing came from the gun, can you, Sergeant?"

"No."

"And that's because your virtually indistinguishable markings were in fact so few in number that they don't permit a comparison. Correct?"

"Yes."

"To make a point, Sergeant, your name has an A. R. in it, doesn't it?"

Stier spoke up from behind him. "Objection. Irrelevant."

Braun let her curiosity overcome her distaste for Hardy. "Overruled."

Faro spoke up. "Yes, it does. F-A-R-O."

"Well, so does mine, Sergeant. H-A-R-D-Y. Does that mean we have the same name?"

"Objection. Argumentative."

"Sustained. Move on, Mr. Hardy."

Braun reminding him that she was aware that she'd been ruling in his favor more often than was her wont, but that his leash was very short now, and tightening.

"Sergeant, how many Glock .40s are there in the world?"

"Objection! Speculation."

"Overruled, Mr. Stier. You qualified Sergeant Faro as a firearms expert."

Hardy fenced with Faro in this vein for a moment before concluding. "In other words, Sergeant Faro," he said, "you can't tell this jury that this casing came from this gun, can you?"

"No. I cannot."

"And in fact, aren't there thousands of other Glock .40s that could have left this casing?"

"Yes, there are."

"Thank you, Sergeant." Hardy kept his face impassive but brought his hands together in muted delight. "Now, as to the bullet itself, the .40-caliber slug that you've identified as the bullet that killed Mr. Vogler. Again, you used the words *consistent with*. Sergeant, did you not run a ballistics test on this slug?"

"Yes, we did."

"And aren't ballistics tests conclusive?"

"Generally, yes, they can be."

"When are they not?"

"Well, when the slug is deformed or mutilated."

"And was the slug deformed or mutilated?"

"No, not too bad. It was embedded in stucco and wood, but it was okay."

"And so, was your ballistics test conclusive?"

Faro shot a quick, impatient look over to Stier, shook his head at Hardy. "No."

Hardy put on an expression of mild surprise. "No? Why not?"

"Because like with the casing, this particular bullet lacked sufficient microscopic detail to permit a conclusive match." Faro seemed to feel obliged to defend his inability to give more conclusive evidence. "This particular type of weapon has a type of unique hexagonal rifling in the barrel that tends not to leave the marks necessary for an exact ballistics comparison."

"So, again, Sergeant, let me ask you. Is it possible that the slug that we have here did not come from the gun owned by Maya Townshend?"

This time, since it was foreordained, and though he clearly hated the pass to which he'd come, Faro didn't struggle with his answer. "Yes."

After a small pause, Hardy went on. "Sergeant, did you and your crime-scene unit get called to the scene of Mr. Preslee's murder?"

"Yes, we did."

A confused frown. "Well, Sergeant, it's true, is it not, that you found not one shred of evidence inside Mr. Preslee's home indicating that Maya Townshend had ever even been inside the place, much less murdered anybody there?"

As Hardy had anticipated, Stier was on his feet immediately. "Objection. Beyond the scope of direct examination. We'll get to the Levon Preslee murder scene in due course."

"Sustained."

Hardy didn't care. He knew he'd gotten on the boards first with that crime at least, making his point in front of the jury. Hardy came back to the witness. "No further questions."

23

The door to the jail's visiting room swung open and Hardy stood as Maya came in. He waited patiently while the female guard asked his permission and then undid Maya's handcuffs with a gentleness that he found heartbreaking. Maya had proven herself time and again to be much tougher than she looked, but Hardy had found that it was the little personal indignities that often broke people's spirits when they were in jail. But this guard was solicitous, even going so far as to touch Maya's arm and give her a confident nod before leaving attorney and client alone in the glass-block-enclosed space.

"I hate this place, you know that?" Maya said as they sat down on their metal chairs. "It's worse than the cell."

"I can't say it's exactly my favorite either." Hardy quickly took in their surroundings. He'd been here many times, and the small semicircular room had a certain familiarity to him. At one time, not so very long ago, the building they were in had been the "new" jail and the polished concrete floors and glass walls lent a sense of openness and light to these rooms that at first had seemed far less oppressive than the rectangular, confessional-sized attorneys' visiting rooms at the old jail.

Over the years, though, this room's diaphanous warmth, too, had dissipated somehow, perhaps under the psychic toll of its everyday use. Now it was just another old room, somehow colder for its modernity, its sterility, its cruel illusion of openness through the glass. "Maybe I should smuggle in some rugs, a couple of plants," he said.

"I could bring them in my briefcase every time. That'd spruce the place right up, I bet."

Unable to fake even a stab at levity, Maya simply said, "I'm not sure it would help."

"No, I guess not." Hardy tried to maintain an upbeat and easygoing style, since he saw no reason to add to his client's pain, but sometimes there was no help for it. "Has Joel been by?"

She nodded, swallowed the lump in her throat. "But outside, at the regular visiting place." This was a long room for friends and relatives—as opposed to attorneys—similar in fact to those seen on television and in the movies, with a row of visitor stations on either side of Plexiglas windows with speakers set in them, rendering any true personal contact impossible. "It doesn't really work out there. He only comes by because he feels like he needs to."

"He comes by," Hardy said, "because he loves you."

"All right." Maya clearly didn't want to talk about it. She bowed her head, lowered her eyes. Then, with a forced interest: "So how'd we do out there today?"

"I was going to ask you."

"I can't believe they keep going ahead with it."

"I know. I've had the same thought myself."

"Especially with Levon. They have nothing at all, do they?"

"Your presence. I guess they feel that's all they're going to need, once they convince the jury on Dylan."

She sat still a moment, hands on her lap. "I just keep thinking that if only he hadn't been carrying that weed with him."

"They probably would have found the stash at his house anyway, and the garden, and maybe the computer records too."

"But if he wasn't selling the stuff out of the shop . . ."

"We can't just keep doing 'if,' Maya. He was."

"You're right, you're right." She paused. "So what about Kathy and Harlen coming down today? Does that help us?"

"I think so, though I wish she'd run it by me first."

Another silence. "Can I ask you something?"

"Anything you want."

"The other person who you said did it. Is anybody looking for him?"

"Well, the cops aren't. That's a safe bet."

"So how about us?"

"How about us what?"

"We look for him."

"Or her. Don't forget her."

"No. I never would. But really."

This gambit, or suggestion, or whatever it was, was heartening in some small way, but Hardy kept his emotional guard up. Though technically it didn't matter what he actually thought about Maya's guilt or lack thereof, she might think it would give him a psychological boost at the trial if she somehow got him believing she was innocent. And this question clearly telegraphed *her assumption* of another murderer, without her having to directly lie to her attorney by saying she hadn't done it.

The problem was, he knew that she'd done something. Something damn serious, about which she obviously was carrying an enormous load of guilt. And he also knew, or thought he knew, what she'd been blackmailed about—robberies or perhaps worse that she must have committed with Dylan and Levon. So unless she'd committed murder in the course of one of those . . .

Whoa, he told himself. Therein lies the path to madness. But then he thought, why not? They'd come this far. And he came out with it. "Maya, yes or no, were you involved in the robbery that got Dylan and Levon sent to prison?"

She straightened her back. "Nobody can prove I was."

"That's not what I asked."

She hesitated. "No." A beat. "Not that one."

"So that is in fact what the blackmail was about?"

She didn't answer, turned her face to look at the wall.

"I ask," Hardy pressed on, "because you should know that unless you committed murder or some other heinous crime during one of these robberies, you can't be charged with anything. Anything else, and the statutes of limitations have tolled."

Her eyes came back to him. They bore a shine that he thought might presage tears. "Why are you so sure they were blackmailing me?"

"For one reason, it's the thing that makes the most sense. You were involved in robberies with them in college. Yes?"

Finally, her shoulders gave an inch. "I've already told you. I did some bad stuff."

"Bad enough for life in prison, Maya? Bad enough to never live with your kids or your husband again?"

She stared through him.

"You want to tell me what it was? Just put it out here between me and you. It's privileged. Nobody else will ever know."

"Don't bully me." Her words had a sudden calm edge.

"I'm not bullying you. I'm saying you can tell me anything you've done."

"What for? So you'd do something different? I don't think so. I think you'd do all the same things, make the same arguments in court, whatever it is you believe I'd actually done, isn't that true?"

Angry now, Hardy did not answer.

And then suddenly, Maya came at him on another tack. "What you don't seem to understand is that I'm being punished," she said.

"For what? By who?"

"God."

"God." Hardy felt his anger start to wane, washed away in a wave of pity for this poor woman. "God's punishing you? Why?"

"The same reason he punishes anybody."

"Because of what they've done?"

She sat mute, facing him.

"Maya?"

"If it's unforgivable, yes."

"I thought his forgiveness was supposed to be infinite."

She answered in a small voice. "No. Not for everything."

"No? What wouldn't it cover?"

"How about if what you harm is truly innocent—" Abruptly she drew herself up and stopped speaking.

"What do you mean by that?"

"Nothing. I shouldn't have said anything."

Hardy came forward in his chair. "Maya," he said, "are you talking about something that happened with you and Dylan and Levon?"

A dead, one-note bark of laughter didn't break the harsh set of her mouth. "If you even can ask that," she said, "you don't have a clue what *innocent* means."

"So tell me."

"Like the unborn. That kind of innocent. How about that?"

That answer called to mind Hardy's discussion with Hunt about whether the blackmail had been about an abortion early in her life, so he asked her point blank. "Is that it?"

But she shook her head decidedly no. "I would never do that. Not ever. But I've already said too much. The point is that whatever happens, however God decides all this has to go, I'll deserve it. I'm good with that now. I'm at peace with it."

"Well, I'm not."

She lifted her shoulders in a small shrug. "I'm sorry about that." She gestured around them. "About all of this."

"I am too."

"But . . . so, can we go back to what I was saying before?"

"What part of it?"

"Looking for who did this?"

A black, throbbing bolus of pain came and settled in the space behind Hardy's left eye. He brought his hand up and pressed at his temple. What was this woman getting at? Hardy could think of several ways to interpret all that Maya had said to him here this afternoon as a kind of confession. And now she was urging him to look for the real murderer.

Who, he believed, very probably did not exist.

He looked across at his client's troubled face and entertained the fleeting thought that she might be legally insane. Should he hire a shrink and do some tests? Would he be negligent if he didn't?

The first day of trial had already been too long, too stressful. It seemed to Hardy that he'd been in constant combat since early in the morning.

And now this.

He squeezed at his forehead. "Maya," he said, "are you telling me straight out now that you didn't kill these two guys?"

Her eyes widened, closed down, widened again, and to his astonishment, she broke into a genuine, if short-lived laugh. "Of course not." Leaving it as ambiguous as ever. Of course not, she was not telling him such a thing straight out. Or, alternatively, of course not, she hadn't killed Dylan and Levon. After which she added in all seriousness, "How could you even say such a thing?"

Hardy left the jail shaken and confused. When he'd gone in to visit Maya, a February ball of pale egg yolk in the western sky was still dripping its feeble light onto the city. When he came out, his head still pounding, it was full night, and that added to his disorientation. The neighborhood around the Hall of Justice felt more than ordinarily bereft of humanity, but the emptiness seemed to go deeper.

A cold, hard wind was kicking up a heavy, dirty dust along with fast food wrappers from the gutters. Hardy had a walk of a few blocks ahead of him to get to where he'd parked his car, but when he got to Bechetti's, the traditional comfort-food Italian place at Sixth and Brannan, he stopped long enough to consider going inside and having himself a stiff cocktail or two—although he knew it was a bad idea when you were in the first days of a murder trial.

Reason won out.

But he hung a left and walked a hundred yards down the street and knocked at a purple door set in the side of a gray stucco ware-house and waited about ten seconds in front of the peephole until the door opened and then he was looking at Wyatt Hunt.

"Trick or treat," he said.

Hunt didn't miss a beat. "I hope you like Jelly Bellies. That's all I've got left." He opened the door and stepped back. He was wearing black Nike-logo running pants and tennis shoes and a tank-top War-riors shirt and there was a shine to his skin as though he'd been working out. He certainly lived in the right place for it.

He'd converted an ancient decrepit flower warehouse into a one-of-a-kind environment. The ceiling was probably twenty feet high. The back third he'd dry-walled off into his living quarters—bedroom, bathroom, den/library, and kitchen. Which left an enor-mous open area, perhaps sixty by eighty or ninety feet, in front. Hardy had been here a few times before but every time was surprised by the fact that Hunt parked his Mini Cooper inside his domicile, just this side of the industrial slide-up garage-door entrance in the same wall as the front door. The other unique feature was the actual half-basketball-court floorboard Hunt had bought from the Warriors the last time they'd upgraded, for the fire sale price of four thousand dollars.

In the space between the court and his rooms on the other side of the court, he had several guitars, both acoustic and electric, out on stands. Amps, speakers, his stereo system. There was also a desk against the wall with a couple of computer terminals glowing with beach-themed screen savers.

But Hardy hadn't gotten too far inside before Hunt called out, "You might as well come out now. I think the jig's up," and Gina Roake—barefoot, wet hair, running shorts, blue Cal sweatshirt—appeared from the back rooms, holding up a hand in greeting, a sheepish smile on her face. "Yo," she said.

"Yo yourself," Hardy replied. "I didn't mean to interrupt. If this isn't a good time . . ."

"Half hour ago," Gina said, no shilly-shallying around, "wouldn't have been a good time. Now the timing's fine."

"You can still have those Jelly Bellies if you want," Hunt said, "but I think I'm good for a beer if you'd rather go in that direction."

"If you're going to twist my arm," Hardy said.

"I'm starting to think she might actually be crazy." Hardy, with his beer, was sitting on one of the tan stressed-leather easy chairs in the den—lots of books and magazines, CDs and DVDs, on built-in white shelves and a large TV. "Now she wants us to go after the killer."

"Us?" Hunt asked. "With our huge investigating team and unlimited resources?"

"That's kind of what I told her," Hardy said.

Gina, next to Hunt, said, "I thought she was factually guilty."

"Didn't she tell you she did it?" Hunt asked. "I thought I'd heard that."

"Not in so many words, but she never really denied it, and then she's been acting all along like if she's convicted, she deserves it. Not exactly an overt confession, but . . ." Hardy sipped from his bottle. "Anyway, so today she tells me she wasn't with Levon and Dylan on the robbery either. Though maybe it was another one."

"Another robbery?" Gina asked. "A different one?"

"Again ambiguous, but apparently."

"Well, then," Gina asked, "what would they have been blackmailing her about?"

"I asked her that. She said God was testing her."

That struck Hunt funny. "Not just her," he said.

Hardy nodded. "Tell me about it. So then she tells me she can't believe I think she did this stuff. I mean, here we are almost a half year into this, and suddenly not only don't we have what she's being blackmailed about anymore, or what we thought it was, but now she wants us to find who really did these guys."

"She's trying to play you," Gina said.

"That's what I thought too. Maybe still think. I don't know. But what's in it for her if she plays me? What? She proves I'm gullible? So what? How's it help her?"

Hunt cleared his throat. "This may be the obvious answer, and I'm not a lawyer of course and maybe don't see the nuances like you two do, but if he or she does exist, and you find whoever it is, doesn't that get her off?"

Hardy was sitting forward with his elbows on his knees, and his shoulders sagged. "In other words," he said, "what if she's not playing me?"

Hunt shrugged. "It's a thought."

"Okay," Gina said. "But why'd this just come up?"

"Didn't you tell me Diz brought it up today at trial? The other dude. Maybe it's the first time she actually thought about that option as something we could do."

"Yeah, but here's the thing, Wyatt," Hardy said. "You know this whole evidence problem we're dealing with anyway? Same holds true if there's another suspect, even a guilty one, hanging out in the bushes. The thing I hate about this, because it's true, is that Maya's got not one, but two, great motives. She was at both places. And,

I don't know, if any of us were being blackmailed for ten years, we might have gotten pretty tired of it ourselves."

"Definitely," Gina said, "I would've cleaned their clocks a long time ago. And I wouldn't have left any evidence either."

"That's my girl." Hunt punched her gently on the leg. "Remind me to destroy those secret videos of us I've been taking." Then, to Hardy, "So what are you going to do?"

"I don't know. If she's telling me now, point blank, she didn't do it, I'm still not sure if I need that to get her off. I just cannot see this evidence convicting her, not in this city."

"Well"—Gina was going to add her two cents—"all other things being equal, Diz, I'd normally agree with you. But you've got the Kathy and Harlen connection . . ."

"There's no evidence about them, either, and that's—"

"Wishful thinking," Gina said. "That is wishful thinking."

"What is?"

"That you're obviously thinking some evidence standard is going to apply, either to Maya in the trial or to Harlen and Kathy and Maya's husband on all the forfeiture stuff. But, as you so eloquently noted in your opening today, this is not about evidence. And I'm not just talking the trial, I'm talking the whole megillah. Stier makes the case, even subversively, that the *reason* there's no evidence is because Maya's got friends in high places who have all the means and power to get rid of evidence, and guess what? She goes down. And them sitting there, the mayor, Harlen—nice show of confidence and all—but it's not helping your client. And it sure as hell isn't impressing Braun, who undoubtedly and maybe truthfully sees it as intimidation."

"I love it when she gets all riled up," Hunt said.

But Hardy wasn't in the mood to laugh about it. "So your point is?"

"My point," Gina said, "is if you've got any chance at all of finding at least a living, breathing human being to introduce as the famous other dude, I'd pull out all the stops trying to find him."

"With no evidence?" Hardy asked. "I wouldn't even know where to start."

"Well, on that," Hunt said, "I might have an idea."

24

"There's nothing to be worried about," Wayne Ticknor told his daughter Jansey.

With her bitten-to-the-quick index fingernail she picked at a little dried blob of ketchup on her kitchen table. The digital clock on the stove read 10:17. "That's easy for you to say, Daddy. You're not going to be testifying."

"True. But they've already told you everything they were going to be asking you about, haven't they? Coached you, even."

"I know. But what if they don't just stick to that?"

"Why wouldn't they?"

"Maybe they want to get me on the weed too. I mean, they mentioned that enough. Wasn't I living off the proceeds? Wasn't I helping with the business?"

"I thought they guaranteed they wouldn't. Wasn't that part of the deal?"

"Well, it wasn't actually a real deal. More like I was just made to understand that if I could help them, they'd help me."

"By keeping you out of the dope side of it?"

"I guess. Yeah. I can't really deny that I knew about it." She pouted and blew out a breath. "Or the defense guy? What if once I'm up there he starts getting into stuff about me and Robert? I mean, if people know about that, it's going to look like we got together pretty soon after Dylan. And then, if they find out it was before too . . ."

"How would anybody find that out?" her father asked.

"I don't know."

"And even if they did, then what?"

"Then they might start putting it together that Dylan was hitting me. So here's a guy who's hitting me that I'm also cheating on. You see what I'm saying? It wouldn't look good."

"Yeah, but, honey, listen. They knew that already and they didn't charge you or Robert with anything, did they? They charged Maya Townshend. They got her gun."

"Okay, but everybody knows Dylan just took that from the shop."

"I don't think the cops do know that, hon. And I don't think I'd volunteer it."

"Don't worry. I'm not going to volunteer anything." Suddenly, running on nerves, she stood up, went over to the sink, wet a sponge, and brought it back to wipe and scour the table—the dried ketchup, a few days' worth of coffee-mug stains, some petrified oatmeal. "It just worries me," she said. "That's all."

"Well, it's natural to be worried."

She stood there squeezing the sponge. "I just don't want them to see how good a thing it was, really, Dylan being killed. I know you shouldn't say that about the dead, but . . ."

Wayne's eyes went black. "You can say anything you want about him to me. You know that. He couldn't have been gone soon enough." Then, with an outward calm, he went on. "They will never in a million years think that you had anything to do with it. Plus, you've got Robert and you saying you were both here the whole morning. You're not a suspect to anybody, hon. And you couldn't ever be. So just answer the questions you know the answers to and leave the rest of it alone. How's that sound?"

She lowered herself onto her chair, letting out a breath. "It sounds like a plan, Daddy. I'll just try to keep remembering that."

"You do that," Wayne said, reaching out and putting a hand over hers on the table. "Now, how are you fixed for money lately?"

She gave him a weak smile. "Okay. I've been talking to the insurance guy. I got the feeling they were waiting for Maya to get convicted. When that happens, they won't have any excuse left not to pay me. So we ought to get the check soon after that."

"After they convict her? Just to rule you out? He didn't say that."

"Kind of. Not that anybody thinks . . ." She let the phrase hang in the room. "He just says if they've got the choice, having somebody else convicted makes it cleaner."

"You'd think somebody else getting arrested would be enough."

She shrugged. "Maybe not, though." She pulled her hand out from under his and sat back in her chair, gripping the sponge in the other hand as though it were a tension ball. "I'd bet a lot from what he's told me that no matter what, they're going to wait until she's convicted. On the chance that she might not be convicted, and then it would still be possible that it was me."

"It was you who what?"

"You know. Killed Dylan."

"I can't believe he would actually say that."

"Not exactly, no. But it's what it feels like to me."

Her father's face closed down. He sat square to the table, fists clenched, glowering. "You got the insurance guy's name? Maybe I'll go and have a talk with him."

But Jansey shook her head. Her father had had a "talk" with Dylan and it hadn't helped at all. "You don't have to do that. I don't think it's him personally. It's like the company policy, that's all."

"You might be surprised," Wayne said. "They tell you it's company policy and then you find out they're just trying to get a bonus or brownie points or whatever by denying benefits until the last possible moment and even then some."

"Well, Daddy, I don't think this is like that. He seems like a nice man."

"Everybody thought your Dylan was a nice man too."

She shook her head. "It's not the same."

"Well, no, nothing's the same, really. But I bet I could talk your insurance company nice man into rethinking his position, or his company policy, or whatever it is."

"I don't think . . . I mean, I appreciate you trying to help me, but I don't think I need it yet with the insurance."

Wayne took a few breaths, relaxed his fists, and laid his palms flat on the table. "You didn't think you needed it with Dylan either."

"Well, as you say, that was different."

"Maybe not so different, though. Somebody taking advantage of your good nature, thinking they can get away with anything. But I look at you, I see the hurt in your eyes, the hurt in your life . . ."

"It's not all hurt. There's good things too. Ben, and now Robert—"

"But no promises from Robert, yet, either."

She shook her head. "Let's not go there again, Daddy. It's a little soon for promises. He's still in med school. And he doesn't treat me at all like Dylan did—"

"He'd better not."

"He doesn't, and for now that's enough, okay? Please."

Wayne reached out and again covered his daughter's hand with his own. His voice, rather suddenly, was husky with emotion. "I just see what you've been through already. And now here's another guy who's essentially living with you and no talk of marriage or responsibility. I don't get it. I don't understand why you let yourself get in these situations."

"This one isn't bad. I promise." And repeated, "I promise, Daddy."

He let out a lungful of air. "All right, if you really think that. And you're okay with money? You're sure?"

She nodded. "Dylan left a lot of cash. I'm using that."

"Drug money."

"Probably."

"You know, if you're spending that to live on and you've got no claimed income, the IRS might ask you how you're doing that. Maybe you should start thinking about a way to claim it."

"I'm sure. Come on, don't worry. I'm not spending that much. It's not like I'm out blowing wads of dollars living high on the hog. All I do is buy groceries and stuff. And the IRS isn't going to care about somebody like me. I mean, we're talking probably less than ten thousand dollars."

This was untrue, and said to palliate her father. In fact, Dylan had put away close to two hundred thousand dollars and they kept it—literally—in a secret place under a couple of loose boards in the crawl space under the house. She checked to make sure it was still there every single night, and several times every day. And no one, not even Robert, knew of the money's existence. But one thing she'd told her father was true—she wasn't worried about cash.

"You've got that much lying around the house? Do you know how dangerous that could be?"

This finally brought a warm smile. "Daddy," she cooed at him, "you ought to be a shrink." She lifted her father's hand and brought it up to her lips. "When you got over here, I was the one all worried about everything. Now it's all you. So now I'll tell you. You don't have to worry. Not about Robert, or the insurance guy, or money or the IRS. Everything's going to be fine. I promise. I really promise."

Craig Chiurco pulled himself up so that his bare back leaned against the headboard of his queen-sized bed. "Maybe I should just find another line of work."

Tamara, pulling a green silk bathrobe around her as she came out of the bathroom, stopped in her tracks. "Let's see. Man makes love to his incredibly beautiful and sexually exotic girlfriend, rolls over, and, lost in the afterglow, says he wants to change jobs. The girlfriend is a) bemused, b) confused, or c) flattered? Hint, it's not 'c.' "

"I didn't mean it had anything to do with us."

"Though, as you might have noticed, we work out of the same office, and quitting your job would be more or less leaving me."

"It's not you."

She made a show of turning around, checking the corners of the room. "Is there someone else here I'm missing that you were talking to?"

"No."

"Good. Okay, that's settled. So why do you want to change jobs?"

"I was just thinking about this Townshend thing. So far, I've embarrassed Hardy and Wyatt by showing up on Vogler's list, and my total contribution to Maya's case has been to confirm the worst piece of evidence connecting her to Levon's murder. It was tons of fun telling the boss, 'Yep, that's her. She's the one I saw there.' Maybe I'll become a vet. No, wait, I hate animals."

"If your girlfriend thought you really hated animals, she would start seeing other men."

"You wouldn't."

"Would too." Tamara sat down on the bed. "But this trial isn't over yet. Maybe you could do something good."

"I'll take any ideas."

"Well, for starters, they don't have her going inside Levon's, do they? And without that, what do they really have?"

"They have her lying, again, to the cops. They get her established enough as a liar, and it seems like they ought to be able to do that easily, then whatever she says on the stand comes across as untrue. And of course it also leaves the question: Why was she there anyway, at Levon's, in the middle of the day?"

"He called her."

"And she just came running? Why?"

"I don't know. Maybe some variation of the blackmail again." Tamara went into a small pout. "So then when you saw her, it must have been right after she killed him?"

"That's what I've been assuming. And I think everybody else."

"So how did she seem? Upset? In a hurry to get away? Any of that?"

Chiurco shook his head. "It wasn't like that, Tam. It wasn't like she posed for me. She was there at the door, turned around, and we were face to face for about a second, enough for me to notice her, but not much more. Then she was gone."

"And you were sure it was her?"

"It *was* her, Tam. She admitted it, remember? And they got her fingerprints on the doorknob. I don't know what you're getting at."

"I'm just trying to get you something to make you feel better." Now with a little heat, "So maybe you could feel like you contributed to casting doubt on what happened. Like if you saw her trying the knob or something, maybe trying to get in, and she couldn't, just before she turned and then you saw her as she was leaving."

"I don't think I'm going to change my story now. I saw what I saw. You want me to commit perjury under oath? I don't think Hardy would want me helping that way."

"No. It's just that you happening upon her just at the one second . . . anybody would believe if you just got there a minute ear-lier and watched her trying to get in. I mean, Mr. Hardy could ask you that anyway."

Chiurco wasn't warming to this idea at all. His mouth had hard-ened down to a thin line. "And then I'd just say no."

"Hey, don't get mad at me," she said. "You're the one who started with how bad you felt about not being able to help her. I'm just say-ing maybe Mr. Hardy could make it seem as if you'd seen her not getting in. Then they don't have that assumption anymore. You didn't see her coming out exactly, did you? I mean, she was just there at the door?"

Suddenly, Chiurco slapped a palm down on the bed between them. "Hey! What's this interrogation? What are you trying to get at here?"

"Craig! Nothing! I'm not trying to get at anything. I'm just talking to you. What's your problem? What are you so uptight about?"

After fighting his emotions for a second he gathered himself and let out a sigh. "Maybe I'm uptight because I'm nervous enough about this to begin with. I'm not going to go changing my story, even a little, even if it might help her. That just gets me in trouble. With Wyatt, with Hardy, with everybody. I don't see how you want me to do that. It's tricky enough as it is."

"What's tricky?"

"Saying what you saw. Keeping it simple. It's not as easy as it seems, especially when everybody's all over you with these little details you never thought about. I got my story and I'm sticking to it."

"The way you say it like that, it sounds like you made it up."

"*I'm not making anything up!* Jesus, Tam, I can't believe you're saying this to me."

"Well, I can't believe you're so touchy about it. It's not that big a deal. We're just talking."

"No, we're not just talking." Now he sat up straight, off the headboard, pulling the blankets up around him. "And it's way that big a deal! You don't see that?"

"Not as big as you're making it." She stood up and walked across to the chair where she'd put her clothes. She slipped out of the robe and started to grab her underwear.

"What are you doing?" Chiurco asked.

"I'm going home. I think we're done for tonight."

"Fine."

"Fine." She had her jeans on, pulled her sweater over her head. "And while we're at it, disagreeing about this and other stuff, I thought we'd decided we weren't going to be smoking weed anymore."

Now Chiurco crossed his arms, shaking his head back and forth, and went silent, rage and frustration smeared across his features.

"In case," Tamara went on, "you think I didn't notice or smell it or anything."

"I wasn't trying to hide it."

"No? A quick toke in the bathroom with the window open? That's not exactly lighting up in front of me."

"I thought you'd be mad."

"Correct, Craig. Mad at you for using it, and mad that you can't stop."

"I don't want to stop, Tam. I've told you. I like it, is the problem. And I could stop anytime I want. Which maybe I don't."

"Maybe I'll believe you when I see it start even a little. And meanwhile, this paranoia problem, don't kid yourself. That's the weed too."

"Now I've got a paranoia problem."

"Your testimony issues? We just had a fight about them? Hello?"

"You're wrong. You're just plain wrong."

"I really don't think so." She crossed over to the door. "I really don't, Craig. And in the meanwhile, I'm just plain gone."

In the living room of his Marina mansion Harlen Fisk hit the remote switch and turned off the television right after the nightly news. He and Kathy had in fact made quite a splash by showing up today in the courtroom, and the networks had played it up in a gratifying way. The city wasn't coming close yet to an election cycle, so in spite of the negative connotations being slung around about his connection to

Joel's development deals and his sister's coffee shop, the general rule of thumb was that the more your name appeared in the media, the better your chances to get elected.

And getting elected was what Harlen was all about.

Still, he couldn't help but be disappointed in his sister. As a matter of fact, *disappointed* was hardly the word.

Well, he told himself, I'm not going to think about Maya now— what her future might be like if in fact she got convicted and sent to jail. That wasn't his fault; it was her doing. Her clueless, stubborn nature.

If she had only kept her mouth shut. That had been Harlen's intent in putting her in touch with Hardy in the first place. A good lawyer should in theory have kept her from admitting anything that put her near any of the murders. But by the time she'd gotten with Hardy, she'd already told the police that she'd been out at church that morning, and somehow the fear that she'd be caught in that lie had led her to compound the injury by confessing to both the lie and her whereabouts near the time of the murder.

Which put her in their sights.

Stop. Don't keep worrying this to death, he told himself. Get up. Go to bed.

But his body didn't respond. He sat there with the reading lamp on next to him, his hands crossed over his comfortable-looking stomach, which tonight felt suddenly knotted with tension.

"Babe?" His wife, Jeannette, looking in. "Are you all right? Are you coming to bed?"

"In a minute."

"What are you thinking about?"

"This trial. Maya. The whole thing."

She came into the room, pulled up an ottoman, and sat on it. She was tall, solidly built, athletic, with shoulder-length blond hair encircling a wholesome, all-American face. "I'll talk about it if you want."

He smiled at her. "I would have thought you'd have been sick of it by now."

"I might be sick of it, but I'm not too tired to talk about it if you want to."

He paused a moment. "I just marvel that she can be so dumb. Sticking with the story that she didn't know much about the weed. I mean, come on, I knew about it, everybody knew about it."

Her forehead creased in a look of concern. "I don't think I knew that. You knew Dylan? How well did you know him?"

He waved that away. "I met him first when he was her boyfriend for a while when they were in college. Then again when Maya hired him, just after he got out of jail. I told her it was a mistake. And of course, she listened to me as much as she always does, which is not at all."

"Harlen, come on. She listens to you."

"Maybe listens, but doesn't hear. I told her this dope stuff could be a problem a couple of years ago, told her to fire him. No chance."

"Why not?"

"She was saving him, I think. This messianic complex she's got. She's got everything and she's so lucky and so she's got to help losers to balance the scales or something. Not realizing, of course, about the people who are covering for her."

"You mean you?"

"Let me just ask you," he said. "Who's got her kids right now?"

"I don't mind that. They're good kids."

"No argument. But they're not ours, are they? And you and me, we didn't sign on for the little darlings, did we?" Sighing, he went on. "She shouldn't even be in this at all. I told her not to go down there. Six in the morning? I mean, what kind of hour for a meeting is that? And why do these things with her become my problems?"

"I didn't know you'd talked to her. When was that?"

Again, he waved off her question. "The night before. She called and asked me what I'd do. I told her to call him back and find out what was so important, but again, naturally . . ." He turned a palm over, meaning she'd ignored his suggestion. He let out a long breath, his head shaking from side to side. "And then there's this Levon thing too."

"The other victim?"

He nodded. "Levon Preslee. Actually not a bad guy."

"You knew him too?"

He faked a short-lived smile. "Hey, I'm a politician. I know everybody."

"So what is this Levon thing?"

"He gets out of jail, he comes to my sweet little sister to help him out, since she helped Dylan when he got out. And if you haven't guessed yet, these guys—Levon and Dylan—still talk to each other. So I know people, right? It's what I do. So way back then I put him in with Jon Francona over at ACT, and it worked out pretty good until . . . well, until last fall."

"Okay."

"Okay. So, well, the point is, why I might be thinking about this stuff right now, and getting a little edgy about it, is Jon Francona died two years ago, so nobody in the world, besides my sister and you, has got or knows of any connection between me and Levon Preslee, and I'm just a little wee bit concerned that along with this forfeiture stuff we're all wrestling with, somebody's going to pull that up and wave it in my face too. And don't get me wrong, I love the publicity and all, but I think that might actually do me some harm."

"Well"—Jeannette reached out and put her hands on her husband's knees—"nobody's going to fault you for helping the poor man out all those years ago."

"Nobody's going to know, Jeannette. Nobody can entertain the thought even for a minute that I knew this guy from Adam." He let out a last deep sigh. "I mean, I keep telling myself Maya put herself in this position. I've got no choice. I've got to let her get herself out of it. I can't cover for her anymore, or else everything we've got is at risk."

"Come on, hon. I think that must be a bit of an exaggeration."

Harlen chewed at the inside of his cheek and pushed himself up out of his recliner. "Not really," he said. "Not too much."

25

Paul Stier's first witness the next morning was San Francisco's ancient medical examiner, Dr. John Strout. The good doctor had been a fixture in and around the Hall of Justice for over forty years and had appeared in court at least a thousand times, maybe more. Tall, with wispy white hair and positively gaunt instead of merely thin, he'd somehow evaded the mandatory retirement he should have taken the better part of a decade ago. But no one was pushing for it, because he remained highly and universally respected. His voice and manner retained a casual authority and easy affability that his Southern drawl only accented.

Now he sat back, comfortable, and waited while Stier positioned the poster board with the mounted autopsy photographs on the tripod next to the witness box, where both Strout and the jury could see. In many trials Strout's testimony, which concerned itself with the cause and basic fact of a victim's death, might have a huge impact on the verdict. The patterns of bruises on the deceased's body could be highly significant. The shape of an injury could identify or eliminate an object as a possible murder weapon. Other, more subtle distinctions— blood alcohol levels, scans for various drugs or poisons—could be spun in myriad ways to cast doubt or lay blame.

But today, no one expected much in the way of fireworks from Strout's testimony. In fact, after the previous day's nearly unrelenting drama, the courtroom—sans mayor and supervisor—had nowhere near the buzz Hardy had expected. And this was a relief. After his conversation with Gina and Wyatt last night, he'd come to accept their mutual view that maybe Kathy and Harlen's presence wasn't doing his client as much good as they'd hoped.

So Strout's testimony was going to establish conclusively that there were in fact two dead people, killed at the hands of another. Nevertheless, you never knew exactly what was going to come up in live testimony, and Hardy was paying close attention as Stier took the small pile of photos from the last juror to have viewed them, placed them with the other marked exhibits, and walked to the center of the room.

"Dr. Strout," he said. "To begin with Dylan Vogler, the gunshot victim. Were you able to determine the time of death?"

"No." He looked over to the jury box, speaking to them in an avuncular tone. "When the medical technicians arrived, he was warm to the touch. That suggests, for example, that he hadn't been in the alley overnight, but I can't say more than that."

"What killed Mr. Vogler?"

"A gunshot wound to the chest."

"Please describe the injury."

Strout did so—the entrance, the exit, the track through the body—and Stier took it from there. "How quickly would an injury like this be likely to incapacitate the victim?"

"The bullet went in his chest and then right through his heart. Most people would collapse immediately from the injury and die shortly thereafter."

"Doctor, would you tell the jury what defense wounds are?"

"Defense wounds are injuries typically sustained when the deceased tries to ward off blows or an attack. Injuries to the hands, for example, or forearms, usually. Sometimes to the legs."

"Did you find any defense wounds on Mr. Vogler?"

"No."

"Any abrasions, scrapes, cuts, or bruises to suggest he had been in a fight or struggle?"

"No. I can't say there were."

"In fact, did Mr. Vogler have any sign of injury of any kind except the gunshot wound that killed him?"

"No." In other words, Hardy thought, Vogler either knew his attacker or was shot without any warning, or both. But Strout had one last word. "It was a pretty efficient killing."

Hardy could have objected to this gratuitous comment—it wasn't in answer to one of Stier's questions—but it wouldn't have accomplished anything, and he decided to let the prosecutor go on.

"Dr. Strout, moving on to the other victim, then, Levon Preslee. Again, can you tell the jury about the cause of death of this victim?"

"Surely. The victim died from injuries sustained by blows to the top of the head from some sort of a bladed object that cracked his skull, causing massive brain trauma and hemorrhage."

"And were you able to determine, Doctor, what time it was when death occurred?"

"No."

Hardy knew that this was a made-for-television question. The public had become so inundated with the pseudoscience of prime-time TV that they expected all sorts of forensic miracles. Stier simply wanted to dispel the popular notion that you could tell when someone was killed and that therefore the prosecution had been negligent in not presenting that evidence.

But Strout amplified anyway. "The body had achieved ambient temperature."

"And again, same question as with Mr. Vogler, Doctor. Were there any signs of defense wounds on Mr. Preslee's body?"

"No."

"And how quickly did this injury kill Mr. Preslee?"

"Just about immediately. He would have been stunned and probably rendered unconscious by the force of the first blow and died soon after. Maybe not as immediate as the bullet through the heart, but pretty quick. Within a minute outside."

Stier checked the jury to make sure they understood the violent, gruesome, bloody nature of this attack, which, if it had been perpetrated by Maya, painted her as a monster. But he wasn't quite finished yet. "A couple of clarifications, Doctor. You said blows. How many times was the victim hit?"

"Twice. Although either one would have been plenty."

Hardy saw the effect this small sentence had on the jury, as a couple of the members actually flinched, imagining the moment.

"And again," Stier went on, "you said the blows were struck by a bladed object. Can you explain what you mean by that?"

Over the next ten minutes Stier and Strout nailed down all the details of the attack on Levon Preslee—the damage done and use of the dull edge of the cleaver, the attack from directly behind the unsuspecting and probably stoned victim. No surprise, Preslee's blood tested positive for THC, the active ingredient in marijuana. Overall, Hardy thought, the effect of the testimony painted a coherent scenario of two apparent friends sharing a doob and then one of them going behind the other and launching a premeditated, grisly, and murderous attack.

That is in fact what had happened, and Hardy couldn't think of a spin in the world that would do any good for his client. He also knew that there was no way he could control Strout, or stop him from delivering those little asides that had such a visceral impact on the jury. So he passed the witness.

Glitsky sat on the corner of Bracco's desk in the large room that the homicide detail worked out of. Darrel himself was in his normal chair at his desk, while his partner, Debra Schiff, was three flights downstairs delivering her testimony in the trial of Maya Townshend.

"It'll bite you," Glitsky said.

"I don't care. I'm doing it."

"I don't see what it'll get you."

"Peace of mind. Very important for job satisfaction."

Glitsky sighed. "What's the exact wording you're going with?"

Bracco looked down at the TR-26.5, the department form that cops were supposed to fill out to explain away their parking tickets. Under Alternative Parking Considered but Not Utilized, he read aloud what he'd written: "Leave car on mayor's lawn with siren on and lights flashing. Walk three miles to crime scene."

"They'll flay you."

"Oh, well." Bracco sat back. "No guts, no glory. Maybe they'll realize the absurdity of all of this."

"Sure," Glitsky said. "That'll probably happen. But meanwhile, why are you even here?"

"As opposed to?"

"Downstairs. I thought you guys were testifying on Townshend today."

"Schiff. Stier wanted her first."

"Why?"

"I don't know. DA strategy. Maybe she's a better witness."

"In what way?"

"I don't know, Abe. More passionate, maybe."

The corner of Glitsky's mouth turned up. "With Jerry Glass, you mean?"

"Maybe a little of that." Bracco stood up and stretched, now closer to eye-to-eye with his lieutenant. "She's probably more convincing than I'd be anyway. I don't blame Stier putting her on. I would too."

"And not you?"

"As I said, maybe later. But maybe not at all." He hesitated, then shrugged. "Either way, it doesn't matter. She'll do fine. She's a true believer."

"I hope you're not telling me at this stage, after the trial's started, that you don't believe in the case you guys have built."

"It's not so much that . . ."

"That sounds like it's still some part of it."

Bracco's eyes scanned the large room, over Glitsky's shoulder, around behind them. Nobody else was around. It was safe to talk. "I don't have any real doubt she did it, Abe. Maya, I mean. But from the time Debra went out and talked to Glass . . ." Hesitating, Bracco made a face.

"What?"

"You ever notice there's this mind-set among certain law enforcement people—I mean we've all seen it a hundred times—I just haven't had it run into one of my cases before. Where anybody who has money and knows a criminal, then that person's a criminal too."

"Yeah, I've seen that. In fact, I've thought it. You know why?"

"Because it's true?"

"Maybe more than you'd think, Darrel."

Bracco rolled his shoulders. "But not always, huh?"

"What are you saying?"

"I'm saying what I started with. That Debra's probably a better witness. Hardy might be able to eat me up on cross, whereas he won't touch Debra, who buys everything Jerry Glass is selling. So does Stier."

"And you don't?"

Another pause. Then, in a more quiet register, "I don't want to rat my partner, Abe. She got the collar."

"I thought you both got the collar."

"If you get technical, okay."

"I don't care about technical. Was there something wrong with the arrest?"

"No. I was there. It was righteous enough. I just . . . if it was me, I think I would have waited a little, that's all. Maybe go to a DA and see if he'd fly it for the grand jury. But Debra just got the news about the fingerprint ID on the doorknob and stepped in."

Glitsky had seen this before too. A relatively inexperienced cop would sometimes arrest a suspect before he or she had built a solid case based on the evidence. Occasionally, this was warranted, as when the suspect was a danger to witnesses or an immediate flight risk and had to be detained until someone could check more facts. Or when someone flat out confessed.

But more often, the best case protocol was as Bracco suggested— build the case and present it to the district attorney, who then—if the evidence was compelling—would get a warrant or get it in front of the grand jury. The alternative was that an inspector could simply go and make the arrest. And only then would the DA's office review the case to see if it would be charged.

"So what happened on this one?" Glitsky asked.

"I didn't think it was enough at the time," Darrel said, "and Debra and I had words about it, but what could we do? It was a done deal. And then, hey, of course Maya gets held to answer at the prelim, right? So we got it. It was going to trial. We had other cases. I stopped thinking about it."

"But you've still got questions?"

"Not really questions, no." Bracco shook his head. "And not really about whether Maya's guilty. I mean, who else? And with her motive and connections to both these guys? Just that she knew both of them, they were squeezing her. She's a liar. It just totally works."

"But?"

"But I think we could have built Stier a better case. Now it's all this other stuff with the forfeitures and political heat. So Maya's a rich person who knows criminals, therefore she's a criminal, and if she's a criminal, then she probably did these guys. I just don't want to have to hold all that together on the stand, that's all, when I don't think we've got the evidence to back it up. Debra'll be way better at it."

That same morning in Chinatown the mood was strained at The Hunt Club.

Tamara Dade sat red-eyed at her computer, unspeaking, unsmiling. Wyatt Hunt had stopped by one of the local bakeries on the way in and had brought a bag of hot, fresh-from-the-oven *cha sui bao*, the delicious pork-filled buns that were a rare treat and Tamara's favorite food on earth, and she told him she wasn't hungry.

After twenty minutes back in his office Hunt stood and opened the door back to the reception area. "Tam," he said gently, "have you heard from Craig?"

She half turned to face him. "He called in sick."

"Sick?" This was decidedly unusual. Sickness wasn't really an acceptable part of the culture of Hunt's business. "What's he got? Tam? Hey. Are you okay?"

Clearly, she wasn't. After the merest glance at her boss, and again without a word or a look back, she rose from her chair and walked out the main door. This led both down to Grant Street outside and to the bathroom, and Hunt wasn't at all sure whether she'd be back until he realized she hadn't taken her purse.

So leaving the door between reception and his office open in case she wanted to come in and talk to him, he went back to his desk, picked up his telephone, and punched some numbers.

"Hey, Wes."

"Hey yourself."

"You talk to Diz this morning?"

"No. He's at trial. He's been going straight in."

"I know. But he stopped by my place last night."

"What'd he want?"

"He wants me to put a press on who killed his victims."

This brought a pause. Farrell was the firm's resident adviser on never believing that your client was innocent. This was because the celebrated case that had made his bones in the city's legal community was one involving his best friend, another attorney named Mark Dooher, who'd been charged with murdering his wife. Farrell had gotten him off, cleanly acquitted. That turned out to have been a bad mistake that almost cost Farrell his own life a while later. "You mean Maya Townshend's victims?"

"Diz doesn't think so. Or at least he isn't sure anymore."

"Since when?"

"Since yesterday afternoon when he talked to her."

"Denied it, did she?"

"Ambiguously, at least. Enough to make him think he might be neglecting or ignoring something important."

"He always thinks that. That's why we made him managing partner. Nothing gets through." Hunt heard a breath in the phone. "Anyway, you're calling me about this because . . . ?"

"Because you knew Vogler."

Another hesitation. "If Diz told you that, I'm going to have to have a talk with him."

"It wasn't Diz. I did some Net searching back when I first heard about this list of Vogler's customers."

"How'd you even hear about that?"

"You know Craig, who works here?"

"Sure."

"He's on it too. Told me about it right up-front in case it was a problem for me. I told him it was nothing I couldn't handle, but he'd be smarter if he didn't do anything overtly against the law while he was trying to get his license. Anyway, I got curious after that, found it in a blog somewhere. Nothing's sacred anymore, in case you hadn't heard. Good news for the PI trade; not so much for everybody else."

"Tell me about it. So, okay, I knew Vogler. So did your Craig. Ask him."

"I would, but he's out sick today. I thought I'd start with you."

"I have no idea, Wyatt, what I could tell you. That's the honest truth."

"I believe you, and that makes us about even. I don't know what I want to know. Not exactly, anyway. I just figured the weed side of the equation's been left out, I mean if somebody on that side killed him. So nobody's talked about how that whole thing worked. How often, for example, did you buy from him?"

"About once a month. I hope you realize this makes me damned uncomfortable, Wyatt. I've been trying to put that all behind me as just another dumb mistake. Sam and I almost broke up over it, too, among other things. What does it matter how often I scored with Dylan?"

"Again, Wes, I don't know. I'm trying to get a sense of how much marijuana he moved, or anything else. If he had seventy regular customers, give or take. What did a bag go for?"

"Mine were a hundred."

"So call it ten grand a month?"

"If you say so."

"I've got to think that's serious enough money to get shot over, in spite of everybody seeming to believe it wasn't about the dope. How'd it get delivered?"

Once again, Hunt heard a frustrated exhale. "You asked for the manager's special, whoever was on the register would call Dylan. He'd go in the back, come out with a sealed Ziploc in the bottom of a regular coffee bag, grind some beans in over it, close it up."

"And how long had this been going on?"

"I don't know. I made the connection maybe six years ago, so at least that long. And I don't really believe I was his first customer."

"And you're telling me that in all that time, none of the employees picked up on it?"

"No. I can't imagine they wouldn't have figured it out."

"But according to Diz that's been no part of the police investigation."

"That's hard to believe."

"Yeah, but I bet I know where some of that ten grand went every month. And I know why the guy had such loyal employees."

"You think one of them . . . ?"

"I have no idea, Wes. Just like when I called you. But at least now I've got someplace fresh to start looking."

Tamara stood in the open doorway, her face blotched, her eyes red. "I'm sorry."

Hunt waved off the apology. He'd known his secretary since the time when, as a Child Protective Services worker, he'd been called to the home of the two Dade children, brother and sister, who'd missed several days of school without an excuse. At the time Tamara had been Tammy, a starving twelve-year-old trying to feed and care for her emaciated younger brother, Mickey, and waiting for her mother—a heroin addict who'd died in her bedroom of an overdose—to wake up. Hunt, a former foster child himself, had followed the lives of both of the kids into young adulthood and, when he'd opened his agency, had brought Tamara along full-time, and began using Mickey as a runner and occasional driver.

Now she said to him, "Craig and I had a fight. I think we might have broken up."

"Is that why he's not in here?"

"I'd guess so. There was just the message when I got in, that he was sick. But he wasn't sick last night."

Hunt leaned back in his ergonomic chair, rocked in it once or twice. "You want to talk about it?"

"I don't know." But she came inside his door and let herself down onto one of the chairs in front of him. "It's just so stupid, is all."

"Stupid happens." He gave the silence another beat. "Do you want to go home? I've got some fieldwork I need to do. We can close up."

"No. I can stay." She raised her eyes and met his. "I hate all dope," she said, "you know that?"

Since her mother had died from an overdose, this shouldn't have been so surprising; but Hunt knew or guessed that she and Craig were occasional pot users. "I'm not too wild about it myself, to tell you the truth. Is that what the fight was about? Stop me if I'm prying."

She gave him a weak smile. "You've earned pry rights." Crossing her arms, she stared into the space between them. "I mean, everybody says a little weed'll never hurt you, you know? It's not addictive, safer than alcohol, blah blah blah. And maybe a little won't, but a lot . . ."

"Craig does a lot?"

"I don't know how much. I don't monitor it. But we told each other we were going to stop. Or at least I thought we told each other that. Maybe we didn't. I don't know. I'm not trying to get him in trouble with you, Wyatt. He doesn't get high when he's working. I know he doesn't do that." She shook her head. "I just wish he could stop."

"He can't?"

"Oh, he says he can. Anytime he wants. He just doesn't want to." From the shine in them, her eyes were on the verge of tears. "It just reminds me so much of what my mom used to say. How she used to act. And I kept telling myself that *that* was different, she was actually truly addicted to heroin, not the same thing as weed at all. But now, I don't know, somehow it seems a lot more similar than not. But I just don't think I want any of it in my life anymore, and I try to say that to Craig, and he's all . . . he just doesn't think that way."

"Even if it means losing you?"

Now a pair of tears broke and rolled down her cheeks. "I don't want to think that, Wyatt, but that's what it seems like is happening. I never meant to make it either me or weed, you can't have both, but I think it's come pretty close to that."

Hunt rubbed a finger against the grain of his desk. "I'll tell you one thing, if he picks the weed over you, he's a bona fide moron."

"But I think he might," Tamara said. "I really think he might."

26

Debra Schiff had given her direct testimony to Paul Stier and now was well into her second hour on the stand. She thought she was holding her own pretty well in the first twenty minutes of cross-examination by Dismas Hardy, most of it dedicated so far to the murder of Dylan Vogler. He might have thought he'd scored some points off her on the gun issue, but she'd stuck to *her* guns, reiterating how Maya had lied to them initially about whether she'd even been in the alley that morning. Beyond that they had Defendant's registration of the gun in her name, and her fingerprints, for God's sake, on the magazine.

What more could the jury want?

In Schiff's mind there was no question of what had happened on that Saturday morning, and she knew that she was conveying it to the jury effectively in spite of Hardy's best efforts. Now he turned and walked back to his counsel table. He turned a yellow legal pad around and appeared to read from it for a moment—although Schiff knew, since both Jerry Glass and Paul Stier had told her, that much of this extraneous physical activity was choreographed so that attorney and witness didn't just transmogrify into talking heads to the jury.

Hardy walked back to the middle of the courtroom, eight feet or so in front of her. "Inspector Schiff," he began again, "I'd like to ask you a couple of questions about the Levon Preslee murder scene. We've seen the pictures. There was a great deal of blood, was there not?"

"I'd call it more a moderate amount, but there was blood, yes."

"A moderate amount, then. But certainly puddles of it both on the table and also on the floor between the table and the kitchen sink, yes?"

"Yes."

"So the blood dripped from the table down to the floor, did it not?"

"That's what it looked like, yes."

"But no blood was found on the cleaver, which Dr. Strout has identified from the deceased's injuries as consistent with the murder weapon. Is that true?"

"Yes. No blood was found on the weapon. It had been washed."

"And how do you know that?"

Schiff, for the first time, showed a brush of annoyance—a small pursing of her lips—gone almost as soon as it appeared. "Well," she said, now directly at Hardy and not to the jury, "it appeared damp at the scene, as if it had been washed, and there were traces of the decedent's blood in the disposal under the sink and in the pipes underneath. And the cleaver was next to the sink in a drying rack."

"So presumably, someone had washed the murder weapon in the sink, is that right?"

"That was our assumption, yes." Schiff cast a passing glance over at Stier, hoping that he might object. She was a little uncomfortable talking about what the crime scene meant, since that was really the provenance of the CSI team. But her ally the prosecutor just offered her a faint smile and sat with his hands crossed on his table.

"All right," Hardy said. "That was your assumption. That the cleaver was the murder weapon, is that true?"

"Yes."

"All right. Accepting that hypothesis for the moment, were there any other clues that indicated to you, a trained investigator, how the murder had actually taken place?"

"I'm not sure what you mean. The deceased was hit from behind with the cleaver."

"Yes, but just before that. The deceased was seated at the table when he was struck, granted. But was there not a water ring on the table?"

"Oh, that. Yes."

"And what did you assume from that?"

"That Defendant was sitting—"

"Excuse me." Hardy, playing with her rhythm, interrupted and looked up at the judge expectantly. "Your Honor, move to strike that last phrase."

"Granted." Braun frowned down at Schiff, who was all of a sudden aware that Hardy had tricked her—she really should have known better. He'd lulled her with these mundane questions and caught her off guard. She would have to be more careful or risk losing her credibility. "Sergeant," the judge intoned at her most sanctimonious, "the jury will decide whether this defendant or someone else entirely was sitting with Mr. Preslee. Just stick to what you observed."

Hardy was graciousness itself. A quick, warm smile, a barely perceptible nod. "Thank you, Your Honor. Now, Sergeant, again . . ."

She wanted to punch him.

"We were talking about a water ring on the table, Sergeant, and your theory of the murder."

Schiff tossed another look at Stier, who'd developed a frown, and then at the jury. "It appeared that the assailant, Mr. Preslee's murderer, had been sitting across the table from him, perhaps just talking, having a glass of water, and possibly smoking marijuana. At some point the assailant got up—maybe on the pretext of refilling the glass—got behind Mr. Preslee, grabbed the cleaver, and hit him."

Hardy stood relaxed in front of her. "Very succinct, Sergeant, and I believe supported by the evidence."

Herself confused by Hardy's comment, Schiff could only manage a small nod. "Thank you," she murmured, and realized that this interrogation had somehow gotten away from her.

Hardy was moving ahead. "Sergeant, what was the approximate distance between where the deceased was hit and the kitchen sink right behind it?"

He was off on another apparent tangent. Schiff didn't see the point of any of these questions, and yet Stier was allowing them. *Why wasn't he objecting to something?* Her sense of dread increased, and she felt a drop of perspiration fall out of her hairline. She brushed it away and tried to narrow her focus. Just relax and stay with the facts, she told herself. And then, aloud, "Not far. Maybe eighteen inches."

"And did the blood on the floor cover any of this eighteen-inch area?"

"You can see from the pictures—"

"Yes, but I'm asking you to calibrate it for us."

"About half of it."

"So, according to your theory of the case, the assailant killed Mr. Preslee, then stood behind him cleaning up the murder weapon in the sink?"

"Yes."

"And the glass?"

"Yes."

"While blood dripped off the table just behind?"

"Yes."

"Did you find any shoeprints in the blood itself?"

"No."

"Or tracks or any traces of blood except directly at the scene?"

"No."

"So according to your theory, Sergeant, the assailant stood directly behind the deceased, with blood dripping onto the floor from the table, into an area only eighteen inches wide. And stood there long enough to wash both the cleaver and the glass. Is that correct?"

"Yes."

Her eyes flitted between the jury box and Stier. *I've got no idea where he's going with this.* The thought unnerved her.

"Sergeant, did you and your partner obtain a warrant to search the Townshends' house?"

"Yes, we did."

Hardy, in no hurry, took another walk back to his table, picked up a piece of paper, then turned again and walked all the way back to her, handing her the exhibit. "Sergeant, do you recognize this?"

"Yes, of course. It's the search warrant we served on Defendant the day after Levon Preslee's murder."

"Wasn't it first thing in the morning, just at seven o'clock, that you served this warrant?"

"Yes."

"Would you please read for the jury, Sergeant, from the affidavit section, what you were searching for with this warrant?"

Schiff looked down at the paper and, suddenly aware of where this must be going, read in a mechanical voice. "Computer disks and downloads, business and banking records, shoes and clothes that might contain blood spatter—"

"Thank you, Sergeant, that's enough. So you were looking for blood spatter, true?"

"Yes."

"And why was that?"

In the witness box Schiff lifted a hand, then cleared her throat. "We thought there might be blood spatter on her clothes and shoes."

"And why is that?"

Schiff drew a breath and made herself sit up straight and face the jury. She would brazen it out. "Because we figured the blood dripping on the floor right behind her would have some spatter, even if microscopic."

"Were you looking for spatter anywhere else?"

"We thought it possible there would be some on material covering the upper body."

"Why did you think that?" Hardy now had Schiff firmly assuming the role she didn't want and wasn't qualified for, that of crime-scene reconstruction expert. But if Stier wasn't objecting, she couldn't very well refuse to answer the question.

"We thought . . . after the first blow . . . the assailant would have to lift the cleaver, which now had blood on it, and swing it hard down again. Some blood might have come off in the swinging or from the second impact."

Now Hardy turned and faced the jury, impassive. Without looking at Schiff he asked, "Sergeant, did you in fact search for blood on the clothes you took from Maya's home early in the morning after the murder of Mr. Preslee?"

"Yes, we did."

"Isn't it true, Sergeant, that you removed all the clothing from the house, including her husband's and children's? And removed for testing the contents of the hampers and laundry room? Everything, in fact, except for what they were wearing?"

"Yes."

"And were there clothes in the washing machine or dryer or anywhere else in the house?"

"No."

"So you got them all?"

"Yes."

She hated this. She knew it was coming across to the jury as some form of police harassment. Even if she didn't have the specific evidence. She knew that it wasn't particularly difficult to be in a room or an apartment, even for a substantial period of time, and leave no physical sign of it, especially if you knew you were going in to commit a crime. She *knew* that Maya had been at Levon's, and if not to kill him, then why? She didn't know what the damned Townshend woman had done with her clothes and her shoes in the time she'd had to get rid of them. And if she hadn't gotten rid of them, Schiff didn't know how she'd avoided the blood spatter. But none of that made any difference to her core belief that this defendant was a crafty and dangerous killer. "We were just trying to be thorough."

"Indeed," Hardy said, "thoroughness is commendable. And you were careful when you seized this clothing to package it appropriately for later testing for blood by the crime lab, were you not?"

"Yes."

"But with all their sophisticated testing, the crime lab found no evidence whatsoever of blood on anything you seized from Maya Townshend's house, did they?"

Stier finally came alive. "Objection. Hearsay."

"Sustained."

"Okay, let me ask it this way, then, Inspector. I want you to assume that lab personnel will testify that they found no blood. That's not consistent with your theory of how this crime was committed, is it?"

Now Stier compounded his error. He should have let Schiff say that maybe the defendant had gotten rid of her clothes, or maybe there just wasn't enough blood to find, but instead he objected. "Speculation, Your Honor. Irrelevant. Inspector Schiff's theories are not evidence."

Hardy couldn't believe his luck. "Well, gosh, Your Honor," he said. "My point exactly. Since the prosecution concedes that Inspector Schiff's theories aren't evidence, and since the prosecution doesn't seem to have anything besides her theories, I have no further questions."

Braun banged her gavel and chastised Hardy for making speeches, but he didn't care.

For the rest of the afternoon Hardy continued to hammer the same point through the other lab witnesses.

"You're a fingerprint expert, right? Did you find fingerprints inside Mr. Preslee's home?"

"Yes. Lots of them."

"Were any of those Maya Townshend's fingerprints?"

"No."

"In fact, there are several fingerprints that belong to people whom you've never identified, isn't that right?"

"Yes."

"Fingerprints at the table where the victim was seated?"

"Yes."

"Fingerprints at the sink where the cleaver was allegedly washed?"

"Yes."

"Fingerprints on the interior door handle of the apartment?"

"Yes."

"And none of these are Maya's, and some of them are unidentified, right?"

"Correct."

Hardy did the same with the DNA—some recovered, some unidentified, none belonging to Maya. When he was finally done with his last cross-examination at quarter to five, Hardy took a long beat and threw a look at Stier, wilting at his own table. The prosecutor had taken a beating today on the Preslee evidence, and he knew it.

But next up, he would be talking about motive. And motive evidence, Hardy knew, was going to be brutal.

27

The apartment door opened and Wyatt Hunt stood looking at his young associate. "What is this bullshit, Craig?"

"What bullshit?"

" 'What bullshit?' he asks. Calling in sick when you look about as sick as I do, except for a little red around the eyes. Are you stoned?"

"Slightly."

"And what do you hope to accomplish by that?"

"Nothing. I'm not trying to accomplish anything. Except figure out how I'm going to get back with Tam."

"You think better when you're loaded?"

"I don't know. Probably not."

"And yet here you are."

"I just thought I'd take a day off and think about things."

"This is thinking about things?"

"No. I felt bad about Tam and was trying to cheer myself up about it."

"Yeah, you're just the picture of good cheer."

"What do you want me to say?"

"There's nothing you can say, Craig. You know the rules. You want a day off, call in and ask for a day off. If I'm not mistaken, you've done that before and it's never been a problem. But you don't call in sick when you're not sick."

"I'm sorry."

"Yeah, well . . ." Hunt hated this, hated Craig at this moment.

"You want to get back with Tamara, it's not rocket science. She wants you to stop with this dope shit."

"She send you here?"

"Nope. I wanted to see how bad it was."

Chiurco blew into the air between them. "It's not as bad as it looks."

"That's great. I'm glad to hear it. Because to tell you the truth, it doesn't look too good right now."

"You going to fire me?"

"I'm thinking about it. I feel a little betrayed, if you want to know."

"Not by me?"

"Yep, by you."

"Wyatt, come on. This is the first time for anything like this in like—what?—five years. We're not exactly in the busiest time we've ever had. I just made a bad decision."

"Couple of 'em. Notice any connection between the dope and the bad decisions?"

"Maybe. A little."

"Maybe a little, yeah. And in the meanwhile Dismas Hardy comes by my place last night and gives us a shitload of work and I'm thinking you and me are going to be humping round the clock on this Townshend case for at least the next few days, maybe a week. Except you call in sick when you're not actually sick at all, and Tam's all messed up back at the office, can barely answer the phone, and I've got no goddamn backup."

"I didn't know that. I couldn't have known that."

"No, I know. Which is why one of the rules is you show up at work when somebody's paying you, so that if there's work to do, you're there to do it."

Chiurco hung his head; his shoulders rose and fell. "Again, I'm sorry."

Hunt waited until Craig's head came back up, then looked him square in the eyes. "Shit," he said. "This is no way to run an airline. Didn't we already have a discussion about this once? How am I supposed to write a reference letter if this is going on? How about, if this is your chosen field, maybe you want to avoid things that threaten it?"

"I don't usually smoke during the day."

"You shouldn't be usually smoking at all, Craig. You might lose your job over it—hell, your whole profession. Worse, you're losing Tam, and you already know that."

"I know. You think I don't know that? That's what I've been trying to figure out all day."

"What's to figure out?"

No answer.

"And beyond that, Craig, while we're on the topic, being high isn't going to help you figure anything out. Especially this. Isn't that pretty goddamn obvious?"

"It should be, yes."

"So?"

"So"—a sigh—"so I'm gonna stop. I mean it. Starting now, Wyatt. I swear to God."

Hunt just stared at him, this discussion already far beyond his tolerance level. "So what do you think I ought to do about this now? About you?"

"You could fire me if you want."

"I know I could. Maybe I should. If this wasn't the first time you screwed up like this, I sure as hell would."

A trace of hope showed itself on Chiurco's face. "I swear to God, Wyatt, it's over. You can tell Tam it's over."

"You can tell Tam it's over, Craig. I've got other work to do."

"I could—"

"No, you can't." He pointed a finger at Craig's chest. "Tomorrow you can if you're straight by then. And this is the one and only warning. Fool me once, shame on you. Fool me twice, fuck you. Clear?"

"It is. I hear you."

"I hope so," Wyatt said. Then, "Get some sleep and be on time tomorrow." He turned on his heel and stalked off down the hallway.

Bay Beans West was open again, business at least back to slow but steady.

Wyatt Hunt, the embers of his anger still smoldering in his gut, stood across Haight Street on this cool and overcast Tuesday lunch hour and watched people come and go for about twenty minutes. The clientele couldn't be more diverse, and Hunt reflected that if we were what we eat and drink, then we human beings were really mostly the same; nothing should really separate us at all, since apparently every ethnic group in the world, both sexes, and people at every economic level drank coffee and lots of it.

Hunt entered at last and got his place, fifth in the ordering line. Getting up to the counter, he ordered a regular with a couple of shots of espresso. Leaning over, he then quickly showed his business card and mentioned that he was an investigator—he specifically did not say police investigator. Although quite often that's what people heard, and he usually didn't correct them. Could he please, he inquired, have a few words with the manager? It was about the Maya Townshend case.

Before he'd had his order filled, a flamboyantly dressed, ponytailed young man with a diamond in his ear appeared at Hunt's side and introduced himself as the manager, Eugenio Ruiz. Thanking him for coming over, Hunt again flashed his business card and this time identified himself as a private investigator working with the defense on the Townshend case.

"Okay, what can I do for you?"

"We're trying to get a little specific," Hunt said, "about the way Dylan Vogler ran the marijuana out of here. Did you know anything about that?"

Ruiz had quick, dark brown eyes, and they flashed over to the register and then back to Hunt. "Dylan pretty much handled all of that himself, I think."

"Really?"

"Pretty much, yeah."

At the counter they called Hunt's coffee, and he turned and smiled. "That's me, be right back. You mind we go sit someplace for just a minute?"

"A minute. Sure."

Hunt got his coffee, turned, and found Ruiz again at his elbow. "There's some chairs in my office," he said. "After me." And led the way.

The room was small and narrow, maybe six or seven by ten feet. A cluttered desk sat along the left-hand wall, and Hunt took one of the two chairs at the far end of it. The walls were papered with posters of coffee-growing locations—Costa Rica, Hawaii, Kenya, Indonesia. Ruiz closed the door behind them, then pulled over a small wooden barrel and sat on it. "I've only got a couple of minutes," he began. "We're getting into a rush out there."

"Seems like you've always got a rush."

"That's pretty much true." A hopeful smile came and just as quickly disappeared.

Hunt took a small sip of his hot coffee. "Really delicious," he said.

"Yes."

"Well," Hunt said, "I guess the big question is how Dylan distributed the money to the workers here. Was it only the assistant managers, or did everybody get a slice?"

Ruiz, to Hunt's gratification caught completely off-guard, opened and closed his mouth a couple of times. "Um, no."

"No, everybody got a slice?"

The quick eyes triangulated the little room, finally came to settle on Hunt. "No, neither. This was all Dylan's thing."

"No," Hunt said. "No, we know that's not true."

"It is true."

"No, it's not." Hunt shook his head in commiseration. "Good try, Eugenio, but Maya's told us in general terms how it all worked. And frankly we're to the point of getting a little desperate to find somebody else who had a motive to kill Dylan. Or the jury's going to decide Maya did it. So she—Maya—wants us to go to the police and start bringing you guys downtown to talk. And really, who can blame her? But my boss thinks we don't have to shake things up that much to get what we need."

"What do you need?"

"I need to know what you and your coworkers know."

"Like what?"

"I don't know specifically, you see. But certainly clients who might have been having a hard time paying, or maybe were making trouble for Dylan some other way. Competitors, people threatening to bust you. Come on, Eugenio, you know. You've been doing this. You don't run a ten-grand-a-month drug business and not have some problems."

Eugenio turned halfway around to check the door. When he came back to Hunt, again he shook his head. "No."

Hunt smiled. "I thought we'd been over that, Eugenio. 'No' is not the right answer. 'No' means you and your guys start going downtown."

"But they say it wasn't about the weed. They didn't steal the weed Dylan had on him."

"There you go. 'They.' 'They' is not 'she.' So who is 'they'?"

The highly strung manager fidgeted on his barrel. "I don't mean 'they' like that."

"So how did you mean it?"

"You know, like a figure of speech."

"Okay. But let me tell you something. The more we're looking at this, the more we're convinced that it is, in fact, about the weed. Maya thinks it's about the weed, since it's definitely not about her. So you see where we're coming from. We're running out of time."

"Yeah, but I don't know any names."

Hunt broke a frigid smile. "Well, that's where you're in luck. Because it turns out we do have names, a whole list of them. We just don't know what kind of relationships some of these people had with Dylan. We need to talk to you some more and other staff members who were part of this thing."

"Nobody was part of it. Nobody sold or handled anything except Dylan."

Hunt leaned back in his chair. "I believe you, Eugenio. But we're not talking sales. We're talking cooperation and payoff. You guys knew what Dylan was doing and you helped him do it, and in exchange he paid you under the table, probably pretty well. Now, I know this and you know it, but it hasn't been the subject of much police concern so far because they've been thinking about Maya and murder. So up to now you're all under the radar. And the really good news here is that talking to me or my colleagues isn't going to get you in trouble. But if the cops come down here and get involved, that's all going to change." Hunt came forward. "Is there something that's unclear about this to you? This is a great deal for you guys, I promise."

Eugenio tattooed out a rhythm on the edge of the barrel. "Do you have that list with you?" he asked. "I could look at it, see if any names ring a bell."

At a few minutes past eight that night Treya and Abe Glitsky were standing over the sink, doing the dinner dishes—Abe washing, Treya drying—in their small kitchen. They had a dishwasher, but it had gone on the blink shortly after Zachary had gone into the hospital, and they'd just never gotten around to fixing it.

Now it was beginning to look as though that might never happen. The simple rhythm of handling the dishes—rinsing, handing the plates and cups and silverware to your partner to dry, talking all the while—had brought to them both an unspoken comfort and even a kind of intimacy that had somehow kick-started their communication during those darkest days when Treya sometimes thought Abe would never really talk again.

Sometime during that crisis time with Zachary, Treya had also instigated a practice she called Parent Savings Time, or PST, and tonight she had put it into practice for the first time in a couple of weeks. The idea, she admitted, was fiendishly simple, and perhaps even inlaid with a tiny element of cruelty. But kids could be such a pain sometimes—even though of course you always loved them—that she didn't feel too guilty laying some payback on them for their own cruel ways.

PST involved going around the house and setting the clocks an hour, or even two hours, ahead. Then, after dinner, you'd look up with surprise, and say, "Oh, my gosh, where has the time gone? It's bedtime already." And you whisk them off to their slumbers.

Now Treya took a dish from the drying tray and began wiping it down. "So what did Diz say?"

"He said it wasn't Schiff's finest moment."

"So what's going to happen?"

"Nothing. Diz says that the Levon count might not even get to the jury."

"Wow. How often does that happen?"

"Not too. Normally you go for a double one eight seven, if the second one's squirrelly, they don't file it. Or maybe it gets dismissed at prelim, but never in the middle of a trial. Still, Diz is talking about a motion to dismiss as soon as Stier rests. I can't imagine Braun granting it, but if she did, it would be pretty huge for Diz." He paused. "It wouldn't be so huge for me."

"You? What do you have to do with it?"

"Well, though you might not know it to look at me, especially the last few months, in theory I run the homicide detail. Which means I have some input on what we bring to the DA. Or not. At least where there's a question."

"You're saying there was a question here?"

"I thought there might be when Debra first went to Glass. But I just couldn't seem to stay focused back then."

"Gee, Abe. I wonder why that was."

Glitsky put his sponge inside a drinking glass and turned it absently around the rim. "The reason doesn't really matter, Trey."

"No, I know. God forbid you have a legitimate excuse or, worse, use one."

"I don't need an excuse. I take full responsibility."

"You? You're kidding."

He handed her the rinsed glass. "Quit busting my chops, woman, would you?"

"I'm not. I'm teasing you."

"I'm laughing. See me laughing."

She put down the glass, put a finger into his belt, and turned him toward her. "Kiss me."

"My hands are all wet."

"I don't care. Kiss me."

After about thirty seconds he said, "Are we going to finish these dishes?"

"I doubt it," she said. "At least not right now."

Wet hair wrapped in a towel, wearing a pale yellow terry-cloth robe, Treya came out into their living room where Abe, in black flannel pajamas, sat on the couch, hunched over a couple of stacks of papers on the coffee table. "Well, look at this," she said.

Shooting her a false glare. "You starting again with me?"

She smiled down at him. "You want me to?"

He patted the couch and moved over an inch or two.

She sat down. "Finding anything?"

Shrugging, he turned a page over, laid it facedown on the second pile. "That's the problem." Another page. And another. "Diz said it was about the blood, and he might be right."

"What about it?"

"There isn't any. Not on Maya's clothes, not in her house. Nowhere."

"Couldn't she have just ditched them?"

Abe put his current page down and sat back on the couch. "Let's see if this flies for you. She kills Levon in a pretty spectacularly bloody way. Spends a few minutes cleaning up, running water in the sink, no doubt splashing, and blood dripping off the table onto the floor like a few inches behind her."

"Okay."

"Okay, first thing, we know she's got some blood on her."

"We do?"

"Got to, Trey. No way with all that splashing front and back can she avoid it. So from there we've got two possible scenarios. One, she doesn't see any blood and just goes from Levon's to pick up the kids and then goes home with them. We've got a timeline for her somewhere in here"—he pointed to the papers in front of them—"that shows her actions from picking up the kids until the next morning. Her story, anyway, but corroborated by her husband and their housekeeper before anybody thought it was an issue. So I'm tempted to believe it. She didn't go out."

"Which means?"

"It means those clothes are at her home at seven the next morning when Bracco and Schiff show up, and luminol's going to show the blood, even if she couldn't see it."

"All right."

"All right. So it didn't show up."

"What's the second scenario?"

"She sees blood and has to dump her clothes. But the problem with that is she picked up the kids promptly at three."

"So she either brought a change with her—"

"Not."

"No, I agree. Or she . . . what? Went home first and changed?"

Glitsky shook his head. "No time for that. And besides which, the maid says she didn't come home first."

"So what's that leave?"

"That's the question."

"All the people who alibi her could be lying."

"That's true."

"But you don't think so?"

Glitsky nodded. "Not that it couldn't happen, but they wouldn't have known what they were covering for when they said it, so it's unlikely."

"So what does this all mean?"

"She wasn't inside. I'm okay with no fingerprints, no DNA, all that. Hard, but doable if you're careful. But if she was there and killed him, she got blood on herself, that's all there is to it."

"You know what, it's good to see you into this." She put her hand on his leg.

He turned to face her. "I'm starting to believe, hope, whatever, that Zack's going to be all right." He leaned forward and rapped on the coffee table. "Knock on wood. Anyway, so maybe I'm not hopeless. Maybe there's something I can do to make sure they don't get blown away on the Vogler side of the trial too."

"Is the evidence better on that?"

"Oh, yeah. No question, basically. But still, if they left anything out, maybe I can help them get it back in."

"Like what?"

"I don't know. Shore up if there's any other weak spots. Whatever they might need."

Treya sat silently for another minute, her hand resting on his leg. "So if the judge dismisses the Levon side, then what?"

"Nothing, really, except that Diz looks good for a media minute, which actually lasts only about thirty seconds."

"No. I mean about Levon."

"What about him?"

"Well, technically, wouldn't he be an open case again?"

Abe's mouth tightened up in concentration. "Not really. I mean, even Diz thinks she looks good for it, even if the DA can't . . ." He ground down to a stop, met his wife's eyes.

"Except," Treya said, "she had no blood on her, did she? She never went inside. Which means somebody else was in there and killed him, doesn't it?"

28

At around nine o'clock the next morning Hardy "no-commented" his way through the crowd of reporters who accosted him as he tried to sneak into the back door of the Hall of Justice. He was in relatively high spirits, having slept well for a trial day—waking up without an alarm at five-thirty as opposed to the more usual three or four.

Even though neither Kathy West nor Harlen Fisk had shown up at the truncated morning session of the trial yesterday, the powers that be had determined that a metal detector was still a necessity. So a line of spectators and more reporters snaked for fifty or sixty feet outside of Department 25. Upon laying eyes on it Hardy was about to backtrack and take his shortcut behind the courtrooms when he heard a familiar voice call his name and, turning, was somewhat surprised to see Fisk striding toward him.

The normally hale and hearty face seemed today to have an underlying pallor, and dark circles under his eyes spoke of a lack of sleep, but if Hardy had a sister on trial for murder, he thought he might lose a few zz's himself. He stepped into the line and extended his hand. "Hey, Harlen. Got the trial bug, do you?"

He tried a smile that mostly failed. "Maybe some of that, Diz. But mostly I wanted to ask you, after yesterday, why can't Jackman just drop the Preslee side of this thing?"

"Careful, Harlen, your politics are showing. The short answer is that Stier's picked this fight for them and they're in it. What I am hoping is that maybe Braun'll do it for them."

"She can do that?"

"She can grant my motion to dismiss when Stier's done with his case. If I can convince her that no reasonable juror could convict on the Preslee count with this evidence."

"What's it going to depend on?"

Hardy chortled, leaned in closer to whisper. "In theory, careful weighing of the evidence. In fact, pretty much whim."

"That's heartening."

"Welcome to Superior Court. But in truth, I think we might actually have a chance. There really isn't anything that proves she killed Levon."

Harlen nodded. "This whole thing is a mockery, if you want my opinion. Always has been."

"I agree."

"And if Braun does drop Levon, isn't that saying Maya didn't do it?"

"Well, not exactly. It means they can't prove she did it."

"So what do they do then?"

"Who?"

"The police. The people investigating his murder."

Hardy's grin had a sardonic twist to it. "Again, we're up against theory versus reality. In theory the police should start looking for more proof, but there isn't any that I've seen. So then, still in theory, they should revisit the investigation and see if they might trip over another suspect somewhere along the way. In reality, since the cops believe that Maya in fact did kill Levon—"

"That's insane," Harlen interrupted. "I *know* she didn't do that."

This stopped Hardy. "If you do, tell me how."

The supervisor, too, hesitated for a second. "What I mean is my sister isn't hitting somebody on the head with a cleaver, Diz. It just flat couldn't happen."

"I'm not saying I disagree with you. It's a stretch for me too. But the cops think that's what happened, even though she avoided all traces of blood, which is a pretty good party trick if she did. Anyway, the bottom line is that in reality, Braun dismisses Levon and nobody's going to do a damn thing about it. They figure they'll get her on Dylan anyway. But the good news—and this really is good, Harlen— is if Levon gets dropped, it's no longer Specials." By this Hardy meant special circumstances—mandated by multiple murder—and because of which Maya would be facing life in prison without the possibility of parole. Without Levon, life without was going to be off the table.

But Harlen didn't take much solace in that. "I don't want her to go down at all," he said. "That's why I turned her on to you in the first place. I never intended for this to happen. You were supposed to stop it from getting to here."

Hardy had seen this before, the family becoming adversarial to the defense as the trial progressed. Still, Harlen was a long-standing colleague—just short of being a personal friend—and the accusation stung. "Well"—Hardy's decent mood by now completely leached away—"I hope you know I'm doing all I can to keep that from happening."

"I know that. I didn't mean—"

"Yeah, you did. It's okay."

"It's not okay, Diz." Harlen swallowed, took a deep breath. "I tell you, these fuckers are killing all of us. Joel and I almost had it out—I mean actual fists—last time we saw each other. He said I was ratting him out with the grand jury. You ever testify for one of those?"

"Yeah. But I wasn't a target."

"Well, here's the good news. Neither am I. Or they tell me that's good news, but you ask me, make me a target anytime."

"So you can take the Fifth, right?"

"Not that I've got anything to hide, really, but it would be a nice option. Instead of letting Glass, last time he got me on the stand, rip me a new one. Then he starts on my tax returns for like ten years ago. And how do I account for this? And how did I really make that? And how do I prove that my sister and I were not actual partners in BBW, and that the dope money isn't really what got Joel's real estate stuff started, or at least bailed him out after nine eleven."

"And you had to answer?"

"Every time or I'm in contempt. I mean, that son of a bitch Glass treated me like I was a major criminal, but I've got nothing to tell him. Then after all that Joel busts my ass anyway." The big man blew out heavily. "And you notice Kathy's lost about ten pounds. Ten pounds on her, that's like fifty on me. And it isn't her new exercise routine, believe me."

"I hadn't heard they'd called her yet."

"No. That's what's so awful. They're keeping the big ax—testifying with the grand jury—over her head. Glass waiting to see what happens down here in court, maybe. I don't know, but it's eating her up too. Like literally. I think that's what more or less got her to come down here. Put the fucker on notice, show him she's not afraid." He leaned in closer. "But let me tell you something, Diz, between me and you. She is."

From his own experiences with Joel—arguing with him over billing, cash flows, trial strategy, his treatment of Maya—Hardy had known that Glass's campaign against the families was taking a serious psychic toll. Now, though, Harlen's totally uncharacteristic outburst—the man was a professional politician, after all, he never lost his temper—had made Hardy realize how deep the knife cut, how threatening the grand jury must be, how very real loomed the possibility of ruined careers and even prison time. Now Hardy took his own deep breath. "Well, Harlen," he said with a mustered calm he didn't come close to feeling, "we're still a long way from done here. That's all I can tell you. We've got to let it play out."

Hardy let Fisk go through the metal detector and then stepped aside out of the line and walked back to the other familiar face he'd noticed in the lobby behind them. Chiurco, in a coat and tie, looked well-rested and clear-eyed as Hardy shook his hand. "Hey, Craig," he said. "You here with Wyatt?"

"No. Wyatt told me to come down here and see if I could be of some use."

This wasn't the most impressive offer Hardy had ever heard. The only thing Craig had to talk about was Maya's presence outside Levon's flat just before or after he was murdered. Which meant that if Hardy put him on the stand, all he could do was damage the case further.

But then, suddenly, unexpectedly, an idea surfaced. "Something you could do," he said. "With all the craziness, you and I never talked about whatever you found out about Levon and Dylan."

"Sure, but I've got to tell you, beyond the robbery and his address, it wasn't much."

"Wyatt didn't ask you to follow up on any of that?"

Craig shook his head. "No. And I don't really know what it would be. I think you guys know all I know."

"Probably," Hardy said, "but maybe you know something you don't know you know. Stuff you might have seen with Maya at the door."

This brought a frown. "Tamara kind of hinted that maybe I'd want to mess with my story if—"

But Hardy jumped all over that. "No, no, no. Nothing like that. I'm not talking about making up a story. Just if what actually happened might change an argument or something."

"Well, whatever you'd want."

"You want to set a time? Give me an hour?"

"Sure. When?"

"Tonight, tomorrow night? Call Phyllis at my office and she can set us up. You okay with that?"

"Of course."

"Good. So now if you'll excuse me"—Hardy indicated the courtroom behind him—"Her Highness awaits."

Upstairs, Glitsky let Bracco and Schiff into his office, closed the door behind them, and walked around his desk to his chair. He had hot tea in his SFPD mug and he pulled it in front of him and cupped his hands around it.

Not that he was cold.

He felt he needed a prop—something immediate and proximately painful—to take the edge off his main emotion at the moment, which was a fine amalgam of embarrassment, disappointment, and fury. As a further subterfuge—to all appearances this was simply a chat about procedures—he'd bought a couple of Starbucks frou-frou coffees downstairs and had put them on the edge of his desk in front of where his inspectors were sitting.

Schiff pretty obviously hungover.

And now, motioning to the coffees, Glitsky said, "I hear those are great. Orange macchiato, or something like that. Treya swears by 'em."

Bracco reached forward, took a cup, removed the plastic top. "Thank you, sir."

"You're welcome. Debra?"

She raised a palm. "Maybe in a minute, thanks."

The tension among the three of them taut as a wire.

"Are you feeling all right?"

A brisk nod. "Little bit of a rough night is all."

Glitsky kept his eyes on her. After a minute he sipped his own tea. "It takes some getting used to, but you can't let that stuff get to you."

She didn't reply.

"You have a tough day of testimony," Glitsky said, "it's part of the job. Comes with the territory. You shake it off and do better next time. At least that's my experience. The coffee might really help."

Schiff sighed and reached for the cup.

"Of course," Glitsky continued, pressing his hands around his mug, focusing on the heat in his palms, "it's preferable if you make sure your evidence is rock solid before you're stuck with explaining something that might not make much sense."

Schiff, her mouth set tight, let a long, slow breath out through her nose. She left the paper coffee cup where it sat on the desk and straightened back up in her chair. "It made perfect sense, Lieutenant. People have been known to cover their tracks, and she did. It doesn't mean she wasn't there."

"No, of course not."

"In fact, she was there."

"Well, in fact, to be precise, she may have been at the front door."

"She *was* at the front door, Abe. Her fingerprints and DNA say so."

"That's true, sir," Bracco said.

Glitsky's eyes went from one to the other. "All right. Still, the Preslee count isn't too wonderful, is it? If it wasn't for Vogler, in fact, you and I both know it wouldn't have been charged. Why do you think that might be?"

Schiff wasn't backing down. "Like I said, she planned it and pulled it off. And let me ask you something. Did you get your take on this from your friend Mr. Hardy?"

The scar through Glitsky's lips went a little pale in relief. "I'm going to pretend I didn't hear that, Debra. It's way beneath you, and maybe just a result of how you're feeling this morning, huh?"

"I'm feeling fine."

"Good. Because I did want to ask you both about something. Never mind your write-ups or your testimony or what Maya Townshend might or might not have done at Levon's place, how do you, either of you, explain to me the complete absence of blood from any of her clothes or shoes or anything else you looked at? And before you start, let me give you my analysis and you tell me where I'm wrong."

For the next few minutes Glitsky outlined it for his inspectors. He wrapped it up by saying, "And this isn't a question of admissible evidence or lack of sufficient proof to convict. I'm talking here the actual fact of what happened."

Schiff didn't even hesitate. "The actual fact is she killed him. Her husband lied when he corroborated her alibi. Either him or the housekeeper. Happens all the time."

Glitsky's mug was tepid by now; it was failing to serve as a calming device. "You're saying she got home, when, before she picked up the kids?"

"She might have. We don't know."

"But we do know, don't we," Glitsky replied, "what time she got the call from Preslee? Couple of minutes either side of two, right? And we know she picked up the kids at three sharp. So you're telling me she gets this call at her house on Broadway, decides on the spot to kill Preslee, drives out to Potrero? And by the way, I did it this morning coming in. No traffic, city streets, twenty-two minutes one way. So anyway, she sits down and drinks some water and maybe smokes a joint with Levon, whacks him with the cleaver, then cleans up with a lot of care, and she's got time to dump her blood-spattered clothes before she gets the kids?"

"She could have done it anytime that night."

"So the husband knew about it?"

"Had to."

Glitsky looked over at Bracco. "Darrel?"

No hesitation. "If she did it, and she did, Abe, then that's what happened."

While a part of him admired the loyalty of his troops to one another, Glitsky felt his stomach roil at this absurd display of professional obstinacy. He was all but certain from his earlier discussions that Bracco thought that they could've tightened up the case before the arrest, and that Schiff had acted precipitously, but Darrel wasn't going to contradict his partner in front of his lieutenant, and that was all there was to it.

Never mind that their convictions flew in the face of the first law of criminal investigation—facts must flow from demonstrable evidence, and not the other way round, where the evidence is massaged or explained to fit a set of predetermined perceptions.

Now, knowing he was defeated in his primary objective—to get his inspectors to admit that they might be wrong, and might want to spend some of their time looking for who had really killed Levon Preslee—Glitsky let out a breath, gave up on his tea, and leaned back in his chair. "All right," he said. "But I think you'll have to admit it's possible that the jury's going to have a hard time with Levon. Can we go with that?"

"You know as well as me, Abe," Schiff replied. "San Francisco juries have a hard time with guilt, period."

"All too true," Glitsky said. "And all the more reason to make sure we give the DA everything he needs every single time."

"He's got plenty here, Abe," Schiff said. "She's going down for Vogler. Even in San Francisco."

"All right, fine, I believe you, and I hope you're right. And you're both confident you've built the strongest case you could on Vogler?"

Darrel was the first to pipe up. "Yes, sir."

"Debra?"

"Absolutely."

"Okay, then." Glitsky pulled a small stapled stack—five or six pages—of computerized printouts over in front of him and flipped it open to the middle. "Then I've just got one last quick question for both of you. Who is Lee or Lori Buford or Bradford?"

The two inspectors traded glances with one another.

"Nobody," Schiff said.

"Nobody," Glitsky repeated. "But I see here a Post-it in the file with our case number on it and that name or one like it."

Schiff, her own blood high by now, wasn't hiding her anger. "You're riding this one a little hard, wouldn't you say, Lieutenant?"

"I'm in charge of this detail, Sergeant, and in my opinion, this case we gave the DA is about halfway down the tubes because we just didn't quite have enough evidence when we made the arrest—correction, when *you* made the arrest. And you want my opinion, we're still a damn sight light on Vogler. And if this *nobody* happens in fact to be somebody you guys in your zeal to arrest just plain forgot to include in your write-ups or reports and who might actually help the DA get a conviction on this Townshend woman, then it's my job to point that out to you. Either of you got a problem with that? 'Cause if you do, we can take it upstairs and have a discussion with the chief. How's that sound?"

Bracco, jaw set, a flush in his face, said, "Lori Bradford. An old woman out in the Haight."

"A senile old woman out in the Haight," Schiff corrected him.

"You didn't take notes when you talked to her?"

After a minute Bracco said, "No. We decided she wasn't credible, Abe. There was nothing worth putting in the file."

Glitsky knew that though strictly against regulations, this was not an uncommon practice. Although inspectors were supposed to memorialize every interaction with witnesses or potential witnesses, either by tape or notes, in practice it often became the call of individual inspectors to include or exclude testimony, for whatever reason or for no real reason, from their reports. It was clear to Glitsky—if only because he was certain that Bracco knew better, but also because of the look of pain on Bracco's face—that Schiff had drawn the short straw to write up the report on Lori Bradford's interview and had decided for reasons of her own to leave it out.

Keeping his voice under control, Glitsky finished the last of his tea. "Nevertheless," he said, "if either of you two remember, I'd be interested in hearing what she might have told you."

29

Before the decision really had a chance to sink in, a smiling and confident Big Ugly Stier, never looking bigger nor uglier to Hardy, rose at his table and—no doubt seeking to undo some of the damage Hardy had done with Schiff yesterday—called Cheryl Biehl to the stand.

Paul Stier had discovered Biehl, née Zolotny, in much the same way that Wyatt Hunt had, by chasing down Maya's college connections in the hope that someone who knew her both then and in the present could shed some light on the blackmail question, and hence on Maya's purported motive for the killings. Now the former cheerleader, conservatively dressed in a tan business suit, clearly uncomfortable in the role of prosecution witness, shifted as she sat waiting for Stier to begin.

"Mrs. Biehl, how long have you known the defendant?"

"About fourteen years now."

"And where did you meet?"

"At USF, freshman year. We were both cheerleaders."

"And have you kept up on your friendship?"

"Yes. Until she got arrested, we usually had lunch together every couple of months or so."

"Mrs. Biehl, did you also know the victims in this case, Dylan Vogler and Levon Preslee?"

"Yes."

"And to your personal knowledge, did Defendant also know both of these victims when you were all in college?"

"Yes."

"Did you ever witness Defendant using marijuana with either or both of these men?"

Biehl cast an apologetic glance across to Maya and nodded to Stier. "Yes, I did."

"And did you ever witness Defendant, either alone or with one or both of the victims, selling or distributing marijuana?"

"Yes, I did."

"Would you characterize this as a more or less common occurrence?"

"For a while, when we were in school, yes. They were the main connection if you wanted to buy pot among our friends."

"All three of them?"

"Yes."

"All right, Mrs. Biehl. Moving ahead several years, in the lunches that you and Defendant had together, did she ever mention either Mr. Vogler or Mr. Preslee?"

"Yes. She mentioned both of them, Dylan quite frequently, since she still worked with him."

"But she mentioned Levon Preslee too?"

"Right. But not really recently."

"Do you remember the last time she mentioned Mr. Preslee?"

"About eight years ago, just after he got out of jail."

"And by jail, Mrs. Biehl, don't you really mean state prison?"

"Yes. Right. I thought prison and jail were the same, I guess. But, yes, it was just after he got out of prison."

"And what were Defendant's comments on Mr. Preslee at that time?"

"Just that he'd gotten in touch with her through Dylan. He wanted her to fix him up with a job or something."

"What was her reaction to this request?"

"It really frustrated her."

"How did you know that?"

"Because she said so. She said she was never going to get out from under these guys."

"She was never going to get out from under these guys. Did she offer any explanation of what she meant by *get out from under*?"

"No, she didn't."

"Thank you, Mrs. Biehl. Now, turning to Dylan Vogler, he was her manager at Bay Beans West, was he not?"

"That's right."

"And in these conversations you had with her, how did she characterize her relationship with Mr. Vogler?"

Biehl hesitated for a long moment before replying, "Unpleasant."

"Was she more specific?"

"Well, a couple of times she told me she just wanted him out of her life and she'd offered to buy him out, but he refused."

Stier, eyebrows raised, flagged the significance of this testimony to the jury. "She used the phrase, *to buy him out*?"

"Yes."

"Did you find that strange?"

"A little bit, yes."

"And why was that?"

"Well, because he worked for her, I wondered why she just didn't fire him."

"Did you ask her about that, why she didn't simply terminate him?"

"Yes. We talked about it a couple of times."

"And what did she say?"

"She said she couldn't. Couldn't fire him, I mean."

"And why was that?"

"She wouldn't say specifically."

"Did she tell you in a general way?"

Another look over at Maya, then Biehl let out a wistful sigh. "She said she could never fire him because he owned her."

"He owned her. Those were her exact words?"

"Yes. She said them more than once."

Stier, to all appearances sobered by the enormity and surprise of this testimony—although he'd guided her directly to it—nodded to the witness, then over to the jury. "Mrs. Biehl, in the few months prior to Defendant's arrest, did you two have lunch together again?"

"Yes, at the end of last summer."

"And did Mr. Vogler come up again in your conversation?"

"Yes."

"How did that happen?"

"I brought him up. I told her I'd been worrying about her situation with him. I'd heard somewhere that he was selling marijuana out of the store, and I told her that whatever it was she was hiding, it would be better just to get him out of there and get it behind her. Otherwise, it was just going to go from bad to worse."

"And what did she say to that?"

"She just kind of shrugged it off and said I shouldn't worry about it. I was right. It wasn't a good situation, but she was going to take care of it pretty soon."

A final repetitious riff to the jury. "She was going to take care of it pretty soon." And then Stier was turning to Hardy. "Your witness."

30

Biehl's direct testimony got them to lunchtime, so there wouldn't be any cross-examination until the afternoon session, and this suited Hardy fine. He didn't have much of an idea of what, if anything, he was going to ask her. Her testimony had been true and probably accurate. Vogler had no doubt been blackmailing Maya. He and Preslee probably both had had their claws into her, so that she wanted to get out from under their control. The strategy he'd decided to adopt called for a steady drumbeat about the lack of physical evidence tying Maya to either of the crimes, but Biehl hadn't offered anything he felt he could refute.

He had a voice mail from Wyatt Hunt on his cell phone, telling him that he'd be having lunch at Lou the Greek's if Hardy wanted a report on what he'd been doing out at BBW, and suddenly—if for no other reason than he was perpetually somewhat morbidly curious about the Special—that seemed like a good idea.

So he hung back until his client and Stier and most of the crowd had dispersed from the courtroom, then snuck out, walked the two flights down to the throbbing lobby where it was too crowded for anyone to notice him. Outside, trench-coat collar up and head down in an overcast chill, he jaywalked across to Lou's, stepped over the sleeping or dead body in the outer doorway, then descended the half-dozen ammonia-tinged steps that took him to the restaurant's entrance proper, swinging double doors covered in red leather.

As usual at lunchtime patrons stood three deep at the bar. Each of the twenty-odd tables was taken as well. Hardy recognized several cops, Harlen Fisk at a small table alone with Cheryl Biehl, five or six of his fellow attorneys, and a couple of members of his own jury at one of the side tables; and somewhat to his surprise, at the largest table in the house, Glitsky and Treya and Debra Schiff and Darrel Bracco along with District Attorney Clarence Jackman himself, scowling and listening intently to whatever Bracco was saying. Nobody at that table looked happy enough to interrupt, and besides, Hunt was holding up a hand flagging him from one of the booths, so Hardy picked his way through the mob and the cacophonous din and slid in across from his investigator.

"Souvlaki lo mein," Hunt said by way of greeting.

"That actually sounds edible."

"It does, I know. But I predict a secret ingredient. Octopus, something like that. All those little legs and the noodles mixed up together so you can't tell which is which."

"Octopus legs and noodles? I could tell the difference."

"You could? How?"

"The legs are probably going to be thicker. And have those little suction cups on 'em. That's the giveaway."

Just at that moment the proprietor stopped at their table. Lou was mid-fifties or so, with thick black hair, short legs, a solid round stomach under his starched white shirt. "Hey, Diz, Wyatt. Lunch or just drinks?"

"We'll have the octopus," Hardy said, "if you can cut the suction cups off the legs for Wyatt here. He thinks suction cups suck."

Lou's face clouded over in something like real pain. "No octopus. Noodles and lamb, maybe some hummus and hoisin. Delicious."

"Can Chiu put some octopus in mine?" Hunt asked.

"Come on, guys, can't you see I'm hoppin' here? We don't do substitutions, you know that. How long you been comin' here? You eatin' or not?"

"Two Specials," Hardy said.

"There you go. Water, tea, beer, what?"

Both men chose water, and Lou was gone, on to the next order. Hardy jerked his head a little out toward the room. "Check out the summit meeting."

"I know. They got here a few minutes after me. I don't think it's a birthday."

Hardy looked over and again noted the tension around the table. "Maybe they just aren't as enthusiastic as we are about the Special."

"Those are our guys, aren't they? I mean our case."

"Schiff and Bracco, yeah."

"Maybe they screwed up."

"They've probably got ten other cases, but we can always hope." The water arrived—pint jars with ice chips—and Hardy took a drink. "So how you doin' on our list?"

"Slow," Hunt said. "But we were right about all the staff being in on it. They really, really don't want to talk to the actual police."

"Are they still dealing out of there?"

"It wouldn't shock me. Though not at the level Dylan was. At least not yet."

"So who? The new manager?"

"Ruiz. Sharp guy. But he says there's a guy, he thinks called Paco, who got in a beef with Dylan while Levon was there maybe a couple of weeks before he got killed."

Hardy sat up. "They were both there together, Dylan and Levon?"

"Oh yeah. Pretty frequently, at least every time Levon came for his pickup."

"Well, there you go."

"Except there's no Paco on the list. I've got Ruiz watching for him if he comes in again, but he says he hasn't seen him since the big day. And, of course, he could be making it all up."

"Of course." Hardy threw another quick glance at Glitsky's table—just as cheerful as last time. "I had a chat with your man Craig this morning, you know."

"Yeah. He called in. Can he do anything for you?"

"Well, so far he puts Maya at Levon's, but he doesn't put her inside. So if I need him for something on the stand, he won't do too much damage with that."

"Actually, it might be a little better than that. The way it sounds to me, she'd just got there and couldn't get in, as opposed to she was just coming out."

"Big difference," Hardy said.

"No shit." Wyatt hesitated for a second. "But how did he seem?"

"Who, Craig? Fine. Why?"

Hunt shrugged. "He and Tamara broke up. I think he's having some problems. But he was okay?"

"He seemed fine."

"Good. Just checking on the puppies." Hunt turned his glass around in its condensation ring. "I did get something else, maybe. Actually, Gina got the hunch from something else I was saying. If it's anything."

"You think you got enough qualifiers in there?"

"I don't want to get your hopes up."

"I'll be on diligent guard. Meanwhile, at this point," Hardy said, "I don't care if Daffy Duck is your source. I'll take it."

"Okay. What do you know about Tess Granat?"

Hardy felt he'd be nothing without his memory, and he had his answer in a second. "Movie star. *Falling Leaves, Death by Starlight.* Died here in the city, didn't she? Hit by a car when she was pregnant, if I remember."

Hunt nodded. "Hit-and-run. Mom and unborn kid both died. Driver never found."

"Okay."

"Okay. Did you know she was Kathy West's sister?"

With his water halfway to his mouth Hardy stopped cold and slowly replaced the jar on the table. The words *unborn kid* went jangling around in his brain. As did the details of his interview with Maya in the attorney visiting room at the jail—when she had talked about the innocence of the unborn but had denied ever having had an abortion. Her words came back at him with a visceral force.

Lou had a lunch staff of two white women and two Filipino men—all middle-aged—that delivered food from the kitchen and never slowed down, and one of the women showed up and plopped their Specials down without fanfare between them, then threw after them their utensils wrapped in paper napkins.

Hardy finally found his voice again. "When did this happen, the hit-and-run?"

"March of ninety-seven," Hunt said. "Maya was a junior that year. It's when things seemed to go south for her."

"How'd you get this?" Hardy asked. "Or Gina?"

"We were just talking about how I got started on all this, and I mentioned running into an article about Tess Granat being Maya's aunt in USF's newspaper. And I ask Gina what was it that happened to her. So Gina, being senior to me, which I never let her forget, remembers the hit-and-run, the whole story, and then it hits us both at the same time."

"There's a connection?"

"Maybe worth asking about."

"So you're thinking the blackmail might not have been about a robbery?"

"I'm not thinking anything. I'm just wondering. Granat's death was a big deal at the time. A huge deal."

A muscle worked in Hardy's jaw.

"They were an item back then, too, you know? Maya and Dylan." Hunt stopped to let that fact settle, then continued. "Although by senior year, or maybe sooner, they broke up, and she goes back to being Junior League and finds religion again."

"It would explain a lot." Hardy getting into it. "If she knew anything about the hit-and-run with Granat and didn't go to the cops at the time, and then her family found out about it later, she's fucked. The family would never forgive her, and she can't forgive herself. Which is why she thinks she deserves whatever happens to her. It's God working in biblical time, just paying her back now for what she did then."

"It's a damn compelling theory," Hunt said, "but the bad news is that it doesn't actually change all that much. Dylan's blackmailing her about that, the bottom line is he's still blackmailing her, so she's got the same motive."

"Not exactly." Hardy was already thinking about how he could get any of this in front of the jury. "If it's not about something she and Dylan did with Levon around dope in college, it takes Levon out of the picture, at least out of *her* picture. She's got no reason at all to kill him."

"Except if maybe Dylan told him."

"Never. Knowledge being power and all, if Dylan's the only one who knows, and my money says he is, then he doesn't dilute it by telling anybody else."

"You're right."

"Only sometimes. But it would be nice if this was one of those times." Hardy pulled his Special over in front of him and poked at it with his fork. "Hmm. Looks a little like Yeanling Clay Bowl." This, probably Lou's most famous and mysterious Special—it didn't come in a clay bowl and no one had any idea what a yeanling was—showed up on the menu about half a dozen times a year.

"You think maybe *yeanling* could mean 'octopus'?" Hunt asked.

But before Hardy could do anything about his latest information, he had to be sure that it was true.

He stood in the wide hallway behind Department 25 and waited, depressed as always by the sight of the shackled prisoners belching from the elevators coming down from the jail above him. Maya, over in the new jail behind the Hall of Justice, would be coming in through the back door in her personal little chain gang.

Her saw her now and walked down to meet her. The months of incarceration hadn't been good to her. She'd asked for a short haircut to minimize the lack of luster brought about by the caustic soap they had in the showers, but the result was just an unkempt, vaguely butch, mop—and now it was even showing signs of gray. Her skin, too, had the familiar jail pallor, although ironically she'd gained perhaps fifteen pounds with the huge servings of high-calorie jail food. And no one would ever mistake the deep creases around her eyes for laugh lines.

He accompanied her into the four-by-eight-foot cage built into the wall and connected to the back entrance to the courtroom, and the metal door clanged as the bailiff closed it behind them. This was where she waited every day, usually all alone, until court was called into session, and this is where they now both sat on the cold concrete ledge that served as a kind of bench.

Braun walked by them, coming back from her lunch, in conversation with one of her judicial colleagues, and she didn't even glance in their direction.

"She's an awful person," Maya said.

"Yes, she is."

"How does somebody like that get to be a judge?"

"Usually the governor appoints them first. Then they just keep getting elected."

"So the qualification is they know a governor?"

"And probably either gave him money or helped him get it. Assuming a male governor, of course."

"And why wouldn't we?" She plucked at her jail suit. "I'm sorry, I'm just a total bitch today. I shouldn't be so judgmental. I'm sure she's trying her best." She sighed. "And to think that's so much the life Joel and I bought into before all this began."

"What's that?"

"You know. Fund-raising. Benefits. Helping people like her get appointed. I'm beginning to think it's really not about justice at all. I wonder what we were doing, what we were thinking, all that time."

"Protecting your interests," Hardy said. "Your assets. And you wind up with people like Braun, and Glass, for that matter, as your gatekeepers. And they take it damn seriously. Problem is, once you're perceived of as outside the loop, you're the enemy. You're the threat."

"Joel's not a threat." Finally, some color came into her face. "He's never done a dishonest or illegal thing in his life. And they're all over him."

"He's going to beat it," Hardy said. "But he's going to need you beating this thing too."

She turned her head toward him. "I thought that's what we were paying you for."

Hardy had heard this kind of thing before, from both husband and wife, even from Harlen, and he showed some of his growing impatience with it. "As we've just been discussing, sometimes money doesn't get you what you think it should. Sometimes you've got to change your vision. Your idea of what you're all about. Like, for example, are you inside that big wall, protecting your assets, or are you going to just let these people take them?"

"Me! Am I just going to just let these people take them? Like I've got any choice in what's happening here? Or out there?"

Hardy put his back against the wall and turned to meet her eyes. There was no warmth in his expression. "You've got all the choice in the world, Maya."

She just stared over at him, shaking her head. "What are you talking about? I've got no choice about anything. Are you out of your mind?"

"Maybe I am, trying to defend you with the wrong theory, the wrong motive, and you sitting there day in and day out watching me do it, letting me do it."

"I don't know what you're saying."

"Yes, you do, Maya. I'm talking about the basic fact of this case. Dylan wasn't blackmailing you because you guys sold drugs in college and, gosh, maybe people would find out. That wasn't it, was it? Although that's what you let me build our whole case on."

"And why would I do that?"

"Two reasons. One, you felt guilty and that you deserved to be punished. And two, you could never tell anybody the truth. Not even your lawyer, because you can't trust him enough." Hardy came forward, his elbows resting on his knees. "Okay, so enough. Now it's time. True or false, Maya. Dylan was blackmailing you because of something to do with your aunt's death, wasn't he?"

Her body gave slightly. No words came.

"What was it, Maya? Did you know who did the hit-and-run and not tell the police? Did you loan them your car?"

Now Maya's mouth went loose, her eyes glassy.

"You were there, weren't you, Maya? In the car with them." Hardy suddenly felt his own head go light as the probable reality hit him. "No," he said. "No, you were the driver."

For a long moment she regarded him as she might her executioner, then all at once a small sound came out of her throat. She hung her head and her shoulders began to heave.

Tears splashed like raindrops onto the floor between her feet.

She'd passed through the sobbing, though the blotched and wet effects of it remained on her face. "What matters is that nobody in the family can know. Which means nobody at all, 'cause whoever knew would tell them." She let out a shuddering, unsteady breath. "How did you find out?"

"Serendipity," Hardy said. "My investigator mentioned Tess Granat and you to his girlfriend in the same breath, and there it was. You've kept this to yourself all this time?"

"Of course. I had to." Then, a hand quickly on his leg. "And you can't tell anyone either. Ever."

"No. I know that. You don't have to worry about that." He hesitated. "But maybe you could, after all."

Her tortured gaze fell on him. "If you think that," she said, "you don't understand my family at all. Or me. Or any of this."

"What about your husband?"

"Tell him I am a murderer? Tell him the mother of his children is a child killer?"

Hardy straightened, his back stiff up against the cell wall. "You're being too hard on yourself, Maya. It was a long time ago."

She shook her head. "It's yesterday," she said. "It's this morning. It's now, for God's sake. Don't you understand? I killed her. My mom's sister. Kathy's sister and her unborn child. Everybody's favorite."

"It was an accident."

"I was stoned and drunk. Both. Loaded. It was murder."

"And you'll never forgive yourself for it."

"Why should I? I did it. Would you?"

"I don't know, to tell you the truth. Maybe after all this time I'd be tempted to start trying."

"Time hasn't made it go away."

"It might if you shared the burden of it. If you told somebody. Maybe you need absolution."

"I pray for it every day."

"It's not going to come without some kind of confession."

"What? Now you're a priest?"

"Not even close," Hardy said. "Just a fellow sinner like yourself. But I was raised a good Catholic. Believe me, I know how the forgiveness thing works."

"You ever kill anybody?"

Hardy nodded. "I was in Vietnam. I killed a lot of people." Including not just in Vietnam, he thought, but also the victims of the horrific gunfight he'd been part of here in San Francisco, the aftermath of which had dominated his emotional stability and career for the next three or four years. So, yes, he'd killed his share of people. And kept his share of secrets too. A plague of them, he sometimes felt. But Frannie, his children, Glitsky, Roake—they all knew what he'd done, had worked through the consequences together, and that had helped.

Maya shook her head. "Vietnam was killing in a war."

"What? Like that doesn't count? It felt like it counted, trust me. I know it did to the families of my victims. I know it did to me." He drew in a breath. "My only point is I think maybe keeping this secret has hurt you enough. Look at the power it gave Dylan Vogler."

"I hated that man."

"I'd imagine so. He was in the car with you?"

She nodded. "It was his car. No connection to me. He just washed it up and never told anybody. The bastard."

"When did the blackmail start?"

"Not until he was out of prison, but right after that. He couldn't get any other work, not that he really tried, I don't think. He looked me up and reminded me how much I owed him for his silence."

"I get it," Hardy said.

"I don't know if you do. I don't know if anybody can." Her chin fell, a puppet's string cut. "It never ends. It's just a constant weight."

"I don't want to beat a dead horse, Maya, so I'm only going to say it one more time. You could let it go. Let Joel in, at least. He's stuck by you through all this, and here maybe thinking you killed somebody too. He loves you. He could handle it."

She had her arms crossed over her chest, hunched over now, rocking on the hard concrete ledge. "God God God."

"It's all right, Maya. It's all right."

"No. No, it's so not all right." Seconds passed and she slowed herself down in her movements, finally became still. "You'd think I would have been on guard against it. I mean, it was the great myth I was raised with."

"What was that?"

"Eve. The Garden of Eden. The tree of the knowledge of good and evil. That's what it all was to me back when I met Dylan. He was the serpent, just so attractive, so much wiser, I thought. Willing to try anything, you know, for the *experience* of it. 'Here, try some of this.' And I was this kid who'd never done anything, who was just—just so simple, and stupid. And you know what the real stupidity was?"

"What's that?"

"I really was happy." She looked over at Hardy, searching his face to see if he understood at all. "I mean, before Dylan. I was a happy person, a good person. But then he'd started challenging and questioning me about everything, about who I was. 'How can you know you're as happy as you can be when you haven't even tried to experience anything outside of your well-ordered little life? Maybe you're just afraid to find out what real life is about. And if that's the case, then all your so-called happiness is just cowardice and sham, isn't it?'" Her eyes pleaded with Hardy. "How could I not see what he was doing?"

"It's seductive, that's why," Hardy said. "If it's any help, I doubt Eve saw it either. She just wanted the knowledge, to taste the forbidden fruit."

"One little taste. That's all I wanted. Just to see."

"Original sin," Hardy said. "And so you're not the first to commit it, are you? It goes back a ways, that fall from grace. Some would say it's the human condition."

"But it wasn't who I was ever supposed to be."

"No," Hardy said heavily. "No, I don't suppose it was."

"That's the horrible thing. And then Tess." Her voice broke again. "If I could just have those days back. That day."

John Greenleaf Whittier's phrase hovered in Hardy's consciousness—"Of all sad words of tongue or pen, the saddest are these: 'It might have been.'" But he merely draped his arm over his client's shoulder and drew her in for a moment next to him. "You've still got lots of days ahead of you, Maya. Better ones. I promise you."

Suddenly, the bailiff knocked from the courtroom side and swung the connecting door open. Recognizing the not unfamiliar tableau—a suspect wrung out with emotion, a face nearly disfigured, swollen and red from crying—he stepped into the doorway and leaned over toward Hardy, asking with an unexpected solicitousness, "Everything okay here, sir?"

"If we could get a couple more minutes, I'd appreciate it," Hardy said. "And maybe some Kleenex."

31

Stier stood looking down onto Seventh Street from the third-floor window in Clarence Jackman's office. "You've got to be shitting me."

Jackman, obsidian black, stood six feet five inches tall and this morning had grunted in satisfaction when his bathroom scale failed to clear the two-hundred-seventy-pound marker. As always, he was dressed in a well-tailored dark suit and white shirt, today with a maroon-and-dark-blue rep tie. Ignoring Stier's profanity, Jackman spoke in his low-registered, powerful, quiet voice. "You needed to be told right away. Get it in front of Marian, put the woman on your witness list."

Stier turned. "Of course. Nothing else to do, really." He shook his head in disgust. "This was Schiff?"

"Apparently, although Bracco says he's just as responsible."

Another dismissive head shake. "Cops. What was she thinking?"

"I really believe she'd convinced herself it was immaterial. The woman seemed senile. Schiff didn't think you'd want some probably untrue random detail screwing up your story."

"I don't care about my *story*, Clarence. I build the case out of whatever story I've got to work with. If it's got inconsistencies . . . but, hell, you know this. And it would have been nothing if I laid it out up front. Now it looks like we buried it."

"I know that."

Stier slammed his hand on the windowsill. "Shit!"

"Right. But I'm afraid there's something maybe worse, if you'd like to sit down."

The request clearly surprised Stier, but this was his boss, so he went where Jackman indicated and sat on the front couple of inches of one of the leather couches. "Shoot," he said.

"Well, let me start out by admitting a personal bias, which I do try to leave out of my professional duties. Nevertheless, I think you may know, Paul, that Kathy West and I go back quite a way. When I first came on here, she walked me through quite a few minefields on the political side, actually was one of my informal advisers."

"Well, I—"

Jackman forged his smile of steel and held up a hand, cutting off the interruption. "If I may. My point is that I've watched this case develop over the past few months with a lot of interest and a bit of a sense of discomfort, not only because of the inherent weaknesses in the evidence, but because of the media blitz that's accompanied all of Jerry Glass's side of things with the mayor and Harlen Fisk and your defendant's husband.

"But I never felt I had to discuss this with you because, as I say, I generally like to stay out of battles where I have a personal stake, but also because you won at the PX, so there was nothing for me to say. The court had ruled."

Jackman slid his haunch off the edge of his desk and went to sit across from Stier in his leather wing chair. "But now, suddenly," he continued, "this new wrinkle—maybe there were two shots and not just one—seems to undermine your basic theory of the case. This is important to me, first because it's no longer personal, and second because, contrary to popular opinion, my job—*our* jobs, yours and mine—that job is not only to prosecute. It's to serve justice. It's to find the truth of what happened. If we find exculpatory evidence, it's our duty to put it in the record, not hide it so we can go ahead and get our conviction."

"I'm not hiding anything, Clarence. I didn't know about this until twenty minutes ago."

"No, I know that. I guess my real question is how does this make you feel about this case, and about your defendant? Does it change anything for you, and if so, what?"

Stier's body language—hunched shoulders, flushed complexion—belied the control he exerted over his confident tone. "Strategically, I'd admit it's a pain in the ass. It's going to give more credence to this testimony than it deserves. But as to the actual facts, first, they probably don't change a lick. You tell me the woman's apparently senile, so she may or may not have heard two shots, and in any event she didn't get to Schiff and Bracco until a couple of days later. Hell, what she heard might not even have been on the morning of the murder. So do I have an issue with my basic theory? No. None. Nothing's changed."

Jackman, hands relaxed and linked in front of him, nodded. "And Mr. Glass?"

"Regardless of what the media's doing with the mayor and all that, Jerry's helping me make the dope case, Clarence, and that's the motive here. I know it's unusual for the feds to get involved in one of our murders, but to me the financial stuff he's got already proves the money laundering, which in turn proves her complicity with Vogler. As for the mayor . . ." Stier met Jackman's gaze. "She's no part of my case. Neither's Fisk. That said, their financial dealings with Joel Townshend are complicated and wide-ranging, and I don't think Jerry's out of line looking into them."

"Well"—Jackman stole a peek at his watch—"thanks for making the time. I see you've got to be back in court in ten minutes."

This was a dismissal.

"Certainly." Stier got up and made it to the office door before he turned. "Thanks for the heads-up on Schiff's witness, Clarence, although I don't think she's going to make any difference in the verdict. And on the other stuff, I appreciate the candor."

Cheryl Biehl considered herself a close friend of Maya's. She'd visited her twice in jail, and Hardy knew that for a nonfamily member to brave the bureaucracy, indifference, cultural challenges, disorganization, noise, and crowds of the jail's visiting room showed a rare and true commitment and friendship. And to do so twice! Biehl's affection for Maya must be genuine. So he was happy that he wasn't going to be grilling her on her earlier testimony to Stier, testimony that had effectively painted her friend as a long-standing user and seller of drugs.

He was also marginally cheered, if slightly perplexed, by Stier's addition of a new witness, Lori Bradford, at this stage in the proceeding. Calling for a sidebar, and admitting as soon as the court had come back into session that he had only been informed of the existence of this witness during the lunch recess, Stier acknowledged that he would in all probability not actually call her. But he told Hardy and the court that a perusal of police procedures during the investigation had revealed that this woman's testimony had not made it into the inspectors' reports, and hence not into Hardy's discovery documents. Painting the oversight as little more than an unimportant technicality, Stier just wanted to preserve the sanctity of the record.

Hardy accepted this for the time being. He would have time to find out everything he might want to know about Lori Bradford and her testimony. And in the meanwhile he had what he hoped would be the simple cross-examination of Cheryl Biehl, where he might elicit some facts about her continuing friendship with his client that might help the jury view her in a better light in the here and now.

"Ms. Biehl," he began, "in the past eight years, have you ever witnessed Maya using or selling marijuana?"

"No."

"When you told her that you'd heard about Dylan Vogler selling marijuana out of Bay Beans West, what did she say to you about that?"

"She said she was sure that wasn't happening. Dylan didn't need to do that."

"And about her statement regarding Levon Preslee, that 'she was never going to get out from under them.' In spite of that comment, to the best of your recollection, did she ever mention Levon Preslee to you again?"

"No."

"So it was just that once, right after he got out of prison?"

"That's right."

"And how long ago was that?"

"I don't know exactly. It must have been seven or eight years."

Hardy took a beat, walking back to his table. Maya, her eyes still puffy from the crying jag, nevertheless seemed to be more engaged, less burdened somehow. He gave her a subtle nod of encouragement. And, in fact, Hardy felt he had cause for a renewed sense of hope. After all, he had two brand-new and unexpected facts with which to conjure—Lori Bradford and Tess Granat—and in his experience facts had always had a way of expanding concentrically, although he couldn't identify as yet the exact territory they were expanding into.

Now he paused.

He'd been considering trying to use Cheryl Biehl's cross-examination as a way to give the jury some kind of a sense of the real reason that Dylan had been blackmailing Maya. Of course, this would be a very tricky strategy on a couple of levels, not the least of which because it left Maya with essentially the same motive—blackmail—to have killed her manager. But these, he considered, might both be mitigated by other considerations. In the first case, blackmail over the hit-and-run took Maya's purported selling of dope and its attendant moral turpitude out of the equation, and this also removed any motive for her having killed Levon. Also, in the real world, and absent Maya's confession—which would never be forthcoming—there was no chance of building a case for the hit-and-run, so that issue was moot.

But somehow the risk of pursuing any of this seemed suddenly too great. Hardy had his own responsibility under the attorney-client privilege to keep any hint of what he'd just learned to himself. He didn't want to play any morally ambiguous games with his fragile client on this score. He was now finally her confidant and confessor, and he couldn't betray her by not-so-subtle implications of other motivations. So all in all, though Hardy thought that getting the fundamental truth about Maya and Dylan before the jury might have its advantages, in the end he decided it was not something he could do.

He turned back to his witness. "Thank you, Mrs. Biehl," he said. "No further questions."

As far as witnesses went, Jansey Ticknor had opened up after they'd charged Maya back in October. In her first interviews with Bracco and Schiff she had been unforthcoming, but during the course of Paul Stier's preparations for the preliminary hearing back in November, she had come to remember quite a bit of what she couldn't seem to initially recall about Maya Townshend and her relationship to Dylan. Now Stier was seeing to it that she was laying as much of it as she could out for the jury. "So Mr. Vogler told you about their earlier relationship?"

Hardy objected on the grounds of hearsay, but as he thought she might, Braun overruled him.

Hearsay was one of the most flexible and confusing concepts in all of jurisprudence—sometimes allowed, sometimes not—and Braun's interpretation today looked like she was going to be allowing Jansey's testimony. She was buying Stier's theory that Vogler's statements were against his penal interest—something so unfavorable to him that he would never have said it if it wasn't true. And this was an exception to the hearsay rule.

Braun also appeared to accept Stier's argument that the statements were admissible for Vogler's state of mind, an argument so arcane that even Hardy couldn't follow it. In any event, whether it was a valid legal call or not, Braun's decision was going to be the rule in this courtroom today, and Hardy had to live with it.

"Yes," she said, "they had been intimate in college."

"And since then?"

This time, in frustration, Hardy held up his hand. "Objection. Relevance."

"Goes to motive, Your Honor," Stier replied. If he wasn't going to convince the jury about the blackmail, he'd take the jilted lover as a backup position.

Braun nodded in her brusque fashion and again shot Hardy down. "Overruled."

"Since they finished college, then, Ms. Ticknor, did Mr. Vogler tell you that he'd had an intimate relationship with Defendant?"

"Yes. Up till a little before he met me."

Hardy felt a tight grip over his forearm and Maya's voice sharp in his ear. "That's a damn lie!" Loud enough for all the courtroom to hear it, and maybe even the one next door.

Judge Braun slammed her gavel.

But Maya, all but inert for much of these proceedings so far, suddenly had come alive. "That's just not true," she said to Hardy, then turned the other way in her seat, toward the jury, and addressed them directly. "That's not true," she repeated.

Bam! Bam! "Mr. Hardy, control your client! Bailiffs."

But before either of the two bailiffs could get to her, Maya had turned completely around to face her husband, sitting in the row behind her. "It's not," she said, "it's not."

"It's all right," he said. "I believe you." And he went to put an arm out to touch her.

But by this time the first bailiff had come up and gotten in between them, knocking Joel's arm away, looking up at Braun for instructions. And as if in response to this escalation the entire gallery seemed to erupt at once over the steady cadence of the gavel.

When at last, after nearly a minute, a restive silence, if not true order, had been restored, Braun glared down from the bench, looking to Hardy as if she'd suddenly aged ten years. Real fright that her courtroom had so quickly gotten out of her control showed in her face, in the set of her mouth. Maybe it hadn't happened to her in a while, but whatever the reason, she had been unprepared. As Hardy's heart pounded in his ear, from one pulse to the next, Braun shifted from intimidated oldster to wrathful prelate. She wielded her gavel, randomly, it seemed, in the near silence, and then dropped the little hammer again, until the silence was complete.

Gathering herself, she summoned Stier and Hardy to sidebar. She spoke with an exaggerated quiet. "Mr. Hardy, any further outburst from your client such as the one we've just all endured, and I will order her removed from the courtroom. She can watch these proceedings on closed circuit TV if she can't control herself. Is that about as clear as I can possibly make it?"

"Yes, Your Honor." He could have gone on with a bit more of a floral apology but decided to leave it at that. If nothing else, his client had just achieved one of his primary objectives—humanizing herself to the jury.

Hardy went back to counsel table and squeezed Maya's hand.

Stier, for his part, seemed to have enjoyed the blowup as well, for his own reasons. He would be happy to grant the defendant's humanity, too, so long as it was a humanity characterized by a hot temper and a dismissive disregard of authority.

He came back to his witness. "Ms. Ticknor, how long did this intimacy between himself and the defendant go on after Mr. Vogler got out of prison?"

"Until he met me."

"And when was that?"

"About six years ago."

Hardy had one hand over Maya's own hand on the table and his other hand firmly holding her arm just above her elbow.

"So they broke off their relationship because of you?"

"Yes."

Maya leaned over and whispered to Hardy. "Why is she saying this?"

Hardy thought he might know, but this really wasn't the time to talk about it, so he shook his head very slightly and squeezed her arm tighter.

Braun frowned in their direction.

And Stier went on. "Yet, after this breakup, Mr. Vogler kept working for her at BBW. As his domestic partner, did you know Mr. Vogler's salary there?"

"Yes. Ninety thousand dollars a year."

A few gasps from the gallery greeted this intelligence.

"Did your partner share with you why he was paid so handsomely?"

"Your Honor"—Hardy showing some exasperation—"hearsay, relevance, facts not in evidence, conclusory. None of this entire line of questioning is probative."

"It all goes to motive," Stier put in, "as will be clear shortly."

"Very well," Braun said. "The objections are overruled. Go ahead, Mr. Stier."

Stier repeated the previous question, and Jansey nodded with some enthusiasm. "She wanted to keep him around because she loved him. She thought she'd get him back."

"And how did you feel about that?"

"I didn't like it, of course. I resented it."

"Did you ask him to quit his job?"

"Several times."

"What reason did he give you for not quitting?"

"He couldn't make anywhere near as much anywhere else. Besides, he could sell the marijuana out of BBW without any hassles. He had the perfect situation, he said. He couldn't be fired. She was paying him just to keep him around."

"So, to your knowledge, did Mr. Vogler tell you that Defendant knew about the marijuana sold out of her shop?"

"Yes, of course."

Another whisper from Maya. *"That lying bitch!"*

Another upper-arm squeeze from Hardy.

Stier paused for a moment. Pure theatricality. "Ms. Ticknor, did anything change between Mr. Vogler and Defendant in the last year?"

"Yes."

"And what was that?"

"They started up an affair again."

"And how do you know about this?"

"Dylan wasn't coming home when he usually did and I called him on it."

"So he admitted it?"

"Yes."

"And what did you do?"

"I moved out. In with my parents."

"When was this?"

"About this time last year. Say six months before—before he was killed."

"And what happened next?"

"After a couple of weeks, he stopped it—the affair. He told me he'd made a mistake and begged me to come back to him, which I did. Mostly because of Ben. Our child. I wanted our son to have a father." Jansey ran a fingertip under one of her eyes, then the other.

"Yes, of course," Stier replied with an admirable sanctimoniousness. He turned to the jury, including them in his heartfelt emotion. Now, returning to his witness, he cleared his throat. "After this second and most recent rejection of Defendant by Mr. Vogler, did things change at BBW?"

"Yes."

"In what way?"

"Now she wanted to punish Dylan for dropping her, to fire him, but he couldn't let her do that. He had too much stuff going on at the store. He couldn't let it go."

"So what did he do?"

"Well, mostly he threatened to tell her husband about the affair, and also some of the stuff they'd done in college."

"In other words, he started blackmailing her."

"If you want to call it that. Yes."

"Thank you." And turning, he said to Hardy. "Your witness."

In spite of Maya's outburst both she and Hardy had known the gist of Jansey's testimony before she'd gone onto the stand—they had heard a similar version of it during the preliminary hearing. Hardy had hoped that much of Jansey's testimony would never in fact be heard by the jury because so much of it was hearsay.

Well, that would show him.

But against the urge to hope, he was always prepared. Taking some pages from his binder, he walked up to his place in front of

Jansey, handing them to her. "Ms. Ticknor," he began, "do you recognize these pages which I've just handed to you?"

She glanced down at them, turned them over. "Yes. They're transcripts of the talks I had with the inspectors."

"You've had a chance to read them and to compare them to the original tape-recorded statements that you gave police?"

"Yes."

"And they are a full and complete record of those interviews?"

"Yes, they are."

"Ms. Ticknor, you've just told Mr. Stier that you knew that Mr. Vogler was blackmailing the defendant, right?"

"Correct."

"And you're absolutely sure about that?"

"Yes."

"Now, Ms. Ticknor, I'd like you to turn to page two and read to the jury the highlighted section." Jansey looked down, found the place, and read in a shaky voice. *"If he was blackmailing her, he could have just asked for a raise, and she would have had to give it to him, right?"*

"Thank you. For the jury's benefit, Ms. Ticknor, the *him* and *her* you use refer to who?"

"Dylan and Maya."

"Good. So you were asking the inspectors a question about *if* Dylan were blackmailing Maya, isn't that so?"

"I guess so, but—"

Hardy cut her off. "So, Ms. Ticknor, if it is true that you knew at the time that Dylan was blackmailing Maya, why did you have to ask the inspector something that you already knew?"

"Well, I—"

"Let me ask you again. Did you know for a fact that Dylan was blackmailing Maya?"

"Well, I don't see how he could have—"

"*Ms. Ticknor.* Excuse me. Yes or no? Did you know for a fact that Dylan was blackmailing Maya?"

"Well, yes, he told me."

"But is it correct that you have no explanation for that passage in the transcript that you just read?"

"No. I guess I was just confused."

"Thank you." Hardy kept right on. "Now you have just testified that Dylan told you that he was not afraid of Maya because he could tell her husband about their affair and she needed him for the marijuana business. Isn't that right?"

"Well, yes."

"Thank you. Now I'd like you to read another short excerpt from the transcript of the same interview. Page four, please, the highlighted section."

Again, the witness found the spot and began to read: "*'You're right, though, about him not being afraid of her, or of losing the job.'*

"*'But he never talked about why?'*

"*'The most he ever said was that she owed him.'*" She looked back up at Hardy.

"*'The most he ever said was that she owed him.'* Are those your words?"

"Yes."

"And you are referring to Dylan and Maya again, right?"

"Right."

"So you're saying that the most Dylan ever said about not being afraid of Maya, or of losing his job, was that she owed him?"

Again, a querulous, uncertain nod. "I guess so."

"This isn't a guessing game, Ms. Ticknor. Again. Either that's what you said or it wasn't. Which is it?"

"Okay, that's what I said."

"The most Dylan said about not being afraid of Maya was that she owed him, is that it?"

"Yes."

"Yes." Hardy turned to include the jury. "But you just testified that he said a lot more than that, didn't you?"

"I don't know what you mean."

"You just testified that he said he could blackmail her for two separate reasons. Would you agree that that's different from that she owed him? Do you agree or not? Yes or no?"

"Well, that's what I meant."

"And how often did you have these conversations?"

"A lot of times." She took her plea directly to the jury. "Just when we talked. It was just stuff he told me."

"But when?" Hardy persisted. "If you didn't know about any of this when you spoke to the inspectors, after Dylan was already dead, when could you have talked about it with him?"

Jansey threw an agonized glance over at Stier. "I don't know. I'm not sure. But we did. I'm sure we did."

The point made, Hardy left it. "One last short reading, if I may. The highlighted section in the middle of page five."

By this time her voice had shrunk to a near-whisper, but she found her place. " *'Did he say what she owed him for?'*

" *'It wasn't like we really ever talked about it.'* "

"It wasn't like you really ever talked about it. That would be you and Dylan, correct?"

"Yes."

"Just one more thing, Ms. Ticknor. Tell the jury what the police found in the attic of your home."

"What do you mean?"

"I mean about a quarter million dollars' worth of marijuana. That's what I mean."

"Well, yes, the marijuana was up there."

"And that's the marijuana that you have just told us Dylan was selling in Maya's business?"

"Yes."

"So naturally, you've been arrested and charged with having a very large stash of marijuana growing for sale in your house, haven't you?"

"Well, of course not."

"But you've just told us you knew it was there?"

"Yes."

"Growing in your house?"

"Yes."

"Providing the money that supported, at least in part, you and your child, right?"

"Well, I never took any dope money."

"But the fact remains, you've never been arrested for or charged with possession of any of that sizable stash of marijuana. Did you ever discuss that possibility with the police?"

"Well, yes, they told me I wouldn't get in any trouble."

"Let me refresh your recollection, Ms. Ticknor, as to the order in which these conversations took place. First, you told the police you knew very little about what had happened, and nothing about the marijuana upstairs. Correct?"

"Well, that was my first statement."

"Then, more than a week later, after police told you that you could go to jail for a very long time if they connected you to Dylan's marijuana business, you recalled information that incriminated Maya Townshend. And then the police told you you wouldn't be charged for the marijuana upstairs. Isn't that pretty much the way it went?"

"Well, okay, but it's not the way you make it sound."

"Thank you," Hardy said. "No further questions."

32

It wasn't as though the media had lost interest in the trial, and today's testimony sent the scribes and pundits scurrying from the courtroom to their telephones and keyboards to report on the newly revealed allegations of Maya's infidelity, her subsequent rejection, and the added motivation this would certainly have given her to have murdered Dylan Vogler.

All this was, for example, on the evening news, which Hardy and his partners, over drinks, were watching on the huge TV they'd had installed in tasteful cabinetry on the back wall of the Solarium. Although as soon as the broadcast was done, Hardy hit the remote and turned the television off. "Never mind that none of it happened," he said, "though I hate to quibble."

Farrell, drinking espresso, was more or less back to being his old self, reconnected with his girlfriend, Sam, getting his hair cut with some regularity. Since it was after business hours, Phyllis had gone home, so Wes was comfortable enough coming downstairs with his dog and wearing his T-shirt, which today read "Eternity: Smoking or Nonsmoking."

"You live to quibble," he said to Hardy. "Quibbling gives meaning to your life, as anyone who knows you will surely attest."

Gina Roake sipped her Oban, neat. "Are you sure?" she asked. "None of it happened?"

"Okay, when they were in college. But not since. Sorry, but I believe Maya."

"So Jansey just perjured herself?" Gina asked.

Hardy, in trial mode, took a pull at his bottle of water and nodded. "All over the place."

"Why?"

Wes chuckled. "I love when you ask that, Gina. Like perjury's a surprise."

"I'm not surprised so much as disappointed it keeps happening. And what's in it for Jansey is, I guess, what I'm getting at."

"I think, first, mainly," Hardy replied, "is she's in no-man's-land and this is her ticket out. Early on, Stier or Schiff or somebody probably told her something like, 'We're not interested in how much you knew about Dylan's dope business, or what you got out of it, or if you're still in it. We're interested in Maya killing him, and if you can help us out on that, we'll just conveniently forget about the rest.' So she's heavily motivated to give them something. And what better than a bunch of stuff Dylan supposedly said to her, which no one can ever check or even refute? It's perfect. And she probably thinks Maya did it anyway, that is if Jansey didn't do it herself . . ."

"You think that's possible?" Gina asked.

Hardy shrugged. "Somebody did. Jansey's alibi's squishy at best. She's got a new boyfriend already, probably had him before. She's one of the best bets to have gotten her hands on the gun. But, though I hate to say it, Maya still doesn't look too bad for it either."

"Attaboy." Farrell had a strong and, it must be admitted, oft-justified prejudice that the client was always guilty. "Don't wimp out on that now."

"Don't worry. I'm pretty secure, although I admit there's a small chance I could still be swayed."

"By what?" Farrell asked.

"Oh, I don't know. A new fact or two."

"Well," Farrell said, "that's not going to happen, not at this stage."

"Actually, it might," Hardy said. "In fact, maybe it already did."

He told them about Lori Bradford, new to Stier's witness list. "I've already sent Wyatt out to talk to her, see what she's got to say."

"What's in the police reports?" Gina asked.

A rueful grimace. "It seems they never got around to writing it up."

"You shock me," Farrell said.

"I know," Hardy agreed. "It's rocked my worldview. But the fact remains, she's got to have something to say or Stier wouldn't have made such a fuss about getting her on the witness list. Even if he's not going to call her. He's hoping I'm going to let her slide too." He smiled at his two partners. "But I'm afraid I'm going to let him down on that. At least until I know what she's got, or not."

Seven-thirty P.M., killing time until Craig Chiurco's expected arrival, Hardy sat at his desk. As was his habit, he was reviewing his files, hoping something among this amorphous mass of kindling might spark. The files now ran to four thick black three-ring notebooks, into which he'd crammed, in some semblance of order, forensics reports, police reports, interview transcripts such as those he'd used with Jansey in the courtroom today, photographs, private notes of Schiff and Bracco—the endless accretion of litigation.

At last, having reviewed his notes on Jansey's testimony—forty-seven pages' worth—for the second time, he closed the binder and leaned back into his chair. Though part of him yearned to recall her to the stand and pick apart individual strands of her testimony that he'd left unaddressed that afternoon—which was, after all, most of it—he also realized that he'd succeeded in doing his main job, which was discrediting her so that all of her testimony was suspect. Besides, he couldn't ignore his gut feeling, his pure instinct, that there was nothing in her perjured story that, were the truth known, would likely change any juror's opinion about Maya's guilt. The basic facts remained—whether Maya had had an affair with him or not, Vogler had been blackmailing her, she'd been paying the blackmail (which meant she was guilty of *something*), she'd gone down to BBW and over to Levon's.

Why? Why? Why?

Jansey was undoubtedly lying, but lying for all of her own, probably very good, reasons. In the end he believed that nothing she said was going to make any real difference.

Hardy got up, walked first over to the window where he looked down on Sutter Street, then came around to another recessed cabinet on the wall across from his desk, this one holding his dartboard. He opened the doors of the cabinet and slid them back into wherever they went, then grabbed his tungsten beauties from their slots and retreated to the dark cherrywood throw line in his polished white oak hardwood floor.

Twenty. Double twenty. Five.

From the board to the line.

One. Five. Twenty. Then one, one, five. Another four or five lost rounds—terrible, atypical shooting—before he finally rang up twenty, twenty, twenty.

Okay.

Leaving those darts where they'd landed, he lifted himself back onto the desk.

Chiurco, again in his coat and tie, sat in a wing chair across from Hardy in the more informal of the two seating arrangements in the office. He seemed nervous, so Hardy did the initial lifting. "So. Levon Preslee."

"Okay."

"Remind me. How did his name come up in the first place?"

"Wyatt had put me on Dylan's old robbery conviction. He thought there might be some tie-in to whatever he was using to blackmail

Maya. Or, even better, we might turn up somebody else who wanted to kill him."

"So how'd you get to Preslee?"

"I just did a Web search. I found Vogler. That gave me the robbery in 1997. And there's his codefendant, Levon. So I run him on the Web and find out he's working for ACT. You're not going to believe this, but he's also listed in the phone book. I figure he works in the theater, he's probably home during the day, so I drove out there. I didn't even know that Wyatt had run across him, too, until I heard about that from you guys."

"You didn't call him first?"

"No, sir. I thought in case he wasn't right with all this stuff, I might get better answers if I caught him off guard."

"So then what?"

"Then I get into his lobby, and there's this woman standing there at the door."

"How'd you know it was Maya? Had you met her before?"

"No, but she's our client. I saw her picture in the paper. It was her."

"As it turns out, you're right."

"But anyway, I didn't know what she was doing there, or what I should do, so I just stood there for a minute."

"Then what?"

"Well, she told me he wasn't home, and walked out past me. Mr. Hardy, honest to God, I think she was jiggling the doorknob like she was trying to get in, but I got there a split second too late, and I can't be absolutely positive. But really, that's what I think I saw."

"Well, then, if that's the best you can do for us, then that's what we're going to go with. At least it's something. If I call you to testify, don't try to improve it. That's what you've got to say. Got it?"

"Got it."

"Okay, then. So write it up just like that and sign it, because if I decide to call you, I'll need to give the discovery to the DA."

"Cool."

"Okay, then. Have a good night."

"You too."

"She's an old lady," Wyatt Hunt said, "but I don't know where they got senile."

Hardy had remembered to call home and tell Frannie he didn't know when he'd be in—common enough during trials—but at the same time he'd remembered that he'd also forgotten to eat. So when Hunt had checked in after his meeting with Lori Bradford, saying he was at his own office just around the corner on Grant, Chinatown's main street, preparing to go out to grab some Chinese, Hardy invited himself along.

Now they sat on high stools, sharing a tiny two-top in the front window, the only two customers, eating shrimp and pork and no sign of souvlaki lo mein à la Lou the Greek's. A good thing.

"So what's her story?"

Hardy chewed and listened while Hunt laid it out. For all of its simplicity the implications, Hardy realized, might be enormous—nothing less than a complete restructuring of the theory of the case. More importantly, there was no set of facts he could imagine that would be consistent with Maya having been involved in this two-shot scenario.

"No," he told Hunt, "think about it. There's only one shot from the supposed murder weapon, right? Right. So what did she do, shoot once—at what? Dylan? Some kind of warning shot? Unlikely. But the main thing is if there's that second shot from the one gun, the magazine would have been light two bullets, and it wasn't, just one. And to get back to that one, she would have had to reload. And that's just plain absurd."

"Stier's going to say it didn't happen, period. He'll even use your own argument of no evidence. No second casing, no second slug, no nothing. It didn't happen. It was a backfire."

"Yeah. Right. I know. But let's pretend for a minute."

"All right. So what do you see?"

"Got to be two guns."

"Two?"

Hardy, into it, put down his chopsticks. "Whoever came to shoot Dylan had his own gun and knew Dylan carried, so he stuck him up at gunpoint for the other gun first."

"Why? Why didn't he just shoot him, bang?"

"He knew him. Maybe first he thought they could talk it out, whatever their differences were. Maybe Dylan tried to stall him somehow."

"So they had a meeting planned? With Maya too?"

Hardy shook his head. "I don't have that one figured yet. How would this woman, the one you saw tonight—"

"Lori."

"Right. How would she be on the stand?"

"Pretty good, I'd say. Sincere and smart. Knew exact times for the shots and remembered the day and date even after all this time. She's no dummy, Diz."

"So. What is it? Did Stier just not believe her? I mean, why leave her out up front instead of trying to find some way to explain her story? And, PS, it's pretty easily explained, as you've already done about a minute ago."

"He might not have known about her."

"Till when?" Then Hardy pointed a finger, recalling the tense lunchtime gathering at Lou's with Glitsky and Jackman and the inspectors. "Maybe lunchtime today, huh?"

"The thought crossed my mind, to be honest."

"This could do it," Hardy said. "For the verdict, I mean."

Hunt popped a shrimp. "It might," he said, then cocked his head with a question. "Is there something else? Besides the verdict?"

"There's who really did it, Wyatt. If it wasn't Maya. And if there were two guns . . ."

The idea set back Hunt in his chair. "Well, now," he said, and stared out the window into the misty street. "An innocent client? Wes swears that never happens in real life."

"I know. He'll be devastated, but he's been wrong before."

After a minute, Hunt came forward again, elbows on the table. "But so, on the other thing, I've been dying to know what you found out."

"What other thing?"

"Tess Granat? The hit-and-run? I Googled it after lunch."

"Thank God for Google," Hardy said, really wishing that Hunt hadn't brought this up again. "Everything that's ever happened, there it is."

"Except Dylan Vogler. His early life, at least."

"What do you mean?"

"I mean that except for the few days right after he got shot, I think our friend Dylan might be the only human being Google hasn't found and chronicled."

"You looked?"

"Diz. Google's half my life, maybe three quarters. It's where you look first. Which brings us back to Tess Granat, who was very real and very chronicled. So what'd you find out?"

Hardy picked up his tea and blew on it. "Nothing."

"Nothing? She wouldn't say, or what? Even if she wasn't involved, she must have known all about it."

Hardy could see there wasn't anything to do but come clean. "It was a privileged conversation, Wyatt. I can't talk about it."

Hunt broke a smile. "Diz. Dude. I'm your investigator. I'm covered by the privilege."

"Well, just because I can tell you doesn't mean I should. And don't think it doesn't break my heart." Hardy put his cup down, moved on. "But, listen, I don't know if we're going to need that anyway. This Lori Bradford, as I said, might do it all by herself. We've got to get her subpoenaed."

"As our witness?"

"Absolutely. And ASAP, I think."

Hunt took a small notebook from his jacket pocket and made a note. "I'll have Craig come by your office for it in the morning."

"That'll work," Hardy said. "I'll make one out first thing and leave it with Phyllis. Give the boy some meaningful labor, work through his problems."

"Well, I'm hoping he's over them. Kids, you know. Love."

"I've heard of 'em both," Hardy said.

"Anyway, if Craig doesn't show, I will. Don't worry. And I got Lori on tape tonight, anyhow, for what that's worth. It's back at the office, locked up."

"Excellent." Hardy put away the last bite of pork and looked at his watch. Quarter to ten. Blowing out heavily, he shook his head. "Sometimes I think I'm getting too old for these things anymore."

"Trials?"

"Not just trials. Murder trials."

"I thought they were the fun part, when lawyers felt most alive."

Hardy gave him a look. "Uh-huh. Only in the sense that when you're suffering, at least you know you're alive."

"Well, there you go."

"There you go," Hardy said.

But suddenly, Hardy realized as he was driving home that the confluence of the two new facts he'd only discovered today—the two-shot scenario at the alley behind BBW, and Maya's involvement with the death of Tess Granat—had, much against his will and inclination, pushed him not just over the line into doubt about his client's guilt, but into a near certainty that she might in fact be innocent.

The key element regarding Tess Granat, which he and Hunt had hinted about at lunch today, was simple and yet profound. Dylan Vogler had known about the accident and had been blackmailing Maya about it since he'd gotten out of prison. Hardy could believe— and in fact had believed—that his client had all the motive in the world to have killed Dylan. She'd also had means and opportunity.

What had changed in the Tess Granat scenario, which had the rather significant advantage of being true, was that to Hardy's mind, it completely eliminated Levon Preslee from the picture. He'd already gotten his one favor, his job, from Maya, and maybe even through Dylan. But that had evidently been enough. That job had worked for him, for a new start on a different life. And in any event, that favor, or whatever it was, had been years before. There was no record or even sniff of a record that Maya had seen or spoken to him in eight years before she suddenly went over to his apartment on the day he was killed.

Again—why?

Because Levon had called her?

In just the same way that Dylan had called her?

Or had someone else called her? Either or both times?

Someone who was connected to both Dylan and to Levon in the present, and who might have had dealings with them in the past as well?

Paco.

33

At ten-fifteen, long after everyone else except the downstairs guards had left the building, Harlen Fisk sat holding a Glock .40-caliber semiautomatic weapon, the twin to his sister's, in his office upstairs in City Hall. Harlen had bought both the guns at the same time, while he was still only a couple of years into his service with the police force. As was the custom, when Glock came out with the new model, they'd offered it at a discount to active-duty cops, in the hope that cops would come to favor the gun and entire cities would order it as the on-duty weapon for their police force. In fact, he'd insisted on buying Maya's for her after they'd had an early robbery at BBW. You needed a weapon if you owned a store in the Haight, even if you weren't planning to use it. It was good for peace of mind.

Back in those days Dylan's time in prison hadn't seemed to weigh so heavily on everyone. Not even to a cop like Harlen. They'd all known each other when Dylan and Maya had been in college, Harlen the older brother, not yet a cop. Sometimes they all smoked dope together, had some laughs. Then Dylan had done something truly dumb, and got caught. But he'd paid for it, and now he was working with Maya, doing a great job. Harlen never considered that he'd go back to crime. Why would he? He didn't need it.

So he'd bought the guns, the Glocks. Harlen hadn't even known or cared about the ballistics quirk—that fired bullets from this model couldn't usually be traced back to a particular gun—until he'd heard about it at trial.

Harlen's office wasn't large, and most of it was filled with the old-fashioned desk and free-standing bookshelves that lined the wall to his right. To his left the view out his large windows across Van Ness included a glorious stretch of San Francisco's somewhat grandiose architecture—the Opera House, Performing Arts Center, and War Memorial. Behind him a framed rogues gallery of himself posing with various other politicians and celebrities—his aunt Kathy, of course, Bill and Hillary, Dianne Feinstein, Robin Williams, Dusty Baker in his Giants uniform—offered mute but compelling testimony to his own popularity and success.

Harlen had made it, in a somewhat tortuous route, and in the most cutthroat of fields, almost to the very top. At least to the city's top—and after that, who knew how far he could go? He'd been a supervisor now for seven years, after starting out as a clerk in Kathy's office just out of college about seven years before that. Through his aunt Kathy's tutelage and influence he'd joined the PD as a uniformed patrolman, and rose quickly, finally making it all the way to homicide for a few months before finally quitting and jumping over to the political side, starting with the low rungs of community activist work—soup kitchen and homeless shelter service on the one hand; victims' rights advocacy, a natural with his police background, on the other. Mix in a couple of stints on various visible boards—the National Kidney Foundation, Friends of the San Francisco Public Library—and a term on the school board, and then Kathy moved up to mayor and he ran for and won her seat on the Board of Supervisors.

And now here he was, gun in hand, wondering if it was all going to end.

The immediate problem was Cheryl Zolotny. No, Biehl now. Sweet sweet girl, and hot hot hot when she'd been younger. In fact, she was still more than easy to look at, and in other circumstances he might have found himself falling into those bedroom eyes—eyes that he'd once known well—over lunch.

But not today.

Today her testimony about all those years ago with Maya simply had made Harlen realize how at risk he still was. This was a woman who'd not only known him, she'd done drugs with him. And so, okay, it had only been marijuana. Lately, and in spite of his long-term support of the medical marijuana laws and parlors in the city, he'd come to appreciate how much trouble a little pot could get people into.

If only Dylan hadn't been wearing that backpack . . .

But he had.

And now Cheryl, from out of nowhere, had suddenly returned full-blown into the picture. Not that she was, so far as he knew, out to get him in trouble in any way. In fact, at lunch she'd been nothing if not inviting, even downright flirtatious, in spite of her marital status. Making noises about how flattered she was that he—a very important man now, in his exalted position—that he even remembered her from back when they'd fooled around a little, when she'd been just a kid.

But what if she talked to somebody, some reporter, anybody really? There was nothing more true about Harlen's business than the fact that you couldn't hide. He took it as a truism as universal as Murphy's Law that a politician with a damaging secret somewhere out in the ozone was a finished politician. It would come out—the fact that he'd known Levon too. Hung with him.

He kept asking himself, so what? So what?

And the simple answer was that he didn't know the consequences— from petty to profound—if the people already hounding him about these forfeiture issues got any more to chew on. No matter what, he thought, it would mean more headlines, and not the good kind. It was one thing to help a poor black kid get a job at ACT after a stretch in prison, but quite another to have partied with him and his doper friends and your own murder-suspect, dope-dealing sister. And even if it wasn't a career-breaking matter to the general public, it would be to Kathy.

It could finish him.

And Cheryl knew all about it. And, yes, she'd told him that of course if it was important to him, she'd keep all that old stuff to herself. But what if . . . ?

What if?

He looked down at the gun in his hand. What did he think he was doing with that? Had he come down here thinking that his career, his life, was really so close to over, that perhaps he was really going to kill himself? What about Jeannette and the kids? What would they do without him?

He had to relax. After all, nothing had happened yet. Maybe nothing ever would. And Cheryl had promised him that she'd keep it between them forever. Just like their other secrets from when they'd dated. She'd never betray him. She understood everything he'd told her and agreed that it was important.

Super important, she'd actually said. And the insipid, Valley girl adjective had brought back one of the other realities about Cheryl the ex-cheerleader. She had been hot hot hot, no doubt, but also dumb, dumb, dumb. Super dumb.

Was she too dumb to understand what she knew? Or should he try to contact her again? Set up an appointment.

Make it clearer.

Robert Tripp, in his scrubs, came out of the bathroom, peeled off his surgical gloves, and dropped them into the trash can in Jansey's kitchen. "I think I got it all." He started running the water in the sink, soaping up his hands. "But that was not a pretty job."

"Thank you," she said. She sat at the kitchen table, a glass of wine in front of her. "I owe you. I just couldn't handle that tonight."

Tripp turned. "What if I wouldn't have been here?"

"I would have quarantined the bathroom and forbidden flushing until I could call the plumber."

"You could always do it yourself."

She made a face. "I do a lot of good-mother stuff, Robert. I really do. But putting my hands in that—"

Tripp held up his hands. "Gloves, then soap. Does wonders."

"Did he use the whole roll, you think?"

"Most of it. Looked like it, anyway."

"Yuck. I'm sorry. But yuck."

"Lucky you got me." He dried his hands and came to sit down across from her. "But other than that, Mrs. Lincoln, how'd you like the play?"

She drank off about half her glass and shook her head. "It's been a tough day, if you want to know. Tough all the way. I look at Maya sitting there across from me, and she looks so harmless, really, so pathetic almost. I think she'd been crying before she came into court. Then I feel like such a beast, somehow."

He reached across and put his hand over hers. "She did it, hon. I thought we were pretty clear about that. No matter what she looks like."

"I know. I know. But there's just all this other stuff."

"What other stuff?"

"You know. The insurance, when they're going to pay out, whether the cops are still going to come after me for something about the business."

"Didn't they say not?"

"Well"—she shrugged—"if you believe them. But I never signed anything, so I guess they still could."

Tripp stood up and came around the table, pulling up a chair next to her. He put his arm around her shoulders and drew her toward him, kissed the hollow of her neck, and held himself there for a moment. "You're just worrying. I love you."

"I just think what if it's not her?"

He pulled away. "But it is her. Who else would it be?"

"I know. I know. But it was just way different actually facing her and saying all that stuff out loud. And I also know—don't think I don't—that once she's convicted, it's way better for us."

"Hey," he said gently, "we're cool. We don't have to worry about us."

"But I do. I mean, if he calls me back again."

"Who's that?"

"The defense guy. Mr. Hardy."

"What about him?"

"Well, he didn't even ask about us."

"Why would he?"

"Well, you know, because . . ."

"Because we're an item?"

She turned to him. "Not because we're an item, now, Robert. Because we *were* an item. I mean, then. That's never come out, and if it does . . ."

"Then what?"

"I don't know. But something, I'd think."

"Why?"

"Because it gives me a reason . . ." She blinked back the starts of tears.

He pulled her again to him, his hand on her neck, whispered into her ear. "You're just worn down, Janz. It's been a long haul, that's all. And it doesn't matter if you've got all the reason in the world to have done him—which, by the way, you did . . ."

"Don't say that!"

"All right. But the fact remains, it still doesn't matter, since I said you were here."

"But I *was* here."

"Of course. But me saying it makes you really here, with an actual alibi, as they call it. You know what I mean." He put a finger under her jaw, gently. Lifted it so that she was looking at him. "We've talked all about this. Lots of times."

"I know. I'm being stupid, I guess."

"Not so stupid." He kissed her. "But really really cute, all upset the way you are."

She pouted, shook her head. "I don't feel cute."

"I bet I could fix that in about five minutes."

She stared past him through the window into the darkness outside. "He never asked me about us at all," she said.

"That's because you and me, we're not what this is about. This is about Maya killing Dylan, and helping the prosecution prove it. That's all it's about."

"You're really sure?"

"I'm positive, hon. Absolutely positive."

Ruiz thought it would have been downright irresponsible, since they had the program in place and working smoothly, to simply abandon the business just because Dylan was gone, along with his steady supply of quality sensimilla. The other long-term employees at BBW weren't likely to find any other job that gave them a monthly bonus even close to what Dylan had paid them for their loyalty and cooperation and Ruiz was, of course, ready to step in almost immediately once the heat just after the shooting had dissipated.

Now, near midnight, Ruiz was in his ten-year-old Camaro crossing Golden Gate Park's panhandle at Masonic, on his way to tonight's meeting with his new source—actually his old friend, Jaime Gutierrez, but who knew he was dealing weed until you looked around?—and pick up some product for the upcoming week. Tuesday was always the night, and earlier on Jaime had left him a text message on his cell with the always different address, same as usual.

So Ruiz had shut down BBW at ten o'clock and swung by his apartment on Parnassus, where he'd picked up his eight thousand dollars cash, which he knew was way too much to be carrying around normally, but it was only once a week and had to be done. He also grabbed the old funky revolver, a six-shooter actually, that Jaime had sold him once they'd done the first couple of deals and it had looked like it was going to keep working.

Of course, Ruiz knew that having a gun hadn't done any good for Dylan, but that's because Dylan had gotten complacent over time. Everybody at BBW knew where he kept it at work and how he carried it in his jacket's inside pocket whenever he was moving either product or money or both. And he was really, at base, such a trusting guy. Made a lot of money, gave a lot of it away, a sweetheart.

Ruiz was smarter. Nobody at BBW knew he even had this gun. Or when he moved the money in and out. Or, especially, when or where he scored his product.

Although, he had to admit, this was the area of the business where Dylan had shown a talent for organization and control, and Ruiz was planning on emulating that model once he could get himself into a bigger crib where he could grow his own in quantity, the way Dylan had done in his attic. Which had meant that Dylan didn't have to go to these weekly buys that always felt a little sketchy. Dylan hadn't had to buy; he only sold, and that made everything so much cleaner. Even after all their years together Ruiz never figured out where he'd stored the cash in or around the store. No one ever knew when he'd show up with the product, or leave with cash.

So, the lesson to take home from that—keep all your logistics to yourself, as Dylan had done. The thing to watch for, Ruiz knew, was one of the other guys in the shop getting ideas that he could take over if Ruiz disappeared. Just as Ruiz had. Dylan had never considered that possibility, or at least never showed it if he did.

Oh, well, times changed. Lives changed.

And now in his new life, Ruiz parked on Turk down by Divisadero—the whole area darkened now since this neighborhood, the outer Fillmore, tended to be underserved by the Department of Public Works. Streetlights were not the biggest priority here—it was hard to say if, in fact, there were any other civic priorities either.

Locking the car, checking for foot traffic—none—Ruiz heard hip-hop loud from a block or two away. The wind was light but very cold, and Ruiz pulled his parka up over his chin, hands in its pockets, around his gun in one and his money in the other, and checked doorways until he got to the address and stopped.

It was an old-style apartment building, four stories. The lobby shimmered under dull ceiling fluorescents, their coverings yellowed with age and neglect. Ruiz tried the front door.

Which was open.

How Jaime found these places, he didn't know.

A large gray cat sat in a litter box just under the mailbox and from the smell, Ruiz was pretty sure it wasn't the only animal that had relieved itself nearby. Maybe even some humans.

He was looking for 3F, so he pressed the single elevator button, but it didn't light up. He only waited twenty seconds or so before he gave up and turned for the stairway. The second floor was dimmer than the lobby, but somewhat to his relief the third was brighter. Sweating now with nerves and the exertion of the climb—he *had* to get going making his own garden grow—he turned out of the stairwell and walked back to 3F, where he knocked twice, then once.

Spy shit. He chuckled at it. Ridiculous.

And in a moment the door opens and here is Jaime, happy as ever, slapping his five, mellow, without a care in the world. Ruiz took a last look behind him on the landing, then stepped in and Jaime closed the door behind them, threw the dead bolt.

An adequate apartment, if a little small—maybe one of Jaime's girlfriends'. Living room, dining room, kitchen. Furnished in Goodwill, but not bad. Tasteful.

Their usual protocol was they had a beer or two and caught up, exchanged money for product, made sure they were good for the next week, and said good-bye, and this is what they did now. The whole thing took twenty minutes, tops.

And then they were saying their good-byes. Jaime was throwing back the dead bolt, starting to open the door, when suddenly it exploded in on them and they were being backed up by two guys in big parkas. Each carried a gun, pointed straight at Jaime and Ruiz. Both guns had extensions on their barrels.

The two parkas advanced, but didn't back up their targets for long, maybe a step or two.

Then they opened fire.

34

"I know you're awake. Pick up."

It was still dark out, 5:42 A.M., and Hardy was having his morning coffee and reading the front-page story in the paper about his day in court yesterday, when Jansey Ticknor had implicated his client in a long-standing and, he was sure, completely spurious affair with Dylan Vogler. For not the first time—and though he already had some marginally serviceable answers—he was asking himself why she had perjured herself so thoroughly and wondering if he had anything to gain by calling her back to the stand and taking her head off.

But at the sound of Glitsky's voice, these cogitations fled and he leaned over and grabbed the receiver. "This isn't what we call a reasonable time."

"You're in trial. I know you're up."

"Frannie's not in trial."

"I didn't call that phone."

"You've got all the answers."

"Got to. I'm a cop. People depend on me."

"Actually, I'm glad you called. I was going to check in with you today about Lori Bradford."

"I figured you would someday, but that's not what I called about. Do you know who Eugenio Ruiz is?"

"Why do you ask?"

"Diz. Don't play games with me, please. Of course you know who he is, right?"

"BBW. The new manager."

"Right. Except now he's the new dead manager."

"Oh, my God, poor Eugenio."

"I don't know, Maya. Maybe not so poor."

"So what does this mean?" she asked him. They were next to one another at the table in the glass-block-enclosed attorney visiting room. It was still a few minutes short of eight A.M. "Besides that, after this, now we're definitely closing the place down. We should have done it before, but Joel wanted to make a stand against Glass. So you're telling me they were still selling dope out of there."

"It looks like it. At least Eugenio was." Hardy shrugged. This was by no means the most important issue of the day, nor the most unexpected. "Dylan had the whole system set up, everybody who worked there probably in on it. It makes sense somebody kept it going."

"Do they have any suspects? I mean for who shot him."

"No. It's way too soon for that."

"I hope Joel has an alibi. If he found out that Eugenio was dealing again after all we've been through, he would have killed him."

"Let's not mention that to anybody, okay? But it wasn't Joel, even without an alibi. There were two different-caliber bullets, so it looks like two shooters. What it looks like, classically in fact, is a dope rip. Somebody followed somebody to where the money and the dope changed hands and just started blasting away."

"That happens over marijuana?"

"Every day, Maya. Every day."

"It seems so strange. Remember when we were younger?"

"I wasn't young when you were, but I know what you mean."

"It's so hard to imagine. I mean, a little grass was like nothing, no big deal at all, and now these people are dying over it."

"It's illegal. So it's prohibition all over again."

"They ought to just legalize it."

"That's a different discussion which I'd love to have with you someday. But let's not make the argument when you get on the stand. How's that?"

The comment clearly offended her. "I'm not stupid, Diz."

"Not even close, Maya." He pushed his chair back a little from the table, crossed one leg over the other. "But you asked me what the killing of Ruiz meant for us. I'd like to pretend that Braun or maybe Stier will see this as the next step in a turf war that began with Dylan and Levon, and one that you couldn't have been involved in, so they'll just decide this whole prosecution and trial is a mistake and let you go. But unfortunately, that is not happening, not in a million years."

"So. What's left?"

"What's left is a guy named Paco, who Eugenio maybe could have identified, and now definitely can't."

"Paco?"

"Ring a bell?"

"Well, actually, yes."

Hardy sat back with a little thrill of surprise and pleasure. "Tell me you know him and where he lives and you could pick him out of a lineup."

She bit her lip. "None of the above, I'm afraid. But I do know that name. He was a friend of Dylan's. And Levon's, too, for that matter."

"All dead guys now, you notice. When did Paco know them? Back in college?"

She nodded. "Sometime back there. Evidently they were all kind of the in crowd before I became part of it. You know, Dylan and his pals always doing this crazy, dangerous stuff. And this kind of legendary guy named Paco."

"So what happened to him? You never met him?"

"No. He was supposedly gone by the time I showed up."

"Dropped out, transferred, what?"

"No idea, really. Maybe he wasn't even in school with us, was just kind of a hanger-on. Except, you know, I'm pretty sure Paco wasn't his real name. It was more like a nom de guerre. Sometimes I got the feeling it was somebody we all actually knew. I mean still knew, and still hung out with. It was just like Dylan to wrap it all up in a mystery and be the one keeping the big secret. Sound familiar?"

"You think Dylan might have been blackmailing him too?"

"I don't know. I kind of doubt it."

"Why?"

"Well, I think first, he didn't need to. He had me. And second, if you don't have a weak and guilt-ridden person like me you're dealing with, blackmail can be a little dangerous. I mean, you'd better know your mark. You threaten to expose the wrong thing about the wrong guy, and the guy goes, 'Uh, no. I think I'll kill you instead.' You know what I'm saying?"

"I do. And Paco wasn't weak or guilt-ridden?"

"Evidently not. His toughness was why he was legendary. He was a real player. He used to go out with Dylan and Levon, like I did later, but was . . . well, he wasn't just a tagalong. They supposedly hit this liquor store once and the clerk pulled a gun and Paco shot him dead."

"This was a different robbery than the one Dylan and Levon went down for?"

"Yeah. Before I'd even met them. But when Dylan told me about it, I thought he was just bragging, making it sound like they were such romantic studs, sticking up places, these fearless kind of Robin Hood guys, getting money from these liquor stores and buying our dope with it, which they shared with everybody. How did I ever get involved with people like that? I just don't know how that happened."

"Maybe by doing robberies with them?"

"You make it sound way worse than it was. It wasn't anything strong arm. It was more just intimidation to get stuff we wanted. Three or four of us putting the press on somebody, that's all. It was mostly just other kids and their dope."

"You just took it from them?"

She didn't answer, looked down at the floor.

"At gunpoint?"

"No! Never with a gun. Dylan wouldn't use a gun after Paco. Said you couldn't predict what would happen and didn't want another mistake."

"Dylan thought it was a mistake, then? Using a gun."

"Oh, yeah, definitely. He saw it as the reason Paco stopped hanging with them. And that really bummed him out. One less guy he had power over."

"So Paco checked out because . . . ?"

"Maybe he grew a conscience about the guy he shot. The way I heard it was Paco hadn't planned to kill anybody. It was all kind of a lark that suddenly went bad." She looked askance at Hardy. "That's the way it happened with Dylan. You started messing around with him and doing crazier and crazier things until you did something awful that you didn't mean to do at all. Just one moment of frailty falling in with these guys, and then somehow later you are in just completely the wrong place you never really meant to be. Me and what happened with Tess. Levon. Maybe this guy Paco, I don't know."

It appeared that Stier wasn't going to let himself be sidetracked by the discovery of Lori Bradford or the murder of Eugenio Ruiz. He had three other witnesses tentatively scheduled to appear whose testimony, Hardy knew, closely adhered to that of Cheryl Biehl's about Maya's collusion with both Dylan and Levon in the marijuana business in college.

But since Stier had skipped from Biehl straight over to Jansey Ticknor, Hardy thought he was probably going to abandon any more discussion about Maya's distant past. Everybody in the courtroom probably believed by now that his client had dealt drugs in college. What Stier had to get to next was her current involvement in Dylan's operation, and to that end, as soon as Braun had taken the bench, he called Michael Jacob Schermer.

Schermer, in his mid-sixties, might have been an athlete in his earlier life, or even still a long-distance runner in this one. Tall, thin, white-haired, and very well dressed for the courtroom in a light green Italian suit, he projected a quiet confidence as he took the oath and went to the witness chair.

"Mr. Schermer," Stier began, "what is your profession?"

"I'm an accountant."

"And for how long have you been in accounting?"

Schermer, genial, sat back to enjoy the experience of testifying, which he'd clearly done many times before. He broke a small smile that he shared with the jury. "About forty years."

"And have you developed a specialty over these years?"

"Yes, I have. It's called forensic accounting." Again, bringing in the jury. "It's kind of like a superaudit, with a lot of computerized analysis and other bells and whistles, if you want to put it in lay terms."

"And you are licensed in this field?"

"Yes. I am licensed and accredited as a CFE, or certified fraud examiner."

"And what do you do in this line of work?"

"Well"—Schermer shrugged—"as the name implies, I'm basically trained to identify fraudulent business practices or financial transactions, embezzlements, misappropriation of assets, questionable bankruptcies, and so on."

"And how do you do that?"

"Well, it gets a little complicated." Here he paused for the jury and gallery to chuckle with him. "But basically I analyze both physical and computerized accounting records to document I and E to—"

"Excuse me, Mr. Schermer, what is I and E?"

"Oh, sorry. I live in a world of jargon, I'm afraid. I and E is income and expenses. So I basically analyze I and E and movement of assets. I also reconstruct I and E to find hidden or illicit income. Stuff like that."

"Money laundering?"

"Yes. That's more or less my subspecialty."

"Good. Thank you. Now, Mr. Schermer, have you had occasion to examine the financial records of Bay Beans West for the six months ending November first of last year?"

"Yes, I did."

"And did you discover accounting irregularities?"

"I did."

Hardy, sitting back in his chair, knew that this was not going to be a high point for the defense. His only early hope had been that the financial testimony itself would be so dry and technical that the jury's interest would flag after five minutes or so. But Schermer's chatty and agreeable style looked like it was going to trump the material itself. A quick glance at the jury verified this view.

"Could you summarize these irregularities for the jury?"

"Well, there wasn't just one kind."

Hardy thought he might as well get in a lick or two if he could, and he objected. "Nonresponsive, Your Honor." And much to his surprise Braun sustained him. Irrationally buoyed by the tiny decision, he straightened in his chair, pulled his yellow legal pad over in front of him, perked up. But only slightly.

Stier turned back to the witness. "Starting from what you consider the most significant irregularity, can you tell the jury what your analysis uncovered?"

"Well, I always start in this kind of a retail business with the cash register, since it will have a record of the primary sources of income."

For most of the next two hours Schermer put on a pretty compelling course—complete with charts and graphs and regressive analyses of cash flows—that to Hardy's perspective, and he was sure to the jury's, proved that BBW was not run, to say the least, according to strict adherence to established accounting procedures. It wasn't simply the personal checks that Maya had written to cover expenses or the lack of traceable reimbursables. During the course of his testimony, in the six months before Dylan Vogler's death, Schermer identified no fewer than sixty-seven individual transactions—cash in or out, payroll discrepancies, simple checking errors, food and beverage cost, and use analysis—that painted the business, and of course Maya as its owner, in at best an unflattering light.

And at worst, of course, as a sophisticated criminal.

And all this before it got personal. "Mr. Schermer." Stier had put away the latest graph and now stood again in front of the witness in the center of the courtroom. "At the time of Mr. Vogler's murder, what annual salary was he drawing as manager of BBW?"

"Ninety thousand dollars."

Though jurors had heard about the salary before in Stier's opening statement, still this number seemed to nearly knock a couple of the jurors out of their chairs, and sent a ripple of noise through the gallery as well.

Stier, knowing he was on to some juicy testimony, pressed ahead. "And what was the approximate gross income of the coffee shop over the past fiscal year?"

"Well, going on the tax records the business filed, the shop brought in, gross, four hundred sixty-one thousand ninety-two dollars and fourteen cents."

"Now, Mr. Schermer, was the salary of Mr. Vogler typical of other employers working similar jobs in the same business?"

"No. It was approximately double the city average."

"Double. And were other employees at BBW similarly compensated, in terms of multiples of the city's average pay for those jobs?"

"No. They made about the norm, which was essentially an hourly rate slightly above minimum wage."

"Let's take the assistant manager, for example, Mr. Schermer, an employee named Eugenio Ruiz. Did he work for an hourly rate, or was he on salary?"

"He was hourly, making twelve dollars and eighty cents an hour, plus tips. About five hundred dollars a week at forty hours."

"So two thousand a month, about twenty-four thousand dollars a year? As opposed to Mr. Vogler's ninety thousand dollars?"

"Yes, that's about right."

"Mr. Schermer, in your professional opinion, was Mr. Vogler's salary as a percentage of the coffee shop's gross income defensible as a viable business practice?"

Hardy knew he could object, but also knew that it wouldn't do him any good. Schermer, with the credentials of a recognized expert witness, was allowed to give his opinion. The jury didn't have to believe it, but the court would permit the testimony. He sat, his hand on Maya's arm, and both of them seethed.

"No," Schermer said. "It was an irregularity of a dramatic nature."

"So would the business running on this model be sustainable over the long run?"

"In my opinion, no. Not given the business's gross income and this salary."

"And as a forensic accountant, does this type of irregularity raise a red flag for you of a certain kind of financial malfeasance?"

"Yes, it does."

"And what is that?"

"Most commonly, it would be money laundering."

"Could you explain to the jury how that works?"

"Certainly." Schermer turned in his chair to face the panel. "Let's say that there is an unreported source of illicit income in a coffee shop such as BBW, such as the sale of marijuana, for example. An employee can ring up any number of coffee drinks on the cash register and not actually pour any of these drinks. So that in the course of a day you might have an extra two or three hundred dollars, or more, or less, on the till. Then you simply supply the cash into the register that you've made on your illicit business and entered as regular coffee income, and it becomes part of the business's legitimate cash flow. Now the dirty money is so-called clean, or laundered, money, and since you can account for the income, it can be redistributed as dividends, profit sharing, or salary."

"Or salary," Stier repeated, loving this. And so, it seemed, was the jury. "Now, Mr. Schermer," he went on, "is there any way to reliably identify the existence of this sort of money-laundering scheme?"

"Yes, there is. That's what my work essentially entails."

"Can you explain?"

"Well, in our example above, I think we can all see that there is actually less coffee poured than there is a record of. So by comparing the amount of raw coffee beans actually bought by the business with the income that would be produced by the sale of that coffee, cup by cup, we can pretty accurately determine if there is a discrepancy."

"And did you find such a discrepancy in your analysis of BBW?"

"Yes."

"And to what extent?"

"Well, based on the actual amount of coffee beans bought, by weight—we've seen this on one of our graphs, if you remember—the maximum gross income from the sale of coffee drinks over the past fiscal year should have been no greater than about three hundred and seventy thousand dollars, as opposed to a reported four hundred and sixty-two thousand."

"So, a difference of ninety-two thousand dollars? Almost precisely Dylan Vogler's salary?"

"That's correct."

"Thank you, Mr. Schermer, no further questions." He turned to Hardy. "Your witness."

But Braun interrupted. "Mr. Hardy, as it's getting close to noon, I suggest we hold off beginning your cross-examination until after our lunch recess. Is that acceptable to you?"

"That's fine, Your Honor."

"All right, then." Braun tapped her gavel. "Court's adjourned until one-thirty."

35

Stier might have simply decided to ignore the Ruiz murder as a factor in Maya's case, but as head of homicide, Glitsky could not do that, even if he was of a mind to. Which he most assuredly was not.

Over the past several months, while Abe had been perpetually brooding over his son's accident and ultimate prognosis and his own karma, Hardy had grown unhappily accustomed to his new, low-affect persona, to the point that now—meeting with him behind a curtain in a private booth at Sam's—the full flower of evident rage emanating from his friend's demeanor struck him as perhaps actually dangerous. To Abe's own health, maybe, but more to his inspectors, the source of this anger.

"And, if you can imagine," he was saying with a guttural intensity, "now Schiff is all bent out of shape because I didn't put them on Ruiz. After what they've done to Vogler and Preslee, they should be happy they're not busted down to robbery, or even patrol. Learn a few of the basics over again."

Hardy smeared butter on some sourdough. "Maybe you could drop by the courtroom after we're done here and share some of these thoughts with Braun. She needs to hear them."

"I'm not saying your client's innocent, Diz."

"No. Of course not. You just asked me here to talk secretly because no one else would have lunch with you. And I can't say that I blame them. Although I'm a little surprised about Treya. You'd think, being your wife and all, she'd at least feel sorry for you." He popped the bread into his mouth. "Why did Schiff want Ruiz? And Bracco, too, I assume."

"Why do you think?"

"Obviously, because it's BBW again. And if that's the case, they've got doubts about Maya."

"No, they don't. Not even one. Don't even ask them."

"How about you?"

"Not so much doubt about Maya, Diz." Glitsky tipped up his water glass and chewed some ice. "I just don't know how they moved the case even this far along."

"*You* don't know? I know. It's Jerry Glass and Schiff. They got the whole thing out of whack. As a righteous murder, much less two, it hasn't made any sense from the beginning. Not that Maya couldn't have actually done these guys, but there's never been any case, evidencewise. You know this."

"Well, at least I'm thinking it now. I just wonder what else is going to pop that's going to make the detail look even more incompetent."

"You mean like Lori Bradford?"

"Close enough. Have you talked to her?"

"Not yet, but Wyatt Hunt did. I put her on my witness list, which is great for the good guys, but not for you."

"Schiff and Bracco knew all about her and decided she wasn't important."

"That's what I gathered. I think, though, she might be."

Glitsky sat back as the tuxedoed, ultimate professional waiter drew back the curtain and took their orders—Hardy's every-time-he-came-here sand dabs and a Crab Louis for Glitsky. When he'd gone, a small silence settled, until Hardy said, "So. You didn't invite me down here to help me get Maya off."

"True."

"So?"

"So the bottom line is the case is starting to look like a loser for us. Certainly the Preslee side."

"As it should be."

"Okay, granted, maybe. That's the problem when things start out so sloppy and get all political."

"I'm more or less aware of that, Abe. What do you want?"

Glitsky took a beat. "I want to know if you've got something I need to know on Ruiz."

"Like what?"

"If I knew, I wouldn't need to ask, would I?"

"If I do know something, how's it going to help my client?"

"It probably won't."

Hardy broke a grin. "Wow, you really make it tempting. What do you have so far?"

"Essentially, nothing. If he hadn't worked at BBW, we'd be at absolute zero." Glitsky chewed another piece of ice. "As you may have surmised, this goes a little up the food chain."

Hardy considered for a second, remained deadpan against the urge to show his surprise and pleasure. "Kathy?"

A nod. "Backstage, of course, and always deniable. But through Clarence, then Batiste." The DA and the chief of police, respectively. Serious high-level pressure from above. "Her mayorship has made her case, especially after hearing about this Lori Bradford fiasco yesterday, that somehow a solid investigation into another BBW-related murder will set Maya free. I'm not so sure of that. It might help on Vogler, though I think she's going down for that, and she won't need it on Preslee. But whatever, Kathy thinks Ruiz is going to open a door, and she's more or less dared us to do something on it, and fast, or maybe a head or two will roll."

"Yours?"

"Not impossible. Maybe even the chief's too. Who, you remember, serves at the mayor's pleasure."

The waiter knocked, opened the drapes, and delivered their plates. As the curtain closed, Hardy said to Glitsky, "So where were we?"

"Kathy West and Eugenio Ruiz."

Hardy forked a bite of fish, taking his time. Finally, he made his decision and came out with his answer. "I might have something."

"Might. I like that."

"I knew you would. Hence my careful locution. I might have something if you've got something to trade."

"Probably not. But what?"

"If you find something based on what I give you, I want it too."

Glitsky didn't hesitate an instant, shaking his head from side to side. "I can't do that."

"Fine."

"Diz."

"No argument, Abe. You can't do it, you can't do it."

"You mean if it helps your case?"

"I mean whatever."

"I can't. You know I can't."

Hardy chewed and swallowed. "Not my issue. My issue is my client."

"What if it doesn't help her?"

"I'll be the judge of that. Sorry, but those are the rules." He hesitated. "Look, if it's any help, give it to Stier too. I just wouldn't like to see whatever it might be disappear, the way Lori Bradford did."

Hardy, by now unexpectedly hopeful at the possibility of having the resources of the entire police department working on his behalf, nevertheless didn't want to push. He had the cards here and Glitsky either would recognize that fact or not. He took a sip of his club soda, pushed some buttered capers onto his fish.

"It would be discoverable," Glitsky said.

Hardy shook his head. "Before that. Under the table—under this very table if you want—but before it goes through Stier and company. From what you say, Jackman's going to back you and so's Batiste."

"They're my troops," he said. "Bracco and Schiff. I undermine their case . . ."

"I get it. Though one could argue that it's already undermined and they deserve whatever happens. But again, Abe, not my problem. And, hey, what I have might be nothing."

It took Glitsky another full minute, maybe more, Hardy eating with gusto and apparent contentment, tasting none of it.

Finally, Glitsky capitulated. "You want me to sign an affadavit, or is my word good enough?"

Hardy put down his fork. Took a steadying breath against the rush. "There's a guy who may or may not be named Paco who knew both Levon Preslee and Dylan Vogler back in college and who showed up from time to time at BBW to buy his weed. But not since October."

"May or may not be named Paco." Now dismissively. "That's what we've been negotiating about?"

Hardy shrugged. "It's what I got, Abe. Ruiz was looking out for him."

"What do you mean?"

"Ruiz was going to get in touch with Wyatt Hunt if he came back into BBW. And by the way, it looks like the whole crew down there was getting cut in."

"Yeah, we're assuming that. We'll be talking to all of them this time, instead of a select few. But this Paco, is he on Vogler's list?"

"No."

"No, of course not," Glitsky said. "He wouldn't be. How'd you find out about him?"

"Well, Ruiz, first. Then Maya."

Glitsky's eyes narrowed. "She knew him too."

"Knew of him. The name. Back at USF. He hung out with Vogler and Preslee and—maybe—killed a guy in a liquor store they held up."

This stopped Glitsky midbite. "Maybe."

Hardy shrugged. It was what it was.

"Where?"

"I don't know. Except it was probably in the mid-nineties—ninety-five or -six."

"It might have been in the papers. There would have been an investigation. Maybe a suspect."

"Knock yourself out," Hardy said.

"Did Paco know Ruiz was looking out for him?"

"No idea. Anybody working there could have told him, though."

Glitsky put down his fork. "You're not making this up?"

"Not any of it."

After lunch Hardy stood and approached the forensic accountant in the witness chair, seemingly as relaxed as he'd been all morning. "Mr. Schermer," he began, "you have given a great deal of technical testimony about accounting practices, working with numbers. Are any of these numbers subject to a margin for error?"

"Well, yes, of course. Some to a greater extent than others, but generally, yes."

"Referring to the analysis you offered on BBW's gross income versus the amount of raw coffee bought over the last fiscal year, would this have a greater or lesser margin for error than some of the other calculations you performed and shared with the jury?"

"Rather on the high side, I'd think. It is, after all, an estimate."

"An estimate, with a margin for error rather on the high side. I see. And is there an industry standard that enumerates the margin for error in this kind of analysis?"

Here, for the first time, Schermer's face creased into something like a frown. "I'm not sure what you mean."

"Well, I mean you take a certain weight amount of a raw product—coffee in this case—and you do an analysis that shows it takes, say, a pound of coffee to make a certain amount of cups, and then you deduce that the business didn't buy enough raw coffee to make as many cups as it claimed it sold. Isn't that the basic idea?"

"Basically, yes."

"Well, then, can we assume that this type of analysis is a standard tool in the industry?"

"In a general way, yes."

"With other products, you mean?"

"Yes."

"How about with coffee? Is this a test with a long history of analysis and comparison with other similar tests?"

"Well, no. This was specific to this one business. BBW."

"Specific to this one business? Do you mean to say that other licensed and accredited forensics accountants such as yourself, and in fact the organization to which you belong, have not established benchmarks to measure the reliability of these analyses?"

"Well, no, not exactly, but—"

"No is sufficient, thank you, Mr. Schermer. Now, can you please tell the jury a little about the methodology you employed to measure the amount of coffee needed to make a cup at BBW?"

Finally given a chance to simply discourse on his specialty again, Schermer leaned back in the chair and faced the panel. "Well, I gathered information from other coffee shops in the city, both chain and individually owned, and took the average of the number of cups of coffee produced from every hundred pounds of beans."

"How many coffee shops did you use for your comparison?"

"Ten."

"And how many different kinds of beans were represented in your answer?"

"I don't know what you mean."

"Well, beans come from a lot of different places. South America, Africa, Jamaica, and so on. So what kinds of beans were represented in your sample?"

"As I recall, most of them were from Colombia."

"And is that the sole source of BBW's beans, Colombia?"

"No, I don't think so."

"They came from all over the world, did they not?"

"Yes, I believe so."

"All right. And do you know how many bags were delivered from all over the world over the course of the fiscal year to BBW?"

"I don't know that, exactly. Perhaps hundreds."

"But several thousand pounds of coffee, wouldn't you say?"

"Yes, at least."

"And did you test to make sure that all of that coffee had the same density? That is, approximate number of beans per pound?"

"Uh, no."

"So the representative sample you used for your analysis might have been stores that used more or fewer beans to make a cup, isn't that true?"

"I guess so. Yes."

"And in fact, BBW was a very popular coffeehouse, was it not?"

"Yes."

"Could that popularity have been based on the flavor of its coffee? That is, that its coffee was stronger or more mild than the shops you used in your sample?"

"I have no way of knowing that."

"All right, then." Hardy glanced over to the jury, all of whom were with him, following the cross-examination with none of the more common postlunch torpor. "Let's talk for a minute, if we may, about the coffee made from these beans. Is there a standard BBW uses for various strengths of coffee? Strong? Medium? Weak?"

"I used medium, which is their house blend strength."

"But do they serve other coffees of different strengths?"

"Yes."

"Both stronger and weaker?"

"Yes, which is why I used medium, to be about average."

"But do you in fact know the percentage of coffee actually brewed there that is weak, medium, or strong?"

Schermer took a breath, no longer enjoying himself at all. "No."

"And what about espresso?"

"What about it?"

"It was a rather large percentage of the coffee sold at BBW, was it not?"

"Yes, it was."

"Do you know the exact percentage, Mr. Schermer?"

"No."

"And espresso is roasted differently than other blends of coffee, is it not?"

"Yes."

Hardy, hammering the man mercilessly, decided to back off for a moment lest to the jury he come across as unsympathetic. He walked back to his desk, took a sip of water, gave half a nod first to his client and then to Joel Townshend and Harlen Fisk, sitting next to one another in the front row. He pulled his legal pad over and pretended to read from it, then turned and came back to his place in the center of the courtroom.

"Mr. Schermer, at the beginning of this cross-examination testimony, you said that your analysis of raw coffee bought versus coffee served was merely an estimate with a margin for error, isn't that true?"

"Yes."

"But there is no industry standard that defines an acceptable margin for error for an analysis of coffee shops, is there? Not for this particular comparison?"

"Correct."

"Would you care now to estimate for the jury, and after the questions I've just put to you, how high the margin for error could go on an analysis such as this, with different density beans, and differing strengths of various coffee drinks?"

"I don't know if I could say."

"Ten percent? Twenty percent?"

"Yes. Yes, I suppose."

"In fact, since there is no industry standard on this margin for error for this particular test, it could even be higher, could it not?"

"In theory, I suppose it could."

"How about fifty percent? Could it be as much as that?"

"Well, I really don't think so."

"You don't think so?" Hardy repeated with just enough emphasis on *think* to make his point to the jury.

"That's correct. I don't think so."

"Okay, then let's go with the twenty percent that you admit is a possible margin of error. Now, if I could just ask you for a moment to revisit the actual income numbers you gave in your direct testimony." Hardy went back to his desk quickly and this time brought back with him his yellow legal pad. "You said the amount of raw coffee bought should have produced income from coffee drinks sold of three hundred and seventy thousand dollars, and instead BBW's books showed an income of four hundred sixty-two thousand dollars, isn't that right?"

"Yes."

"And would you agree, sir, that twenty percent of three hundred seventy thousand dollars—the margin for error we've been discussing—is seventy-four thousand dollars?"

"That sounds right."

"It is right, sir. Which means that, according to your own calculations, BBW's coffee drink income from raw coffee bought could have easily been as high as four hundred forty-four thousand dollars, or only sixteen thousand dollars short of the reported income, isn't that right?"

Thoroughly dispirited by now, Schermer stared down at the floor in front of him. "It sounds like it."

"Well, Mr. Schermer," Hardy said, "given your direct testimony outlining sixty-seven simple accounting errors, does a sixteen-thousand-dollar discrepancy on a gross income of between three and four hundred thousand dollars strike you now as necessarily indicative of money laundering?"

Stier started to rise, but before he could object, the witness replied. "Not necessarily, no."

The judge let the answer stand, and Hardy whirled, smiling. "No further questions." Stier had no redirect.

"Mr. Schermer," Braun said, "you may step down. Mr. Stier, your next witness."

Stier threw a look over at Hardy, back up to the judge. "Your Honor, the People rest."

Braun nodded once and looked up. "Very well. Mr. Hardy, I believe you'll have a motion?"

"Yes, Your Honor."

"All right. Ladies and gentlemen of the jury, I'm going to give you a longer recess than usual. Please remember my admonition not to form or express any opinion about the case or discuss it among yourselves or with anyone else until the matter is submitted to you. Come back in forty-five minutes."

Ten minutes later, with Braun back on the bench, Hardy made his 1118.1—his motion to dismiss the charges on both Vogler and

Preslee. Normally, this is a pro forma motion made at the end of the prosecution case in every criminal trial. But at least as to the Preslee count, Hardy actually thought he might have something to talk about.

"Your Honor," he said, "no reasonable juror could possibly convict my client, particularly of the Levon Preslee murder."

Stier defended the charges. "In spite of Inspector Schiff's admission about the lack of physical evidence in the Preslee slaying, there is no net change in the prosecution case. Admittedly, it is light on physical evidence, but as you know there are other kinds of evidence, and they can be compelling. Eyewitness testimony, for example. Consciousness of guilt. This is circumstantial but compelling evidence."

"Yes, Your Honor. But the burden of proof is on the prosecution to prove not just that Maya was in the hallway, but that she was inside the apartment, and more than that, that when she was in there she killed Levon Preslee. They have nothing remotely approaching that. You don't just convict the person with a motive who happens to be closest to the scene of the crime, especially in a case like this where you have no idea who else might have had a motive. Or, for that matter, who else had been inside. I don't have to prove that Maya wasn't inside that apartment. Mr. Stier has to prove she was. And there simply is no such proof. Letting the jury consider this evidence in this count would not be only an error with respect to the Levon Preslee charge, it would inevitably taint any verdict on the Vogler count."

Hardy was pushing it pretty hard here. Normally a judge could figure that if the evidence was really as weak as the defense claimed, the jury would simply acquit as to that count, and the defense would have nothing to appeal. But Hardy was taking that out away from Braun. By tying the charges together Hardy was arguing that the judge would be tainting any verdict on Vogler, even if the jury acquitted on Preslee.

So Braun was actually going to have to make this decision or expect to hear about it on appeal later. Hardy had her in a corner and she knew it. She took in the situation with a reptilian silence, her eyes closing to mere slits. Turning to her recorder, she said, "Ann, I'm hoping you got all that."

"Yes, Your Honor."

"Mr. Stier. Comment?"

"Your Honor, the prosecution rejects Mr. Hardy's efforts to tie these counts together like that. Each count stands on its own, each count is supported by the evidence, and that's how the court should rule."

"Nobody has put Maya inside the place, Your Honor," Hardy said. "You can't ask the jury to decide she was there if there's nothing putting her there."

"I can do what I want in my courtroom, Mr. Hardy. I could get up on my desk and do a tap dance if I want to."

"Yes, of course, Your Honor, I didn't mean you couldn't—"

"That's what you said, Mr. Hardy."

"I'm sorry, Your Honor. I misspoke."

"Apology noted." And now Braun surprised him. "All right. Mr. Hardy, you raise a colorable point. Give me a moment, please." She came forward and put her elbows onto her desk, her fingers templed over her nose, her eyes closed. Finally, her shoulders heaved and she brought her head back up. "This issue is too complex to decide on the spur of the moment. Court is in recess for another half hour. I'll have a decision for you before the jury is seated again."

36

Hardy had a message on his cell phone that Craig Chiurco was outside in the hall, having escorted Lori Bradford down on her subpoena as a courtesy—service with a smile from Freeman, Farrell, Hardy & Roake.

Now, with the court in recess, Hardy walked out through the gallery, accepting congratulations from Joel and Harlen and some of his associates who'd shown up as they usually did when one of the bosses was in a big trial, to see how it was done. All and sundry agreed that he had just kicked some serious ass with Schermer, and between that cross-examination, his lunch at Sam's with Glitsky, and Braun's unexpected consideration of his motion to dismiss, Hardy had to fight to keep himself from getting cocky.

It still and always was going to come down to the jury, and without another suspect for them to even consider, Maya remained in a precarious place. Hardy had to get Paco or someone like him into the testimony somehow, and now with Ruiz dead, that was going to be problematic. Maya's purported knowledge of the man was hearsay anyway, and even if it weren't, she certainly couldn't put him at BBW or with either of the victims.

Outside, in the hallway, Chiurco sat on one of the wooden benches with a white-haired woman dressed in a light blue pantsuit. The two appeared to be in a somewhat animated discussion, enjoying each other's company, as Hardy approached. Seeing him, Chiurco got up and gave him his signed statement from their conversation of the night before, then touched the woman's arm and introduced her.

"Thank you for coming down on such short notice," Hardy said.

"Thanks to this young man for bringing me."

Hardy grinned. "I'll see he gets a raise right away."

"And did you say Dismas?" she asked. "Dismas? The good thief?"

"That's him, though too few people seem to know it."

"I don't believe I've ever actually known a Dismas."

"Well, you do now. I hope it's good for you."

"You're cute," she said.

"So are you." Hardy sat down next to her. "Has Craig here explained what we'd like to talk to you about in the courtroom?"

"What I saw, or heard, that morning."

"You remember the date, don't you?"

"Of course. October twenty-seventh, two thousand seven, to be exact."

"Exact is good. We like exact."

Her eyes brightened with the adventure. "And two shots. One at six oh eight or nine and one at six ten."

"Very good." He leaned in toward her. "I was hoping to call you to be a witness pretty much right away, if that's all right with you."

"Of course it's all right with me. That's why I'm here."

"Good. Now, I've already heard what you said in your talk with Mr. Hunt, and that will be the basis of your testimony, but if you don't mind, maybe we could just take a minute here before we go inside and run over some details?"

"Sure, of course," she said. "That would be fine."

In spite of the glimmer of hope he'd begun to entertain about his motion to dismiss, Hardy wasn't particularly shocked, nor even greatly disappointed, when Braun came back to the bench and ruled against him, denying his motion in its entirety.

Still, he was buoyed by his belief that Lori Bradford was going to be an important and powerful witness, offering a completely alternative version of the bare facts of the case. He had given some thought to the phraseology and tenor of his opening questions, wanting not only to get to this witness's information but to alert the jury to the homicide inspectors' wily and discreditable ways.

Now, already having established a solid rapport with her, one that he hoped the jury would recognize as between equals—as opposed to a young man condescending to a senile witness—he began his questioning. "Mrs. Bradford, where do you live?"

"I live in a second-story apartment on Ashbury Street here in the city, on the west side of the street, right up from Haight. It's also," she added, coached by Hardy, "right across the street from the alley that runs behind Bay Beans."

"Can you see that alley from your apartment?"

"The first twenty or thirty feet of it, out the living room and dining room windows, yes."

"Now, Mrs. Bradford, do you remember anything unusual and specific about the morning of Saturday, October twenty-seventh?"

"Yes."

"And what was that?"

"At a few minutes after six o'clock I was in bed in the back of the apartment, but already awake for the day, when I heard a loud report, like a firecracker, although for some reason I remember thinking that it might be a gunshot. So I got up and was in the hallway going to the front windows and then—*bang!*—there was another one. About a minute later."

"And what did you do then?"

"I got to the window and looked down into the street and across to the alley."

"And did you see anything unusual down there?"

"No. Nothing. It was still pretty dark out."

"Did you call nine one one?"

"Not then. No. There didn't seem to be any emergency. It was just the two noises. Although, of course, when the police cars started getting there, I realized something must have happened. By then it was too late to call nine one one."

"But you did eventually call the police, did you not?"

"Yes. A couple of days later."

"And why was that? The delay, I mean?"

"Well, mostly because the news reports were all saying that there had only been one shot, and I thought they'd want to know that I'd heard two of them."

"You heard two shots?"

"Yes." Lori, God bless her, added the word Hardy had recommended. "Definitely."

Raising his eyebrows for the jury's benefit, he went on. "And so you called the police to tell them about this information?"

"Yes."

"And did you speak to some inspectors?"

"Yes. Two of them came by the apartment and we talked about it."

"You told them about the two shots, did you?"

"Yes, I did."

"And what was their comment about that, if any?"

"They thanked me and said that the information might be enough to change the entire theory of the case."

"I see. And then did you hear from them soon after that?"

"No."

"No?" A pause for the effect. "Not even back in November after they'd arrested the defendant, and they were preparing for the preliminary hearing?"

"No."

"And not as this case went to trial?"

"No."

"Hmm. When the inspectors did speak to you at your home, did they tell you that they didn't believe your testimony, or your eyewitness account?"

"Objection. Irrelevant."

"Goes to the witness's state of mind, Your Honor." This didn't make a lot of sense, but Hardy had learned from the testimony of Jansey Ticknor that Braun didn't have a real good grasp of what this hearsay exception meant. He figured if Stier could use it to get stuff in, he might be able to as well.

It worked. "Overruled."

Hardy asked permission of the judge and then repeated his question. "Mrs. Bradford, did the inspectors tell you that they didn't believe your testimony, or your eyewitness account?"

"No. To the contrary, as I've said, they talked about it changing the theory of the case."

"And yet they never called you back, or served you with a subpoena, or asked you to come down here and testify in court, correct?"

"Objection. Asked and answered."

"Sustained."

"Thank you, Mrs. Bradford. I have no further questions."

Stier was on his feet before Hardy was back at his counsel table. "Mrs. Bradford," he began, "did the inspectors you spoke to ask you if you'd seen anything in the street on the morning of Mr. Vogler's death?"

"Yes."

"And did you in fact see anything down in the street, or in the alley?"

"No, as I've already said."

"Now, as to the noises you heard. Are you familiar with the sound of gunfire?"

"No. Not particularly."

"In your testimony with Mr. Hardy you said that while you were in bed, you heard a report, and this is a direct quote, 'like a fire-cracker.' Unquote. Isn't that true?"

"Yes, it is. I thought it might have been a firecracker. Or a back-fire."

"And yet you told Mr. Hardy that you definitely heard two gun-shots, did you not?"

"I did."

And here Stier, in his enthusiasm and lack of respect for this wit-ness, made his big error. "So let me ask you this. How could you know they were gunshots?"

Hardy had asked Mrs. Bradford that very question in the hall and had fervently hoped Stier would be foolish enough to ask it in front of the jury.

"Well, they were identical sounds. And we know for sure that one of them was a gunshot from the alley across the street, don't we? That's when Mr. Vogler was killed, wasn't it? Right when I heard the shots."

Rule Number One, Hardy thought—you talk to every single wit-ness yourself, every single time. Hardy saw Stier's shoulders slump as some of the jurors came forward and the import of this testimony hit home. He turned hesitantly toward the panel, stopped, came back to the witness. He finally said, "But can you say for certain that the sec-ond sound was in fact a gunshot, and not a backfire, or even a fire-cracker?"

She thought about this for a second. "I can say for sure that the two sounds were exactly alike. If the first one was a gunshot, the second one was a gunshot. And vice versa."

Stier decided to quit before he made it worse. "Thank you, ma'am."

Lori Bradford got up from the witness chair. "And they really did sound like gunshots," she added with a believability and sincerity that cemented her complete defeat of The Big Ugly.

The three partners—Hardy, Farrell, Roake—and Wyatt Hunt were at the Freeman Building after the close of business, gathered around the large round table in the Solarium considering options. The overhead lighting was on full against the encroachment of the misty darkness that gathered outside the glass panes. A bottle of red wine stood open on the table, although Gina's choice was her Oban and Hunt, next to her, was having an Anchor Steam.

Hardy was running out of time if he wanted to get any sort of "other dude," Paco or anyone else, into the consciousness of the jury. Before Ruiz had been killed, he'd half planned to call him as a witness both on the Paco question and to counter the allegations that there had ever had been anything romantic going on between Dylan and Maya. But now, of course, that option had been foreclosed by events.

Other witnesses for Maya's defense were few, if any, and far between. This was why Hardy had grabbed so desperately at Lori Bradford. At least here was a real bone for the jury to gnaw at. Nothing in the prosecution's case contemplated or explained a two-shot scenario, and that fact, if taken as fact, created a glaring hole if any jury member cared to look hard in that direction. But since there was no second bullet, nor casing, nor even gun for that matter, there was no guarantee, nor even a likelihood, that this would happen.

And as for Maya, her alibis were flimsy and unsupported. Nobody had seen her either kill anybody or not kill anybody. And there were still the huge and unresolved questions of why she had been at both murder scenes. The time, in Dylan's case, and the location, in Levon's, pretty well eliminated any consideration of the idea that she'd simply been in the respective neighborhoods. She'd gone to both places on purpose, apparently summoned—or setting up—the victims. And if she hadn't gone by to kill them, then why?

"I've got to call her," Hardy said. "Let the jury hear her story."

"Maybe I'm missing something," Gina said, "but what is her story? I mean, does she even have any explanation for why she was at these places?"

"Dylan called her, and then Levon called her."

Gina sipped her drink. "And she just went? No reason? When was the last time she'd even seen Levon?"

"I know," Hardy said. "It's weak."

"*Weak*'s one word for it." Farrell leaned back in his chair. "You might just want to go to argument. I mean, the theory is that they've got to prove something and you don't."

Hardy reached for his glass. "I'd just like to give 'em something, anything at all."

"Well," Hunt said, "there was Lori."

"And God love her," Hardy replied. "But two shots kind of goes nowhere without another story to go with them. And that I don't have."

"How about Glitsky?" Hunt asked.

Hardy had informed them all of his lunchtime deal with Abe, but like everything else about this case, it was looking like anything Abe could bring to the party was going to be a day late and a dollar short. "We're supposed to talk again tonight, but if he had anything live and pressing, I think I'd have heard."

"Maybe you could call the homicide guys Abe put on Ruiz," Gina offered. "Talk about another weed-related murder at BBW, this one while Maya's in jail and couldn't have had anything to do with it. There's an element of doubt. Something else going on, at least."

"That's an actual thought," Hardy said. "Although Abe would have me killed if I called his guys in the middle of this."

"Yeah, but at least you'd be killed by professionals," Farrell said, "so it wouldn't hurt much." He went on. "Braun wouldn't let it in anyway. Ruiz is six months removed from our victims here. That's a tough sell." He took a healthy drink of red wine. "I'm back to closing argument. You've just got to argue that there's no evidence. That's all you can do."

"Well, not to get picky," Gina said, "but there is evidence. There's Maya's gun, her fingerprints on it, fingerprints on Levon's doorknob." She shrugged. "It's not much, granted, but it's hard to explain away. Any other jurisdiction in the state, given the motives, I think she goes down. Here, maybe you'll get your one juror, but on argument alone, I wouldn't get my hopes up."

"Well, on that cheery note." Hardy tipped his wineglass up and pushed himself back from the table. "I'm on all my phones all night if anybody gets any ideas."

"The clerk, I'd bet," Glitsky said, "was named Julio Gomez. Twenty-four years old when he died in ninety-five. The place was Ocean Liquors."

Glitsky, going out of his way to stop by Hardy's home, had interrupted his friend's seemingly unending perusal of his trial binders, and now, just past nine o'clock, they stood in the kitchen waiting for the microwave to beep for Glitsky's tea.

"Was there an investigation back then?"

"No," Glitsky said sarcastically. "Homicide just decided not to look into this particular murder. It seemed like too much work." A beat. "Of course we opened an investigation."

"And?"

"And we closed it about a month later."

"No suspects?"

"Not a one." He pulled an envelope from his inside jacket pocket. "I copied the file and brought it around for you, though as you can see, it's a little thin." Then, gesturing back to the dining room where Hardy's binders were spread out on the table, "Not that it looks like you need much more reading material. I gather that's your case in there."

"What there is of it." The microwave's timer sounded and Hardy crossed over, took the cup out, and handed it to his friend. "Santé. How about witnesses?"

"Witness. One. You can see him in there. Old Asian guy, coming out of a bar across the street, twelve-thirty on a Tuesday night. And the fog was in, evidently heavy. Plus, he'd had a few. Anyway, he heard the shot, saw somebody run out of the store, get in a car, then take off." He pointed down at the envelope. "It's all in there."

"Yeah, but, so a driver? More than one guy? Two guys waiting in the car?"

"He doesn't say. And I know what you're thinking, that this is your Paco."

"It could be. Is this the only liquor store shoot-up in those years?"

"No. There were actually six of them, homicides. But believe it or not, we got four of the guys, all solos, although to be fair, two of 'em got shot themselves by guys they shot behind the counter, which made it a little easier. The other one was a woman, never caught. That left whoever killed this guy Gomez. Maybe your Paco, after all."

Hardy nodded with satisfaction. "That's pretty thorough. You ought to do this stuff for a living."

Glitsky blew over his tea. "I'm motivated. But none of this ancient history is helping much with Ruiz."

"You haven't got anything?"

"Well, we've talked to most of the workers at BBW. That's going to go on for a while. But so far, not much, just everybody shocked that Ruiz could have been involved in drugs."

Hardy chuckled. "I can imagine. But none of this helps Maya either."

"I never thought it would."

Sitting at his dining room table, having already scrutinized his binders all the way through again until he was nearly blind, Hardy accepted a kiss on the cheek from his wife at around ten-thirty and told her he'd be up in a while.

"This is going to be over soon, isn't it?" Frannie asked.

"One way or the other, a day or two."

"That'd be neat. I've been thinking it really wouldn't be so bad having a husband again."

"I know."

"It's why I've stayed married to you. To have a husband."

"I know."

She kissed him again. "I'll probably still love you."

"Good. That'd be good."

But in reality barely hearing her, kissing the air in front of her face, reaching for another pass at one of the binders.

Nothing. Nothing. Nothing.

He closed the black binder and stood. Going back into the kitchen, he opened the refrigerator, closed it back up, cricked his back, and saw Glitsky's envelope on the counter. This Gomez killing thirteen or fourteen years ago wasn't his case, Glitsky had given him the summary, and even if it had been Paco, so what? So he'd left the envelope and gone back in to try one last time to find something in his binders.

Standing at the counter, he pulled out the half dozen or so pages—
incident report, copies of some pictures of the deceased, autopsy,
ballistics, two pages of testimony from Mr. Leland Lee, pretty much
as Glitsky had described it.

More nothing.

He started through the pages again, his routine, more slowly this
time. Eyes burning, he forced himself to read every line.

Wait a minute. Wait.

He turned back to first the autopsy, then the ballistics report. The
bullet that had killed Julio Gomez was a .40-caliber. A handwritten,
barely readable scrawled notation by an unidentified ballistics lab
worker read: "Probably Glock .40. Ballistics markings unidentifiable."

Okay, he had to make some assumptions, but they seemed warranted.
And what other choice did he have anyway? Somehow these long-ago
and near-invisible events and relationships, he was sure, were at the
heart of the case that had consumed his life for the past six months.
It was all about, perhaps not Maya at all, but certainly Dylan and
Levon and the mysterious Paco.

Back at the computer in his family room he suddenly realized that
although Hunt and Chiurco had looked into them, he himself had
never really pursued any of the details in the robbery that Dylan and
Levon had been convicted of.

And why should he have? It was, at best, tangential to Maya's situation, and again in the far distant past.

But now he suddenly realized what he should have considered a
couple of days ago, when he'd first become aware of the existence
of Paco—that if there had been a trial back then, or even a plea
bargain, there would have been both witnesses for the prosecution
and possibly friends for the defense, friends and witnesses whose

association with Dylan and Levon might have extended back beyond when Maya had met and hung out with them, back when Paco had been in their crowd, and as a real human being, not a nom de guerre.

In fact—

He pulled his legal pad around and wrote a note to call Wyatt Hunt and leave him a message and instructions for tomorrow as soon as he'd finished his computer search here. He'd just realized that Cheryl Biehl and the other three female witnesses that Stier had never called might fit into this same category—of people who'd been at USF back then and had known Dylan and Levon. And who might have known Paco under his real name.

But in the meanwhile he could do a quick search for the case that had involved Dylan and Levon, and armed with that he might be able to have Hunt or Chiurco identify the actual case files, the officers involved, other witnesses.

He went to Google and typed in Dylan Vogler's name, recalling even as the short page came up that Wyatt Hunt had told him that there was little mention of Vogler on the Net other than the recent details about his death. Shifting over to California Inmate Record Search, he again entered Dylan's name and there he was, at Corcoran State Prison in 1997 for robbery. Likewise, here was Levon Preslee in the system, starting two months into Dylan's time.

Did any of this mean anything? Or help Hardy in any way? Certainly, these facts told him nothing about the actual crime they'd committed together. He spent another fifteen minutes or so searching the various criminal databases to which he had access. He found Dylan and Levon in several of them. What he didn't find was any indication that they had committed their crime together, or had gone to trial together. That information had apparently vanished into the mists of time.

And if that was the case . . .

Suddenly, staring at the screen, the issue that had nagged at him for days came into focus with a startling clarity, bringing with it a jolt of adrenaline so powerful that it threw Hardy back into his chair, suddenly breathless, blood pounding in his ears. He brought his hand up to rest over his heart.

Thought it all through, beginning to end. It had to be.

It had to be. There was no other option.

And, late though it was, he reached for the telephone.

37

Hardy didn't know if it was because of her recent, albeit clandestine, interaction with the DA and the chief of police, but for whatever reason, Kathy West with her attendant entourage was back in the first row of the gallery when Hardy entered the courtroom from the holding cell with his client. Sitting between Joel Townshend and Harlen Fisk, she had also brought her trail of reporters, and once again the gallery was filled to overflowing.

In this Friday morning's paper the mayor had gone public with her suspicions, completely unfounded by any evidence Hardy had seen or heard about—and he'd heard plenty by now from Glitsky—that the Ruiz murder was intimately connected to the events surrounding Maya's trial and the deaths of Dylan Vogler and Levon Preslee. And this, of course, had ratcheted up the sense that something dramatic was going to take place in the courtroom today. Something, perhaps new evidence, that would remove once and for all the Townshend/Fisk/West family connection from the slanders of the past several months.

And the mayor wanted to be there for it. To show her face for her niece, if for nothing else. Kathy West didn't believe that Maya had done anything wrong, and she was going to make sure that the jury understood that clearly before they went in to deliberate.

But such was Kathy's gravity in the city that the mere rumor, much less the actual fact, of her presence again in the courtroom served also to draw in a host of the politically involved, the suddenly interested, the professionally concerned, the simply curious—DA Clarence Jackman, Police Chief Frank Batiste, U.S. attorney Jerry Glass, Glitsky, even the wheelchair-bound *Chronicle* "CityTalk" columnist Jeffrey Elliot. Gina Roake sat halfway back next to Wyatt Hunt, ashen-faced and presumably as sleep-deprived as Hardy himself. Catching Hardy's questioning eye, Hunt gave a short and solemn incline of his head. The entire gallery sounded to Hardy's ear like a race car, loud and thrumming at the pole. The jury, collectively, seemed to be mesmerized by the energy level, the shifting planes of volume, intensity, and nerves playing out in front of them.

At the prosecution table, and since Debra Schiff had already given her witness testimony and it was allowed, Stier had brought her back in as moral support to sit next to him, and the two of them were head-to-head in conversation as Hardy, Maya, and the bailiff crossed in front of them. And then, after a few words of forbidden greeting to her family members in front of the starstruck and forbearing bailiff, Maya was at last in her seat and Hardy was arranging his papers when the clerk entered and, clearing his throat, spoke up loudly. "Ladies and gentlemen, Department Twenty-five of the Superior Court of California is now in session, Judge Marian Braun presiding. All rise!"

Getting three new names approved onto his witness list had entailed another small battle with Braun and Stier this morning in the judge's chambers, but in the end Hardy argued that he had discovered new evidence that, in the interests of justice, the jury would need to hear in order to reach the correct verdict.

Of course, this announcement had aroused Stier's deep suspicion and ire, and he'd demanded to know the substance of the prospective testimony. Hardy acknowledged that in the first case—Jessica Cunningham—it was fingerprint evidence; and in the second—

Jennifer Foreman—Stier already had had access to everything she might know, since she was on his original witness list. Indeed, she was one of the three uncalled old college friends of Maya.

Finally, Hardy said, "You know Chiurco. He's one of my investigators. And here's what he's going to say." And he handed the prosecutor Chiurco's short signed statement. Stier grumbled for a moment that he should have gotten these witnesses at the beginning of the trial, but everybody knew that this was a nonissue. The witnesses would be permitted to testify. But, Braun warned him, Hardy had better be sure he was talking about introducing new evidence and not spending a lot of time rehashing.

But—the bottom line—he was going to be able to get it all in. And now, his palms wet, his mouth dry, Hardy lifted his exhausted body from his chair. "The defense would call Jessica Cunningham."

The bailiff disappeared out through the back door of the courtroom and returned a moment later with a young woman in a police officer's uniform. She made her way up the center aisle and into the bullpen, where she took the oath and then moved around to the witness seat.

"Ms. Cunningham," Hardy began, "will you tell the jury what you do for a living, please?"

"Sure." She turned to look at the panel. "I'm a technician in the police department's lab here in the city."

"In that capacity, do you have a special expertise?"

"I do. I do fingerprint analysis."

"Identifying people by their fingerprints, is that right?"

"Yes."

"And how long have you been doing that?"

"About six years."

For a few more moments Hardy established Cunningham's credentials as an expert in this field. Then he began to bring it closer to home. "Did you have occasion several months ago to analyze the fingerprints found in the home of one of the victims in this case, Levon Preslee?"

"Yes, I did."

"Can you tell the jury what you found?"

Of course, this testimony had already been cursorily addressed in the testimony of Debra Schiff, but now he had the lab technician herself on the stand, and a completely different approach. Cunningham, enthusiastic and professional, nodded and again spoke directly to the jury. "Well, as in most locations, we found many fingerprints."

"How many separate prints in all did you locate?"

"Oh, maybe fifteen or so."

"Could you identify any of them?"

"Yes. Six came back from the victim."

"Were you able to identify any of the other eight or nine?"

"A few, yes."

"But not all?"

"No."

"Is it unusual to find fingerprints at the scene of a crime that you cannot connect to any individual?"

"No."

"And why is that?"

"Because, first, not everyone has their fingerprints on file. Secondly, sometimes, or really quite often, the fingerprints are not clear enough to match the computerized records. And finally, there are a limited number of databases we typically use to try to get our matches. Most of the time, for example, we're trying to match a fingerprint to a known suspect, and in that case it's a simple one-on-one cross-check."

"Did you compare the defendant's fingerprints to the remaining unidentified fingerprints at Mr. Preslee's?"

"Yes, of course."

"Trying to see if any of those belonged to the defendant?"

"Right."

"And, just to restate it for the jury, you did not find any of the defendant's fingerprints at Mr. Preslee's, did you?"

"No."

Hardy threw a gratuitous look over his shoulder at Stier's table, where he and Schiff sat in miserable proximity. "Now, Ms. Cunningham, as far as you knew, back in November when you ran these comparisons, did you compare the unknown prints to anyone's besides the victim, Mr. Preslee, and the defendant, Maya Townshend?"

"Yes. The other victim, Dylan Vogler, and Mr. Preslee's friend, Brandon Lawrence."

"So two more people?"

"Yes."

"Could you identify any of your unknown prints from the crime scene to any of those?"

"Yes. Two of those fingerprints came back to Brandon Lawrence."

"Leaving you with seven unidentified prints. Correct?"

"Correct."

"Were you able to identify any of your remaining seven latents?"

"Actually, we identified four of them because they were in the criminal database, which is our primary tool."

"So there were three that remained unidentifiable, is that right?"

"Yes."

"Good. Now, Ms. Cunningham"—Hardy closing in on it—"have you had a recent opportunity to revisit the fingerprints you originally lifted at Mr. Preslee's home?"

"Yes, I have."

"And when was that?"

"Just this morning."

Hardy felt some sonic energy begin to shoot through the gallery, but he spoke over it. "And how did that come about?"

"Lieutenant Glitsky of homicide reached me at home this morning and asked me if I would come in early and go back to the unidentified fingerprints and compare them to a specific other single set of fingerprints from another database to see if there was a match."

"And was there a match?"

"Yes, there was."

"You mean there was a specific individual who had left his fingerprints in Mr. Preslee's home and whom this investigation had not discovered until just this morning, is that right?"

"That's correct, yes."

Braun gaveled down the now nearly constant, if low-pitched, hum of the gallery. After silence had been restored, Hardy came back at the witness. "Ms. Cunningham, did Lieutenant Glitsky ask you to review any other fingerprint findings this morning?"

"Yes."

"And what were they?"

"There was a partial fingerprint on the brass bullet casing that was picked up at the scene of the Vogler murder."

"A partial print? What does that mean?"

"Actually, most prints are partial prints. It's rare on a forensic sample to get an entire fingerprint from somebody. But this print was a smaller section even than most."

"And can that be useful for purposes of identity?"

"Often not."

"And why is that?"

"Because it's incomplete. Certainly a computer can't read it, so you have to have the known prints of an individual, you have to do a

manual comparison, and you have to find enough points of identification on the forensic sample to compare to your known prints."

"Now, Lieutenant Glitsky asked you to run a manual test against
the known fingerprint of a single individual whose prints were in
Levon Preslee's home, did he not?"

"Yes."

"Did you find a match?"

"I'm sorry. The testing is not completed. As I said, it's a very small
sample and I just haven't had enough time yet."

Hardy would have given his left arm to know the final results of
this test. But this was it. If he was going to spring this trap, it was going
to happen right now before anyone got wind of what he was up to. He
had to press ahead. "All right. So now, Ms. Cunningham, can you give
us the name whose fingerprint you identified in Mr. Preslee's home?"

"Yes, I can."

"And whose fingerprint was it?"

"One of your investigators, Mr. Hardy. A Craig Chiurco."

While the bailiff went to get the next witness, Stier asked Braun if
counsel could approach, and at her impatient bidding both attorneys
got up and walked to the bench.

"What do you want now, Mr. Stier?" Braun asked, clearly at the
limit of her forbearance.

"Your Honor," Stier began, "I haven't got a clue as to what Mr.
Hardy is up to. This seems irrelevant, immaterial, and just plain a
waste of time."

"I'm going to wrap this up, Your Honor, within the hour. Two
more witnesses and I'm done." Turning, and hoping to provoke an
already rattled Stier, Hardy smiled sweetly. "I have to give you the
discovery, Counselor. I don't have to explain it to you."

"That's enough, you two!" Braun snapped, nearly loud enough for the jury to hear. "I'm tired of this bickering. Mr. Hardy, you're going to call your witnesses and we're going to get this thing done. Return to your counsel tables."

Hardy wasted no time calling his second witness, and by now, as he approached the witness seat, his fatigue had dissipated. Jennifer Foreman had been another one of the USF cheerleaders—friends of Maya and Dylan back in the day—that Stier had originally put on his witness list and then elected not to call for direct testimony.

Late last night Wyatt Hunt had worked his magic and, in spite of the hour, had persuaded her to talk to him. Now, on the stand, and obviously dealing with a serious case of nerves, she appeared not to have had a great deal of luck getting back to sleep in the intervening hours. Or maybe it was the fact that Hardy and Hunt had asked that she check in upstairs, then wait at Lou the Greek's, accompanied by Gina Roake, so that she wouldn't come into contact with any other witnesses until she was called to the stand.

Still, she came across as poised, well dressed, competent and, always a plus, very attractive, as these ex-cheerleaders tended to be. A good, solid witness if Hardy could direct her where he needed to go. Hardy stood five feet in front of her and gave her a reassuring smile. "Mrs. Foreman," he began, "you were a classmate of the defendant, Maya Townshend, at USF in the mid-nineties, were you not?"

"Yes, I was."

"Were you in the same class?"

"No, I was a couple of years ahead of her."

"But you were friends, were you not?"

"Yes, I thought so. We were cheerleaders together."

"And during the time you were cheerleaders, did you also spend time with both of the victims in this case, Dylan Vogler and Levon Preslee?"

"Yes, I did."

"Did you ever personally witness them smoking marijuana?"

"Your Honor!" Stier was standing up. "Mr. Hardy has promised us that he has new evidence, but this is all old news and irrelevant."

But by now, after the previous witness, Braun was fully engaged and inclined to let Hardy go on, even without a strict evidentiary base. He'd already presented compelling fingerprint evidence that Stier hadn't been able to supply, and even if the meaning of that was still questionable, there was no doubt about its possible relevance. "The objection is overruled, Counselor. Go ahead, Mr. Hardy."

"Thank you, Your Honor. Now, Mrs. Foreman, should I repeat the question?"

"No. Did I ever witness Dylan and Levon smoking dope? Yes, of course."

"Many times?"

Here Mrs. Foreman broke a small chuckle. "Pretty much all the time."

Hardy let the moment of levity run its short course. "Mrs. Foreman, how did you meet Dylan and Levon?"

"We had a mutual friend in my class who everybody called Paco. He turned me on to them." She shrugged and added to the jury, "If you'll pardon the phrase. He was kind of the leader of the other, younger guys."

"And this Paco, to your personal knowledge, this friend and leader of Dylan and Levon, was also a regular user of marijuana, was he not?"

"Yes."

"Mrs. Foreman, you've said that everybody called this person by the name of Paco. But was that his real name?"

"No. It was just like a street name, something he thought was cool."

"And you also knew him by his real name, did you not?"

"Yes."

"And what name was that?"

"Craig Chiurco."

Again, Hardy let the considerable tumult recede before he filled his lungs with air, glanced one last time at the assembled crowd in the gallery, and threw a look over to Stier.

Who looked as though the roof had fallen on him. Now he clearly knew what was going to happen, but didn't know how to stop it, or even if he should try.

Hardy turned to the bench. "The defense calls Craig Chiurco, Your Honor."

Braun scowled for a second, wondering about the decorum in her courtroom, but eventually raised her eyes to the back of the gallery. "Bailiff, call the witness," she said to the officer standing just inside the closed back door, and she opened it and disappeared out into the hallway.

After, to Hardy, an agonizing half minute, enough time for the gallery to begin to hum again, Chiurco entered in his trademark coat and tie, looking confident and, as opposed to his bosses Hardy and Hunt, well rested. He'd been waiting with Bracco upstairs in the homicide detail for the sign that it was almost time and he should move down to the corridor outside the courtroom. Now, passing up through the bar rail, by the defense table, he proffered a quick, silent greeting to Hardy, who was already standing in his spot before the witness chair.

But Hardy, intent and self-absorbed, didn't look up.

The clerk swore him in.

Craig looked expectantly at Hardy, who carefully walked him through the statement he'd prepared about their discussion two nights before. Upbeat, Chiurco gave every indication that he was glad to be testifying. "Now, Mr. Chiurco, to backtrack a bit. Just a moment ago you told the jury that you had been assigned by your employer, Wyatt Hunt, to locate Levon Preslee, did you not?"

"Yes."

"Up until that time, had you ever heard of Levon Preslee?"

"No."

"To your knowledge, had you ever met him?"

"No."

"And you did, in fact, locate Mr. Preslee, did you not?"

"Yes."

"In a matter of hours?"

"Right."

Hardy went back to his table and picked up a piece of paper. "I think you told us how you found Mr. Preslee. Didn't you just say that you had done a Web search and found out that Mr. Vogler was convicted for robbery back in 1997, and that he had a partner in that crime named Levon Preslee? Does that sound about right?"

"Yes."

"In other words, your employer did not tell you that Mr. Vogler's partner was Mr. Preslee?"

"No."

"And why not, do you think?" This was technically objectionable, but as Hardy had hoped and predicted, Stier remained silent, certain that Braun was not going to interrupt.

Chiurco's expression wavered briefly, a moment of indecision. But Hardy exuded encouragement, and Chiurco gave him his answer. "He didn't know it, not at that time."

"Mr. Hunt didn't know Mr. Preslee's name, that is?"

"Right. We just knew that Vogler had a partner in the robbery he'd committed. We didn't know who it was."

"So again, how did you find that this partner was Mr. Preslee?"

"As I said," Chiurco still cooperative, but some exasperation breaking through the veneer, "I did a Web search."

"You looked on Google or Yahoo?" Hardy asked. "That type of thing?"

"Yes. I don't remember precisely which one."

"Do you mean you don't remember which search engine you used?"

"Yes. There are a lot of them. Prison databases, city and county records, and so on."

"And looking on one of those databases, you found a site that somehow informed you about the crime that Mr. Vogler and Mr. Preslee had been convicted of, is that right?"

"Yes."

"So you must have checked on Mr. Vogler's name first?"

"That was the only name I had, so yes."

"And then keying off Mr. Vogler, you found a related site for Mr. Preslee, correct?"

"Yes."

Nodding, Hardy again went back to his desk and picked up another couple of sheets of paper, then came back to the witness. "Now, Mr. Chiurco, I have here in my hand a copy of the cover page of the criminal proceeding that resulted in Mr. Vogler's conviction and sentencing back in 1997." Thanking his stars for Glitsky and his access, Hardy stepped closer to the witness box. "Would you please read for the jury the title of this case? Right there inside the bracketed area."

Now with a bit of reluctance, Chiurco came forward and accepted the paper. "*The People of the State of California v. Dylan Vogler.* Case number SC-137804."

"Thank you." Hardy held out his hand, and Chiurco handed him back his copy. "And now, if you please, would you read the title of this other case, which for the jury's benefit resulted in Mr. Preslee's conviction and sentencing?"

Working to regain a semblance of cordiality, Chiurco took the next sheet of paper. "*The People of the State of California v. Levon Preslee.* Case number SC-139504."

Hardy again took the paper back. "As you can see, Mr. Chiurco, and as you've just read to the jury, these are different case numbers, are they not?"

"Yes. Obviously."

"Obviously. But, if these cases are indeed separate and unconnected, this leads to the question of how you referenced one of them and had it lead you to the other. Can you tell us how you did that?"

Chiurco sat back, his face set, and bounced his shoulders a few times. "I don't exactly remember. They showed up together in one of the Web sites. That's all I can tell you."

"And from that you got Mr. Preslee's name and then were able to find his address and go out to his house, is that right?"

"Right."

"A house where you had never been before. Is that correct?"

"Yes."

"A house that you'd certainly never been inside?"

"Right."

"A house where police could never, under any circumstances, have found your fingerprints. Is that correct?"

Chiurco's face had gone dark now, and he turned to the judge, then back to Hardy. "What's this all about? What do my fingerprints have to do with anything?"

Hardy stepped closer to the witness. And after the earlier two witnesses Braun clearly was inclined to give him his head. "Mr. Chiurco," he said, "did you not already know who Mr. Preslee was, and that he had been Mr. Vogler's accomplice in the robbery that sent them both to prison, when you received your assignment from Mr. Hunt?"

"No, I did not."

"In fact, didn't you request the assignment from Mr. Hunt so that you could keep from Mr. Hunt the reality of your relationship with Mr. Preslee?"

"No, I did not."

"Are you saying you did not have a relationship with Mr. Preslee?"

"Yes, that's what I'm saying."

"You hadn't been to his home before as a guest?"

"That's right. I've already said that."

"Yes, you did," Hardy said. "Then perhaps you can explain the testimony we just listened to this morning from Officer Jessica Cunningham of the San Francisco police lab, who identified your fingerprints inside Mr. Preslee's home."

Chiurco's eyes shot out beyond Hardy, past Hunt, to the back door, over to the side doors. "Obviously, she either made a mistake or she lied. I've never been inside the place."

Hardy moved a step closer to him. "Are you telling the court that you hadn't seen both Mr. Vogler and Mr. Preslee together at Bay Beans West in the last weeks of their lives?"

"I don't know where you get any of this."

"If I were to tell you there were two witnesses—"

"Well, they're lying, too, whoever they were."

Hardy now hung his head, half turned briefly to the jury, his face impassive. "Mr. Chiurco, isn't it true that you attended the University of San Francisco here in the city between 1992 and 1995?"

Suddenly, at this gambit, Chiurco's back went straight, his head snapped quickly from side to side. Hardy, aware of the bass rumble behind him starting to develop in the gallery, nevertheless pressed the attack. "Mr. Chiurco? Your Honor?"

Braun glared out to the gallery, her gavel poised. Then leaned over the bench. "The witness will please answer the question."

Chiurco shrugged into his sports coat. "Yes."

"And while you were there, were you not acquainted with both Mr. Vogler and Mr. Preslee?"

This time, as the gallery fairly erupted behind Hardy, he stood locked into eye contact with Chiurco while Braun gaveled the crowd back into silence.

"Mr. Chiurco?"

"I think they were both there when I was, yes."

"And if we just heard from a witness, who said she knew all of you back then, testify that you were close friends of both of them, would that witness have been telling the truth?"

No answer.

"That's the truth, isn't it, Paco?"

All belligerence now. "Who's Paco?"

"You are, Mr. Chiurco, or you were, weren't you?" Hardy kept waiting for the judge to step in to advise Chiurco of his Fifth Amendment rights, but if she wasn't going to do it, he sure as hell wasn't going to do it for her. This man had killed at least two people, probably three, and had tried to frame his client, and Hardy couldn't possibly have cared less about his rights.

Chiurco, still unresponsive, pulled at his tie, cleared his throat.

Hardy let a few seconds pass, silence settling into the room until it was complete. "Mr. Chiurco," he asked, "where do you buy your coffee?"

"All over the place."

"Have you ever bought coffee at Bay Beans West on Haight Street?"

"I might have. I can't say for sure."

"Mr. Chiurco, did you not tell your employer, Mr. Hunt, that you were a regular customer of Mr. Vogler's marijuana business at Bay Beans West? If you'd like, we can have Mr. Hunt come up here and so testify."

The witness did not move, did not speak.

"Mr. Chiurco?"

"I don't have to answer that question. It might tend to incriminate me."

"So you're invoking the Fifth Amendment?"

"Only against whether or not I bought marijuana, yes."

"All right," Hardy said. "Let's move to another topic. Do you own a handgun?"

Chiurco brought his hands up to his mouth, pulled at the sides of his face. "All right. I own a gun. So what?"

"What make of gun?"

But Chiurco just shook his head. "That's all. I'm not saying anything else."

The already heavy stillness seemed to take on an oppressive weight in the packed courtroom. Chiurco stared stone-faced into the space between him and Hardy.

"I'm not answering," Chiurco said again. "I'm taking the Fifth."

Hardy nodded, took another step forward to within spitting distance of the witness. "Isn't it true, Mr. Chiurco, that you used that same Glock .40 to kill Dylan Vogler and a liquor store clerk named Julio Gomez during a robbery in 1995?"

At this the gallery fully exploded behind Hardy. And over that tumult, finally Stier found his voice again. "Objection, Your Honor. The witness has taken the Fifth."

She banged with her gavel, again and again, her voice strained as she tried to make herself heard. "The objection is sustained. That's enough." *Bam! Bam!* "Sustained." Now standing, leaning out over the bench, at the top of her voice. "I want order in this courtroom! Order!" And the sound of gavel pounding rang out again and again.

At last, a semblance of silence. Braun, still on her feet, shaking with rage, now asserted her authority, order after order. "The jury is to retire to the deliberation room. Bailiffs, clear the courtroom. Clear

the courtroom! Mr. Chiurco, you will remain on the witness stand.
Counsel, stay at counsel table!"

The gallery's removal took the better part of ten minutes, much of
the crowd objecting and even refusing to move until Braun had more
bailiffs called in to help from neighboring courtrooms.

When, finally, the last spectator had been cleared, Braun pointed
down at Chiurco. "Sir, as a witness in this courtroom, you have asserted your Fifth Amendment rights. You need to talk with your attorney. You will consult with counsel and return to this courtroom
with your attorney on this coming Monday at nine A.M."

But Hardy, still standing in front of Chiurco, couldn't let that go
unchallenged. "Your Honor, with respect, that's unacceptable. Mr.
Chiurco should be taken into custody."

Now she raised her gavel as though it were a weapon. "That's all,
Mr. Hardy. How dare you try to tell me what's acceptable or not in
my courtroom. That's absolutely all from you." And now unnecessar-
ily banging her gavel on every note for emphasis, she added, "You . . .
will . . . not . . . disrupt . . . this . . . courtroom . . . further!"

And again at last in total control, the master of her domain, Braun
looked around in a kind of stunned disbelief at what her pronounce-
ments had wrought. "Bailiffs," she said evenly, "the defendant goes
to the holding cell. Mr. Chiurco, you go find yourself a lawyer. Counsel, in chambers. Right now. It's quarter of." Then, with another
glance out at the empty gallery, "Bailiffs, you may readmit the spectators. This trial resumes again in precisely fifteen minutes."

In Braun's office Stier was near apoplectic. "Talk about no evidence!
In spite of all of his self-serving rhetoric Mr. Hardy presented no evidence out there just now, Your Honor. All that was just a blatant at-
tempt to find a handy scapegoat to distract the jury."

"Ridiculous, Your Honor. Fingerprints at the crime scene are evidence, particularly when the person whose fingerprints they are says they couldn't be there. What's your theory, Mr. Stier? Did Chiurco loan somebody his fingerprints? Did his hands take a walk without him? The fact is," Hardy said, "that I've presented more evidence this morning that my client is innocent than Mr. Stier has presented in his entire case against her."

"She's not innocent until the jury says so," Stier said.

Hardy held out a hand in a behold-the-ass gesture: "Actually, Your Honor, Mr. Stier's got it exactly backwards. Maya's innocent until the jury finds her guilty. I think they still teach this in law school in this country."

Braun had finally lost all pretense of a judicial demeanor. "God damn it! No more!"

But Stier kept on. "Mr. Hardy can split hairs, but I'm confident the court understood what I was saying, Your Honor. And this testimony from Ms. Foreman that Mr. Chiurco maybe used to be called Paco? On what planet does this rise to the level of evidence?"

"The same one," Hardy shot across at him, "that you landed on when you had Cheryl Biehl testify. I'm just, frankly, stunned that you think you've still got a case."

Stier harrumphed. "To the contrary, Your Honor, since Mr. Chiurco does investigative work for Mr. Hardy's own law firm, I wouldn't put it past them to have colluded to put on this entire elaborate charade just so the jury would have to consider an alternate suspect." Then, directly to Hardy, "So, how do you do it? You give your guy a bonus when this is done for the inconvenience you put him through?"

"That's the most ridiculous and insulting accusation I've heard in all the time I've been practicing law, Your Honor. It's beneath contempt." Hardy, finally reaching his limit, raised his own voice. "Here's what I did, Paul. I paid your police department to plant his fingerprint inside the scene of a murder and maybe on the casing from a cartridge at the scene of another murder. What kind of a bonus would you recommend for someone who's willing to put themselves in prison for life?"

Braun slapped a palm down on her desk. "That exchange, gentlemen, just cost you each a grand. Want to go for another one?"

Hardy, dizzy with adrenaline, fighting to reassert his rationality. "The plain fact, Your Honor, as I said out there, is that Chiurco ought to be under arrest right now. He's a danger to himself and to the public. The police should be searching his stuff for spatter and Preslee's place for his DNA. We need to continue this trial at least into next week, or even longer, to let the police finally conduct a real investigation."

Braun hated this whole thing. She hated Hardy's provocative and believable theory. She hated Stier's entire presentation of the case, the sideways involvement of Jerry Glass, Schiff's sloppy investigating, the political ramifications, the testimony about things that may or may not have happened as much as fifteen years before.

Above all, Braun hated the idea that she might have to tell the jury that this trial might be prolonged another week or even longer. There was no way she could accept a police investigation at this stage into another suspect without dismissing the charges against the current defendant.

"Well, gentlemen," she began in a cold fury, "it seems we've gotten ourselves into—"

At that moment the first gunshot echoed from somewhere close by, inside the building. And they heard a woman scream.

38

Chiurco didn't move from the witness stand for a short while after he'd been dismissed. Things had happened fast, but the judge had told him he could go, so long as he returned to court next Monday morning. He heard the back door of the courtroom open behind him, watched Hardy and Stier march solemnly past him on the way out. Still he didn't move.

At last, though, since the audience had returned en masse to the gallery—in fact, if anything, with the news of the drama, the crowd had increased—the noise level was gearing up again. The mayor and Fisk and Maya's husband came forward off their seats and Maya had turned around, the bailiff hovering in hesitation about obeying the judge and bringing her back to the holding cell. Everybody talking about his testimony, what had just come down.

Glitsky and DA Jackman were on their feet, stretching their backs, deep in discussion. Debra Schiff, over at the prosecution table, sat hunched over, head down, fingers at her temples. Chiurco's boss, Wyatt Hunt, had disappeared behind some other standees, everybody up and talking talking talking.

It was now or never.

Chiurco got to his feet, his shoulders squared, face set. Completely within his rights, he got out of the witness chair and crossed the open courtroom. Opening the bullpen gate, he stepped into the center aisle of the gallery, now clogged up with the overflowing crowd. A reporter grabbed at his elbow and said something, but the

world had turned into a blurry tunnel that ended in the doorway
about thirty feet away in front of him, and he shook the reporter off,
moving forward, moving.

Off to his side, in conversation with Jeff Elliot, his damn wheel-
chair in the aisle slowing everything down, Hunt and Gina Roake, at
first barely noticing him except, now, for Hunt's double take as he
passed. And hearing, as though muffled through water, Wyatt's
cry—"Abe!" Then louder, "Abe!"

Chiurco getting physical in the crush, pushing at someone, getting people out of his way.

"Hey!"

Now, from Hunt, an actual cry. "ABE!"

Chiurco was so close to the door, five or six steps, but still others
clogged the way before him, blocking him as they were filing out for
the bathroom, a smoke, a phone call, gossip.

He was stuck.

And so he pushed someone else, took another step, kept moving.

But the door was open, and one small Asian female bailiff had
come in from her post at the metal detector outside and was now
standing by it. Chiurco tried to squeeze around a fat man, couldn't
move him, got a sense of some activity in the rows behind him.

Hunt pushing his own way out? Trying to stop him?

And then, suddenly, Glitsky was standing on his chair, his voice
cutting through it all. "Bailiff! Hold that man! Stop that man!"

The judge may have ordered Chiurco released, but Glitsky on his
own had the power of arrest, and with the support of Clarence Jackman, standing next to him, he had decided he had heard enough to
at least hold Chiurco for further questioning.

But that was not going to happen, not if Chiurco had any say
about it, and he did. He was getting out of here. Pushing again now
at the heavy body in front of him.

Glitsky's rasp again. "Mr. Chiurco! Hold up! Bailiff!"

She had come in from the hall to intercept Chiurco as he tried to make it out of the courtroom, but now the same fat man was trying to make it through the door before him and suddenly she was directly in front of him, blocking his way.

Turning around for a glance, Chiurco saw Hunt coming at him out of one eye, Glitsky out of the other, the lieutenant pushing his own way out of his row toward the aisle, pointing at him, desperation in his voice. "That man! The last witness! Hold him there!"

With the fat man still inside, but pushed out of Chiurco's way, the bailiff was the last obstruction as she now pulled the door shut. But she was so small it was no contest. Chiurco lashed out, struck her a rabbit punch on the side of the neck, and she would have gone down at once except that the fat man saw what had happened and found himself holding her up.

There was nothing else Chiurco could do.

Though San Francisco bailiffs on courtroom duty didn't carry guns, this particular hallway bailiff was armed because of her duty outside the courtroom by the metal detector. Now, unsnapping her holster, Chiurco grabbed, pulled out her gun, with all of his might tried to push the fat man and the bailiff to one side, then fired a shot into the ceiling.

Someone yelled out. "Down! Everybody get down!"

And a woman screamed.

The fucking fat guy still in his way, Chiurco pushed again, got his hand on the door, and behind him heard a woman's voice. "Drop it! Drop the gun now!"

And turning, he saw Schiff by the prosecution table, now with her own weapon drawn, on the far side of the bar rail, taking aim at him over the ducking crowd. No time to think, he brought the gun up, his hands together, and squeezed off two quick shots, textbook. The inspector went down, her gun clattering over the floor.

Chiurco turned to finally get out, but another blast from by the defense table exploded the wood on the door just over his head. And Chiurco, looking left, opened fired again at the big man in the business suit standing in the front row who'd perhaps just fired, and who fell back over the rail onto the floor by the defense table.

And revealed the actual second shooter, the other bailiff, standing, holding Schiff's gun, over where Maya Townshend lay prostrate on top of her shot brother, sheltering him on the tile. The bailiff had his gun extended in a two-handed grip, drawing another bead.

His hands already up in the classic firing position, Chiurco once again fired twice in rapid succession and the bailiff, too, staggered backward, dropped Schiff's weapon, and fell.

And then someone out of nowhere grabbed Chiurco's gun arm and chopped viciously at it. The female bailiff, trying again to restrain him, took another swing at his face, a glancing blow, and now he swung his gun at her. It went off accidentally as the fat man clutched at his shoulder and spun around and down to the ground next to them.

Now Chiurco only needed another step and he'd be outside and free, but the damned bailiff woman was holding on to his leg, so he reached down, got an arm around her neck, and pulled her up against him, holding her there, waving his gun threateningly around at the room at anyone who dared raise his or her head.

But to get the door he had no choice. He needed either to release his hostage or lower his weapon.

He couldn't let go of the hostage, though. She would attack him again.

He had to let down the gun.

Which gave Glitsky, fifteen feet away, and waiting for just such an opportunity, one and only one clear shot.

It was all he needed.

39

City Talk

By Jeffrey Elliot

City officials are still trying to piece together how security procedures in the Hall of Justice could have gone so awry as to allow the series of events that last Friday resulted in the deaths of four people, including two law enforcement personnel and City Supervisor Harlen Fisk, and the wounding of another man in one of the city's courtrooms.

This reporter was present during the events that transpired and can relate that even before court was called into session that morning, a palpable tension reigned in Department 25, the courtroom of Judge Marian Braun, scene of the murder trial of Maya Townshend. Both Mayor Kathryn West, Mrs. Townshend's aunt, and Fisk, her brother, were present in evident support of the defendant, and the attendant media presence as well as rumors of surprise, last-minute witnesses for the defense had packed the gallery.

Mrs. Townshend had been charged with the murders of Dylan Vogler, the manager of the Bay Beans West coffee shop that she owns, and another past associate of hers, Levon Preslee. The trial to date had focused upon evidence of Mrs. Townshend's apparent motive for these murders, and experts had opined that it was particularly light on physical evidence implicating the defendant. So when

defense attorney Dismas Hardy's first witness, a fingerprint specialist
at the police laboratory, identified one of Hardy's own investigating
team, Craig Chiurco, as having been present at the scene of Preslee's
murder, and perhaps having left a partial fingerprint on the bullet
casing at the Vogler murder scene, the gallery grew tense with antici-
pation of what was to come.

It didn't have long to wait, as Mr. Hardy briefly questioned one
other witness who established Mr. Chiurco's earlier and previously
undisclosed relationship to both Vogler and Preslee, then called Mr.
Chiurco. Apparently, not knowing what was taking place in court, he
had been waiting outside in the hallway to take the stand. Mr. Hardy's
questions, and Mr. Chiurco's responses, grew increasingly heated as
Hardy tried to tie his associate to these crimes.

In the end, with Chiurco invoking his Fifth Amendment right
against self-incrimination, Mr. Hardy accused him point-blank of
these murders, and pandemonium broke out in the courtroom. It
took Judge Braun several minutes to restore order. Rather than having
her bailiffs hold Chiurco for the police, Braun ordered him to consult
an attorney and keep himself available for further examination if necessary. At that, the judge and the two lead attorneys left the room to
confer in Judge Braun's chambers, leaving Chiurco unguarded on the
witness stand.

A few moments later the folly of Braun's decision became apparent as Chiurco rose from the stand and started to make his way
through the crowd that by now blocked the aisle of the gallery. He
had nearly made it to the back door when Lieutenant Glitsky, chief of
the city's homicide department, called out and ordered one of the
courtroom bailiffs, Linda Yang, to restrain Chiurco. But the desperate witness—now suddenly revealed as a murder suspect—struggled
with the bailiff and managed not only to disarm her but to gain possession of her service weapon and to fire it into the ceiling.

As members of the gallery dropped to the floor or took shelter behind their chairs, homicide sergeant inspector Debra Schiff, who'd been seated at the prosecution table, fired a shot at Chiurco, which he returned, fatally wounding her. In the next few seconds another bailiff, Rolfe Hagen, fired at Chiurco again from inside the bar rail, and in response to that, Chiurco got off a flurry of shots that killed both Supervisor Fisk and bailiff Hagen before Lieutenant Glitsky saw an opening and fired one shot into Chiurco's chest, killing him. Glitsky has been placed on the automatic administrative leave that follows any officer-involved shooting.

But the violence that could and did erupt with such tragic results even in a guarded courtroom leaves officials pondering a host of questions: Shouldn't courtroom bailiffs in San Francisco be armed, as they are in every other jurisdiction in California? Or, on the other hand, should guns, even in the hands of police personnel, ever be allowed in courtrooms at all? Is there an adequate number of bailiffs in San Francisco courtrooms? Was Judge Braun negligent in affording a potential murder suspect the opportunity to escape and/or take hostages?

Above all, how was an innocent woman arrested and brought to trial for two murders in a San Francisco courtroom, based on an investigation that could be described, at best, as incompetent, and at worst, as grotesquely negligent?

The evidence of Maya Townshend's innocence was right in front of the police and the prosecution during this entire investigation. Yet they chose to ignore it in what the unkind might describe as the pursuit of a political vendetta. In this reporter's opinion it is a travesty that this case was ever allowed to be brought to trial at all.

40

"Actually," Glitsky said, "I'm enjoying the time off. Getting quality time with my little rat here." Zachary, the rat in question, still wore his helmet but otherwise looked and acted as healthy as any normal kid as he played with his sister in the sandbox in Glitsky's backyard. "Rebonding."

"Don't kid yourself. You never unbonded."

"Maybe not, but it felt like it. Unbonded from the world."

"Yeah, well . . ." They sat on the top step, their usual spot, looking down over the backyard and the greenery of the Presidio beyond. "You came back just in time, so I wouldn't beat myself up over it."

"I won't. I thought I told you. I'm done with beating myself up."

Hardy threw him a sideways glance. "If that's true, how will I recognize you? You'll find something else to beat yourself up over, you watch. It's just who you are. Screwed up, but probably worth saving. Marginally. In the long run."

"Thank you."

"You're welcome. But, in fact," Hardy added, "not that I don't have anything better to do on a Sunday afternoon, but you did call."

"I did."

"And you're going to make me guess again?"

"If you want, or I could just tell you what we found at Chiurco's."

"You mean besides blood spatter on what . . . his shoes?"

"Shoes, check."

"And a Glock .40 hexagonal-barrel semi?"

"Nope, but three live rounds and a cleaning kit that would fit that gun. Besides those?"

"I give up. No, wait. Weed."

"You're good. You want to guess how much?"

"Nope. I quit when I'm ahead. Weed is good enough. But what else?"

"You're going to like it. You want another few seconds?"

"Okay." A companionable silence settled for the better part of a minute, until finally Hardy said, "What else?"

"Newspaper clippings. Old ones."

"Julio Gomez."

"Right."

"I could have got that if I'd have thought a little more."

"Just like you got Chiurco knowing Preslee."

"No. I should have seen that long before I did. I mean, Wyatt told me all about Dylan not being on Google until recently, so how could Craig have found Levon? The answer was that he couldn't have. No way, no how. Especially when I realized that they'd gone to trial separately. So he must have known Levon before. And I even knew Craig had been at USF and knew Dylan and was on his weed list. I mean, flags everywhere and I couldn't see them."

"Yeah," Glitsky said, "you're a little slow. It's amazing you keep getting clients."

"I marvel at it myself. Still, though"—Hardy let out a sigh—"what a fiasco at the end there."

"I hear you. Though that's one of the things I'm not going to beat myself up over. I've made up my mind."

"Probably smart. You had no choice."

"Really. None."

"I know. I believe you. You just wonder sometimes how things get to where they are. I mean, why did Maya even get charged? And because of that Harlen's dead? And Schiff? And even Ruiz. To say nothing of Chiurco and those poor bailiffs. What's that about? All those victims."

"And everybody still goes on calling it a victimless crime, don't they?"

"It's the crime part," Hardy said. "Take away the crime, make the stuff legal . . ." He looked at his friend. "But you being a cop and all, I don't suppose that's going to be your issue, is it?"

"Good guess." Glitsky chewed at his cheek. "But as to how things got to where they did, part of that, you want to be honest, was me. Bailing on the job. Worrying about Zack."

"That would have been a very small part. But I'm proud to see you're already back on the road to beating yourself up." Hardy glanced at his watch. "You made it about forty-five seconds, a new record, I think."

"No. I know it was mostly Schiff, and God knows she paid for it."

"What about Bracco? You talk to him?"

"Not since right after."

"How is he?"

Glitsky let out a breath. "Talk about beating yourself up. He said he knew he should have stepped up, said something, but he wanted to be loyal to his partner."

"Cops and loyalty, huh?"

"Don't I know? I just hope he can talk himself into staying on, but I'm not betting on it. On the other hand, Treya had some fun news the other night you might not have heard about."

"She's pregnant again."

Glitsky gave him the bad eye. "Don't even kid. Think DA's office."

"Clarence is stepping down and she's taking over."

"Incorrect. Think Paul Stier."

"The Big Ugly?"

Glitsky nodded. "The big, now-between-jobs ugly. At least until he can hook on with Glass or somebody."

"I don't know. I think Mr. Glass might be having his own problems lately. Having taken on the mayor, stirring up all this shit, and really coming up with squat. Rumors abound. And speaking of which, the word is that you're back in the saddle next week."

"Might be. Might not."

"Let me guess. You're not beating yourself up over it?"

Glitsky nodded. "Close enough."

Tamara Dade knew that Craig Chiurco's shell-shocked and disbelieving parents had taken his ashes and scattered them under the Golden Gate Bridge. She hadn't wanted to intrude on them in their own hours of grief; and besides, she did not come close to forgetting that she and Craig had broken up. A serious and, she had felt, irrevocable breakup. So she wasn't with the family and didn't want to be.

But she had her own grieving to deal with.

Now, four days after the memorial service, she found herself at the pier behind the Ferry Building, waiting in line again for the boat to Sausalito. She hadn't come in to work, nor had she called, since the day of the shootings. Instead, four days ago she'd started to come out here after her mostly sleepless and crying nights, and she'd ride across the bay, sit alone on the Sausalito jetty and watch the water, then take the ferry back by about noon. She'd then repeat the round trip in the afternoon, getting back to the city after darkness had descended.

Today was bleak, windy, and bitter cold. As the ferry left the protection of the shore, whitecaps piled up and flung their foam across the open front deck. This was where Tamara had taken to standing, but on this day, even with her raincoat, it was too wet, too miserable. She turned and went back inside, bought a hot chocolate, and found a seat at one of the bolted-in tables by a window, where she could look out and . . .

What?

Imagine what life would have been like with Craig? Wonder why they had never progressed to a committed relationship? Try to understand what he'd done, and why? And what, simply, had happened in the courtroom?

None of it made any sense to her. She found it nearly impossible to get her mind around the stark reality that he'd murdered Dylan Vogler and Levon Preslee, and apparently another liquor store clerk years ago. That he had been able to live with letting Maya Townshend get all the way to trial.

Who had he been all this time, and how had she not seen it?

She didn't have any answers. Except that it would be a long while before she would trust her romantic instincts, or even her fundamental human instincts, again. Maybe forever, she thought. She stared out into the windswept, gray-green, white-capped chop.

"Is this seat taken?"

The familiar voice startled her and she turned her head quickly to verify the presence of her boss, Wyatt Hunt. After doing so she turned back to the window and her shoulders rose and fell as she blew out a long breath. "How'd you find me?"

"I'm a private eye, Tam. Finding people is what I do. If you don't want me to sit down, I'll go find another spot."

She turned back to him. "No. It's fine. You can sit here." Then, when he had, "I don't know if I can come back to work."

"Okay. That's not why I'm here. I wanted to make sure you were all right."

Her lips turned up fractionally and she let out a dry, one-note, half-laugh half-sob. "I don't know what that means, *all right*. Not anymore. I can't believe Craig's gone. Even more, maybe, I can't believe what Craig was."

Hunt nodded. "I've been having some issues with it myself."

"So were we both just blind?"

"I don't know. I suppose so. Although, how were we going to know? What did he show us that could have tipped us off?"

"I don't know. But I keep thinking I should have known. I should have seen something. I mean, I knew he was confused, and he had his bad moments, but he was almost always nice to me. To everyone, really."

"You never threatened him. Thank God."

She let out another deep sigh. "So he really did do it? I mean Vogler and Preslee."

"I don't think there's any doubt about that, Tam."

Turning away from him, she looked out the window at the churning bay and, at the farthest extent of vision, the spectral shape of Alcatraz, the old deserted prison with its decrepit buildings. "I really don't know what I'm going to do, Wyatt. About work, I mean."

"How about if you don't have to decide for a while?"

"Even still. I don't know. It's like the world is all different. Maybe I should be in a different field, around different people."

"Maybe you should."

"You wouldn't hate me?"

He put his hand over hers. "There's nothing you could do that could make me hate you, Tam. You've got to know that."

She turned back to him and tried to smile. "I don't feel like I know anything anymore, Wyatt. I feel like he stole my innocence or something. I just keep waiting for a break in these clouds, but I'm not sure there's going to be one."

"Except that there always has been before."

"No," she said. "The clouds have never before been this thick. And I really hate him for that."

Hunt patted her hand. "Time," he said.

She attempted another wan smile. "God, I hope so."

On the third Friday after the last day of Maya's trial, the phone buzzed at Hardy's elbow in his office, and he punched the button to speak to Phyllis. "Yo." Taking a moment's immature pleasure from his receptionist's exasperated sigh—senior attorneys do not answer the phone informally, since that causes a disruption in the force— he checked that it was indeed four-thirty and again stole Phyllis's thunder when he added, "Send the Townshends right in."

It was both of them, holding hands, Maya looking so radiant and lovely that he might have passed her on the street and not recognized her. Her hair and her cheeks glowed. She'd lost the weight she'd gained on the jail food, as well as the cellblock pallor. Joel, for his part, wore a sense of comfort, a confidence, and an easy smile that Hardy hadn't noticed before.

Not that there'd been much to smile about over the past six or seven months, but something in the couple's body language toward each other spoke of a renewed connection, an ease, a true rapport. No longer rich, successful husband and subservient, stay-at-home wife, but true partners now. A lot to grab from a first impression, but Hardy decided to believe it was true.

The occasion—final payment for his legal services—could have been handled by a check in the mail, but they'd wanted to come down and deliver it in person, and he was grateful for the opportunity to see them again, in this setting, with their ordeal behind them. So he offered coffee and condolences about Harlen, both of which they accepted, and they made small talk, until they were all settled in the formal seating area closest to Hardy's desk.

At which time Joel reached into his inside pocket and proffered an envelope embossed with his corporation's logo.

"Feel free to open it now, if you'd like," Maya said.

"That's all right." Hardy broke a small grin. "I trust it's pretty close."

"Maybe not." Maya, with an impish smile of her own, made it sound like a dare.

So Hardy shrugged, opened the flap, pulled out the check, and looked up with some surprise. "This is, um . . . I don't remember the last time I got tongue-tied."

"It's a bonus," Joel said.

Maya was outright beaming now. "We thought Dylan's salary for a year would have a nice symmetry."

"It's got a lot more than symmetry," Hardy said. "Are you sure this is . . . I'm afraid I'm just a little overwhelmed. This is more than extremely generous."

Maya nodded. "You saved my life, Dismas. In many ways." She reached over and put a hand on her husband's knee. "I told him."

"Good for you," Hardy said. And turning to Joel, "And I bet you weren't even tempted to leave her."

He put his hand over hers. "Not even close. I never would. No matter what. I don't know if she ever really believed that before. But we all make mistakes, huh? Do things we're ashamed of, and worse than that."

"I know it's happened to me," Hardy said. "Though if you'd keep that in this room, I'd appreciate it. My associates would be shocked and dismayed."

"In any event," Maya said, "I . . . we just wanted to thank you so much. It has been such a burden for so long and now I don't have it anymore. I feel like a different person."

Joel hadn't let go of her hand. "The same person, only happier. And better."

She looked contentedly across at him. *"Arrête un peu."* In French. Stop a little. But not too much. Then, back at Hardy, with a sigh.

"Anyway . . . if you don't mind, I've got one last little thing that you could explain that I wanted to understand, and just really don't."

"If I can, I will."

She let out a small breath. "Why me?"

"Why you what?"

"I mean, with Craig Chiurco. How did he pick me to frame? I never met him, I never even had heard of him, and suddenly he picks me out of nowhere and tries to ruin my life. I just don't understand what happened. How that happened."

Hardy picked up his coffee and took a sip. He knew that it was an excellent question, and that she deserved an answer. But there was no certain answer. Craig was dead, and no one would ever really know for sure. Hardy just hoped that the one he had—and he'd given it a lot of thought—was good enough for her.

"Well," he began, "here's my best guess. Dylan was in the blackmail business, and he was a greedy man. For a long time he was happy stringing you along, selling his dope, keeping up on his customer list. But remember, he also knew that Craig had killed the Gomez boy. Now, the fact that he'd done it in connection with a robbery they were both involved in made it a little squirrelly, since technically, legally, they'd both be guilty of that murder, whoever it was that pulled the trigger.

"But he liked pushing the limits, Dylan did. And what I think happened is that they were all together at BBW that day a few weeks before he got killed, and Dylan brought it up again. And here's Craig going for his private eye license, straight all these years, thinking his past is all behind him, and then Dylan ups the stakes. Somehow. Tells him what he's been doing with you, maybe without any of the specific details, but enough to make Craig know that you've got every reason to want Dylan removed too.

"So he decides to kill Dylan, and all he needs is to have you show up soon after."

"So he called me? That was him?"

"I don't know for sure. But Dylan had a Brooklyn accent, which isn't so hard to mimic. Craig calls you late at night and makes it short and sweet, saying it's an emergency he can't talk about now . . . well, you came running. He knew what time Dylan got to the alley every day. He knew he'd have your gun with him. In any event, it all worked. If you want my opinion, you're damn lucky he didn't wait around to kill you too."

"I thought of that. I'm kind of surprised he didn't."

Hardy shook his head. "Two dead people, and the police still left looking for who killed them? Too much to orchestrate. He wanted to keep it simple."

"So what about Levon?"

"Levon would have remembered the conversation at BBW, their fight that Eugenio Ruiz witnessed, remember? So he goes to Levon's, pulls his gun, has Levon call you on his cell phone and invite you over, walks behind him and . . . well, you know the rest."

"So he didn't know me at all, and just did that?"

"That's what I think," Hardy said.

"That's about what I told her too," Joel added. "She just said that sounded like the essence of evil. She doesn't want to believe that people could really be that bad, in their souls."

"I mean," she said, "we all make mistakes, sure. Even terrible ones. But this wasn't a simple mistake. This was a conscious decision to just destroy somebody he didn't know at all."

Hardy nodded. "That's right."

"I don't want to believe that people can actually be like that," she said.

"Not all of them. And thankfully, maybe not too many. But definitely some," Hardy said. "Definitely some."

Acknowledgments

It is almost impossible for me to imagine that this is my twentieth book! And so my first acknowledgment is to all of you, my readers, who have been so enthusiastic and supportive of my work over all these years. I never forget that I owe my success—never anticipated to this degree, and tremendously appreciated—to those of you who buy these books, pass them to your friends and relatives, discuss them at work and at home, take them to your hearts. Having such a dedicated core of readers is one of the great thrills of a writer's life, and I am humbly grateful to each and every one of you. Thank you. Thank you. Thank you.

This book began in an e-mail discussion with one of my correspondents, Dr. Jack Crary, who had been intrigued by some of the medical issues in some of my earlier books—particularly the effect of traumatic injury on family members of those who'd suffered it. That correspondence led me to Abe Glitsky's reaction to his son's accident, and got me off and running in Chapter One. Thanks, Jack.

As the story got under way, I encountered, as usual, a great dearth in my knowledge about what I was hoping to write about. For insights into business perspectives that were foreign to me, I'd like to thank my neighbors (and fellow Piscators) Tim Lien and Tim Cronan. These gentlemen connected me to a U.S. attorney in San Diego, Bruce Smith, who was a forthcoming and generous source on the uses of forfeiture in connection with the drug trade. After the first draft was finished, I turned to a very talented writer and author, John

Poswall, and a couple of other colleagues of his who prefer to remain anonymous, for further insight into government prosecutions and grand jury proceedings.

None of my books would be what they are without the ongoing assistance and first-draft revision suggestions of my dear friend, San Mateo assistant district attorney Al Giannini, whose general expertise on all things criminal, exquisite taste, and refined judgment contribute mightily to the finished product. Like no one else, Al is a true collaborator in the Dismas Hardy–Abe Glitsky series, and my debt to him cannot be measured.

Of course, any book owes its life to its publisher, and I am blessed to have worked with a wonderful staff at Dutton now for the past nine books. This is a fantastic group of enthusiastic, bright, committed people—starting with the publisher Brian Tart; marketing whizzes Lisa Johnson and Beth Parker; Erika Imranyi, Trena Keating, Kara Welsh, Claire Zion, Rick Pascocello, Susan Schwartz; and the wonderful cover artist and designer Rich Hasselberger. Saving the most personal until last, I'm knocked out by the style, taste, and talents of my editor, Ben Sevier. His support in many conversations was crucial throughout the book's gestation, and his comments and suggestions as we approached a final manuscript were consistently pithy, germaine, and critical. Ben is the real deal as an editor, and I consider myself blessed to be able to work with him.

My writing life wouldn't be half as productive without the load taken up by my assistant, Anita Boone. Besides possessing one of the most even-keeled and sunny personalities in the world (a major plus when working with sometimes gnarly authors), she is truly the right arm and majordomo of many, many aspects of my life in the business of writing, and I couldn't do what I do without her.

As many have attested, the writing life can be solitary. Without close friends to keep perspective on the other things that are important, and that hopefully help to keep the writing fresh, the creativity wouldn't flourish, nor would the experience be joyful. And so for keeping the spirit alive, here's to the perennial best man, Don Matheson; to author/bon vivant Max Byrd; Frank and Gina Seidl; Sandy and Peter S. Diedrich, M.D., M.P.H.; and my two children, Justine and Jack.

Several characters in this book owe their names (although no physical or personality traits, which are all fictional) to individuals whose contributions to various charities have been especially generous. These people, and their respective charities, include: Stacy and Mark Wegzyn, Holy Family School; Katherine (Kay) Hansen, Thrillerfest (International Thriller Writers); Michael J. Schermer, the Sacramento Public Library Foundation; Deborah L. Dunham and Chuck Cunningham, the Davis, California, Chamber of Commerce; Mrs. Jacky Glass, H.E.L.P. (Healthcare and Elder Law Programs Corporation); and Mickey Friend (Sonoma Paradiso).

Finally, my literary agent, Barney Karpfinger, is the rock of my career and of my professional life. A great friend, a tireless advocate, a beacon of taste and intelligence, Barney is simply the best in the world at what he does, and I'm endlessly grateful for my relationship with him. Thanks for everything you do, Barney—you're an amazing and wonderful human being.

I very much love hearing from my readers, and invite all of you to please visit me at my Web site, www.johnlescroart.com, with comments, questions, or interests.

About the Author

John Lescroart is the author of nineteen previous novels, including *Betrayal, The Suspect, The Hunt Club, The Motive, The Second Chair, The First Law, The Oath, The Hearing,* and *Nothing but the Truth.* He lives in northern California.